ISABELLE WEBB

THE GRECIAN PRINCESS

a novel

OTHER BOOKS AND AUDIO BOOKS
BY N. C. ALLEN

Faith of Our Fathers Vol. 1: A House Divided

Faith of Our Fathers Vol. 2: To Make Men Free

Faith of Our Fathers Vol. 3: Through the Perilous Fight

Faith of Our Fathers Vol. 4: One Nation under God

Isabelle Webb: Legend of the Jewel

Isabelle Webb: The Pharaoh's Daughter

OTHER BOOKS PUBLISHED UNDER
NANCY CAMBELL ALLEN

Love Beyond Time

No Time for Love

A Time for the Heart

Echoes

ISABELLE WEBB
THE GRECIAN PRINCESS

a novel

N.C. ALLEN

Covenant Communications, Inc.

For my mom, Kari Gundersen Campbell
April 13, 1945–May 3, 2012
I love you

Acknowledgments

Writing can be hard to do when you're not a solitary person by nature. My eternal thanks go to my writer friends who attend Write Nite and provide an atmosphere of camaraderie and support, namely Josi S. Kilpack, Jennifer Moore, Marion Jensen, and Robison Wells. (With special thanks to Josi for providing the office and Jen for providing the little cabin in the woods.)

My thanks also go out at this time to the readers who have asked for Isabelle's last book—without you, I think I might have put the whole thing to rest. And now, I'm really glad I didn't because Isabelle had a lot of loose ends to tie up.

It goes without saying that I thank my family for their support and love. To my husband, a special thanks for being my cheerleader from the very beginning. His support of my writing career has never wavered, and I am so grateful.

Prologue

The princess took the stones she had mined with her own hands and placed them in the box. Her enemies had discovered the existence of the stones, knew of their purpose and value. Trembling, she crept from her well-appointed suite of rooms, the marble floor cool beneath her feet. She passed the guards, who slept heavily on the wine she'd given them earlier.

The cave wasn't far from the palace, and she knew the way there by heart, even in the dark. Making her way into the depths of the cave, she found the place she'd already searched out and laid the box in the recessed crevice. Placing a large stone in front of it, she stood for a moment, staring at the spot and trying to still the frantic beating of her heart.

If the soothsayer was to be believed, the entire city would soon see its destruction. As the princess stared into the darkness of the cave for a final moment's reflection, she wondered if she would be able to save herself long enough to escape with the stones . . .

***

In which the reader is reacquainted with the intrepid Isabelle Webb

When Pinkerton spy Isabelle Webb embarked on a journey in 1865 with her ward, Sally Rhodes, she sought to leave behind memories of a failed attempt to save the president of the United States from assassination at the hands of one John Wilkes Booth. Although the memories encroached at inopportune times, she found herself slowly achieving her goal.

In India, Sally and Isabelle had met James Ashby, a blacksmith from Utah with broad shoulders and an irritated mien. He'd been searching for his brother, Phillip, who had been duped by one Thaddeus Sparks into believing he was the key to a quest for a mysterious jewel that granted the possessor untold wealth and wisdom. Isabelle and Sally soon joined in the search, making the acquaintance of a distinguished but troubled British military official and his spoiled daughter, Alice Bilbey.

The end of their adventure in India found Phillip well, but Alice and Sally were abducted and put aboard boat to Egypt. James, Isabelle, and Phillip followed, in possession of the Jewel of Zeus. Egypt held surprises for the group—Isabelle's former guardian, who revealed her true identity as Isabelle's grandmother, was now funding an archaeological dig along the Nile and had already met up with Alice and Sally, enticing the lot of them into staying for a time in order to enjoy the adventures of Egyptology and the lure of hidden treasure.

Thaddeus Sparks still needed Phillip to aid in his quest. He joined forces with a powerful entity, the Federation, who also sought the jewel, and learned that there were three jewels, not just one. In addition to this tantalizing fact, Sparks also learned that, while Phillip bore a birthmark that reacted when in close proximity to the jewels, true success in the search came in the form of females who also bore the mark, and Alice was one of them.

Isabelle's group expanded to include a French professor of linguistics, Jean-Louis Deveraux, and a British secret agent, Jackson Pearce MacInnes, who had infiltrated the upper echelons of the Federation; the group found the second jewel, the Jewel of Poseidon, only to have it stolen by Thaddeus Sparks and spirited away to Greece, where he hoped to find the third.

So in possession of the Jewel of Zeus, needing to retrieve the Jewel of Poseidon, and hoping to find the Jewel of Hades, Isabelle and her crew boarded a steamer just after Christmas and headed for Athens—running from the long arm of the Federation and multitudinous others seeking the jewels for personal gain.

With only their knowledge of Sparks's methods, coupled with information from Jack MacInnes's recently deceased grandfather, who was an expert on the legend of the jewels, they moved forward in a race against time and villains who sought to rule the world.

1

THE STEAMER PITCHED FROM SIDE to side, the wind and waves tossing it about like nothing more than a child's toy. Isabelle Webb sat up in her bed looking in vain for a source of light inside the small cabin, but the world outside the porthole was black. She winced as she listened to Alice Bilbey, her young seventeen-year-old friend, lose the contents of her stomach for the third time that night.

"Alice," Isabelle said as she touched her feet to the floor and began to grope on the side table for a light. "Can I do anything for you?"

"Kill me," came the muttered response, the cultured English accent still discernible despite the misery of the tone. "And do be quick about it."

Isabelle's fingers found the lucifer matches, and before long she had a lantern lit, its glow chasing some of the darkness from the small room.

Sally Rhodes, Isabelle's ward and also seventeen years of age, sat up in her bunk and rubbed a hand across her eyes. Blinking, she stared in confusion for a moment at Isabelle and Alice before flinching at the sight of Alice doubled over on the floor, her face in the bucket that had become her constant companion.

"Oh dear," Sally said. "Alice, you ought to have awoken me. Is the washcloth still on the nightstand?" Sally's Virginia accent was in sharp contrast to Alice's normally quick British cadences.

"No," Isabelle told her. "It's over on the washbasin. I'm going to wring it out again after securing the lamp."

"I'll get it." Sally rose from her bed and made her way across the floor of the swaying ship, staggering and smacking into the wall only twice. She dipped the small cloth into a basin and wrung it out then stumbled her way to Alice and placed the cloth across the back of the other girl's neck. Gathering Alice's hair in her hands, Sally pulled it away from the girl's face as Alice heaved once more.

Isabelle pinched the bridge of her nose with her fingers, feeling a headache building. The weather leaving Alexandria, Egypt, had been pleasant for the first two days. But as they had made their way farther into the Mediterranean, the storms had whipped into a frenzy that had Alice begging for death and had left Phillip Ashby, across the hall with his brother, in much the same condition.

"It's that wretched stone," Alice said, spitting and gratefully accepting the handkerchief Isabelle handed to her. She wiped her mouth and her forehead and groaned as she straightened her back and moved off her knees to sit flat on the floor. "The Jewel of Zeus! It's Jonah avoiding Nineveh. I say we throw the horrid thing overboard!"

Isabelle's lips twitched. "The jewel isn't causing the bad weather. Captain Whitney said storms are common this time of year."

"Fat lot he knows," Alice muttered. "He's not aware that we're traveling with a cursed menace."

"At least it's not in our cabin," Sally said and began braiding Alice's hair to keep it off her face. "And it shouldn't be bothering Phillip either. Jean-Louis took it. He and Jack will keep it from now on."

Alice closed her eyes and attempted a nod which she quickly aborted. "How many more days until we reach Athens?" she said, her brows drawn close together.

"Three, hopefully," Isabelle said.

"I shall be dead by then."

"No, you won't be," Isabelle told her. "You can do anything for three days."

"You don't understand, Belle. I would rather be dead."

"I'm sure you would, but that's not an option."

Sally finished braiding Alice's hair and stood, helping the sick girl rise unsteadily to her feet. "You take the bottom bunk," Sally said to her. "Here, keep your bucket close, and just get through the night. We'll attempt to go up on deck in the morning. I think that will help."

Alice's eyes filmed over, but she acquiesced and fell unsteadily into the lower berth as Sally clambered up to the higher one.

Please, dear God, supposing You're there and accessible, do help Alice get some rest, Isabelle thought. Mercifully, her prayer must have been heard because Alice fell asleep within minutes.

***

The distinguished Egyptian sat in his well-equipped study while his informants stood before him, trying not to fidget. He was powerful and fierce; he headed an international organization of equally powerful men—leaders devoted to a single purpose. Their efforts to locate the elusive jewels had come to naught, despite the growing network of informants and foot soldiers they'd either hired or bullied into service.

He quietly considered the news his informants had just given him—information they'd tortured out of a member of the British consulate in Cairo.

"His name is actually Jackson MacInnes, a British operative," he finally said. "Posing as an Italian man of affairs." He drew his fierce eyebrows together; the dark eyebrows were in direct contrast to his head of silver hair. "You're certain he is Dr. Pearce's grandson?"

"Yes, sir." One of the informants nodded quickly, twisting his hat in his hands.

The Egyptian sat back in his chair and picked up his cigar, which rested on a crystal ashtray. "That is an interesting turn of events," he said. "Perhaps not so much of a coincidence as we might suppose."

He dismissed the informants with a flick of his hand. They were nervous, and that was to their credit. People were always nervous around the head of the Federation, if they were wise. He squelched the flare of anger that rose in his gut and slowly exhaled. He needed to use the information to his advantage. Have the man killed too early and they may be missing out on an opportunity to reap the benefits of his labors.

Interesting that the British were seeking to ferret out his affairs. The man he'd once trusted as his eyes and ears concerning the hunt for the jewels was actually an operative, clearly sent to infiltrate the organization, steal information. Perhaps lay hands on the jewels himself for the British government.

The Egyptian had to tip his hat to the man; his Italian had been flawless, the act convincing enough to have fooled the Federation thoroughly. The Egyptian had begun to suspect the man had ulterior motives but had assumed from communication from the worm, Thaddeus Sparks, that the Italian had decided to strike out on his own in pursuit of the jewels. That the man had been an operative had never crossed the Egyptian's mind, and he was a very suspicious man.

And now MacInnes had thrown in his lot with the American treasure seekers. They would be dispensed with eventually. Accidents were easily enough arranged—especially since the group traveled en masse. And when he was no longer of any use, Jackson MacInnes would suffer for having betrayed the Federation. It was time he sent his best man to Athens, the Egyptian decided.

***

Genevieve Montgomery turned over on her cot for what seemed like the hundredth time. It was comfortable as cots went, but she couldn't rest well for more than a few hours at most. Isabelle had been gone from Egypt for just a short while, but Genevieve's senses were on high alert. She had always had dreams about her granddaughter—some good but most fraught with danger that left her heart pounding when she awoke.

She sat up in the dark and wiped a hand across her forehead. It was no use. The dreams had increased both in frequency and intensity. Isabelle's intrepid group of treasure hunters was doomed to fail, and Genevieve did not like situations she could not control. She had sent Isabelle off with plenty of money—but a fraction of the girl's inheritance—but gold wasn't the issue.

"What is it?" A muffled voice came from the darkness.

"Maude, I cannot stop dreaming."

Genevieve's good friend Maude Davis rustled about on her own cot. "Isabelle again?"

"Yes." Genevieve rose and lit the lantern that sat atop her small writing desk inside the comfortable tent. The Egyptian dig she was funding had done amazingly well since the discovery of Princess Ibis's tomb.

"You do seem to have a sense about the girl," Maude said with a yawn. "It's why we're here, after all."

Genevieve sat in the chair at the desk and pulled a piece of paper out of her box of writing materials. Jotting a few notes to herself, she said, "I need to send a telegram in the morning."

"To whom?"

"To Claire. She's on her way, but the last I heard from her was over two weeks ago. I had hoped to see her reunite with Isabelle, but then they'd had to leave for Greece immediately. If Claire's still delayed in London, there's a chance I can reach her before she books passage for Egypt. I'll instruct her to travel straight to Athens instead."

Maude raised a brow. "And will she heed your instructions?"

Genevieve frowned. "One can hope."

***

The ship's library was empty save a handful of passengers. The walls were lined with shelves of dark oak that held a fair amount of books and newspapers picked up at each port visited. The items were held behind glass doors that clicked shut to avoid messes when the seas turned rough.

The room boasted comfortable seating and a few small desks at which to write correspondence. Isabelle sat at one of them and opened her journal, thinking to update it. Alice was resting comfortably in the cabin, and Sally had gone ahead to the dining room for an early breakfast.

Isabelle noted Alice's discomfort in her diary and made a few comments about the quiet of the last few days, which was especially refreshing in light of the mayhem that had preceded their boarding the ship in Alexandria, Egypt.

There are three jewels, she wrote, *rather than just the one we had supposed in India. We found the second, the Jewel of Poseidon, in the tomb in Egypt, but Thaddeus Sparks again showed his vile face and took it. That he didn't kill us all in the process was a miracle. Now we are chasing him to Greece—he is at least two days ahead of us—and I have hopes we can track him down fairly quickly. We've done so in the past; I believe I'm becoming familiar with his habits.*

Isabelle paused and tapped the cap of her fountain pen against her lip. *Our little entourage has added two members: Jackson MacInnes and Jean-Louis Deveraux. Jean-Louis is fairly proficient in Greek and will be a valuable asset in communication. He and Alice are enamored of each other although they both seem to think that nobody else notices.*

Isabelle doodled in the margins of her journal for a moment, absently drawing a heart and then smiling when she realized she'd written *James* inside it, with much swirling and decoration. Such effeminate silliness was unlike her, but as much as she wanted to scoff at herself, she couldn't. She looked at her left hand and moved it slightly, appreciating the sparkle of the diamond as it caught the light.

Engaged, she wrote under the heart. *I am to marry the best man on earth.* Her heart caught and tripped, but she felt a surge of joy at the fact that it was more a feeling of excitement and happiness than the fear she'd felt in Egypt. When she had come to the conclusion that if she were ever to have a happy relationship with James Ashby she would have to trust him completely with her heart, she finally obtained peace.

Isabelle rose and stretched, preparing to join Sally and the others for breakfast. She walked slowly next to the shelves as she made her way to the door, glancing over the titles of the library's collection, most of which were old and had seen some use. There were many tales of mythology, histories of the Mediterranean countries, and a few contemporary novels of the day.

On a whim, Isabelle pulled an Austen novel she'd not yet read from one shelf and a book on Greek history from another. Cradling them both in her arm, she placed her journal back into her reticule and left the room, swaying with the motion of the ship and hoping very much that Alice was still sleeping.

***

"I've certainly encountered storms on the Mediterranean before," Captain Whitney was saying as Isabelle took her seat at one of the dining room tables, "but this is unusual. Even for this time of year." The captain was pressed and crisp in his uniform, his hat held carefully under one arm and a rueful smile on his face. Isabelle had made herself familiar with the crew on their first day aboard and found the captain to be a pleasant sort.

"Oh dear," Sally said, her brow wrinkling. "Are we expecting more bad weather?"

The captain nodded. "I'm afraid so. We will likely see rough seas in another hour or two."

Isabelle looked at James, who was also seated at the table with Jean-Louis Deveraux and Jackson MacInnes. "And how is Phillip this fine morning?" she asked James.

He shook his head. "He's been better, for certain."

"He still doesn't want company?" Sally asked James.

James shook his head with a half smile. "I'm afraid he would be mortified should you see him in his current state."

Sally nodded slightly and returned to her food, downcast. Isabelle couldn't help a sympathetic smile. Phillip had been as seasick as Alice from the moment they'd boarded the ship. Sally hadn't seen him in all that time, and it was apparently all her young, enamored heart could take.

James took a bite of toast. "It's odd," he said, wiping at the crumbs with his napkin. "I've never known him to be so sensitive before. He doesn't usually have problems with motion sickness."

Isabelle glanced at James as a server set a plate of food in front of her. "He was ill when we traveled from India to Egypt," she said. At James's nod, she continued. "Did he mention being seasick when he crossed the Atlantic with Sparks?"

James shook his head. "He hasn't ever said. But I've also not thought to ask."

Sally must have followed Isabelle's train of thought, "Alice wasn't sick when we traveled to Egypt," she said slowly.

Conscious of the captain's presence, Isabelle glanced up at him and with a smile said, "Well, perhaps they'll recover their former constitutions, then."

"I do hope so," he said. "I wish I could do more to see to their comfort. Enjoy your breakfast." With a smile, he replaced his hat and moved on to the next table.

When the captain was out of earshot, Jack leaned in slightly, wincing at the movement. "You believe there's a connection, then? Between those two and our cargo?"

Isabelle shrugged and looked at James, who did likewise. "I don't know," Isabelle said, turning her attention to her food. Poached eggs, toast with marmalade, a slice of ham. European traffic was high on the Mediterranean, and the steamers that traveled here accommodated their passengers' tastes. "It does seem odd, doesn't it?"

"It does," Jack murmured in a low voice as he pushed his food around on his plate with his fork, his other arm in a sling. He was still recovering from a gunshot wound to the shoulder from a few weeks earlier when they had caught Thaddeus Sparks sneaking into the burial chamber at the dig in Egypt.

Jack frowned and sat back in his chair. "The sooner we have done with this business, the better. I can't shake the feeling that we're being watched." Jack spoke in his natural Scottish brogue, which was at odds with the Italian nuances he'd mastered as a spy within the Federation's hierarchy and with the proper British Oxford professor identity he'd taken on when he'd joined Isabelle and the others at the dig. The ruse had allowed him access to the dig to search for the Jewel of Poseidon for his true employer—the British government. Isabelle was learning that his true personality held less élan and more grit.

Jean-Louis polished his spectacles with his napkin and replaced them on the bridge of his nose. "Surely the Federation was not able to have us followed aboard this ship," he said quietly. "We used the utmost care in avoiding them when we left Egypt."

"We did," Jack said with a nod. "You may not realize, however, just how far their hands reach."

"Forgive me, Jack," Sally said, "but wouldn't you be dead by now? And perhaps the rest of us as well?"

Jackson's smile was grim. "The voyage isn't over yet." He paused and then changed the subject. "I've sent for my grandfather's papers. Just before we boarded the ship, I cabled Oxford and requested they send a packet to Athens. I'm hopeful it will not be too far behind us."

Isabelle looked at him in some surprise. "That is an excellent idea," she said. "His research on certain legends, I would assume?"

Jack nodded. "We need more information than we have, and there may be something that will help us . . . conduct our research."

"Will the university be willing to part with his papers, do you suppose?" Jean-Louis asked.

"I hope so. I'm his legal heir, and I know his assistant well. Although my grandfather only just passed, I'm fairly certain Mr. Andrews will be comfortable sending me the documents."

Isabelle nodded slowly. It was as though a ray of light had shot through the clouds. It had been chafing at her for some time that they were so very much in the dark concerning the legend surrounding the three mystical jewels; perhaps Jack's grandfather's research would answer questions that had been accumulating for a while now.

"What information was your grandfather able to find, Mr. MacInnes?" Sally asked him.

Jack's glance flickered almost imperceptibly, and Isabelle recognized a kindred spirit as Jack scanned the room, appearing completely at ease enjoying the company of his companions. Isabelle's work as a spy during the Civil War had taught her skills that were very similar to those she often observed in Mr. MacInnes.

"More information than we can imagine, I'm sure," Jack said. "When I last saw him, he had collected quite a portfolio of stories, notes, conversations, newspaper clippings. He would be so amazed to realize . . ."

Sally nodded. "I'm sure he would. He sounds like a wonderful grandfather."

Jack nodded, a bit stiffly. "I will miss him."

"How well do you know Athens?" James asked the two men. "You've both been recently?"

They nodded. "My Greek is passable. We should be able to find what we're looking for," Jean-Louis said. "Provided, of course, we know what that might be."

"To me, it's fairly simple," Jack said quietly, leaning in again. "We find the two missing items, we join them with the third, and we destroy the lot."

Jean-Louis nodded slowly, and a muscle worked in his jaw. "You feel that this is the only course of action, then."

Jack looked at him. "I do. We must be all of a mind on this, Mr. Deveraux. Are you going to be squeamish about destroying history?"

Jean-Louis's nostrils flared slightly, but he held his ground. "Of course I am going to be squeamish about it, sir. I have built a career around studying things of the past. This is why I want to be absolutely certain there is no other alternative. Having seen the . . . the magnificence of the item firsthand . . ."

Jack nodded, his eyes hard. "This is exactly why you must keep your emotions separate from what we are about to do. We absolutely must not hesitate. I've seen the men who lust for this thing . . . It's unholy, to say the least." Jack sat back in his chair again and propped one ankle over the other knee. "You do understand, I hope."

"I do indeed," Jean-Louis said, clearly insulted. "Just as I hope you understand, sir, the travesty of your actions should you be wrong."

Jack's gaze narrowed slightly. "I am not wrong."

2

JACK MACINNES HAD HIM SPOOKED; that's all there was to it. James looked over his shoulder at every little thing and found himself more paranoid than he'd ever been in his life. Every shadow, every figure that seemed the least unpleasant, every person he passed that didn't return a smile was a possible assassin.

It was evening, and Sally had coaxed James's brother, Phillip, and Alice out from their sickbeds and taken them topside to get a breath of fresh air. Both of the invalids looked like walking death, but James had decided not to tell them that. It was unseemly to say such a thing to a woman, for one, and there was also the fact that, while Phillip might be ill, he probably wouldn't be averse to planting a fist in James's face, conveniently using it as an outlet for his frustration.

James reached Deveraux's cabin and knocked on the door. It opened presently, and the Frenchman beckoned him inside.

"The cargo is safe, I presume?" James asked him.

"Safe and sound." Jean-Louis pushed his spectacles up on his nose, his finger holding the place in a book he was reading. "Is Jack still planning on taking it tonight?"

James nodded. "The farther away it is from Phil and Alice, the more rest they seem to get at night, even being sick."

"It is certainly no problem for me," Jean-Louis said and stretched, checking his pocket watch.

"Alice is up on deck with Sally," James said. "She asked about you."

The Frenchman's face lit up and he paused midstretch. "Oh, well I shall go up right away, then. I wasn't aware she'd left her cabin."

James smiled and turned to go. On impulse, he turned back. "Deveraux, if you don't mind, I have a question for you."

"Certainly."

"When the time comes, will you truly be prepared to part with the cargo?"

"I will hate to see it happen, but yes, it is for the greater good, and I know this." Jean-Louis hesitated and frowned. "I wish there were another alternative. Do you understand the significance of what we have? It is ancient."

James nodded. "I am aware. Ancient and dangerous."

"I'll not stand in the way," Deveraux said, "as much as my instincts scream otherwise."

James bade him farewell and walked down the length of the passageway to the stairs at the end. He rotated his head from shoulder to shoulder and put a hand at the back of his neck. The stress was already beginning to mount and they hadn't even reached Athens. Not only was he concerned about harm coming from outside their group, now he also had to wonder if Deveraux would find the strength to be as good as his word when the time came.

He climbed the stairs and made his way to the lounge, taking a seat next to Isabelle, who was flipping through the pages of an old book.

"Restless?" she asked him, glancing up at his face.

He tapped his fingers against the arm of the chair. "Not really. A bit, I suppose."

"What are you pondering?"

"Nothing specific—anxious to find Sparks and be done with it."

She nodded. "And Sparks is only the half of it. If we don't find the final item, this will never go away. Phillip, and now Alice, will never be left in peace. Someone will always want them."

"Thank you for helping to assuage my concerns and calm my feelings."

She smiled. "It will be like a walk in the park."

"Now you're just being silly."

"You can't have it both ways. Either you take the truth, hard and fast, or you dance around it and pretend—sad, pathetic, and oblivious to reality." She winked.

He reached over and captured her hand, entwining their fingers. Leaning back in his chair, he stretched his legs and crossed them at the ankle, wishing they were alone. "That's what I love about you."

"What?"

"You make me smile." He glanced over and felt a thrill at the softening of her expression. She had been so unsure of their relationship when they were in Egypt, and to have her now at peace with him, with his ring on her finger—it was a victory hard-won. The problem was, though, that it wasn't over yet. Nothing in their past escapades led him to believe that the road before them wouldn't be fraught with disaster. If something were to happen to her . . . it didn't bear contemplation. He couldn't imagine a future without her.

"I think Deveraux will have a hard time of it when we reach the end of our journey," he said. "I have a vision in my head of having to bodily force him to comply."

Isabelle nodded with a half smile. "Now that would be a sight worth seeing. I believe you might have the right of it though. He does love the relics. I wish you could have seen his face when we went back into the princess's chamber after Sparks had wreaked havoc," she said, speaking of their recent time spent in Egypt. "He was nearly physically sick." She paused. "He's a good man though. I trust him."

"I hope you're right. I would hate to have to face the wrath of Alice for harming her beloved."

"Shh, silly. We're not supposed to know they are fond of one another."

He laughed. "Then they should learn to hide it better. Lovesick fools. I pity them. I have certainly never been so obvious in my affections." He winked at Isabelle as she laughed.

"Never, indeed," she said and squeezed his fingers.

"How's your diamond?"

"A perfect fit."

He leaned over and kissed the back of the hand he held. "I would have your word, madam, that you will use caution and good judgment in Greece."

"When have I ever done otherwise?"

"Shall I actually bore you with a list?"

"I always use caution and good judgment. At times, extenuating circumstances prevail upon me to act to the contrary."

"I want you do something for me, then. No 'acting to the contrary.' Truly, Isabelle, I am this close to claiming you for my own. I will be justifiably angry should something befall you."

"Should that happen, simply pry the diamond off my finger and give it to one of the other thousands of women you will be at liberty to take to wife."

"You are demented and not taking me seriously at all."

Isabelle sighed. "I do take you seriously, James. I will use caution and will take every care possible. I might ask the same of you. As it stands, only one of us has been shot during the course of our journeys, and it's not been me."

"No, but your leg was broken before you even left the States."

She glanced at him with a pout. "How gauche of you to mention it."

"Not at all. I find it attractive."

"The fact that I was wounded—you find it attractive? I, kind sir, am not the demented one."

He smiled at her, taking in her dark hair and eyes, finely sculpted face, and full lips. "I like your strength. You are beautiful and petite, and you dash in where angels fear to tread. Just don't do it anymore."

She tipped her head back and laughed. "Seems foolish to abandon the very part of my character that you find attractive."

"I find that I like you in one piece more than I like the idea of you outrunning bullets."

"I can do both."

"Your word, Isabelle. I will have it."

"Very well. You have my word. I shall not outrun any bullets unless you're at my side."

He tipped his head to one side. "Not exactly what I was hoping for, but I suppose it will suffice."

"Good." She smiled and leaned in for a kiss. He suddenly felt as though she'd won and he'd been played for a fool. As her lips met his, he smiled in return and figured there were worse ways to lose.

***

Alice tossed in her bed, feeling a sense of nausea even in her sleep. The images crowded in, bits and pieces she couldn't quite manage to place. A woman, young, wearing a white tunic held at the shoulders with gold clips . . . carrying a box under her arm as she fled through the streets in the dead of night . . . finding her way into a cold cave, moving farther into it, deeper, darker . . . water swirling around her ankles . . .

The sense that she was in danger was so strong that when Alice awoke with a start, her breath came in uneven gasps and she strained in the darkness to see something—anything.

The movement of the ship was relatively smooth and steady, which was a welcome change. She sat up in the bunk and wiped at her forehead with the sleeve of her nightgown. The sense of foreboding, of imminent danger, didn't fade with the last dregs of the dream.

She reached behind her head, and grasping a fistful of her nightgown, she pulled it up and over her head, sending the thing flying through the small cabin and leaving her dressed in a thin cotton undershirt that went to her knees. Bunching her black hair up on top of her head, she inhaled slowly and deeply and blew at a few errant strands of hair that escaped the mess she held in her fist.

Nothing was certain anymore. Her parents were dead, she was far from the only home she'd ever really known in India, and she was suddenly a key to a centuries-old mystery that had an odd, supernatural twist. She had been sick for days, and now the dreams were starting. This marked the third time she'd awoken from the same images, drenched in sweat and feeling as though she were running for her life. Or should be.

At least the birthmark on her back didn't hurt. The Jewel of Zeus was in Jack's cabin, which helped, and she wore her talisman religiously. She placed her hand just below her throat where the small silver necklace hung and rubbed it between her thumb and forefinger. It had been given to her by an old woman, a stranger, in an Egyptian village. The woman had told her it was a protection, and having felt the soothing effect it had on her burning birthmark when in close proximity to the jewel, she now never ever took the necklace off.

The first time she'd had the dream, she had been able to dismiss it as a possible side effect of her illness. By now, though, she was beginning to reassess. The dream never changed—if anything, it became more vivid, more detailed each time.

She listened carefully in the dark and heard the reassuring sounds of Isabelle's and Sally's even breathing as they slept. She was fine; she was safe. The cabin door was locked—there were people around her who cared for her. She was not alone.

Alice closed her eyes and focused on relaxing, on slowing her breathing and convincing herself that there was nothing to be afraid of. She finally loosened her grip on her hair and let it fall down her back and around her shoulders. With a sigh, she slowly lay down and closed her eyes, praying for good dreams as she'd done as a child. It was with a sense of relief that she sank gratefully into quiet oblivion.

***

Thaddeus Sparks walked with firm purpose out of the antiquities museum in Athens. He was of medium height and build, unremarkable in feature and form with the notable exception of his brilliantly green eyes. Those eyes looked right and then left, taking in details and making a mental note of his surroundings. He was observant, and that quality had always served him well.

He thought of the stone that lay hidden in the trunk in his rented room. The accommodations were not what he would have hoped for, but his funds were beginning to dwindle. If he parceled it out carefully, he might be able to make the money last until his objectives were met.

Sparks had been on a mission to find the elusive Jewel of Zeus for months and hadn't managed to track it down in India. His traveling companion, Phillip Ashby, had borne the mark that identified him as one with the potential to locate the jewel, but that plan had gone awry when the elder Ashby brother had arrived on the scene and ruined everything.

Sparks made his way thoughtfully to the Acropolis. He had been surprised to find that there were actually three jewels, not just the one; that discovery had given him new purpose, additional drive. Thanks to his quick thinking and timely intervention in following the Ashbys and their growing entourage to a dig in Egypt, he now possessed the Jewel of Poseidon. It had been hidden for centuries in an Egyptian princess's tomb. He knew from overheard conversations that the third jewel, the Jewel of Hades, likely resided in Greece. Once he had secured it, he would return to India and resume his search for the first.

When he had the three jewels together, the world would be at his feet. He believed the legend—the possessor of even *one* stone would be gifted with untold knowledge and thereby wealth. His heart tripped when he considered what he might be able to accomplish with all three.

He made his way through the city and found a small café situated in the busy market district. He sat outside under the shade of a brightly colored awning and ordered a light lunch. He continued to watch people as they passed by, absently wondering if any one of them bore the mark. He shook his head. A fat lot of good it had done him the last time he'd found one such person. Truth be told, he now knew two. He had tried to take Alice Bilbey with him but had failed. It was yet another issue on the growing list of complaints he planned to take to the Ashby brothers one day. With deadly force.

He felt a small amount of satisfaction at that image and turned when a server carried his food to him. Looking up at the man, Sparks dropped his cup of tea, and it splashed down his front and onto his lap before crashing to the floor in pieces. The waiter quickly moved his feet to avoid the mess and glanced at Sparks in irritated surprise.

Sparks swallowed, waiting for some sort of recognition to dawn on the other man's features. When none was forthcoming, he finally spoke. "Ari? Ari Kilronomos?"

The man's face went ashen at the question, and he slowly set the small tray of food down on the table. His color quickly returned as he pulled a chair out and sat opposite Sparks. With a clenched jaw, he said, "What do you know of my brother?"

3

THE AEGEAN SPREAD BEFORE THE ship—blue, sparkling, and alive as it lapped around the sun-drenched isles and hurt the eye with its brilliance. The passengers thronged the upper deck, standing at the rail and taking in the splendor that spanned the view in every direction.

Isabelle stood with the others on the deck: Alice, Sally, and Jean-Louis to her immediate left, Phillip and Jack to her right. She gripped the railing with both hands, unconscious of her intensity until her hands began to ache. The scene before her took her breath away and left her speechless. When she finally found her voice, she told James, who stood behind her, "It's the most incredibly beautiful sight I've ever beheld."

He seemed equally awestruck. "Amazing," he murmured as he placed a hand at the small of her back, his chin lightly brushing the top of her head. She felt her temperature rise a few degrees at the subtle intimacy.

As the ship neared the islands, continuing its way toward the mainland, white stone buildings were visible, clustered together near shorelines and climbing up hills. Doorways were painted brilliant blues, yellows, and pinks, and flowers decorated homes, storefronts, and streets in joyful bunches.

Isabelle closed her mouth for the third time. "People live here!" she finally exclaimed. "When they come outside in the morning to greet the day, this is what they see! I can't think of a time I've felt more envy."

"Incredible," Alice said. She stood beside Isabelle, one hand holding the rail and the other arm threaded through Sally's. "It's just lovely."

Isabelle glanced at the girl. She was pale and drawn, but her eyes finally showed a spark of hope. "You'll be glad to disembark, I imagine," Isabelle said to her.

Alice nodded and looked at Isabelle, a gentle breeze blowing tendrils of dark hair across her neck. "If I ever board another ship, it will be too soon. I cannot wait to find my feet on solid ground."

"I agree wholeheartedly," Phillip said. He seemed equally entranced with the scene unfolding before them. "I've never been so sick in all my life." He too looked rather gaunt. Though Phillip usually cut a dashing figure, his recent illness had clearly taken its toll.

Jack MacInnes stood to Phillip's right. He looked out over the horizon, his expression serious, his arm still cradled in the sling that served as a constant reminder of the danger they faced. They were a banged-up lot, to be sure: pale, sickly, gunshot ridden, birthmark cursed. Fate had brought them together in an odd manner, and Isabelle couldn't help but smile.

"Oh, look!" Sally pointed down to the water at the porpoises that jumped in the ship's wake.

"Carefree, are they not?" Jean-Louis said, standing to Sally's left. "Not a worry in the world."

"Except, perhaps, for the occasional shark," Phillip said.

"The caldera will explode again, unlike anything we have seen for thousands of years."

"I'm sorry?" Isabelle said and looked over to Jean-Louis, who shrugged and tipped his head to his left, where a man stood, looking out over the water at the islands.

The man nodded and pointed. He looked to be Greek in feature and dress, and his English was heavily accented but discernible. "Santorini," he said. "She was destroyed once before and will again burn."

Isabelle studied him with raised eyebrows. He was well-enough dressed and didn't seem out of the ordinary. His clothing was clean—that of a merchant—and he had no other oddities to mark him as unusual or one of society's outcasts. Aside from a ring on his right hand that gleamed in the sunlight, he wore no adornments.

"Are you a student of geography?" Jean-Louis asked the man after clearing his throat in the silence that had followed the odd pronouncement.

"I am a student of the past and the future."

"If he offers me a necklace or tells me I'm in danger, I shall likely scratch his eyes out," Alice muttered into Isabelle's ear.

Isabelle patted Alice's hand absently as she looked at the odd gentleman, trying inconspicuously to get a better look at the insignia on his ring. Raising the spyglass again to her eye, she made a slow scan of the horizon, dipping the glass down on the man's hand just before lowering it completely and assuming a neutral expression even as her heart thumped once, hard.

"I, also, am a student of the past," Jean-Louis told the man. "Won't you tell us more about Santorini?"

The man turned his gaze from the islands and looked at the group. Finally, he smiled. "The weather acts up at times. We never know exactly what to expect."

With that, he turned and left the railing, disappearing into the crowd.

Isabelle stirred and prepared herself to discretely follow the man as James briefly closed his eyes and with a shake of his head muttered, "Why must everything be so blasted cryptic?"

"Do you think there was a message in that?" Sally asked him, shading her eyes with her hand against the brim of her hat.

"I'm sure there was," Isabelle said, watching through the crowd as the merchant neared the stairwell leading to the lower decks. "Did you see his ring? It bears the symbol." She made to follow him and James stopped her with a hand on her arm.

"I'll go." Before she could protest, James was swallowed by the crowd.

Isabelle turned the man's odd phrases over in her mind, at a loss. Phillip moved to stand with the girls and Jean-Louis, and murmured discussions ensued. Jack looked at Isabelle, his expression grim.

"What are you thinking?" Isabelle asked him.

"That whatever he meant, it can't be good."

"Did Federation members wear rings to identify themselves?"

He shook his head. "Not any of those I worked for."

"Not the Federation head, even?"

"No. Never—I would have noticed. I was with him all the time."

It was some time before James returned to them at the deck railing. "The man is gone," he said. "I can't find him anywhere."

***

Greece had been an independent state for roughly thirty years and Athens was her newly proclaimed capital. The city lay at the foot of the Acropolis, a large platform of land that rose two hundred feet above the modern town. The ancient buildings atop the Acropolis were familiar to Isabelle from photos and illustrations, and the fact that it now spread before her in all its splendor was overwhelming and awe-inspiring.

The weather was comfortable—even in January. The temperatures were known to be moderate but, in some places, rather cool. It had been quite warm in both India and Egypt—what they lacked in clothing they would have to purchase in Athens.

Their first stop once they arrived on the docks at Piraeus was at the British embassy, where Jack spoke with authorities regarding his identity and their plans to find Thaddeus Sparks, who was wanted for abduction in India and theft in Egypt. They next made their way to the national bank, where they exchanged money and Isabelle opened a temporary account. Genevieve's advance on Isabelle's inheritance was generous—Isabelle's mind boggled when she thought of it.

After taking the advice of a bank employee and seeking out one of the city's largest hotels, well used to accommodating the needs of American and European travelers, they booked a suite on the second floor that totaled three rooms: a bedroom for the women that adjoined a large sitting room, and on the other side, a room for the men. Water closet facilities were just down the hallway and shared with the suite next door.

At Isabelle's request, the hotel concierge ordered a light tea sent up from the kitchens, and it was delivered by a shy young woman who introduced herself as Leila and a younger boy named Theo, who seemed mortified to be relegated to serving tea. They spoke halting English, and Isabelle learned that they were siblings who worked to help support their mother after their father had died from a protracted illness.

Isabelle helped the two disperse the meal in the sitting room, and she noted Leila's blush when Jack thanked her warmly for his cup of tea. Giving the siblings a generous tip for their services, she was gratified to see them beam and exchange a quick look of delighted shock as they left the room and she closed the door behind them.

"I feel as though we've been here before," Isabelle said as she turned back to the assembled group.

Sally wrinkled her brow. "In Greece?"

"No. Chasing Sparks." She retrieved her own cup of tea and a small, open-faced sandwich on flatbread with sliced tomatoes and cucumbers, drizzled with olive oil.

"That's because it's exactly where we were less than six months ago." James frowned and scribbled with his fountain pen. "Now then," he said, "we have a basic idea of how the man operates. According to Phil, Sparks formulates a plan, a theory of where the jewel might be and how it would have arrived there, and then he runs in with all guns blazing."

"Do you have any inkling of how much Sparks may know of the legend?" Jack asked Phillip. "He now knows there are three jewels as opposed to one, but did he ever say anything that might lead you to believe he has the wherewithal to reason a logical location?"

Phillip shook his head. "In India, he was convinced the British army had been in possession of the jewel during the Sepoy Rebellion of '57, so we visited sacred sites and museums in each of the rebellion's key cities. He was wrong though." He paused. "It's probably safe to assume he will try museums again. He's intelligent enough to know where to ask about pieces of antiquity."

"I believe we would be well-advised to do as we did in India," Isabelle said and turned to Jack. "We went around to places of potential interest—temples, museums, and the like—and left a description of Sparks with people likely to pay attention to the movements of a foreigner."

"Mostly street children," James clarified. "They proved to have the best eyes and ears. They also responded well to bribery."

Jack nodded. "We shouldn't have to wait much longer for my grandfather's papers to arrive. There was a message from Mr. Andrews waiting at the telegraph office when we arrived. He put a large parcel in the post the day he received my request. From this point, I'll have him cable the hotel directly."

"So, we check the museums for Sparks and wait for the parcel?" Alice asked.

Isabelle nodded. "And while we wait for the parcel, we should be doing some detective work of our own. Not only must we divest Sparks of the thing he took from us, we also need to beat him to the third. Also," she added, "be especially aware of that odd ring. The man aboard the ship most definitely had the symbol—the rectangle encasing the three oval stones—on his."

***

Directly following tea, the group set out to scour the town. They stopped at temples, gave a cursory examination of ruins, and gave coins to children and anyone else looking to benefit from the money by sharing any information concerning an American man with bright green eyes who was looking for antiquities. Jack directed those they bribed to leave any messages at the telegraph office, where he would check twice daily, rather than at the hotel.

After spending a considerable amount of time in their efforts, Isabelle noted the yawns that many in the party tried to hide. Suggesting they rest before dinner, she led them back toward the hotel. A scant block from their lodgings, Jean-Louis noticed a small, plain, whitewashed building with a single sign above the door. It proclaimed itself a museum and antiquities shop, and when Jean-Louis expressed an interest in entering, Isabelle told him she'd join him and sent the others ahead to the hotel.

Entering the museum after being in the bright sunlight had Isabelle blinking in an effort to adjust to the darkened interior. Jean-Louis followed her as she ventured farther into the small lobby and wondered where they might find the curator.

"Perhaps they are still at lunch," Jean-Louis said as he examined the room, which had seen some wear.

"The door was unlocked," Isabelle said, following his gaze along the cracks in the walls and chipping plaster. "What does that notice say?"

Jean-Louis squinted at a piece of paper propped up on a small desk that likely served as a reception table. "The price of admission," he said. "And a warning to refrain from handling the artifacts."

Isabelle glanced at him. "I wonder if we should just take a look around . . ."

Jean-Louis regarded her with an unreadable expression.

"Aren't you curious about the artifacts?" she asked with a smile.

"Well certainly; however, I would prefer to wait until someone knows we're here."

"We might see more if they don't."

Jean-Louis shifted his weight from one foot to the other and looked beyond Isabelle to the open doorway at their left.

"What is the cost of admission?"

He read the sign and told her, and Isabelle rummaged through her reticule until she found the required amount for the two of them; he protested and reached for his own wallet. She waved away his concerns and placed the money on the desk, motioning with her head. He looked at her for a moment before slightly shaking his head and following her through the open doorway.

The room was arranged with shelving along the walls and with tables in the center. There was clearly a system in place, but the artifacts were piled high and called out for more space. Potsherds covered the surface of the shelves nearest the door. There were also more complete pieces of earthenware pottery and broken bits of larger mosaics sprinkled into the mix.

Isabelle watched Jean-Louis as he made his way along the first wall, taking in the items with wide eyes. He leaned in for a closer look and stretched out his hands, stopping himself inches away from a small piece of statuary. Instead, he placed his hands in his pockets with a frown.

"I'm relatively certain that you will not harm these pieces," Isabelle told him with a wink. "Of anyone to enter this room, you're likely the most reverent."

He glanced at her and finally smiled a bit. "We are in here without permission," he said in a whisper. "I'll not add insult to injury."

"So," she said, indicating to the overflowing shelves as they continued to move slowly down the wall, "do you suppose these are authentic?"

He shrugged lightly. "I am hardly the expert the Stafford brothers are," he said in reference to the conservators they had worked with at the dig in Egypt. "They would likely have them identified and catalogued before I could even determine a reasonable range of dates. Still, many of these pieces do seem particularly interesting." They explored the museum in a companionable silence until he continued, "You mentioned seeing the three ovals inside a rectangle while in India, correct?"

Isabelle nodded.

"And then, of course, we saw the same symbol in Egypt, both in the Great Pyramid and again in Ibis's burial chamber. I believe it would stand to reason that if there is indeed something similar hidden here in Greece, we should see that same symbol. Somewhere."

Isabelle nodded, and Jean-Louis continued his perusal of the items in silence for a moment before speaking again. "Do you know what will happen to Alice when we are finished here?" he asked Isabelle, his eyes still forward on the shelves as they walked.

"I suppose she will return to England to be with her brothers."

"Is the eldest brother of the age of majority?"

"I don't believe so. Colonel Bilbey had a brother—likely he will have guardianship until the eldest is of age." Isabelle watched him surreptitiously as she ran an eye over the items on the shelves. The man was clearly fascinated with antiquities, but he had the entire room at his disposal and he was distracted by thoughts of Alice? She smiled. *Smitten* was the word that readily came to mind.

His brow creased in a frown. "Do you suppose . . . do you suppose . . ."

Isabelle tipped her head to one side and waited.

"I am concerned for her health. I don't like the notion that she is to play such a key role in this . . . drama." He flushed. "Not as though I have any claim to intimate worry for her. I just, I suppose I . . ." The Frenchman paused, faced her squarely, and dropped his voice. "I don't like it, Isabelle. I am uncomfortable with this turn of events. She is young and innocent. What will happen if she falls into the wrong hands?"

Isabelle raised a brow. He was indeed serious if he was finally willing to use her first name. She had given him leave to do so quite a while back, but he had remained very formal and respectful. "I understand, Jean-Louis, truly I do. I am equally concerned. We must keep her close to at least one of us at all times. I will guard her with my life—you must know this by now."

He nodded. "I do know you would. I would not suggest otherwise. I just . . ." He ran a hand through his hair. "I care for her very much." He gave a short laugh. "I don't even know to whom I should declare my intentions."

"And what are those?"

"I should very much like to court her."

Isabelle smiled. "Even in these odd circumstances? It's a bit difficult to meet in her parlor for tea and cakes."

He returned her smile. "Then I suppose I shall have to make do."

They resumed their study of the room in silence. Isabelle wondered if it were little more than an exercise in futility. What were the odds that they would actually find what they were looking for?

A few words barked in rapid Greek pulled her gaze to the door. A stout man stood in the doorway, his hair a tousled gray mop. Jean-Louis stiffened and made his way to the man, his words tripping over themselves in a hodgepodge of English and Greek.

After a fair amount of loud speaking and gesticulating, the short man finally seemed moderately placated. The red color that had suffused his face was beginning to recede, and Isabelle was glad they wouldn't have to summon a doctor.

"Might I assume you told him we left our money on the desk?" Isabelle asked Jean-Louis as she made her way over to them and offered a hand to the Greek.

"I did," Jean-Louis said. "This man is the proprietor; his name is Demitrios Metaxas." Jean-Louis introduced Isabelle formally to the man, who had clasped her fingers in greeting.

Metaxas said a few words in Greek, looking at Isabelle.

"He says you are very beautiful, that surely you have Greek blood."

Isabelle smiled, one brow raised. While she had never considered herself beautiful, James constantly told her that she was and she found herself coming to believe it. This man, however, was a charmer and a rogue. "My maternal grandmother was from Spain."

Jean-Louis translated, and the response was a comment on how that would have to do, that he supposed Spain was close enough, and that perhaps it was the fact that she was a foreigner that gave her such exotic appeal. Isabelle's lips twitched and she fought to keep her expression neutral.

Further conversation revealed that while the establishment was a museum, for the right price Metaxas was willing to sell pieces of interest. Through Jean-Louis, Isabelle asked him if it would not put him afoul of his government. Apparently, Demitrios Metaxas wasn't worried about such entanglements. He dismissed the concern with a wave of his hand and a few telling gestures.

"Jean-Louis, I wonder if you would ask our friend if he has ever seen the symbol," Isabelle said.

Jean-Louis spoke slowly, at times apparently searching for the right words. He pulled a small notebook and pen from his pocket, drawing the man a small sketch.

Isabelle watched Metaxas's reaction. His eyes lifted from the drawing to Jean-Louis's face. He spoke briefly in Greek, at which point Jean-Louis turned to Isabelle.

"He says I'm the second man to ask him about the symbol this week."

4

"Described him perfectly," Isabelle told James and Jack when she and Jean-Louis returned from the museum. "It was definitely Sparks, so we're on the right trail." She paused. "Metaxas also said his brother owns a shop about two miles away where we can purchase firearms."

James quirked a brow. "Some of us already have weapons—do you really believe we'll need more?"

"Can't hurt," Jack muttered.

The three of them sat by a window in a small café near the hotel and looked out over the city that had darkened with nightfall. Gas lanterns twinkled to life, giving Athens a cozy glow.

"Have you identified yourself to the Greek authorities?" James asked Jack in an undertone.

Jack nodded. "I went in this afternoon. The statement we managed to get from the Egyptian police at the dig will help, but we can only hope the locals here will be willing to go through with the extradition process once we catch Sparks. At my suggestion, they are requesting further proof of Sparks's criminal activities from Egyptian authorities. When we capture him, should they find cause to release him . . ."

Isabelle nodded. They would hardly be able to hold Sparks captive themselves—they were forced to rely on the help of the Greek authorities.

Isabelle stirred her tea and furrowed her brow in thought. Alice, Sally, Phillip, and Jean-Louis were at the hotel together. They had all agreed that, for the time being, Alice and Phillip should remain as inconspicuous as possible but had thought of it only after they had been parading around Athens all afternoon. Isabelle was forced to wonder if such a course was counterproductive, and she said as much to the gentlemen at her table.

"I don't know." James looked grim and glanced at Jack, who was equally solemn. "We know Sparks wants Alice, especially since he tried to take her with him when he left the cave in Egypt. Placing her into the open might draw him out."

"Or place her right in his line of fire," Isabelle said.

"If we're careful," Jack offered slowly, "we might be able to accomplish our objective and still keep both her and Phillip safe. We remain together as a large group whenever Phillip and Alice are out."

James nodded. "We will have to think of something. Neither one is going to stay cooped up in the hotel forever."

Isabelle drew a deep breath. "So we'll all continue our 'sightseeing' together. There are seven of us, and with Sparks knowing what he's looking for, we shouldn't have to wait long before he shows his face."

Jack nodded. "What of the other museums? Are they worth pursuing?"

"Yes," Isabelle said and poked at her dessert with a fork. Her stomach was tied in knots, and as delectable as the food was, she didn't think she could eat it. When she offered it to him, James took the plate from her with eager relish, and she felt a smile tugging at the corners of her mouth as he attacked the dessert.

She nodded and continued. "According to Metaxas, the museums here in Athens are finally coming into their own, with more artifacts and antiquities catalogued daily. Now that Greece has her independence from the Turks, there seems to be a renewed local interest to restore their treasures and build places in which to showcase them. I believe they are worth the time it would take to examine them."

Jack leaned in a bit, bracing his good elbow on the table. "What, exactly, do the stones mean? I keep asking myself this question. We know that the pharaoh's daughter was guardian of the one in Egypt, but how did it come to be there? We know the one owned by the Bilbey family was found in India. It was supposedly taken to the Bilbey estate in England by an ancestor who had nothing to do with the legend, but eventually Alice turns up in the family line bearing the mark. The hieroglyphs seem to suggest that the three stones belong together. So why were they separated? And who did it?"

Isabelle looked out of the window at the dark Athens night and finally shrugged. "I would love to find someone who knows. Someone who knows and is willing to speak of it."

James nodded and wiped his mouth with a snow-white linen napkin that had been embroidered along the edge with bright blue and yellow flowers. "One can hope we might learn of it here. For some reason, they all three seem to lead to Greece."

***

"You want me to deliberately set out to find another batty old woman?" Alice demanded of Isabelle as the seven travelers left the hotel the following morning.

"So far, the help we've received from those 'batty old women' has meant something valuable. Since this seems to be the trend, I'm suggesting we put you out there in the market to be seen. If you happen to feel a tug or a pull to any one person, you let me know. Mr. Metaxas told us to watch for a woman named Elysia, and he said she is a self-proclaimed expert of Greece's legends and myths, even obscure ones. She sells fruit at the market with her niece." Isabelle didn't mention that Metaxas had made a swirling sign with his finger near his head, indicating his opinion of Elysia's mental health.

Alice frowned but refrained from further comment. The stroll through the marketplace was everything the tourist in Isabelle hoped it would be—everything she'd ever imagined. Though much like Cairo in that the stalls and storefronts were close together and crowded with people, the feel of the place was uniquely Greek. Whitewashed buildings glistened in the morning sun, and the light emphasized the bright colors of the clothes and accessories on the people who shopped, bargained, chatted with friends, and teased friendly rivals.

Alice walked slightly ahead of the group with Jean-Louis close behind and Sally at her side. The girls linked arms, and Isabelle noticed Alice's eyes moving over the crowd of people, even as she conversed. Rather than look like a cowboy's posse, the other members of the group did their best to act as though they had not a care in the world outside the marketplace.

They stopped periodically to buy small trinkets and food, chatting amiably and laughing.

It wasn't long before Isabelle noticed an older woman who was seated next to a fruit vendor. She held needlework in her hands, but her eyes were on Alice. As the girl moved down the street, the woman's gaze followed. Alice turned her head, made eye contact with the woman, and paused. She began moving again when Sally tugged on her arm to show her a bundle of bright head scarves.

The woman eventually stood and moved toward the girls. By now, Alice had turned her head around again, and she didn't seem at all surprised when the woman reached them and touched her arm.

Isabelle quickened her step and reached them as the old woman, in a heavy accent, said, "Good fruit." She gestured toward the stall where she'd been sitting and pulled on Alice's arm.

"I am in the mood for some good fruit," Isabelle said. "Why don't we, girls?"

James, Phillip, and Jack moved on, pausing at a shop just beyond the fruit stand. Sally, Isabelle, Alice, and Jean-Louis followed the old woman back to her perch, where she took her seat again on a tall stool and, speaking in Greek, gestured to the owner.

The stall owner smiled and nodded at the group. "You would like some fruit?" she said in easy English. She was younger than the woman who had approached them: Isabelle's best guess placed the woman somewhere around forty-five to fifty years old, with beautiful features that would only be enhanced with continued age. Her hair was pulled back into a smooth twist at the nape of her neck and showed surprisingly few strands of gray intertwined with a color so black it was almost blue. High cheekbones and hazel eyes complemented her classically Greek style.

"We would," Isabelle said with a smile. "How much for the nectarines?"

The woman told her, and Isabelle counted the money into her palm and handed it to the woman, who smiled and put the coins into a small cash box at her elbow.

Polishing a particularly large nectarine, Isabelle took a satisfying bite and chewed thoughtfully, looking at the old woman, who was staring unapologetically at Alice. Her gray hair was pulled into a chignon similar to that of her younger counterpart, but despite a few similarities in their features, Isabelle assumed they were not mother and daughter.

The old woman introduced herself as Elysia Floros and the stall owner as Helene Petrojanis, her niece. Jean-Louis made the introductions for Isabelle, Alice, and Sally, after which Elysia turned to Jean-Louis and asked him a question in her native tongue. Jean-Louis easily answered her, engaging in conversation with his beginner's Greek, which was sounding more and more fluid to Isabelle with each exchange he had with the natives.

Jean-Louis smiled at the older woman as he turned to Alice. "She says you are here looking for something. She recognizes you."

Alice frowned a bit. "Tell her I've not had the pleasure of an intro-duction before today."

"You'll forgive my aunt," Helene Petrojanis said, her face slightly flushed. "She often forgets herself."

"Not at all," Isabelle said. "We certainly take no offense."

Elysia said something else to Jean-Louis, and Helene opened her mouth to interject but stopped when Elysia put up a hand for her silence. With a purse of her lips, Helene sat back on her stool and cast an apologetic glance at Isabelle.

Jean-Louis told Alice, "She believes you recognized her as well."

Alice stiffened for a moment, and then her shoulders relaxed, almost as if in resignation. She sighed. "I suppose I felt a certain . . . I don't know. I knew she was there."

"I wonder, would you mind if we ask your aunt about local legends and lore?" Isabelle said to Helene.

The younger woman sighed, sounding much like Alice. "Only if you have the time," she said. "And I must apologize in advance."

Isabelle smiled at her. "Your English is very good."

"I spent the last thirty years as a governess to a family in England. When Elysia's only son died last year, I returned home to care for her."

"Miss Petrojanis," Jean-Louis said, "would you mind terribly if I translate for your aunt? I am working on my Greek."

Helene gestured with her hand. "Of course," she said. "I will enjoy the respite."

"And you will correct me if I'm wrong."

"Only if you wish it," Helene said with a smile.

Jean-Louis turned his attention to Elysia and relayed Isabelle's request for her knowledge of Greek legends. The woman's wrinkled face broke into wreaths of smiles. "She says she knows everything that has ever happened here from the beginning of time," he translated.

"Excellent! Perhaps she knows of the mysterious legend of the jewel?" Isabelle spoke to the older woman and kept her face pleasant, approachable. Lighthearted.

Elysia looked at Isabelle for a moment, her smiling visage becoming thoughtful. Jean-Louis translated for her, saying, "She would like to know how a foreigner from faraway lands knows of the legend." Her gaze again came to rest on Alice.

"Worthy legends travel the world," Isabelle said.

Elysia raised her eyebrows and assessed Isabelle, finally nodding once. "There was a princess," she said through Jean-Louis. "A princess who lived in a beautiful land with a father who was wicked and cruel. He and his close advisors lived in debauchery and decadence, and they worshipped the dark one. The queen had died, leaving her mountainous riches and special abilities to her daughter, for she knew her husband was unworthy.

"The princess knew that she would one day reign, and she told her trusted circle of friends that she intended to use her wealth and influence for good, to restore the kingdom to its proper place, a place of learning and joy. She was betrayed to her father, who began to plot her death.

"The princess knew her father would kill her, so she began spiriting away her treasures and wealth in a hidden cavern along the shore so her father would be unable to use them to further his intentions to wage war on neighboring lands and inflict further pain upon the people. She wanted to be certain that the hiding place would remain secret until long after the king's death, but she also knew that without her to again uncover the cache, it would remain lost. She crafted three stones from the walls of the cavern and infused them each with properties that would guide the bearer back to the resting place of the treasure when all were combined and placed within a special alabaster box."

The woman's voice had taken on a mesmerizing quality, and Isabelle found herself swaying toward the bench of fruit separating her from Elysia. A glance at the other young women proved that they too were under the same hypnotic spell.

"The princess gave the location of the box with the three stones to her trusted handmaiden, telling her to disperse them far and wide should anything happen. Within time, of course, the king arranged the princess's death. It looked as though she had fallen down a flight of stairs and met her doom simply; however, close observers noted the bruising around her throat. Seeking self-preservation, they said nothing.

"The king's rage knew no bounds when he found that the treasury had been depleted, and in his wrath he called upon the one he worshipped to destroy the kingdom. The volcano erupted and the earth shook. The handmaiden escaped with the box and three stones, terrified and alone as the kingdom was besieged by the elements, the likes of which the world had never seen. The fiery storm, sent by the dark one, buried the entire kingdom under the waves of the sea.

"Fearing she had not been the only survivor, the handmaiden hurried to honor her princess's last wishes. She left one jewel in Greece, took one to what would become India, and the other to that which is now Egypt. The jewels would find their way to families whose firstborn daughters would guard them well. Daughters with the mark. One identical to the princess's. A star upon the back."

Isabelle's mouth dropped open and she hastily closed it. She looked at Alice, whose fingers had gone slack, dumping her apple back onto the piles of fresh fruit.

Isabelle cleared her throat and asked, "What of men? Do they also bear the mark?"

Elysia listened to the question and nodded with a shrug, watching Alice's face. "They can," Jean-Louis translated when she spoke, "but they are never the proper guardians. Only the eldest female of the family is capable of discerning the whereabouts of the ancient kingdom when she holds the three jewels in their box."

"Treasure?" Alice said softly. "The stones lead to the princess's treasure?"

Jean-Louis again answered for Elysia. "She says yes, but only one who is worthy will find it. And should the time come that the followers of the dark one come close to obtaining the combined stones, the elements again will rage. It will fall to a guardian to destroy those stones."

"Destroy them how?" Alice asked, breathless.

"The tapestries tell."

Elysia's eyes took on an assessing look as she watched her audience's reactions. She looked at Isabelle and then Alice when she said, "You know of the jewels."

Isabelle blinked. "You speak English?"

Elysia held up her thumb and forefinger, positioning them close together. "This much."

"We do know of the jewels," Isabelle said. To lie to the woman would be futile. She had eyes that likely saw everything.

"Danger," Elysia said with a nod. She turned to Jean-Louis for a lengthier explanation.

"She says that evil men have always sought the jewels because of the promise of ultimate knowledge—knowledge of the treasure's whereabouts. There were a handful of survivors—the King's Men—who had spied on the handmaiden and learned of the jewels. They formed a fraternity determined to recover the jewels and find their way back to the treasure. The society has continued throughout the ages and is no less evil now than it was then." Jean-Louis paused at Elysia's next comment. "They wear a ring," he said.

With a flash of memory, Isabelle recalled the strange man at the railing of the ship and asked, "What of the curse?"

Elysia nodded at her. "The curse, yes. A . . . a . . ." She turned to Jean-Louis, who again spoke for her.

"A ruse, she says—rumors circulated to warn people away from the jewels. A ploy to keep them from the wrong hands. But she also says that there do seem to be odd happenings with the jewels . . . or so she's been told."

"Do you believe in the legend, Mrs. Floros?" Isabelle said to her. "Truth?"

Elysia Floros nodded, her expression serious. "Oh yes. Legend is truth."

"How does she know?" Sally whispered wide-eyed to Jean-Louis while watching Elysia.

"Indeed," Helene Petrojanis muttered under her breath.

With an irritated glance at her niece, Elysia turned her wise gaze onto Sally. "I know," she said. She said something further in Greek, and when Jean-Louis hesitated uncertainly, Helene offered an encouraging nod. "People are afraid to speak of it," Elysia continued through Jean-Louis. "The streets have eyes and ears. But I am not afraid. I am selective though."

A shout from passersby pulled Isabelle from the cocoon Elysia had woven around the small group and back into the present. Suddenly noises seemed louder, colors brighter; everything was more pronounced and she blinked a few times.

"Elysia," Helene said and rapidly followed with something in Greek. Jean-Louis raised a brow but refrained from translating.

"I find your story amazing," Alice said to Elysia.

"You come back," Elysia said. "We talk again. Come tomorrow morning. To my home."

Isabelle looked at Helene. "Miss Petrojanis, we wouldn't want to impose," she said genuinely. The niece clearly had frustrations with the aunt.

Helene waved a hand and smiled. "Please, call me Helene. And truthfully, I would enjoy the company. I am not planning to be here at the stall tomorrow morning—I do this mostly to get my aunt out of the house anyhow. Would you join us for breakfast?"

Telling her they would love to, Isabelle again turned her attention to the old woman as Jean-Louis retrieved a notebook and wrote the address and quick directions to the women's house. Elysia continued to study Alice, who watched over Jean-Louis's shoulder as he scribbled in his book.

"Walking distance from here, then?" Alice asked Helene, who nodded.

"And a beautiful view of the city," Helene said with a smile. "We shall dine on the rooftop. Oh, and Mr. Deveraux, your comprehension of our language is most impressive."

Jean-Louis gave her a nod of acknowledgement, a satisfied smile twitching at the corner of his mouth.

With a promise to meet them in the morning, Isabelle herded her charges out from under the awning and back into the bright sunlight.

5

LATER THAT AFTERNOON, JACK MACINNES walked the short distance from the hotel to the post office and requested that the worker check to see if a parcel from England had arrived in his name. There were a fair number of people in the lobby, milling about and either sending or signing for packages. Sounds of the Greek language flowed around him in a comfortable way; for the most part, people seemed content.

Jack's heart picked up its pace as he watched an employee reappear from a doorway and motion to him. The man was holding a parcel wrapped in brown paper and tied with heavy string. The return identification showed his grandfather's office address from Oxford, care of Lawrence Andrews. Jack signed for the package with a hand that trembled, and he thanked the employee.

He quickly walked the half mile to the hotel with the parcel under his arm, conscious of the fact that he was alone and going against the group's pact that they would always travel in pairs at least. He had been so desperate, though, for something—anything—that would provide him with a physical tie to his grandfather. Jackson Pearce, the man for whom Jack was named, had been dead for nearly two months, but Jack had been on his assignment in Egypt and unable to say a proper good-bye. He had been closer to his grandfather than anyone else in his life; the loss was still staggering and he didn't like to think about it.

Jack reached the hotel and crossed the lobby, waving a quick hello to the hotel proprietor. Climbing the stairs to the second floor, he found all of his companions in the common room, finishing their tea and scones with honey.

"It's here," he said and made his way to the coffee table at the center of the room. The low table sat centered to the fireplace and was flanked by chairs and sofas on three sides. There was a scramble of excitement as the others cleared a space on the table for him to place the box. Sitting next to Isabelle on a sofa, he pulled a small knife from his jacket, cut the parcel strings, and pulled the paper back.

An envelope sat atop a thick, black, leather-bound journal and a heavy stack of papers that were held together with thin twine. Lifting the whole of it, he set it on his lap and opened the black book, which showed his grandfather's neat handwriting communicating from beyond the grave. Jack's eyes burned and he found himself wishing that he were alone.

"Would you like a moment?" Isabelle whispered.

He managed a smile. "No, but thank you."

The ensuing pause was a bit awkward, but Isabelle covered it nicely for him. "Let's get down to business, then, shall we?"

Using his knife, Jack slit the envelope open and withdrew a paper that was folded and slightly bent, as though it had been shoved into the envelope. He opened the paper and read the brief missive, a frown creasing his forehead and deepening as he reached the end of the note.

Jackson,

I must apologize for the state of disarray in which you will find the contents of your grandfather's files. His office has been burglarized twice in the past fortnight, and I fear these papers were the object of the thieves' quest.

I will write more tomorrow, but for now, I send this bundle to you without delay.

Take care, and I remain,
Your faithful servant,
Lawrence Andrews

Jack glanced up at the faces that watched him expectantly and then returned his gaze to the letter, reading it aloud. When he finished, silence filled the room.

"Burglarized?" Sally said. "Who in England would want your grandfather's papers?"

Jack scanned the message one more time, feeling a sense of unease creep up his spine. "I don't know," he said, and he was struck by a thought that left him feeling sick. If the Federation had discovered his identity and somehow tied him to his grandfather . . . that may well explain the burglary.

***

Isabelle read into the late hours of the evening, absorbing facts and poring over Dr. Pearce's meticulous records. The man had indeed been thorough; his journals included conversations he'd had through the years with persons who were supposedly knowledgeable about the legend of the three jewels. He also had maps of Greece and the Aegean with notes scribbled in the margins, along with sketches, newspaper clippings, and comments taken from bits of anecdotes heard whispered from this or that source.

It would take days to fully understand everything the man had compiled; as it was, she, Jack, and Jean-Louis had been at it for hours and had barely scratched the surface. They sat on the floor, chairs shoved out of the way, surrounded by documents, and Isabelle had opened her own journal to jot down details she felt relevant to understanding the legend.

"Quite a few maps of the Peloponnese," she murmured as she examined the map in her hand.

Jean-Louis nodded. "I've found at least three," he said.

"Here's another sketch of Santorini," Jack said and turned the paper he held toward Isabelle and Jean-Louis. "Didn't the man on the steamer say something about it?"

Isabelle nodded. "That it would blow or explode . . . erupt?" She rubbed her eyes and looked at the mantel clock. It was well past the dinner hour; James and Phillip had taken the young women to the hotel dining room for supper sometime earlier.

Phillip and Alice were slowly regaining their appetites—they seemed to experience less nausea and fatigue each day. Isabelle wondered about the difference. In Egypt, Alice had experienced discomfort from her birthmark when near the jewel, but she hadn't been ill. It must have been due to the ocean voyage.

After dinner, the girls had decided to settle down for the evening in the bedroom; Isabelle had told them she would be along momentarily.

Momentarily had disappeared two hours ago.

Jack had thrown himself into the task of deciphering the documents and trying to place them in some sort of logical order. She suspected his drive stemmed from a desire to ignore the fact that his grandfather wasn't alive to tell him about the papers himself.

James and Phillip had gone for an evening stroll after dinner despite the fact that they'd only just decided Phillip and Alice were to never be outside without all of the other five surrounding them. Phillip had said something about needing fresh air and now returned looking none the worse for the wear.

"You weren't accosted, I see," Isabelle said as they entered the room.

Phillip snorted. "Rather wish I would have been. Better that than hiding and waiting for Sparks to do something."

"What have you learned?" James asked, motioning to the piles of papers stacked on the coffee table in several categories.

Jack sighed and leaned back against the front of the couch from his sprawling position on the floor. "We have information, some of which we already knew, on all three jewels: the Jewel of Zeus was found in India, the Jewel of Poseidon was found in Egypt, and the Jewel of Hades is supposedly here in Greece."

"And thanks to Elysia Floros, we know how the jewels reached the destinations they did," Isabelle said.

"If you believe the ramblings of an old woman," James said.

"One thing is certain—the details she offered us match completely what we already know. I think she may continue to be a good source of information." Isabelle had jotted the details of Elysia's story in her journal.

James sat down on the floor opposite Isabelle and stretched out his long legs, crossing them at the ankles. He leaned against a chair and tipped his head back, closing his eyes. "We have the Jewel of Zeus, Sparks has the Jewel of Poseidon, we don't know who has the Jewel of Hades, and the Federation wants all three."

"Not only the Federation, but a local group who also seeks the jewels—they consider themselves blood descendants of some sort," Jack said and rubbed the bridge of his nose. "I found a sketch of the ring we saw on the man who spoke to us aboard the steamship."

"Perhaps descendants of the King's Men—those who sought the princess's life. If we are to believe the ramblings of an old woman," Isabelle said with a wink at James.

"And how are you organizing these stacks?" Phillip asked, motioning to the coffee table.

Jean-Louis placed a sketch on the center pile. "A stack for each jewel and a stack for regional information about Greece. Maps, diagrams, and the like."

"And is it all fairly self-explanatory?" James said.

Isabelle stretched her neck around in an attempt to ease the stiffness that had settled in from sitting so long. "Not all of it. Some, but other things, like the maps—he offers no reason as to why he collected them."

Jack frowned. "I believe I shall send a cable in the morning. Ask Andrews a few questions about the parcel. He did say in his note that he would be sending a letter the next day. Perhaps we'll see it soon." He paused. "I have an inkling that we may be in for rough seas ahead."

James closed his eyes for a moment. "When are we ever not?"

6

HELENE OPENED THE FRONT DOOR to a charming home that perched on the side of a hill overlooking the city. The outer walls were brilliantly bright, and the door a deep blue. There were flowers in abundance at the windows and near the door and fruit trees in the side yard. The steps were wet as though they had recently been washed clean.

Helene smiled widely as she dried her hands on her apron. "One moment," she said and reached to a side table where she'd placed a tray of food. "Let's go up to the roof. My aunt is already there," she said and motioned to the stairs that climbed from the front around to the side of the house.

Jean-Louis motioned for Isabelle, Sally, Alice, and Helene to precede him up the stairs and in the end convinced Helene to let him carry the tray for her. "You will spoil me," she said with a laugh.

Isabelle caught her breath when they reached the roof. It was surrounded on all four sides by a waist-high wrought-iron fence. There was a round table with surrounding chairs tucked into one corner, shaded by a large yellow umbrella that was adorned along the edges with bluebirds. Elysia sat comfortably under the umbrella and rose when she saw them approach.

She gave each of the girls a kiss on the cheek and allowed Jean-Louis the privilege of kissing her hand after he returned the tray of food to Helene. When they were seated and Helene had dished up offerings of hot milk, fresh bread, jam, honey, and a healthy side of fruit and nuts, Isabelle took a moment to examine the view, which was spectacular. The ancient city lay against a vividly blue sky that was populated with large, white clouds. The air was cool enough to warrant a light shawl but certainly pleasant enough to enjoy a meal alfresco.

Isabelle turned her face toward the sun and briefly closed her eyes, forgetting for a moment that they were involved in anything other than a tranquil vacation to the Mediterranean. Jean-Louis was busy translating Elysia's comments to the girls, and as Isabelle turned her attention to her plate and enjoyed her first bite of warm bread with honey, Helene leaned close to her and murmured, "Incredibly beautiful here, is it not?"

Isabelle sighed. "Did you miss it while you were in England?"

Helene nodded. "I did. I came home for holidays and found it hard to return."

"And now you are home for good."

"I am; although I spent so much time in England that the family there became more familiar to me than my own." Helene looked at her aunt, who was speaking with animated gestures and making the girls smile. "She needed someone here, and I was the most likely choice. I never married; I have no children."

Isabelle smiled at her. "So therefore, the assumption is that you haven't a life of your own."

Helene laughed a bit. "I'm afraid it's true. The only other family members are Elysia's two brothers and their families," she said and lowered her voice as she added, "They wanted nothing to do with her, I'm afraid."

"And your parents?" Isabelle asked.

Helene took a sip of her milk and wiped her mouth with a napkin that was embroidered with the same bluebirds that adorned the umbrella. "They passed five years ago. A boating accident just off the coast."

"I am sorry for your loss," Isabelle said.

Helene gestured subtly with her fork. "And what of the two young women you travel with?"

"Orphans, both," Isabelle said, forgoing lengthier discussion about them in light of the fact that they were both within earshot, distracted by Elysia or not. "As am I." With a smile, she lifted her glass and clinked it against Helene's.

"We all find ourselves in good company then, do we not?" Helene said with a laugh as she drank to Isabelle's salute.

"Were you close to your aunt as a child?" Isabelle asked.

Helene nodded. "She and my mother were twins; Elysia's older by two minutes. We spent time together, all of the family. I was always here—this has been her home since marriage. My home with my parents was just down that street," she said, pointing. "My brother and his family live there now."

Helene frowned. "She is not as . . . perceptive as she once was. She says odd things. I must apologize again." Helene shook her head with a glance at Elysia. "I nearly choked yesterday when you asked her about the legend. She is convinced of its truth and will talk about it for hours if prompted. And sometimes if not prompted."

Isabelle paused. "Is she lucid, would you say? Does she seem to live in the present?"

Helene's brows drew together as she took a bite of her bread. "Her mind travels back and forth between the past and present. And she is very forgetful about things and people."

"Does she remember you?"

"Thankfully, yes. Although there are times when she asks me how my mother is doing. She attended the funeral but doesn't remember." Helene sighed. "Which is why, I suppose, I grow weary of her mumblings. It is painful to remember the vibrant woman she once was. If I allow myself to dwell on the years when she taught me to embroider, to cook—it is sad for me."

"It must be difficult," Isabelle said and looked at Elysia, who thoughtfully chewed her breakfast and smiled at something Alice had said. The old woman's hair was neatly swept into a bun, her clothing sparkling clean and pressed. "You care for her very well," Isabelle told Helene.

"I do try. I would hope someone would have done the same for my mother."

"She had one son, you said?"

"Yes, and she always wanted a daughter as well. It is the reason she loved me so much, I think. And my mother was willing to share," Helene finished with a laugh. "I was a bit of a handful, or so I've been told."

"Helene," Isabelle said, "did Elysia speak of the legend of the jewels when you were young?"

"Oh yes. It has always been something she took seriously. It was a bone of contention between her and my mother, who thought it utter nonsense." Helene looked up into the distance for a moment, her eyes unfocused. "In fact," she continued, "Elysia once threw a man from her home—a dinner party, it was—for wearing a ring she said made him an enemy. She said he was one of the evil King's Men. Now mind you, she was of sound mind at the time." Helene shook her head. "My mother was furious over it. The man was a colleague of my father's."

"Oh dear," Isabelle said, smiling. "Must have caused quite a ruckus."

Helene rolled her eyes. "You can't imagine. I was horrified. And what of you? Why do all of you have such interest in the legend?"

"We've come across it in our travels—threads from India to Egypt. Curiosity, I suppose, is what drives us at this point." Isabelle smiled at her, wondering how shrewd the woman was.

"India and Egypt," Helene repeated. She looked at Isabelle for a moment. "Hmm."

Isabelle waited for half of a heartbeat to see if Helene would elaborate. When nothing was forthcoming, she added, "Sally and I were looking for adventures. We gathered new friends along the way." She gave Helene an abbreviated version of their activities, omitting several key elements.

"You are very good for the girls," Helene said. "They are fortunate to have you."

"And I am fortunate to have them," Isabelle said and glanced at Sally, whose attention was clearly divided between the conversation with Elysia and Isabelle's exchange with Helene. She winked at the young woman, who returned it with a smile.

"Mrs. Floros has been telling us about how much the city has grown in her lifetime," Jean-Louis said, drawing Isabelle and Helene into the conversation. "And she says that since they ran the Turks out of town, things have been much better."

Helene shook her head with what looked like a reluctant smile. "True enough," she said. "We have sought our independence for hundreds of years. It is nice to finally be our own people."

"Do you remember that time, then?" Isabelle asked Helene.

"I was fourteen years of age," Helene said, lifting a pitcher to refill the guests' drinking glasses. "There were celebrations like no other." She paused in the act of filling Isabelle's glass and looked at Elysia for a moment before shaking her head almost imperceptibly.

Elysia returned Helene's brief assessment with one raised brow. Elysia nodded to the pitcher of milk that Helene still held in her hand. She said something to her niece, who finished filling Isabelle's glass.

Jean-Louis spoke in Greek to Elysia, who waved a hand at him with a laugh. *She must have been a beauty in her prime,* Isabelle mused. She could imagine a younger Elysia in a similar social setting, gently flirting with a gentleman caller. It was a shame that her mind had become so spotty.

Throwing a mental note of thanks to Jean-Louis for distracting the old woman, Isabelle glanced at Helene, who was busy wiping crumbs from the table. A light frown marred her features.

"Are you well?" Isabelle asked in an undertone.

Helene looked at Isabelle, her face smooth and a ready smile in place. "I am, thank you. Just old memories."

Before Isabelle could pry further, Sally interrupted with a question Elysia had asked—something about Isabelle's heritage—and the moment was lost.

***

Jack carried Mr. Andrews's second letter back to the hotel in the breast pocket of his jacket without opening it. He knew whatever information it contained was going to be upsetting. As he entered the hotel lobby, the employee behind the desk motioned for him.

"Mr. MacInnes," the young man said in heavily accented English. "A telegram for you."

The sense of foreboding that had settled over him when he'd retrieved the letter from the post office doubled as he took the paper from the man with a nod of thanks. He read it as he began climbing the stairs, only to stop short halfway to the second floor. His vision dimmed slightly as the blood drained from his head. He felt cold suddenly, his extremities tingling as he sat heavily on the step. He was still sitting there when James and Phillip approached from the dining room, having just eaten lunch. He heard them talking as they neared him, their voices echoing as though from a faraway place.

"Jack," James said and put a hand on his shoulder. "What is it?"

Jack swallowed, absently thinking he needed a drink of water. "I'm thirsty."

James shook him, looking closely in his face. "Jack!"

He swallowed again. "Someone murdered my grandfather's secretary." He swallowed again and closed his eyes. "That means that my grandfather's death was definitely not an accident. What are the odds?" He opened his eyes and looked at James, whose grim face offered no contradiction.

Jack took a deep breath and stood, following the Ashbys to the second floor. He opened Mr. Andrews's letter and read it through twice, catching his bearings and preparing to brief the others on the contents. James and Phillip gave him the space he needed to gather his thoughts. By the time the others returned, he felt composed.

***

Leila made her way back inside from the alley behind the hotel to the servants' lounge near the kitchen, having dumped her container of trash. Her hands shook violently, and she gripped them together once inside the room, which was blessedly vacant. Leaning against the wall, she closed her eyes. The man had been forceful—but even that fact alone might not have convinced her. It was when he threatened the life of her mother and younger brother that she realized she had no other alternative. And as proof that he could make good on his threats, the man had shown her a lock of blonde hair that had blue-tipped ends. A lock of hair that clearly belonged to her mother, who had accidentally dyed a section of her hair with the blueberry stain that she used to color the fabrics she sold at the market.

It had been late at night while her mother had been working. She had released the tight coil of braids at the base of her neck to allow the long strands to flow freely down her back and shoulders, sighing in pleasure at the release from the pins that had held the coiffure in place.

Leila had laughed with her mother when a good portion of the hair had swung forward into the large bowl of dye, and with her usual good humor, her mother had declared it wasn't a problem as she never wore her hair down in public anyway.

As Leila stood trembling in the lounge, she fingered the bound lock of hair in her apron pocket, where the man had placed it. He had been in their home in the dead of night while they slept, and none of them had even realized it. A cold shaft of fear pierced her insides and she began to shiver.

"Familiarize yourself with them," the man had told her, "so that they do not question your services. I will contact you daily with instructions. For now, all you do is pour the tea."

***

Isabelle felt the tension in the air as soon as she entered the sitting room. She glanced at James, who gave her a subtle nod toward Jack, who stood at the fireplace, one shoulder propped against the mantel. He held a couple of papers in his hand—and an envelope.

Jean-Louis had entered with her and the girls. She looked at him and he gave her a slight shrug in answer. She pulled her gloves from her fingers and removed her hat, smoothing a hand over her hair. "Well," she said, "between Helene and our hotel's fine chef, I don't think I'll need to eat again for a week."

"I agree," Alice said as she and Sally followed suit, removing their gloves and hanging their hats on the hat rack in the corner of the room. "My mother would be horrified to see me eating everything put on my plate."

Sally gave a delicate snort. "I got so hungry during the war that I doubt I'll ever again pass up a plate of food, regardless of what's on it." She looked at Isabelle expectantly. "Are we going to rest for a bit and then venture out again later?"

Isabelle nodded. "However, we do need to discuss some of the things we've found in Dr. Pearce's papers first. And I suspect Jack received the letter he was expecting from Mr. Andrews?" She looked at Jack, gauging his expression. Whatever the letter stated, it couldn't be good.

Jack cleared his throat and nodded. "I did receive the letter from Mr. Andrews. He sent it the day after he posted the parcel, as he said he would."

Isabelle sat down on the settee, and Alice and Sally took the couch. The men remained standing—too agitated to sit, perhaps? "And what does Mr. Andrews have to say?"

"Well, the long and short of it is that my grandfather's office was burglarized several weeks ago, but nothing was missing. His files had been thoroughly ransacked, and it was clear that the person or persons had been after something specific."

Jack ran a hand absently through his hair and shifted his weight, glancing down at the papers he still held. Isabelle fought the urge to snatch them out of his hands and read them herself, but she waited for him to continue.

"Apparently, just before my grandfather died, two men approached him after he finished teaching for the day. They asked him about his files on the legend—wondered how much he would sell them for. When my grandfather refused, they visited him the next day and were much more firm in their insistence that he sell them the files. He refused again, and later that night he and Mr. Andrews locked the files in a safe he had hidden behind one of his bookcases."

Jack frowned, his brows drawn tightly together. "My grandfather died two days later—a heart attack supposedly—and that's when his office was ransacked. When Mr. Andrews realized that nothing had been stolen, he theorized that the same men who had harassed my grandfather must be responsible.

"He cleaned the office and organized the files—except for the ones in the safe—preparing to turn them over to the department chairman. He was wondering what to do with the papers on the legend when he received my request to send the papers to us in Athens. He informed the chairman of his intentions, and the man agreed it would be appropriate as I am my grandfather's heir.

"The following day, he arrived at the office to find it again in disarray. Everything he had placed in boxes for the department chairman had been dumped and apparently pawed through. Mr. Andrews then retrieved the material from the safe and left the building as classes were changing, intending to make his way to the postal offices, when he was attacked by two men who knocked him to the ground and took his satchel. As luck would have it, there were three bobbies in the crowd who saw the incident and tackled the man with the satchel. The papers flew to the ground, but Mr. Andrews retrieved them and ran to immediately put them in the mail."

Jack shook his head and sat in a chair near the hearth. "Thus the hurried note he sent with the papers explaining their misfiling. He apparently wrote this letter that very afternoon and posted it the next morning."

Isabelle considered what he'd said. "You mentioned the bobbies catching the man with the satchel. What of the other one?"

"He escaped capture. The other was arrested and placed in jail."

Isabelle studied Jack for a moment as he paused, leaning forward and bracing his arms on his knees. Recognizing the second piece of paper in his hand, she asked him, "And what of the telegram you're holding?"

He glanced up at her, a muscle working in his jaw. Jack wasn't one for theatrics—his distress was clearly genuine. "Mr. Andrews was murdered in my grandfather's office the next morning, according to the date mentioned on the telegram." He flicked the wrist holding the papers he held and added, "I just received this from the concierge downstairs."

Isabelle's brows raised high. That, she had not been expecting. "Who sent you the telegram?"

"The department chairman. He says he thought I should know."

"Sweet mercy," Sally murmured. "Jack, that is horrible. I'm so sorry."

Alice whispered her agreement, her face pale, her eyes big. "Who would want those papers?"

Jean-Louis broke the silence that followed with a question of his own. "Who wouldn't?"

7

"How is he?" Isabelle asked James as they trailed behind the group ascending the stairs to again meet in the sitting room after eating a dinner the women had sworn they would be too full to even look at. "You spoke to him alone earlier?"

James nodded and offered her his arm. "The shock has lessened. I believe he is grateful for the distraction of solving this mystery—it keeps him from thinking overmuch."

After Jack's stunning revelation that afternoon, Isabelle decided that perhaps some quiet time might be welcome for everyone and suggested as much. The hours before dinner were spent either napping, reading, or embroidering. Attempts at all activities were largely unsuccessful—Sally tossed and turned, trying to get comfortable; Alice stabbed her finger repeatedly and cursed at her fabric, dotted in red; and Isabelle read the same page of her novel three times before finally giving it up as hopeless. The men verified their efforts had met with a similar end.

"He is a professional," Isabelle said to James now as she watched Jack converse with Sally and Phillip while turning the key in the lock to the suite. "Investigative work has its uses—sometimes the fact that it can be all consuming is to one's benefit."

"Do not remind me," James muttered as they followed the group into the sitting room. "I'd rather you didn't know that firsthand."

Isabelle gave him a wry smile and again went through the routine of divesting herself of hat and gloves, wishing for a moment that it were already time for bed so she could climb out of the voluminous skirts and petticoats that fashion demanded. To say nothing of the corset.

"So let's hear it," Phillip said as the group settled in and got comfortable. "What have you learned from these papers that the whole world seems to want?"

"Some of it we discussed late last night," Isabelle said, "but I'll review everything for the girls." She flipped through some pages in her journal and found what she was looking for. Taking a deep breath, she began.

"What we've gathered from the doctor's notes corroborates what Elysia told us at the market. The legend begins with a Grecian princess. She lived many years ago and created the stones for a reason Dr. Pearce doesn't mention. She bore a peculiar mark on her back in the shape of a star.

"The princess's life was threatened," Isabelle continued, "and the stones were dispersed by a trusted handmaiden. They were given over to the care of three women, one each in India, Egypt, and Greece.

"According to Dr. Pearce, when combined, they lead to something incredible, but he was never able to ascertain exactly what it was. Elysia told us they lead to the princess's treasure, and not only that but the lost kingdom itself, somewhere under the ocean. There's also a sketch, here," Isabelle said, pausing as she sifted through papers until she found the one she sought. "It's a box that apparently holds all three stones. This must be the alabaster box Elysia spoke of."

She lifted the paper and showed the others, her brows raised. "Is this looking familiar?"

Alice's mouth dropped open. "It's the rectangle," she said and grasped the silver necklace that hung just below her throat. "The box is the rectangle around the three ovals on my necklace and also in the tomb and the pyramid in Egypt."

Isabelle nodded. "I suspect so. I also saw it once at a temple in India. It stood out to me because it was different than the other symbols carved around it. It meant nothing to me at the time, of course, but now it makes perfect sense. Among other things, we should definitely continue to keep an eye open for that symbol.

"Dr. Pearce also has slips of paper collected from various sources— newspapers, a travel guide—and this one here offers a brief history of our own Ibis, the Egyptian princess. It doesn't say she was the guardian of the Jewel of Poseidon, but there are enough details here that the good doctor was able to theorize about her role. Of course, he had made a thorough study of it—he knew what to look for."

Jack nodded. He stood by the fireplace and occasionally paced the length of it. "He shared pieces of it with me when I was young. I always knew there were three stones, for example, and I knew that people believed them to be of amazing power . . ." He rubbed the back of his neck. "He didn't advertise his interest in the legend, but he was a professor for many years. I wouldn't be surprised if he said something in a class that just the right person—or wrong person—happened to hear . . ."

An uneasy silence settled over the room, and Isabelle looked at the stack of papers sitting on the coffee table. "We should lock these in the safe," she said. "I'm disgusted I didn't think of it this afternoon. At any rate," she continued, "this document here is a British newspaper from 1799 that describes the discovery of the Rosetta stone. At the end of the article, the author includes a funny aside from an older gentleman on the streets, who, when asked what he thought of the Rosetta Stone, commented that he was waiting for someone to find the magic stones from Greece and wouldn't *that* be a newsworthy story.

"And there are numerous maps of Greece—both of the Aegean and the Peloponnese—and information about a Venetian fortress in Monemvasia but no reason for its inclusion."

"In the doctor's journal, we also found a story of a noblewoman in India," Jean-Louis added, "who was said to be a soothsayer of sorts—she bore a particular mark and was supposedly in possession of a great treasure."

Isabelle nodded. "The stories and anecdotes are countless. The journal is full of little details that confirm what he must have suspected all along— that the three jewels do indeed exist and that their value is incomparable."

"I never thought he really believed the legend," Jack said absently. Isabelle glanced up at him. He was looking out the window down onto the street below. "This much information though—it must have been more than just a passing hobby."

"Who told you it was a heart attack?" Isabelle said quietly.

He turned away from the window and looked at her. "You tell me. Genevieve was the one who received the news and she told you. I happened to overhear."

"Have you not been in contact with your family?" she said.

He shook his head. "I didn't want to risk it while we were in Egypt. I am . . . was . . . so deeply incognito." He ran a hand through his hair. "For all I know, the Federation is aware of exactly who I am. Maybe they've known all along. It would be typical of them to play me. To use me to get to my grandfather. Mr. Andrews's letter confirmed that the cause of death had been listed as heart failure, but I don't think he believed it. I don't."

Isabelle took a deep breath and looked at the others in the room. "If Elysia is to be believed, not only is the Federation looking for the stones and box, but descendants of the ancient King's Men are as well. They are referenced in the papers as 'the King's Men.' I believe a visit to our friend Demitrios is in order today. We would be wise to call on his brother's store to obtain a few firearms."

James looked at her with his eyebrows raised. He pointed dubiously at Sally and Alice. Isabelle nodded in response. "They need to be able to defend themselves. As do each of us."

"Isabelle, I've never fired a gun in my life," Sally told her.

"I have," Alice said and all heads turned toward her. "My father taught me to shoot," she said, looking defensive. "I was raised in the wilds of India, for heaven's sake."

Isabelle blinked a few times. "Well then. We needn't worry about teaching Alice to shoot." She looked at Sally. "Really? You've never fired a gun? How about all that time after your mother died—you never had to defend your home from invaders?"

Sally shrugged. "Mostly I just scowled at people and they left us alone. We weren't really invaded until you came along, Belle."

Phillip laughed. "Are you speaking of Isabelle or the Yankees, Sally?"

Isabelle shook her head with a brief eye roll. "One and the same, Phillip."

Sally laughed and opened her mouth to respond when Alice nudged her with an elbow. "I'll teach you to shoot," she said. "There's nothing to it, really. Especially if your target is close enough."

James groaned and put his head in his hands. Jack left his perch by the window and approached Isabelle, hands in his pockets, mouth cocked into a half smile.

"You are sure about this? You really want everyone armed?"

"The Federation is far-reaching, Jack. You've said it yourself. And now we face a local group—that man aboard the steamer seemed to have already ascertained our purpose. What other choice do we have?"

His smile faded slightly and he lifted a shoulder. "Very well. Armed to the teeth we shall be."

***

The next morning dawned bright and clear, with air just crisp enough to require a light coat. James cast an eye about his surroundings as the group approached the Panathenaic Way, the gateway to the Acropolis. After some consideration, they had invited the museum curator, Demitrios

Metaxas, to act as a guide, as well as Elysia and Helene, who provided interesting bits of information about the history of the ancient city, beginning with the fact that *acropolis* meant "upper city."

Demitrios, who was very clear that even the young women should feel free to address him by his first name, fell quickly and comfortably into the role of tour guide, beginning by showing them the Athena Nike, the small temple nearest the *propylaea*, or entrance.

The Acropolis was peppered with grass and wildflowers that seemed to spring forth from multitudinous cracks in the ground, which was impressively green given the fact that it was January. James sucked in a breath at the majesty of the ruins up close. The Erectheon, with its famous porch and pillars that were actually statues of maidens, or *caryatids*. The Parthenon, huge in size and damaged by years of war and weather. The photos he'd seen had not done it justice in the least.

Isabelle had mentioned she hoped to catch sight of Thaddeus Sparks as they visited typical tourist destinations. The odds were long, and James had told her as much, but she'd looked at him and said, "What else are we to do?"

He could only agree.

"Where are you, little worm?" James heard Isabelle mutter as they trailed along with the group, moving around other gatherings of people— largely American and European.

"Sparks?" James said. "He would be wounded to hear you address him in such a way."

"He's going to be wounded when I find him again," she said with a scowl. "Where could he be right this very moment? As much as I hate subjecting Alice to danger, I will be disappointed if our forays into the city don't draw him out into the open. With all of the excitement about the parcel from Oxford, I had almost forgotten our mission is twofold." She glanced at Elysia and Helene and murmured, "Threefold."

Groups of tourists had gathered around the Parthenon, and James kept Alice and Sally in his sight as they moved slightly away from it. Isabelle quickened her pace beside him and called to the girls to wait. "This is when we would lose her," she said to him referring, under her breath, to Alice. "In a crowd."

Phillip walked next to Sally and conversed with Jean-Louis, who flanked the girls on the other side. "She's safe for the moment," James told Isabelle. He pulled her forward by the arm and crossed the distance between them and the others.

"The thing that makes the legend somewhat unique is that the three named gods are the three first Olympians—Zeus, Poseidon, and Hades," Jean-Louis was murmuring to Alice as Metaxas pointed to the pillars of the Parthenon and explained the building design to Sally and Phillip. "As Greek mythology goes," Jean-Louis continued, "Zeus, Poseidon, and Hades were siblings. They were Kronos's children, and they overthrew him, imprisoned him in Tartarus with the other Titans, then drew lots to see who would rule where on earth. Zeus became the supreme leader and ruled the sky, Poseidon drew the sea, and Hades drew the underworld. Whether or not this has symbolic representation in the three stones, I don't know."

Alice drew her brows together. "Wasn't Kronos the god who ate his children?"

Jean-Louis chuckled. "Yes, all but Zeus, who was hidden by his mother, Rhea. When Zeus grew to adulthood, he forced Kronos to vomit up the other children he had eaten, among them Poseidon and Hades."

Alice nodded. "So there we have the parallel. The Olympians over-threw their evil father. The princess crafted—" Alice looked over her shoulder and lowered her voice. "You know. To outsmart her father."

Jean-Louis nodded. "That may well be." He scanned the architecture with an eye that James knew was accustomed to study and research. James found himself wondering, as he had aboard the steamer, if the Frenchman would be able to part with the stones when the time came. Jean-Louis occasionally pulled a journal from his coat pocket to jot notes or sketches. The fact that this habit had also found its way to Alice and Sally as they had traveled from Egypt to Greece was to his credit. They, also, had become scrupulous in their attentions to journal keeping.

His mother would be impressed, James mused. She had a shelf full of diaries she'd kept since her days as a young girl. She recorded everything that had ever happened to her, to their family—he knew he could flip to any chosen date in those books and find more details than he probably needed. He unconsciously touched a finger to his cuff links—they had belonged to his father, who had died when James was ten. Thinking of his mother's diaries brought old memories to the surface, and he wondered if his father would have been proud of the man James had become.

He looked at the blue sky overhead and the ancient structures that stood against it. His father would have been amazed that not only one, but both of his sons had taken themselves to the other side of the world.

He had never wandered far from home, though he'd attempted to cross the American plains, only to have his life cut short at a place called Haun's Mill.

Shaking off the maudlin thoughts, James focused his attention on Demetrios, who was pontificating about the temple's virtues while leading them around the relics with an ease that spoke of a lifetime of familiarity. That James was a long way from home was an understatement. He laced his fingers with Isabelle's and looked down at her. They had yet to experience normal circumstances together, circumstances that didn't involve constant travel, danger, and intrigue.

"A penny for your thoughts," Isabelle said to him.

He smiled a bit. "I want to take you home."

***

Isabelle gave James's arm a gentle squeeze and winked at him. He looked . . . intense. She knew he was weary of the chase and constantly on edge with worry about her and Phillip and the girls—everyone and everything he thought he should be able to protect.

She had left the States with one objective, and that had been to escape the ghosts that haunted her from experiences during the war. Her relationship with Sally had been the one thing that had given her a renewed sense of purpose, and when they had embarked for India, she hadn't had the slightest intention of following any sort of itinerary or schedule. The mayhem that had ensued from the moment they'd met James Ashby had been worth every heart-stopping minute because now she didn't mind the thought of returning home. The prospect of starting her life with him in the Utah Territory, away from the eastern states that still plagued her dreams, sounded divine.

A glance at Helene and Elysia showed them conversing with Phillip, Jean-Louis, Sally, and Alice, and clearly agitating Demitrios, who must have felt the Greek women were stealing his tour-guiding thunder. Isabelle had invited Elysia and Helene with the intent of learning more of the two women. She trusted the pair, and her instincts were rarely, if ever, wrong. But before she was willing to open up about the group's purpose in Greece, she needed to know exactly who the women were. She also hoped, at some point, to be able to coax Helene into divulging the insight Isabelle knew the woman had experienced at breakfast on the terrace— the insight she had quickly squelched and dismissed as nothing.

Isabelle released James's hand and wandered a bit from the group, casting an eye over the view of the city from the Acropolis, wondering where a man like Sparks would hide himself. He had to be running low on money unless he had been extraordinarily careful with the funds he'd received in Egypt from the Federation when they'd hired him to spy on the Ashby brothers. She knew exactly how much he'd earned—Jack had been the one to pay Sparks when Jack had still been undercover posing as an Italian and the Federation head's right-hand man.

Sparks was slightly unhinged but resourceful. And the dratted man had the second jewel. She had held it for but a moment before he'd taken it at gunpoint, and she had relived the scene in her mind ever since. If only she had paid closer attention to the cave entrance . . . if only she'd had her gun at the ready . . .

A figure moved at the edge of her vision and caught her attention. As quickly as she had seen him, he was again gone. It could have been any of a number of tourists or Greek nationals, but were she a betting woman, and occasionally she was, she'd have wagered the pot that it was someone she'd not seen since the jungles of India. Something about him seemed eerily familiar, and her heart thudded in her chest.

She craned her neck for another view of the man, who had lost himself in the crowd. She caught another glimpse as he turned to pick up a handkerchief a woman had dropped. He stood and said something to the woman, who smiled and took the cloth from him, clearly charmed. The same good looks, the same dashing demeanor . . . it couldn't be.

It absolutely could not be him.

As the man bid the woman farewell, he turned and Isabelle caught his eye. His face showed no recognition, but he held her gaze as she stared at him. He frowned and tipped his head slightly, as if in question, and a crowd of people crossed between them. Several long moments passed before the crowd cleared, and when they did, he was gone.

Old instincts made their way to the fore, and moving farther away from her group, she looked from couple to couple, from family to tour guide, but to no avail. She was preparing to lose herself in the crowd and give chase when she heard James call out behind her in a quiet hiss.

"Who did you see?" he asked, his brows drawn together as he reached her side.

Isabelle opened her mouth to answer him, only to snap it shut and then try again. "James, I do believe I just saw a dead man."

"What?"

"Ari. I saw Ari Kilronomos."

James stared at her for a moment before closing his own mouth. He looked above her head and through the crowd, turning first to the right and then the left. "Belle, are you sure?" he said in a low tone. He moved closer to her and grasped her arm when she would have moved farther into the throng of people. "Ari was very classically Greek in his appearance. Perhaps you've mistaken someone else for him."

Isabelle looked near the pillar where she'd seen the man. Slowly, she shook her head. "It wasn't just his face. It was the way he moved."

"But you saw him die."

"I thought I did. His head struck the rock when he fell, the snake was coiled around him, but I left the jungle before I saw for certain . . ."

"You said that snake was massive. The colonel determined from your description that it most certainly would have eaten the man. And his body was gone when the soldiers went later to find it."

"Maybe they looked in the wrong place." Isabelle frowned with a wince. "I do hate unfinished business. It didn't sit well with me then and doesn't now." She blew out a puff of air and motioned to the others in their group, who were watching in concern. "There's no hope for it now. He's long gone." She paused. "I don't like it."

In India, Sparks had worked with Ari Kilronomos to abduct the girls for ransom and search for the Jewel of Zeus. Ari had carried a small black journal that Isabelle had stolen from his room one night, and Phillip later had it translated into English. Isabelle still had the translated version, and she determined to look through it upon returning to the hotel. There might have been something she had missed. Addresses, names, anything . . .

She narrowed her eyes at the throngs of people and cursed her hesitation. Had she moved sooner, she might have at least kept him in sight enough to follow him. She realized James was coming to know her all too well when he said, "You aren't familiar enough with the city to tail him anywhere. You would be lost and I would be furious."

Frustrated, she looped her arm through James's and returned with him to their friends. At Sally's questioning stare, she shrugged. "I thought I saw someone I recognized. Shadows must be playing tricks on me."

8

BALTASAR METAXAS WAS A TALLER, handsomer version of his brother, Demitrios. He spoke some English and was charming, boisterous, and well versed in weaponry of all shapes and sizes. He possessed a lavish shop from which he outfitted each member of the group with a gun suited to his or her size and strength—and smiled all the while. James couldn't decide if he liked the man or merely found him obsequious. He seemed genuine enough; the two employees that shadowed him like puppies and jumped at his every command certainly seemed devoted.

All of the purchases complete, James followed the younger women outside, Phillip and Jack on his heels, while Isabelle and Jean-Louis obtained directions from Baltasar to a shooting range where they could do some target practice.

"For the love of heaven, don't let her put that thing into her reticule loaded." James watched Sally hold her tiny new handgun between two fingers as she looked at it with her nose scrunched. He felt a small measure of relief when Alice took it from her and, with a quick flip of her fingers, removed the ammunition.

"For now, keep these separate," she told Sally. "We'll practice shooting later."

"But suppose I'm accosted today," Sally said as Alice dropped the bullets into Sally's reticule then took the gun from her, also placing it into the small purse.

Alice pulled the drawstrings tight and looked at Sally, returning the purse to her. "Point the empty gun at them. They won't know it's not loaded."

"She's going to end up shooting herself in the foot," James muttered to Phillip.

Phillip shrugged slightly, watching the two young women. "I must admit a grudging new respect for Miss Bilbey," he said. "For one who was raised in relative luxury, she seems remarkably proficient in her knowledge of firearms." He turned to James. "Do you know, she told me I ought to consider purchasing a Winchester 1866 lever-action repeating rifle? That it's better suited to a man's abilities and more efficient from a distance?"

James released an indrawn breath, still watching Sally with a wary eye. "I suppose I shall either come to eat my words and be grateful for this turn of events, or I will be spot-on in my predictions and we'll find ourselves scrambling to mend her foot." He grimaced. "Or mine."

Phillip chuckled. "Sally is very adept. She has a certain amount of savvy she probably learned during the war."

James reluctantly nodded. Sally had indeed managed to keep herself and Alice alive while running from their abductors in the streets of Calcutta. Isabelle and Jean-Louis had finally exited the shop, and James moved in slightly to hear what Isabelle was now telling the girl.

". . . you dare even think about loading that thing until I show you how to use it."

Sally sniffed. "Well thank you ever so much, Belle, for your confidence in my common sense. Alice has already removed the bullets and offered to show me how to shoot. Later."

Isabelle turned to the group in general. "No time like the present. There's an area just outside the city where we can practice shooting. I have a map from Baltasar, who recommends it as very safe." She glanced at Sally, who gave an inelegant little snort in response.

James looked at Phillip, who shrugged with a grin and then made his way over to Sally, who looked up at Phillip with her heart in her eyes.

James stifled a groan.

***

After a rousing session of practice shooting, the group spent the rest of the morning scouring antique shops, churches, and museums. While they saw many fascinating historical relics, anything regarding the stones or the legend itself remained frustratingly elusive.

Midday saw the group famished, tired, and discouraged. They sat atop Filopappau Hill with a large picnic spread in the shade of a tree, comprising a variety of food and supplies they'd picked up from market vendors. The view of the Acropolis was breathtaking, and Isabelle took a moment to enjoy the scenery as she slowly chewed her chicken souvlaki while the others finished dishing up their food. Squinting in contemplation, she eyed the ruins carefully.

"Penny for your thoughts," James said, repeating her earlier comment as he sat beside her on a blanket she'd found in a shop boasting fabrics of all textures and colors.

"I'm thinking about one of the papers in the files," she said, still staring at the ruins. "It looks to be a blueprint of sorts on one side, and the other side looks like a map of some ruins. There are no identifying marks that name the place, however, and I've been perplexed by it. I feel fairly certain that if I knew in which file it belongs, its relation to the other documents would be clear."

Several of the others gradually joined James and Isabelle. "I don't recall seeing that page," Jack said. "How did we classify it?"

"I believe I placed it in the pile containing the maps." Isabelle nodded. "Yes. When we return, I'll show it to you. I'm thinking Dr. Pearce would not have gone to the trouble of adding it to the collection without a good reason."

"Perhaps something is hidden there?" Sally said as she joined the group with a plate of food.

Isabelle nodded. "It's possible." The scattered papers of the good doctor's files were like an enormous puzzle with no guarantee of a solid fit, even when combined.

"What do we need yet to accomplish this afternoon?" Jack said.

Still holding her skewered chicken, Isabelle fished in her reticule for her small diary. She flipped it open and skimmed down her daily list with her finger. "We've visited every antique shop we can find," she said with a sigh. "We have three more museums to see, and we need to call on Demitrios Metaxas to ask if he's seen Sparks again."

Phillip finished the food on his plate and set it aside, stretching out on his back. "Pity Eli Montgomery isn't with us," he said. "My description of Sparks goes only so far. Eli could at least draw us a decent sketch."

Isabelle nodded, thinking fondly of her uncle who was still in Egypt with her grandmother.

"The easiest way by far to recognize him is those green eyes of his," James said, "and we certainly offered up enough bribes. Someone will see him—it's only a matter of time."

"I really would like to go back to the hotel and examine that map some more," Isabelle said, finishing her food.

"Why don't you go back with the girls," Jack offered, "while the rest of us finish the tasks around town."

Isabelle nodded. "If you don't mind. Phillip, would you care to join us? Don't look at me that way. It's not a punishment."

Phillip snorted. "Not a punishment, exactly, but certainly a case of sending the vulnerable one back behind the line of fire."

"And is that really such a terrible way to pass the time?" Sally said to him, one brow raised.

Phillip grinned. "Your accent is much more pronounced when you're irritated." He held up a hand at her retort. "And no, it's not such a terrible way to pass the time. But I don't like being one who needs protection."

"You're protecting us, then," Isabelle said as she stood and brushed the crumbs from her dress. "There. All better, and you're none the worse for the wear."

Phillip looked at James, who shrugged. "Sounds to me like you're going back to the hotel with the women," he said.

***

Sally and Alice busied themselves with their journals in the sitting room while Isabelle and Phillip carefully sifted through Dr. Pearce's papers. Aside from an occasional murmured comment, the room remained quiet, its inhabitants working in companionable silence.

Isabelle found the map she sought and looked carefully at it. She finally shook her head. "I wonder that I didn't realize it sooner—it's a structure within a fortress," she told Phillip. "The ink is faded, and the writing identifying the individual buildings is tiny, but see?" She showed it to him and turned the paper over to examine the back. "And this is another level. Lower, perhaps?"

The drawing was ornate, showing detail upon detail, and Isabelle wondered what she was missing. "It almost looks like an island except for this one strip leading out to it."

Phillip squinted at the writing, his brows drawn together in concentration as he bent his head over the paper. "I suppose I'm looking for an 'x marks the spot' somewhere."

Isabelle reached for the small magnifying glass she had procured from the hotel manager. "I can't even make out the letters," she murmured as she examined the paper.

James entered the room and Isabelle glanced up from the document. "Do you have the sketch of the box?" he asked her.

"Yes," she said and flipped through a stack of papers until she found the picture he wanted. She extended it to him and he took it with a nod.

"What are you doing with it?" Phillip said as James turned again for the door.

"Showing it to Demitrios. He thinks he might know what it is."

Isabelle dropped her jaw. "Could we really be so lucky?"

James lifted a shoulder in a light shrug. "One can hope. And, Brother? You're sitting awfully close to my fiancée."

Phillip choked on a laugh. He smirked and laid a casual arm across Isabelle's shoulders. "I've been banished with the women, remember? I'm doing my duty by keeping them safe."

James raised a brow and left the room, letting the door close firmly behind him. Phillip laughed and Isabelle elbowed him in the ribs with a wry smile.

"Shameless," she said to him.

"Of course. It's part of my charm."

Isabelle shook her head at him, indeed charmed in spite of herself. The Ashby brothers were dangerous. Phillip, the more gregarious, people pleasing of the two, and James, strength and power leashed inside a gentleman's suit. "You must have given your poor mother fits," she said to him as he dropped his arm from around her.

"I'm not ashamed to say I did," he said, still smiling. "But I also made her laugh."

Isabelle nodded. "That is its own blessing. You're a good son."

His smile faltered a fraction. "I was until I got carried away in a scheme hatched by a madman. I don't like to think of the worry I've caused her."

Isabelle patted his arm. "No need for that. She knows you're with James."

"Ah yes. James had to come to my rescue."

Isabelle glanced at him. "Are you still sulking over the same old thing? It doesn't become you, you know."

Phillip's eyes flickered to Sally, who quietly conversed with Alice over a hieroglyph she had neglected to identify in her journal. "I'm ever the younger son," he said to Isabelle. "James will always be the responsible one."

"Have you learned your lesson about embarking on adventures with strangers?"

Phillip rolled his eyes.

"Then why can't you be the responsible one too now? Enough with the wallowing, Phillip. Truly. You must trust me. Releasing past ghosts is one of the best things I've done in my life."

"But what will I do when I return home? I'm not suited for much of anything. James always worked hard, and I was the perpetual student and general ne'er-do-well."

Isabelle considered him for a moment. "Why don't you enter the political arena? Put your charm to some good use."

Phillip put his head back and laughed.

"I am serious!"

"You think I should run for an office?" he said, still laughing.

"Whyever not? You're a person who gets on very well with others, Phillip. And my guess is that you had your finger on the pulse of all things social at home."

"Yes," he admitted with a shake of his head and a chuckle.

"So put your skills to constructive use. Turn your attention to larger issues and see what you can do with it."

Phillip stared at her. "You really are serious."

"Give it some thought. You might enjoy it."

"Isabelle, there aren't too many politicians I admire," he said, finally sobering.

"I knew an amazing one," she murmured. "And the world needs more like him." The thought of Lincoln brought the familiar stab to her heart, but the pain was less intense, the guilt less invasive than it had been. She had been so close to saving the president, so very close. But not close enough. She rubbed her leg absently.

Phillip noticed the gesture and put his arm around her shoulders again, this time clearly in sympathy and affection. "And now who's wallowing?" he asked her with a small wink and a gentle squeeze.

She smiled at him. "Touché."

A knock at the door prompted her to rise, and Isabelle opened it to see Leila carrying a tea tray. "Oh," she told the girl, "thank you, but we've just eaten."

Leila's smile was strained. "It is compliments of the manager," she said, "as valued guests. May I?"

"How very kind," Isabelle said, studying the girl. "Is this standard for all of your guests?"

"No, only the ones in the largest suites," Leila said as Isabelle opened the door wider to let her in. "Oh, but you are not all here?"

Isabelle shook her head. "The others are still out."

Leila looked momentarily flummoxed. "All is well with you, Leila?" Isabelle asked her softly.

By this time, Sally, Alice, and Phillip were all watching the girl, whose cheeks turned pink.

"I—I must do well at my work," she stammered. "I need to earn money and must do a good job."

"You're doing very well," Isabelle said and crossed the room to her reticule, where she pulled out a few coins. "Here," she said and placed the money in the girl's hand. "Thank you for thinking of us."

Leila paused. "Would you like me to pour the tea?"

"No, no. I will do it. Thank you, however."

Leila nodded and turned to leave. Isabelle followed her to the door, troubled on her behalf. The young woman gave a little wave as she began descending the stairs, and Isabelle called after her, "Thank you, again. It is much appreciated."

***

James made his way back to Metaxas's museum with the sketch of the alabaster box folded in his inner coat pocket. The Greek had admitted to knowing a fair amount about the legend—a fact he had skimmed over the first time Isabelle and Jean-Louis had asked him about it—and James had the impression that the man was a little uncomfortable discussing it in great detail. The legend seemed to invoke a certain sense of unease with many people; the job would be so much easier if it wasn't so hard to get straight answers.

When he reached the museum, he found Metaxas and Jean-Louis in deep discussion about something—conversation with the little man was always animated. Jack looked on with his brow furrowed in apparent confusion. Jack's command of the Greek tongue was little better than James's, and it made for an amusing tableau.

James handed the sketch of the jewel box to Demitrios and watched the older man's reaction. He spoke rapidly in Greek, nodding and glancing up at Jean-Louis, who translated.

"He says this is the one," Deveraux said, looking first at James and then at Jack. "He believes it is rumored to be hidden at the old fortress on Monemvasia."

"Rumored by whom?" James asked. "Does he consider it general knowledge? Is this place a common target for searchers of the jewels?"

Metaxas shook his head when Jean-Louis translated James's questions, glancing to the front door of the museum and then to the main room, where a few tourists wandered among the artifacts.

"It is not common knowledge, and he knows this because someone he knows is a credible source. We mustn't say where we've obtained our information," Jean-Louis said when Metaxas had finished speaking, "because it might mean unpleasantness for him."

James frowned. "Why is he helping us, then?"

Metaxas shrugged a shoulder and looked at James when he spoke. He finished his comments with a smile and a waggle of his bushy eyebrows. "He feels we are pure in heart," Jean-Louis said, "and we will surely reward him for his help when we find what we are looking for."

"No?" Metaxas said.

James fought to keep his expression bland when he wanted badly to roll his eyes. "Of course," he said. "Rewarded well."

"With what?" Jack muttered to James.

James glanced askance at the Scotsman. "Our charm. I don't know."

Jack moved toward the door with James as Jean-Louis finished the conversation with Metaxas. "Isabelle has money," Jack said.

"We're using enough of Isabelle's money," James said, perhaps a bit more sharply than he'd intended. "She's funding much more than I'm comfortable with."

"You're not exactly resting on your laurels," Jack told him quietly as they reached the door and exited, waiting for Jean-Louis outside, "and she knows full well she can't take this all on by herself. Every person in this entourage is a crucial piece, and we couldn't do it without her resources. I have my government's backing, but I can't do it alone either. I don't mean to suggest we bleed Isabelle dry of her gold," he finished with a scowl at James. "I am suggesting she has made it available should we need it. And if that little Greek museum owner continues to feed us useful information, he will need a reward."

James thrust his hands in his pockets and exhaled, looking back through the museum's front door. It contained a large, thick glass panel that was warped, giving Metaxas a slightly distorted appearance. "I wonder how much he is to be trusted. If this box is at Monemvasia, why has it not been discovered yet? How do we know it hasn't been?"

"I don't suppose we have a choice but to look. I wonder whom he uses for a source," Jack said. "I've not seen a ring on his hands that matches those of the King's Men."

James shook his head. "Perhaps he wouldn't wear it in the open."

Jack shrugged. "And why not? Others don't have any compunction about doing so. I should think it might be rather like a symbol of power."

James frowned as Jean-Louis shook Metaxas's hand and made his way outside. "I don't trust anyone anymore," he said. "Life was much simpler when I didn't question the ulterior motives of everyone I met."

"Well, that certainly seems to follow our fated path thus far," the Frenchman said with a small sigh as he joined James and Jack. "Danger will follow any who look for the box. Furthermore, Metaxas has information for us about the green-eyed man. Sparks visited Baltasar Metaxas today, looking to buy a weapon."

9

ADELPHOS KILRONOMOS EYED THE AMERICAN, Sparks, with a certain amount of distrust. "You tell me you have the jewel, but I am not about to believe it until I see it. You are asking me to risk much to help you find the others, but I am not yet certain I believe you have even the one." The American was slippery, and Adelphos was leery every time the man opened his mouth.

Sparks said nothing but clenched his jaw before he finally responded. "Very well," he said and retreated to the corner of the bedroom, where he had a small portmanteau stashed atop a chair. Glancing over his shoulder, he withdrew an object and returned to Adelphos. "If this goes missing, I will know where to find it."

Adelphos rolled his eyes but looked with interest as Sparks unwrapped the cloth-bound object. The jewel that spilled into his hand was oval in shape and a beautiful iridescent orange. Adelphos stared at it for a minute, his heart thumping painfully, before extending his hand and looking at Sparks. Sparks handed him the stone with obvious reluctance, expounding, "The Bilbey woman told me she had something that she was willing to sell. It was the Jewel of Zeus."

Adelphos's heart rate increased as he turned the stone over in his hand. He was holding the Jewel of Poseidon, a piece of the earth that was more valuable than anything he had ever seen, something for which people had shed blood for centuries. "And the Bilbey woman died before meeting you. You don't know where it is."

"It's in India. It must be. I am going to find the last jewel here in Greece and then return to Calcutta."

"If I agree to help you with this, I want half."

"Of course."

"And you're certain the Bilbey girl is the key?"

Sparks nodded. "She bears the mark. And females are led to the jewels. She was the reason they found this one in Egypt." He reached for the jewel and took it from Adelphos's hand. Adelphos had to fight to keep from closing his fingers around the stone and holding tight.

Wrapping it in the cloth again, Sparks replaced it in his bag and snapped it shut.

"Tell me again who is responsible for my brother's death." Adelphos eyed Sparks closely, watching his every expression. He wasn't altogether certain that Sparks himself hadn't killed Ari.

"Isabelle Webb. I've told you. He chased her into the jungle, and she came out by herself, telling everyone what had happened. I was forced to go on to Calcutta without him. It was pure serendipity that the two young women ended up aboard the very steamer we had planned for them. Ari's proposal was that we sell them to his contact in Egypt." Sparks scowled. "At least I was there to follow them. Without Ari, the plans were nil. His contact wouldn't have known me from Adam, and I had no control over the young woman at that point anyway."

"How unfortunate that his death spoiled things for you."

Sparks waved a hand absently. "It's neither here nor there now. We have at least one of the jewels. Where would one begin looking in this fair country of yours for the third?"

Adelphos looked at Sparks for a moment before slightly shaking his head. "There are rumors of treasure in Olympia."

***

"Seems fairly simple to me," Jack said once they were all again assembled in the sitting room at the hotel. "We go to Monemvasia."

"And I agree, to a certain extent," Isabelle said. "However, our mission is multifaceted. We find Sparks, retrieve the second jewel, and locate the third jewel hidden somewhere here in Greece. To do this, we need to keep cultivating the relationship we have with Helene and Elysia. I also wonder at the wisdom of abandoning Athens right now when Sparks is likely still here. As far as we are aware, he knows nothing of this box. He never mentioned it to Phillip."

Phillip confirmed her statement with a shake of his head.

Jack frowned. "We are not very efficient like this. Suppose two of us go to the fortress."

James was seated on the floor, leaning against the end of the divan where Isabelle sat. He also shook his head. "I agree we are not using our resources to their best advantage, but I'm reluctant to divide the group. We've already decided that there is safety in numbers."

"We needn't divide it in half," Jack said and motioned to Jean-Louis. "Deveraux and I will go."

"Well then, so shall I!"

"Alice," Isabelle said, exasperated, "surely we've not corrupted you so thoroughly. You cannot travel unchaperoned with two unmarried gentlemen."

Alice's face flushed. "I certainly didn't mean to suggest anything improper! I merely would like to see this fortress myself."

"Out of the question," James told her. "You need to stay with the larger group."

"He's right, you know," Sally said, sotto voce. "You really should stay here."

Alice made a noise sounding suspiciously like a growl, and Isabelle would have found it amusing if she weren't preoccupied by the suggestion of splitting the group apart.

"I'm not entirely settled with the idea," she said, "but it does make a certain amount of sense. If Jack and Jean-Louis go together, they stand a better chance of escaping a troublemaker than Jack would alone."

Phillip nodded. "And we can keep searching here for Sparks and any more clues to the third jewel."

Jean-Louis also nodded his assent. "I don't believe we should be gone long either. I looked on this map," he said, lifting a large paper that had been folded in fourths. "It's ninety-nine kilometers away by steamship. We should arrive in one day—I calculate the voyage should take approximately ten hours. We wander about town, compare it to the drawing, and see what transpires."

"Suppose the building you seek doesn't give tours to the public?" Sally said.

"Well then, we become resourceful." Jack clapped Jean-Louis on the back. The latter looked bemused, and Isabelle wondered at the wisdom of the pairing. Jean-Louis had been uncomfortable about entering Metaxas's museum without permission even when they'd left the payment for admission in clear sight. Truthfully, she would be a much better partner for Jack's undertaking, but she highly doubted that James would appreciate it. And of course, there was the fact that it would be no less scandalous for her to travel with unmarried men than for Alice. Scandal didn't worry her overmuch—she had dressed in disguise for years working for Pinkerton and knew she could avoid it—but she hadn't had a fiancé to think of then. It complicated matters.

She glanced at James, who shook his head at her. "Heaven help you, Isabelle Webb, if you're contemplating what I think you are."

"I didn't suppose you would be happy with it."

"You were correct."

"If I were to go in disguise, however—"

"It would leave the girls here, unchaperoned, with two single men." James's tone was flat. "You said yourself, it's unacceptable."

"We could kill two proverbial birds with one stone and ask Helene and Elysia to stay here," Jack suggested.

James glanced at Jack in what Isabelle recognized as annoyance, and she winced. "We are just going to blindly trust two women, whom we all admit we don't know very well, to be with the girls while Phil and I go about Athens searching for an ancient jewel and a madman," James said.

Jack's nostrils flared slightly. "No. You stay together as a group. Leave the girls alone with the women only if you feel comfortable doing so."

"I don't like it." Phillip's tone matched his brother's. "The moment we leave them unattended will be the moment something happens again."

"We have guns," Sally said, and the group collectively turned to look at her. "Well, we do! We can easily defend ourselves."

"Absolutely not," Isabelle said.

Jean-Louis cleared his throat. "And why, exactly, do we need to go to all of this trouble when we had determined Jack and I would go by ourselves?"

Isabelle scrunched her nose a bit, wondering how to avoid offending the man. "I just thought that since I have experience sneaking into and out of places and I have no compunction about doing so, it might be a good idea if I also went to the fortress."

Jack nodded. "It's a sound idea."

"It is not a sound idea," James ground out.

"We should all go," Alice said, her face mulish. "Then we avoid all of this nonsense."

"Then we're back to the same problem as before," Phillip said. "Let her go, James. You and I can hire an armed guard to stand at the door while the girls rusticate in here."

"I don't want to rusticate. At what point did we become invisible?" Sally said to Alice.

James rubbed the back of his neck and winced in a manner that Isabelle recognized as a pending headache. "How long of a journey, did you say?" he said to Jean-Louis.

"Likely three days, there and back. Provided we can quickly find what we're looking for. However, I should like to know my purpose if Isabelle and Jack are going to break into something."

James glared at Jack. "You're *his* chaperone."

Jack opened his mouth to retort, only to be cut off by Alice. "I do like the idea about Elysia," she said. "She knows the legend, she seems to know me. I haven't felt uncomfortable with her even once. She and Helene could even stay with us overnight to keep tongues from wagging."

In the end, it was decided that Isabelle would pose as Jean-Louis's British wife. Jack would accompany them as Isabelle's brother. Alice and Sally would remain under lock and key ("With our guns!") in the hotel room with Elysia and Helene, and Jack would use his position as a British agent to request a guard from local law enforcement for those times when James and Phillip were out.

James approached Isabelle as the group disbanded for the night and prepared for bed. "A word with you." Placing a hand at the small of her back, he led her out the door and into the hallway. The lights had been turned down and there were shadows on the walls. Nobody else was around—Isabelle wondered if that was a good thing as a muscle worked in James's jaw and he seemed to be carefully choosing his words.

"I'll not tell you what you can and cannot do," he said. "That I am unhappy about this plan is an understatement of epic proportion."

"James," she said softly, "it makes sense; if you but give yourself a moment to ponder on it, you'll realize that Jean-Louis is ill equipped to enter any place without express permission. His personality doesn't allow for it. I don't think the man is entirely comfortable with his firearm either. Did you see him at shooting practice? He winces and fights to keep his eyes open just long enough to mark the target—and he usually misses."

"Belle, you gave me your word that you would be safe this time."

"I gave you my word that I would not get myself shot unless I was with you. So I must endeavor to avoid such a thing." She smiled.

James leaned toward her, shifting just a fraction of space really, but suddenly he loomed large in her sight, and very intimidating.

Ridiculous.

She straightened herself to her full height and looked him in the eye.

He moved closer by small degrees until she imagined she could feel the heat radiating off his chest and shoulders, which filled her vision. She was forced to tip her head back to continue meeting his eyes, and she opened her mouth to say something, but he cut her off.

Grasping her around the back of her neck, he leaned down and captured her lips with his own. The kiss was different—desperate, demanding even— than those he had given her before. She had always known he loved her and that he was physically attracted to her, but the intensity of the kiss left her physically and emotionally breathless. She felt branded, and to her everlasting surprise, she was at peace with it.

Behind James's veneer of civility, he was possessive and she knew it. She saw it in the way he fixed his eyes on gentlemen who looked at her when they were in public. He would wait until they glanced at him and then hold the gaze with a flat expression that eventually had the men looking away first, flustered.

If she wasn't walking with her arm in his, he stayed behind and watched the group as they meandered along the streets and into and out of shops. On the few occasions where they had been sightseeing and gentlemen had tipped their hats to her or loitered overlong in a polite exchange of "good day to you," he materialized by her side with a hand on her back or a gentle but insistent grip on her elbow. He was taller than the average man and wide through the shoulders and arms. What didn't scare other men off in his implacable expression did by virtue of his sheer size. She often found herself fighting a smile after such episodes, and he would look at her innocently with a raised brow.

When he broke the kiss, he didn't move more than a few inches from her face. "I'll not have you forget who waits behind for you. And I'll not have you forget whose ring it is you wear."

She drew in a shuddering breath. "As if I ever could." She looked at his face, still so close to hers, and drew her brows in thought. "What is it that has you so concerned?"

"You're traveling alone with two men, one of whom is very similar to you in temperament and vocation. You have much in common with him. And I daresay most women find him handsome."

Isabelle blinked. She hadn't seen shades of James's temper since they had first met in England. He had been worried about his brother then, and she'd come to realize that because of those circumstances his rope of patience had been very short. After they found Phillip, he had relaxed, and his natural charm had begun to surface. Surely he couldn't be so aggravated about her trip with Jack and Jean-Louis that the smoldering temper would return?

She almost laughed. Placing her hands on his chest, she opened her mouth to say something, only to shake her head and put her hand around his neck this time, pulling him toward her for a searing kiss of her own. "Silly, silly man," she said when she broke the contact. She laid her forehead against his and closed her eyes. "You think, for even one small moment, that I would betray you with Jack?"

He ground his teeth. "The thought did cross my mind."

"Well, cast it out. That is complete and utter nonsense."

"Not from where I stand."

Isabelle trailed her hand from behind his neck to rest on his cheek. "You don't trust me?"

"I trust you," he growled. "I do not know him well enough to trust him."

"I'm not worried about leaving you here with two attractive young women."

"Isabelle, that is reprehensible."

"They are of marriageable age, James."

His disgusted expression had her mouth twitching at the corners. She wound her arms around his neck and pulled him close again for a tight embrace. He didn't resist, and she was relieved. Instead, he wrapped his arms around her, one hand running slowly to the small of her back and up again. She suddenly felt very warm. His hands spanned her waist, pulling her marginally closer. Shutting her eyes, she tried to remember what else she'd been about to say.

"James," she tried again.

"Hmm?" His voice was a low rumble in her ear.

"You know this is a very public place."

She felt him smile. "It's dark, and there's nobody about."

"James?"

"Yes."

"I'll think of you every moment."

"See that you do."

10

THEY DINED IN THE SITTING room the next morning, the entire group subdued. Leila and Theo had delivered a sumptuous array of food that Isabelle's nerves wouldn't allow her to eat but that the Ashbys attacked with relish. Leila seemed more in control of her fears than the last time Isabelle had seen her, and Isabelle noted with some amusement that the girl made a point of serving Jack his tea first.

As to the finer details of the pending excursion, Isabelle quickly learned that not only was Baltasar Metaxas proficient in selling firearms, he also had a knack for forging official papers. It wasn't long before "Monsieur and Madame Guillaume Monteforte" were traveling with Madame Monteforte's brother, "Robert Prince," on a small steamship bound for Monemvasia. Madame Monteforte was a London native who had met her husband during her tour of the continent soon after her debut six years earlier. Provided nobody realized that the groom would have been but age seventeen at the time, they were safe. It would have made much more sense for the men's roles to have been reversed, but a dark look from James had solidified the current pairing.

The steamship departed from Piraeus in the late afternoon, with an anticipated voyage totaling ten hours. Isabelle spent the bulk of her waking hours at a table in a small lounge, studying the many notes she'd made in her journal since leaving the United States for India. Finding something that might make sense of the current riddle would be welcome. On a whim, she'd given James the small black journal that had been translated from Ari Kilronomos's diary before they'd left India. If she hadn't seen Ari that day at the Acropolis, it was someone who looked just like him. And if she had seen him, chances were that Sparks might also. He and Sparks had been allies once upon a time, and it likely wouldn't take long for the relationship to resume.

Isabelle sat next to her "husband," who was also going through his note-book, making notations and pausing to think. Across the table from them sat her "brother," who often rose to look out the small porthole, pensive.

"What are you thinking?" Isabelle said to Jack late in the evening after they had dined and resumed their familiar seats in the lounge.

"I am very . . . unsettled," Jack said. "I feel as though I'm awaiting the grim reaper. Again."

"When was the first?" she said.

"Catherine Throckmorton. Telling us in Egypt that the Federation was going to have me killed."

Isabelle frowned and kept her voice low. "Do you suppose they know of your actual identity?"

"I don't know. My cover was very deep. The only person who knows who I really am works with the British consulate. I am hopeful the Federation merely suspected me of striking out on my own—that would explain why they sent an assassin after me. If they know . . ." He paused. "I'm fooling myself. If I really believed they didn't know who I was, I'd have maintained my Italian identity." He shrugged.

Isabelle nodded. It was a familiar fear and one that had been no stranger to her during her active years as a spy. Behind the confidence that came with playing a role and doing it well was a tiny concern that never really went away: a fear of being discovered. People didn't often take well to being duped. They tended to regard it as a very personal slight. Jack's enemies were ruthless, and she didn't envy him his position.

The fact that they were all in danger because of their association with him also occurred to her. He was such a vital piece of the puzzle though, and by now they were all entwined. The thought of just packing up and returning home was laughable. She could no more turn her back on Alice at this point than she could on Sally.

It was some time later when the three decided to call the day finished and return to their cabins. With a good night to Jack, who entered his cabin across the hall, Jean-Louis turned his key in the lock to his and Isabelle's cabin. Isabelle supposed it was a good thing that her feelings for Jean-Louis were strictly familial. There was a certain amount of intimacy to sharing a cabin, and the fact that it wasn't with her fiancé, at least, was odd.

Jean-Louis opened the door to allow her entrance first after which she turned up the gaslight near the door. Her eyes narrowed as her gaze traveled across the little room, past the small bed near the door, and across the narrow space to the other bed, on which she'd placed her portmanteau.

The latch was slightly unhinged, and she had most definitely snapped it shut.

"Someone has been in here," she murmured to Jean-Louis.

His face paled, and he quickly closed the door, locking it behind them. "How do you know?"

Isabelle crossed the space to her bed and looked closely at the bag. It appeared innocent enough—it hadn't moved at all—but she knew that hands other than her own had pawed through it. She placed a hand on her hip and with the other rubbed the back of her neck.

Jean-Louis joined her and stared at the bag. "What is it?"

"Someone is either careless or sending me a message."

His brows creased in a frown. "Is anything missing?"

"I don't know."

"Are you going to open it?"

Isabelle sighed. There were no smudged fingerprints on the soft, tan-colored leather, no outer sign on the bag itself that might give her a clue as to who had been in it. "I might as well," she finally said.

Cracking it open, she looked inside to see her handkerchiefs, lotions, and other incidentals all undisturbed. In a side pocket, she had placed a few papers—brochures of Greece's finer attractions mostly—and the map of Monemvasia.

"That's what he looked at. The map." She felt Jean-Louis's curious gaze and glanced up. "That's not how I left it."

"How did you leave it?"

"Large crease up. Look at it."

He looked over her shoulder to see the document, folded in fourths and four edges of the paper facing upward with the crease at the bottom of the bag. "You're certain?"

She gave him a flat stare.

"Yes. Of course you are." He drew a deep breath. "Well then."

She nodded. "It begins."

***

Alice fought to breathe. She swam for the mouth of the cave, knowing she had to get inside it but fearing her lungs would burst before she could reach it. The sense of despair at failing to reach what lay inside was nearly as potent as the urge to inhale. Her lungs burned, and stars formed before her eyes, narrowing her vision until she could barely see the cave. She clawed forward, her frantic movements sluggish in the water, her legs tiring as she kicked toward the enclosure. The stars finally filled her vision completely, eventually turning the world black.

She sat up in bed, gasping for air. Coughing and gulping, Alice kicked her way out of the bedsheets that had twisted around her torso and legs. She staggered toward the washstand and poured herself a glass of water from the pitcher, very nearly setting the glass down again when the swirling liquid reminded her of the horrid dream.

"Alice, what on earth!" Sally sat upright, rubbing her eyes. "Are you ill?"

Alice guzzled the water in defiance, holding a finger at Sally to wait. She took a breath when the glass was empty and coughed again. "I had a dream," she said.

"Oh dear," Sally said as she flopped back down onto her pillows. "Again?"

Alice stared at her reflection in the mirror above the washstand. She looked pale and drawn. With a frown, she pinched her cheeks before realizing the futility of the gesture, given that her hair looked like a domicile for a dozen rats. Her ghostly complexion was the least of her worries.

"You go back to sleep," she said to Sally. "It's early yet. I'm going to ring for some tea and take it in the sitting room."

"I'll join you," Sally said, her voice muffled by her blankets as she snuggled back into her bed.

Alice shook her head as she grabbed a brush and furiously began to drag it through her dark hair. "No, truly. I find myself so angry at the moment that I'm hardly fit company."

She made quick work of her messy hair, smoothing it into submission, and dressed with hands that shook slightly. In a huff, she opened the connecting door to the sitting room and was surprised to find Elysia already sitting there.

"Oh! Good morning," she said as she closed the bedroom door behind her. She tried repeating the phrase using the little Greek Jean-Louis had taught her, but the words felt awkward on her tongue.

The old woman nodded. "Good morning." She said something in Greek then that was beyond Alice's perfunctory understanding.

Alice grabbed a Greek-to-English phrase book sitting on the coffee table and handed it to the woman with a smile. When Elysia found her chosen key words, Alice shook her head. "I didn't sleep well at all," she said. "I had a disturbing dream." She fumbled in the phrase book for the word *dream*.

"Ah," Elysia said with a sage nod and patted the spot next to her on the small sofa. She spoke again in Greek, shaking her head at the phrase book, and looked up in clear relief as the door opened and Helene entered. "She tell," Elysia said to Alice.

"You had a bad dream?" Helene said as Elysia spoke. "My aunt says it's to be expected."

Alice frowned and walked over to the bell pull. She tugged on it once and resumed her seat. "Why would she say that?" Alice said.

"Guardians of the stones are rarely at peace."

Alice raised a brow. "But I don't have the stones," she said and then abruptly cut herself off, thinking of the Jewel of Zeus tucked away in the safe that was hidden behind a painting on the wall next to the fireplace. She fought to keep from looking at it.

Elysia watched her closely and then nodded once. Helene turned to her aunt, but Elysia continued to regard Alice in silence for a moment before asking about the young woman's mother.

"My mother?" Alice repeated when Helene translated. "My mother is gone."

"And your father?"

Alice nodded. "My father also. I am alone." The sting was easing a bit, but underneath her brave facade, she was still a raw wound.

Elysia smiled and told Alice that she was also an orphan, to which Alice laughed. She returned to the sofa and grasped the woman's hand, feeling the gnarled knuckles that had seen years of work. Had someone told her she'd one day feel affection for old women, she'd have called them daft.

A knock on the door proved to be a member of the hotel staff. "Leila?" Alice asked the young girl who was becoming a familiar face and was rewarded with a nod and a smile. Alice gave the girl instructions in clear, plain English and included a request for tea and food for her guests as well.

The two men Jack had arranged as guards stood at attention in the hallway on either side of the door, watching the exchange closely. James and Phillip had said the night before that they were going to go out early in the morning and were having a carriage from the hotel sent to pick up Helene and Elysia. Light was only now beginning to show through the windows.

Alice turned back to see aunt and niece conversing in hushed tones. Helene seemed hesitant, Elysia insistent. Alice would have given her left foot to speak the language. Well, perhaps not the whole foot. Maybe just a toe.

***

James squinted against the early morning sunlight as he and Phillip walked down the narrow street. He angled his hat to better shield his eyes as he cast a glance over the folded newspaper he held in his hand, trying not to think about Isabelle on a steamship with two single men, one of whom he considered a distinct threat. To the casual onlooker, he hoped it appeared that he and Phillip were tourists out for a casual morning stroll.

"You're certain this is the street?" Phillip said as he twirled his walking stick.

"According to Metaxas, the house should be at the end here, just before the street turns the corner." James had found an address in Ari's journal that Isabelle had left with him, and the men asked the museum owner for directions to it.

"And what are we going to do if we suddenly see the man?" Phillip said.

"I'd say we best decide quickly," James muttered and veered toward the left and onto a small side street as the house in question opened up and deposited one Ari Kilronomos look-alike onto the front stoop. James hadn't had more than a second or two to look at the man but could well see Isabelle's bafflement at her earlier sighting of him. It was either the Ari Kilronomos they had known in India, or it had to be a relative. The resemblance was uncanny.

"We're going to lose him," Phillip muttered as they continued walking.

"We can hardly walk up and say hello," James said. "At least we know it's the correct address." He picked up his pace as he caught the man in his peripheral vision. "He's walking this way. If he recognizes me, we might as well have knocked on his door and stated our intentions." Ari had spent time with James and Isabelle in India, acting as a concerned friend while, in reality, harboring a hidden agenda. He would definitely know James on sight.

With a whistle and swing of the walking stick, Phillip gently nudged James onto yet another side street, and once out of sight of the other man, James followed as Phillip broke into a trot, jogging up one alley and yet another until they were quite hopelessly lost.

"Well," Phillip said as he slowed his pace and looked around. "I don't see him anymore."

James glanced at Phillip out of the corner of his eye. "I don't see anything familiar anymore. Where are we?"

"I believe we're still in Athens."

James rolled the newspaper in his hand and tapped it against his thigh as he removed his hat and scratched his head.

"Oh, I know where we are," Phillip said as he pointed to the left.

James followed him around the corner and down a street where the whitewashed homes and brightly painted front doors marched side by side in picturesque splendor. "It's Baltasar Metaxas's shop. Where we bought the guns."

James nodded and felt his bearings return. "If we follow the road along that way, then—"

Phillip's eyes narrowed and his jaw clenched. He looked at a point over James's shoulder with a hiss that had James wondering if Phillip had allowed an evil spirit the temporary use of his body.

"What the devil?" James said in confusion. "What is wrong with you?"

"Sparks," Phillip hissed and moved forward.

James caught his arm and pulled him back with some effort, tugging him against the nearest house as a man left the gun shop. "Are you sure?" James murmured.

"I'd know that man anywhere," Phillip said. "This is our chance, James. Are you mad? Let me at him!"

"And then what? He's not going to just hand over the jewel. We need to see where he's staying."

Falling back as far as he dared, James motioned to Phillip and followed Sparks as the man navigated several streets until he came to a busy downtown marketplace. The brothers watched as Sparks purchased a piece of fruit from a vendor and a newspaper from the man who had sold James a month-old copy of the *London Times*, then argued with a young boy who appeared to be begging for change, and headed away from the market.

Fifteen minutes of discreet following led James and Phillip to the very door they'd sought at the beginning of their foray into the city's surrounding neighborhoods.

"So," James said. "Sparks is staying at Ari's house." He looked at Phillip, who still wore an expression bent on murder and mayhem. "I'd say we can be fairly certain they've found each other."

11

MONEMVASIA PROVED TO BE A mountain island of sorts that had functioned as a fortress with an upper and lower level. One road connected it to the mainland, the name *Monemvasia* itself meaning "one entrance"; Isabelle's gaze traveled over the island as she turned a full circle, examining the place. She squinted against the glare on the blue ocean and stopped turning as her eyes rested on the upper level of the island, figuring that the box they sought was most likely somewhere up there, where the bulk of the religious ruins was located.

Jack carried his and Isabelle's portmanteaus to a small table outside a café, where she sat and made a pretense of checking her complexion in a hand mirror while surreptitiously examining everything in front of and behind her. Jean-Louis had spoken with a dockhand, who told him where they might obtain lodging for the night, and he was off procuring it.

The homes and other structures were built into the mountainside in a combination of white and light sand-colored stone. Isabelle noted flower pots and neatly swept porches as she inhaled deeply of the rich ocean air. It wasn't long before Jean-Louis located them and told them he'd spoken with the proprietor of a small lodging who had rooms to rent.

They followed him through a stone archway and into a narrow alley to a set of aged double doors bearing glass panels adorned with starched, white crocheted curtains inside. The doors opened into a common room with stairs leading to an upper level on the right. A married couple of middle age welcomed them—the man wiry and slight, his wife a bit more substantial. Their clothing was serviceable and practical, pressed and tidy. They both wore wide smiles and nodded in greeting as Jean-Louis introduced Isabelle and Jack, his "wife and brother-in-law."

After telling the couple that they wished to see the town's sights, the woman hustled to a side table and picked up a brochure she handed to Isabelle, telling her through Jean-Louis that it contained a map and highlights of the area's finer points.

The woman, who told Isabelle to call her Callidora, led them up the narrow staircase and to a short hallway with four doors. Isabelle opened her and Jean-Louis's bedroom door to see two small beds separated by sturdy wood nightstands and kerosene lanterns. A bureau stood near the door, with drawers for their clothing or other items and a larger compartment in which to hang dresses or trousers.

Isabelle smiled at Callidora and thanked her in Greek—one of the few phrases she actually remembered—and Jean-Louis placed a coin in the woman's hand. She tsk-tsked him and returned the coin with a cheerful remonstration. Jean-Louis answered and laughed a bit with her, and Isabelle envied him his easy aptitude for languages. His comprehension and respect for other cultures served him well. It was a good decision to have included him in the venture; where she and Jack had stealth and ethically questionable skills, Jean-Louis had polish and an ease with people.

Isabelle placed her portmanteau on the floor of the bureau and noted the lock on the tall door. It would hardly keep out determined hands, but Isabelle figured the only item of interest in her belongings had already been examined. Still, she took the map of Monemvasia and her diary and placed both in a small purse that clipped to a loop at the waist of her dress.

After they'd settled their belongings, they met Jack in the hallway and made their way down the stairs. Gratefully accepting an apple from Callidora as they headed out the door, Isabelle took a bite of it and considered their options. Once outside, she said, "I suggest we begin with the churches. There seems to be a religious theme that runs through each piece of this puzzle."

Jack glanced at her as he polished his own apple on his sleeve. "I suppose it's as good a place as any to start. There are churches down here on the lower level—let's begin here and work our way up."

"Yes," she nodded. "The upper level is where we will find ruins. My guess is what we're seeking is likely up there." They began walking toward the stone-paved path that led to the Greek Orthodox church situated on the lower level. "However, can't leave any rock unturned—yes, I intended the pun—so we must rule out every possibility."

"What makes you believe it's hidden in the ruins?" Jean-Louis said.

"I'm not entirely certain, but wouldn't it seem logical that if something were hidden in a functioning church where people constantly visit, it would have been discovered by now?"

Jean-Louis shrugged. "Perhaps it has been."

Jack shook his head as they neared a church that looked as old as its surroundings. "I don't believe it has. I never heard even the smallest mention of it during my time with the Federation."

"Would you have been privy to such information?" Jean-Louis said.

Jack shot the Frenchman a look similar to the one Isabelle had given him the night before. "I listened, whether privy or not."

Isabelle hid a frown as she shaded her face against the sun with her hat. Jack truly was a man marked for death if the Federation had come to realize the extent of his knowledge. "There's a Byzantine church up there called Agia Sophia," she said as she pulled Callidora's brochure from her purse and unfolded it. "When we finish down on this level, I suggest we examine it next."

The church that the trio entered was cool and dark and required a moment of stillness as their eyes adjusted to the limited light. Icons of the Virgin and Child hung on the walls, and the interior was similar in decor and feel to numerous others they had seen in Athens.

"No priest in attendance today?" Jack murmured.

Isabelle moved slowly to the interior of the building and began circling the perimeter of the room. Lanterns placed at intervals along the walls cast a gentle glow that flickered as she moved past. She glanced at the two men—Jack made his way around the room in the other direction, examining walls, arches, and icons much as she was doing. Jean-Louis watched them uncertainly, continually looking to the front door as though expecting a Turkish invasion.

Isabelle drew her brows together in a frown as she neared Jack on the other side of the room. There was no evidence of their mysterious symbol anywhere, no large arrows pointing to a spot on the floor with signs that said, "Ancient jewel box buried here!" The icons and paintings were just that—nothing out of the ordinary, all frustratingly normal.

Jack motioned with his head toward the door. "Onward."

The three made their way out of the church and walked the streets of the lower town, Isabelle holding Jean-Louis's arm and speaking in a British accent when people were close by. The accent came naturally enough—after listening to Alice for months, it was nearly second nature.

Jean-Louis, to his credit, acted well the part of doting husband. Jack strolled with them, hands in pockets and a jovial smile on his face. He was very good. Isabelle knew the strain he was under, and only rarely did she see it flash in his eyes. His Scots brogue had given way to clipped British accents that had her giving him a mental nod of approval.

"What is that?" she asked as they neared a building, octagonal in shape and made of marble. She reached for her pamphlet, but Jean-Louis supplied the information before she could consult the guide.

"It is a mausoleum," he said. "It's similar in design to others I noticed in Athens even though this was initially a Venetian fortress. Architectural styles are so varied in this country, and they all stand side by side."

"Do we need to secure permission to enter it?" Isabelle asked him. Trampling on private family spaces in broad daylight wouldn't garner them favor with the locals.

"I don't believe so. This one is fairly large—it looks communal."

Jack reached the door to the mausoleum first and opened it for the other two. Inside, Isabelle noted everything she would have hoped for in a suitably spooky resting place—it was cold and dark; vaults in the walls were secured with square marble markers bearing family names.

They each took up positions around the room and began examining the markings cut into the stone squares, eventually making a sweep of the entirety and finding nothing of note. Isabelle gave a small shrug when Jean-Louis sighed and made his way toward the door. "If it were easy to find, someone would have done so by now," she told him.

He nodded and held the door open for her, waiting as Jack finished a final sweep of the room. Once outside, Jack motioned with his head. "Up."

The church at the top of the hill, Agia Sophia, was intact but surrounded by ruins of former churches, public cisterns, small mausoleums, and abandoned noblemen's residences. The "blueprint" portion of the Monemvasia map from Dr. Pearce's collection showed a building either round or octagonal in nature, but the print was so light as to be almost indiscernible. And furthermore, as Phillip had noted, there wasn't an x marking the spot where the box lay hidden.

Agia Sophia was beautiful in its design and construction. Jack reached it first and motioned them inside. There was a small group of European tourists within, following a cleric who described the church's origins. There were images of the Christ on tapestries that hung on the walls, and there were alcoves closed off with dark wooden doors that bore simple wooden crosses as their only decor.

In terms of other churches Isabelle had seen in Greece, it was significantly less ornate. The structure of the walls, which were a combination of square and rectangular rocks mortared together, was simple in its design, and she appreciated it. She noted repeated arches recessed into the walls and moved to examine each closely as she slowly made her way around the room. There was a small hallway leading to another door at the side of the church, and narrow windows at the back showed the sheer drop-off into the Mediterranean below.

Passing an icon of the Savior, she paused and, feeling a bit foolish, thought, *Bless us all, please.* She closed her eyes for a moment and then moved forward, hoping nobody had noticed her brief prayer. Figuring she'd best try to acquire a bit of religion before meeting her fiancé's mother, she fought the discomfort of the moment and managed a plea for forgiveness at her lack of spirituality.

Thinking of James's mother made her aware of the fact that he was ten hours away by ship. They had spent nearly every moment together from the time they had met months before in England. She shook her head. Pining as though she couldn't manage one little foray away from him . . . it didn't bear acknowledgment. She recalled their last warm embrace, the feel of his lips, his whispers in her ear, the look on his devilishly handsome face when she'd said something that made him laugh . . .

Isabelle scowled with a muttered curse, and it was with no small sense of relief that she was distracted by a sharp intake of breath. She glanced over to Jean-Louis, who stood across the small room from her, bent over and looking into an alcove. She flicked a quick look at the cleric and his tourists, relieved to find him still droning on about the church to the small flock. Jack had also spared the group a glance and met her gaze. She made her way to Jean-Louis's side and squatted next to him.

"What is it?"

"Could it really be so simple?" the Frenchman said to her.

"Highly unlikely," Jack muttered as he looked down over Isabelle's shoulder. "What do you have?"

Jean-Louis traced his finger over an engraving in a square brick. Clearly the symbol to which they had all become accustomed—the rectangle surrounding three ovals—this time pictured under an arch.

"Why is it that you can never keep track of your jewelry?" Jack said loudly to Isabelle. "Honestly, Sister, some things will never change!"

Isabelle lifted her eyes to see the cleric approaching. "You are losing something?" he said to them, his thick brow furrowed.

"My silly sister has *again* lost her charm bracelet," Jack said. He helped Isabelle rise by placing a hand under her elbow. "That marks the third time this week!"

"It's the dratted clasp," Isabelle said with a pout. "And my darling gave it to me on our anniversary."

"There, dearest," Jean-Louis said as he patted Isabelle's hand. "I shall buy you another in Paris next month." He had deliberately thickened his French accent and played the doting spouse very well. Pulling a handkerchief from his pocket, he handed it to Isabelle, who sniffed delicately and dabbed at her eyes.

"But I did so love that one," Isabelle said as Jean-Louis turned her aside with an apologetic look at the cleric. Jack shrugged and rolled his eyes. With a shake of his head and a quick apology to the man, he followed his sister and her husband out into the bright sunlight.

Isabelle felt the cleric watching them for some time before returning to his tourists.

**

James was beginning to feel as though he could certainly qualify as one of Isabelle's Pinkerton contemporaries. He hadn't seen Sparks since the day before when he and Phillip had watched the man enter Kilronomos's house. He had, however, been spying on "Ari" Kilronomos for hours, dogging the man's footsteps. The most he had learned was that the Greek had a penchant for both liquor and ogling women of questionable moral fortitude.

James fought a yawn as he read the same newspaper article for the third time without really seeing it. He tossed back the last bite of his baklava and wondered how many more he would have to order to justify remaining at the café for as long as Kilronomos decided to.

Finally, the Greek threw some coins on his table and rose to leave. After waiting a few minutes, James did the same and made his way down the street in the same direction. He chatted with vendors and wandered into and out of shops as his prey made his way through the market district.

James didn't think much of the fact that they were nearing his hotel, where Phil and the young women were preparing for dinner—it was on a common thoroughfare after all—until Kilronomos stopped in front of it and stared at the upper windows for a moment. A very long moment. He then turned and made his way down the street with a whistle.

James followed the man back to his home, standing in the shadows for some time, his heart pounding in anger, before turning back to the hotel.

How the two men knew Phillip and Alice were in town was a mystery, but it didn't matter. Isabelle had seen and recognized Kilronomos, Phillip and James had seen Sparks. Given that they were all actively looking for each other, perhaps it wasn't such a mystery after all.

As he walked down the street in the gathering dusk, the air cooled and he angled his hat against a slight breeze. He pursed his lips and considered his options. He could further his foray into Isabelle's world of intrigue and break into Kilronomos's home to try and find the Jewel of Poseidon that Sparks had taken from them in Egypt. There was, however, the pesky fact that he didn't know how to open a lock without breaking it, and he was large of frame and made noise even when he walked on tiptoe. Isabelle had a way of disappearing into thin air when she wished.

He likely ought to move the lot of them to a new hotel. But what were the odds that they could stay hidden? Unless he kept Phil and Alice under lock and key, Sparks and Kilronomos would find them. He shook his head and forced himself to unclench his jaw, which was starting to ache from stress he hadn't realized was manifesting itself. He released a pent-up breath and rolled his shoulders, knowing his attempts at relaxation as he slept that night would likely give him little more than a stiff neck in the morning.

Madness. It was all madness. Isabelle was always in his thoughts, hovering at the back of his mind no matter what he was doing. He imagined her now as he had seen her, close in his arms the night before she had left. Stifling a groan, he shook his head as the hotel came into sight. It was with a renewed sense of urgency he decided that, before long, he was going to determine whether or not Sparks still had the jewel in his possession. Isabelle was miles away from him and her absence left an ache in his chest. When she returned, he fully intended to tie her to him— with a length of rope if need be.

***

The Egyptian sat for a moment and studied the paper in his hand, considering his options. Sparks was a snake, and not necessarily a smart one, but he had to admit the man did have a certain amount of sly cleverness—it was likely the only reason such ineptitude continually landed on its feet. And now it seemed the lucky villain had found himself another Kilronomos to use.

"We do nothing but watch," he murmured then called for his man of affairs to write a letter. "We watch and follow and then move when they have found that which we seek." And perhaps it was time to manipulate some "helpers" into place. There were always those who were desperate enough for bribes or vulnerable enough for blackmail. But it would require some finesse—for the time would definitely come when he would make an end of Jackson MacInnes.

**

Isabelle fidgeted until night finally fell. She, Jack, and Jean-Louis had been going over their plan and possible pitfalls for well over an hour. They were all on edge—the thought that the room aboard the steamship had been broken into and the map examined hovered like a dark cloud.

Isabelle had donned a pair of thin linen trousers and a thigh-length tunic, both midnight blue in color, that she had purchased in India. Black, practically fashioned shoes from Egypt and a cap that hid the hair she'd braided into a rope completed the ensemble. She would not only fade into the dark of the night, to the casual eye she would resemble a boy. To their credit, the men's surprise at Isabelle's attire was relatively subdued. Jean-Louis had raised both brows, Jack, only one.

"We are agreed, then?" Jack said as he looked out the window. Isabelle followed his gaze across the town that twinkled with lights and gentle laughter and out over the massive expanse of the water.

"Yes," Jean-Louis said quietly. "But I am not comfortable with it."

Jack turned to look at the Frenchman. "You mustn't hesitate, man. I will have your word."

He was met with silence.

"Jean-Louis," Isabelle said, a little more sharply than she'd intended. "We must be united in this."

Jean-Louis stood and paced the room. "How is it," he said, "that if you don't return, you expect me to go to Athens in the morning and explain to James why I left you behind?"

"Only should it become necessary," Isabelle said, softening her tone. "If Jack and I find what we're looking for and encounter trouble, we will separate. Whichever of us has the box will return here to you, at which time we leave and cross over to the mainland."

"And leave the third person behind to face . . . whatever happens." Jean-Louis stopped moving and placed his hands on his hips. "Isabelle, this plan is pure folly." He shook his head. "I know you will disagree, but I believe you should stay here at the inn and I should go with Jack."

Isabelle let out a breath. "Dear man, I appreciate your concern. Truly, I do." She sat down on her bed. "I know you seek to protect me from harm, but I can handle myself. I am extremely familiar with my gun and have used it more than once. I have been trained to run about in the dark and hide from people. I commit details to memory—I know every rock and tree between this building and Agia Sophia. One of us must remain behind to collect our belongings should we need to leave suddenly. If Jack and I are pursued, we won't be able to return here."

"And we've agreed," Jack stressed, "that should neither one of us be able to return here, we will meet you on the mainland tomorrow morning by the six o'clock hour at the small café near the docks. The steamer leaves at half past six. Whoever has the box is on it, sailing for Athens. The other one or two of us will board the next available ship."

"I don't like it," Jean-Louis insisted.

"Nor do I!" Jack glared at him. "But do you have any idea what will happen if we are unable to round up those cursed stones and send them to the hell they deserve? In the wrong hands—" He shook his head. "We must not fail."

Jean-Louis narrowed his gaze, his jaw clenched. "Very well," he finally said.

Isabelle released a sigh. She knew it was no small thing to be the one left behind while others went out on an operation.

Jean-Louis cleared his throat, looking miserable. "You have your money with you?" he said to Isabelle.

She gave him a smile and rose, taking him in her arms for a brief embrace. "I do," she said and pulled back, framing his face with her hands. He was a brilliant young scholar and a gentleman. What she was asking of him—that he not only throw chivalry to the wind, but also help destroy ancient relics—was more than what was fair. "I'll be fine—you must believe me. If you don't see me later tonight, I'll meet you at the café in the morning."

Jack, looking out the window again, glanced down at his pocket watch and hefted a black fabric sack up on his shoulder. "Ready, then?" he said to Isabelle.

She checked to see that a small pouch with a few items was securely tied about her waist underneath the tunic. With a final pat to Jean-Louis's arm, she nodded. "Ready."

12

"Now?" James asked the old woman. He turned to Elysia's niece. "Helene, she wants to go the docks right now?" James, Phillip, Alice, and Sally sat with the Greek women in the hotel lounge after returning from a delicious dinner in a terraced restaurant that sported a stunning view of the Acropolis.

Helene spoke to her aunt rapidly in Greek, but Elysia was insistent. Helene turned back to James with slightly flared nostrils and a reluctant shrug. "She says it is best experienced at night."

"What is best experienced at night?" Alice said.

"Her destiny."

James shook his head. "I don't follow. Whose destiny? And I don't think it's a good idea to go out to the docks this late. We were just going to see you home and then turn in for the night."

Helene spoke to Elysia and then turned again to James, her eyes closing briefly. "She says Miss Alice is the Guardian of the stones, and as such she must know where to take them."

"I do think that would be a good idea," Alice said.

James looked at her. "What is this 'Guardian' business?"

Alice glanced at Elysia. "I am, apparently, a Guardian. I have the ability to find the stones, and she seems to think that I can also take them to where they belong."

"And where would that be?"

"Well, I'm sure I don't know, James, which is why we should go with her now."

Phillip leaned forward in his chair. "Alice, we don't even have all of the stones," he said in a low tone. As a seeming afterthought, he added, "And why am I not a Guardian?"

Elysia chuckled, her face wreathed in wrinkles. She spoke a few words, which Helene translated with a smile. "You are not to feel slighted, young man. You are a Detector. Just not a Guardian. This duty falls to the firstborn girl."

Phillip sat back in his chair with a *humph*. "Detector," he muttered. "Hardly impressive at all. So what can a Detector do, then?"

Elysia held up a gnarled finger to emphasize her words. "A Detector has the power to locate the stones. A Guardian," she said through Helene, "can not only find the jewels but is also to keep them safe. Away from those who would seek them for nefarious gain. And Guardians are to keep the stones apart from each other until the time is right." There was a long pause as Elysia looked out the window at the night sky. "She also has the power to return them to their home."

"And what would be the point of that?" Sally said, breathless.

"It would keep the world safe forever by destroying them. Never to be again retrieved by human hands. But it must be during the eruption. And they must be together in the box."

Elysia continued speaking in Greek, and Helene listened to her with her head cocked to one side as though in contemplation. "She says," Helene finally translated, "that the instructions for returning the jewels to their home is found on two small tapestries."

James held back a groan. Not another missing treasure. "Dare I hope she has the tapestries?" he asked Helene.

"You know, I believe she used to." Helene turned to her aunt and spoke briefly to her, and at Elysia's affirmative nod, she turned back to James and the others. "They used to hang in her home. I remember seeing them when I was very small. She said they disappeared one day, and she always blamed Demitrios and Baltasar's father for it. Says he stole them from her for his museum. He never did admit to it. And then he died suddenly, and Demitrios took over the museum ownership—and it's been a disaster ever since."

Even if Helene hadn't translated, James figured he could get the gist of what the old woman was saying in her facial expressions alone. She was clearly not enamored of the Metaxas family.

Elysia pulled insistently on Helene's arm and again spoke rapidly. Helene turned to James and said, "I am so sorry. She is still insisting on going to the docks."

James sat back in his seat and considered his options. He could go along with the old woman, who may or may not be batty, or insist that they call it a night and turn in. He could even have the police guards, playing a rousing hand of gin in their hotel sitting room, accompany the two women home and save himself the trip.

"Well then, to Piraeus we go," he said and stood up. "The omnibus doesn't run this late, so we'll have to flag down a hack."

Phillip gave him a long look. "You feeling well, Jimmy boy?"

Sally and Alice snorted with laughter as they stood and gathered their shawls and bonnets. "Jimmy boy," Sally repeated and elbowed James.

"Phil," James said, "you would be well-advised to sleep with one eye open tonight."

***

A short thirty-minute carriage ride later had Alice looking out over the black expanse of ocean that stretched before her. Elysia stood next to her and gripped her hand tightly.

"You'll not see it from here," Helene translated for the old woman, "but the island will erupt. It is in that direction," she said, pointing off to the south.

"How do you know these things?" Alice murmured.

"You know it too," Elysia told her. "Close your eyes."

Alice obeyed her and shut her eyes. She tried not to cry out in surprise as the old woman began spinning her in a circle. She turned several times until she was completely disoriented and dizzy.

"Now," Elysia said in English. "Eyes closed. Point."

Alice stood still for a moment, trying to get her bearings. It was behind her. She turned a half circle on unsteady legs and pointed straight ahead, gripping the arm of the closest person.

Phillip whistled under his breath as she opened her eyes. He patted the hand that rested on his arm. "A Guardian, you must be," he whispered to her as she looked to see that the graceful line of her arm pointed to the very spot Elysia had indicated.

Alice frowned. "Likely just a coincidence. Luck."

Sally shook her head. "I don't think so, Alice. It was like you knew."

"But where is it? I don't even know what I'm pointing at," she said.

"Santorini," the old woman said quietly. "It erupted once. It will again." She tensed for a moment and then turned back to the carriage. "We go," she said. "We must go."

The carriage ride back into town was quiet, and as they neared Elysia's house, Alice noticed that Helene appeared drowsy, but the older woman was alert, looking out the window as if watching for something.

James exited the carriage as it came to a halt in front of the women's small home. Helene smiled at the girls, and the women bid the occupants farewell. Alice looked out the window opposite the house and stared down the street, noting gas lamps that chased the darkness for a few feet before giving way to the night. Shadows danced, and she wondered if it was the breeze in the trees or something else.

"There's someone out there," she murmured to Sally. "Someone is watching us."

The wind shifted and blew, lifting the tendrils of hair off of her neck. It carried with it a scent, a mixture of men's cologne and cigar smoke. It smelled familiar. She turned to Sally as Phillip and James escorted the women to their front door. "Someone has followed us from Piraeus," she whispered.

***

Isabelle handed Jack his grandfather's parchment that showed the map of the island. He turned it over and glanced at it under the moonlight as they stood at the deserted doors of Agia Sofia. "I don't think it's in the church itself," he murmured as he squinted at the paper and brought it closer to his face.

"Why not?" she whispered.

"Because this isn't the church," he said, indicating the diagram on the back of the map. "This is probably one of these." He gestured to the centuries-old ruins that dotted the landscape around them.

Isabelle took another look at the diagram and wondered how they were going to determine which of the many crumbling remains it once matched. "The carving on the stone inside the church shows the box under an arch."

Jack nodded. "Which means it could be in any one of several buildings that had arches."

They looked at the landscape before them and looked at each other. There were arches aplenty dotting the mountaintop. Trying to orient themselves using the map was useless; the print was faded and nearly illegible in places. And the map didn't indicate the location of the building that was diagramed on the back side of the parchment.

Isabelle took a deep breath. "Well then we keep to the shadows as much as possible and start looking at every arch in sight."

"You begin here, near the church. I'll start over there on the far side, and we can work our way down the slope."

She nodded and with a quick glance stepped away from the ancient church's shielding entryway and onto the rocky expanse. The moon provided ample light, which was both a blessing and a curse. A flash of memory hit her as she skirted from shadow to shadow—an image of her portmanteau on the steamship, unfastened, with the map having been perused without her knowledge, the map of the very hillside she now examined. She paused for a moment and stilled her breathing, listening. The night was quiet, and she briefly closed her eyes, wishing she dared take the lack of noise as a sign of safety.

The countryside sloped downward from the church and was littered with the remains of numerous buildings that hadn't seen habitation for many years. The landscape began blending together after Isabelle had combed it for over an hour, systematically, but to no avail. Every now and again she and Jack met back at the church, shared a few comments on where they'd each looked, unsuccessfully examined the map hoping for new clues, and then separated again.

Isabelle frowned at what she assumed was once the stately home of a medieval nobleman and left it after scanning the interior archways. She hadn't heard anything unusual; for all intents and purposes, she and Jack seemed to be the only two living beings at the top of the mountainous island. Perceived reality was often an illusion—she knew that well enough—and the longer it took them to find the box, the more tension she felt in her neck and shoulders.

It was to Jack's credit that she was unable to find him right away as she again climbed the slope that led from the church; he must have heard her because he stepped out from behind a rock wall as she approached. She gritted her teeth at her clear lack of stealth.

"You heard me?" she mumbled.

"More like I felt a shift in the air."

She nodded. That she could understand. It was better than the thought that she hadn't been quiet enough, and she couldn't well do much about the fact that she occupied space and displaced air as she walked.

"Let me see the diagram," she said. "It could be the mausoleum over to the left. Have you checked it?" She pointed to the building in question.

He nodded but handed her the paper. "I didn't see the symbol anywhere," he whispered, "but we must assume it will be small. We may have missed it twice over by this point."

Isabelle narrowed her eyes, shifting the diagram in the moonlight. "See," she murmured. "This round structure drawn right here . . ."

Staying in shadows, she headed across the countryside and made her way to the ruins she'd noticed the first time they'd climbed the hill. It was a small domed structure made of stone with four thick, arched walls supporting it. Consulting the diagram again, she nodded. "I think that," she whispered with a gesture to the stone building, "is this here," and she pointed to a large circle on the diagram. "Obviously, the rest of this is long gone. It's no longer a functioning mausoleum—just a shell." And for that, she supposed, she should be grateful. The prospect of trying to find the box by pawing through ancient bones wasn't one she relished.

Jack looked at the building's remains for a moment then entered, standing inside and examining the ceiling and four arched walls. "The light doesn't penetrate well in here," he murmured as she joined him. "We'll have to strike a lucifer."

Isabelle took a tin from her small bag and withdrew a Swiss safety match, grateful for its evolution. The forerunner to the present matchstick had thrown sparks and had often been unstable upon lighting. The resulting odor had also been offensive, and if anyone were within sniffing distance, the smell would have given them away immediately.

She pulled a small white candle from the bag as well and lit it with the flame that flared to life as she struck the lucifer. Using the candle's feeble light, she immediately began searching the closest archway for any sign of the familiar symbol. She made it to the ground on one side and back up again before moving on to the next arch.

Jack followed suit, and the two continued in silence for several moments before Isabelle's gaze fell on a rock near the base of the arch that opened to the sea. The moonlight caught upon it rather like a shaft of angelic light, and Isabelle glanced heavenward and wondered if her earlier prayer had made her a candidate for blessings. Truly, the symbol itself was a mere two inches square and barely noticeable, even upon closer examination.

With widened eyes and a shrug of her shoulders, she called quietly to Jack. "Here it is," she whispered as he squatted down next to her on the ground. Using the tip of her finger, she outlined the symbol, which was etched into a rock at the base of the arch.

"Nicely done," Jack murmured and reached into his black bag. He withdrew a small hammer and chisel as he examined the stone closely. "Looks like we may have guessed well on the size."

Isabelle nodded. "I believe so." She held her hand out and studied it. The two stones she'd seen were identical in size and shape, and each fit in her palm. If the box held three of them, it could conceivably fit behind the marked rock. The other option might be under the ground, she supposed, which could prove a bit more difficult. The shovel Jack had brought was rather on the small side.

Jack placed a piece of thick fabric over the end of the chisel and began tapping at the stone's edges. Even with the noise muffled, Isabelle tensed and stood to maintain watch, moving from arch to arch. She didn't worry about the arch where Jack worked—there was only a scant yard or so before the ground gave way to a sheer drop into the ocean below.

The world outside the mausoleum was quiet and still. Moonlight shone bright on the ruins, throwing shadows behind walls and doorways. Trees were scant, but bushes, shrubs, and weeds scattered along the ground waved subtly in the soft breeze. Isabelle inhaled deeply of the rich ocean air and rotated her head. They didn't appear to have attracted any unwanted attention, but that didn't mean someone wasn't watching. Her nerves were taut, stretched to breaking. Clandestine activity had been easier during the phase of her life when she hadn't been in love, hadn't been the guardian to a young woman whom she loved like family.

Isabelle maintained her vigil for a good thirty minutes before she finally heard a gratified sigh emerge from the fourth arch. With one eye still on the landscape outside, she made her way to Jack's side and glanced over his shoulder to see that he had very nearly dislodged the rock, which was large enough on the surface but proved to be substantially thinner than she had previously guessed.

The stone scraped, and Isabelle saw Jack wince as he carefully maneuvered the carved rock out of place. Once it was gone, he lay nearly flat on the ground to look into the body of the thick stone arch. He looked up at Isabelle with a quirked brow, reached his hand inside the enclosure, and pulled out an object that was wrapped in cloth and measured roughly eight inches in length, six in width, and three in height.

Isabelle caught her breath and felt the grin spread across her face. She dropped next to Jack and touched a finger to the fabric, pulling it aside on one corner to reveal an alabaster box—white and translucent. "Amazing," she whispered. She lifted her glance to Jack's face; he was already scanning the area outside the small enclosure.

After replacing the stone he'd dislodged, he reached into his black bag, pulling from it an identical, folded drawstring bag, which he then opened and used to house their find. He handed it to Isabelle, who looped it over her head and across her midsection. Jack then placed the tools inside his fabric bag, after which he withdrew a dark, wooden box that was surprisingly close in dimension to the one they'd just unearthed.

That was a good guess, Isabelle mused as Jack placed the decoy under his arm and strung his bag across his torso as Isabelle had.

"Let's get out of here," he muttered.

He looked at her before they left the confines of the mausoleum. "We stay true to the plan," he told her. "No variations."

"Agreed."

They stepped out of the mausoleum's shelter and snaked their way around the exterior, clinging to the shadows. Isabelle crept along behind her comrade as they made their way along the landscape, hugging the sides of walls and buildings.

When the bullet hit Jack, he stumbled against her with a sharp exhalation of breath.

13

"Go!" Jack grunted at Isabelle as he staggered but maintained his balance.

Isabelle cursed their luck under her breath and ran to her right for the safety of a rock wall that had once been part of a family home. A bullet ricocheted behind her, splintering the stone and sending shards of it flying. Ducking behind the relative safety of the structure, she ran along the edge and out what remained of a back entrance, hearing gunshots from at least two weapons.

A quick glance behind her as she ran for the safety of another ruin showed Jack stumbling into an awkward run in the opposite direction with a dark shadow on his heels. Isabelle reached inside the pouch hanging from her waist and clasped the handle of her weapon. She dove behind a crumbling wall on a slight crest nearing Agia Sofia and took a deep breath, hoping she'd shaken her own pursuer for the moment.

Daring a glimpse around the corner of her protective wall, she braced herself and took aim at Jack's assailant. *Please, please don't let me hit Jack.* It had been an awfully long time since she'd shot at a moving target.

Her first shot was off but caught Jack's pursuer off guard enough that he slowed and stumbled for a fraction of a second that allowed her to fire another that hit him in the thigh.

Knowing she'd given away her own position, she ran for the safety of Agia Sofia and darted around to the side, hoping to find it unlocked. Mercifully, the old door opened and she slipped inside, making her way into the darkened interior. She was concerned at the fact that she had been forced to run away from the winding path leading to the lower town. Agia Sofia stood at the very far edge of the upper level, its whole back side dropping off and down into the depths of the sea below.

She felt rather than heard someone enter the building. It was as Jack had described it—more of a disturbance in the air than anything she could put her finger on. She quietly inhaled and exhaled, willing her heart to slow and her hand to steady. Softly edging her way into the interior of the church with her back against the cold stone walls, she made her way to the arched alcove where Jean-Louis had spotted the symbol earlier in the morning. Pulling the cloth bag close against her side, she melted into the alcove and waited.

***

Jean-Louis paced the small room, checking his pocket watch repeatedly. Waiting for Isabelle and Jack's return was the hardest thing he'd ever done. Every time he thought of leaving to find them, though, he considered what might happen if they returned and he was gone. He stood at the window and looked out over the water—inky black with the midnight hour but with a swath of moonlight bisecting it. He closed his eyes. Life had been so much simpler when he had been at home in France, living a quiet life as a professor at a French university.

Leaning his head against the window pane, he exhaled, hoping the next few hours would find his friends alive and well. An image of Alice floated through his mind—jet-black hair, deep blue eyes, feisty spirit, and latent intellect that had been manifesting itself increasingly since Egypt. She was safe in Athens with the Ashby brothers, and he missed her.

***

Sally registered a scraping sound on the fringes of her consciousness and turned over in her bed. A soft breeze wafted in and she welcomed it. She had been uncomfortable, and in addition to being overly warm, she suspected she was missing Isabelle. She hadn't been entirely at ease since Belle had left for Monemvasia, and Sally would be glad for her friend's return. Phillip was wonderful, and James was kind, as always, but Belle was her security.

Alice thrashed in her bed. Sally rubbed her eyes and tried to awaken her friend from what was clearly another nightmare. "Alice," she mumbled.

As Sally moved to prop herself up on one elbow, a shadow crossed into the moonlight. She convinced herself she must be dreaming because the face that gradually came into focus was one she'd not seen for months. She opened her mouth to scream when he moved forward and swiftly covered her mouth and nose. She struggled for a moment, kicking and scratching and eliciting a muted groan from her assailant before the sticky-sweet smell on the cloth over her nose finally began pulling her under its influence. Alice's muffled cry hovered on the air and then all was quiet.

***

Isabelle stilled her breathing and listened to the quiet footfalls that sounded on the stone floor of the church. She hoped her pursuer would neglect to search her hiding place; she wasn't keen on the thought of shooting first and asking questions later. There was once a time and place where that had been her regular mind-set; however, shooting people at close range had never been on her list of preferred activities. She slowly extended her arm, her weapon hand steady despite the fear that spread through her limbs at her worry for Jack. She was nothing if not practical, however, and war had a way of taking on many different faces. Leaving a bloody mess in Agia Sofia was bound to raise questions, and she was tired and didn't feel up to trying to heave a body over the side of the cliff.

The church was dark—barely any light entered through the windows high in the ceiling. A shadow slowly made its way across the room and Isabelle held her breath. The figure kept to the far wall and inched his way along it as his head turned slightly, listening.

She was in the shadows, well concealed. He would find her, though, if he examined each nook closely, and she would have no choice but to pull the trigger. She clenched her jaw.

The man's gun arm was extended as he moved from one alcove to the next. As he passed through a slit of moonlight, it glittered for a moment on a ring he wore—a ring Isabelle was fairly certain she'd seen once before. Unless her instincts were off, she figured she was in Agia Sophia with one of the King's Men.

A series of gunshots resounded across the hilltop outside the church, and her stalker moved quickly to the front door. Isabelle took the opportunity to slip out of her hiding place and move down the hallway to the side door she'd entered. Easing it open ever so slowly, she slipped out when she had just enough room to fit through the opening.

Isabelle skirted the side of the church and ran for the closest outcropping of ruins, seeing no sign of anyone, including Jack. She thought of their pact and fought every instinct she possessed to stop and search for him; instead, she made quick work of crossing the hilltop, dodging from rock to building until she reached the iron gate at the top of the winding path that led to the lower town. Quickly passing through it, she flew down the path, her gun arm holding tightly to the bag at her side.

She wound a circuitous route through the streets and alleys of the lower town so thoroughly that she was afraid she'd not only lost her pursuers but herself. It was with a sense of relief that she recognized the café they'd visited earlier. Her bearings intact, she ignored the stitch in her side and made her way to the inn.

Jean-Louis opened the door to her with widened eyes. He pulled her into the room and clasped her close for a minute as she tried to catch her breath. "Where is Jack?" he said when he released her, flushing slightly.

"Shot," she said as she braced her hands on her knees, concentrating on inhaling and exhaling.

"Shot?" Jean-Louis leaned forward and looked her in the face. "Shot?"

Isabelle stood and pulled the bag from across her body and over her head. "This is the box," she told him and explained what had happened at the top of the hill.

"So we leave him?" Jean-Louis mumbled, holding the bag in his hands and staring at her. "That was the plan."

Isabelle nodded. "I'm altering the plan," she told him. "You're going to return to Athens with the box. I'm staying here to find Jack."

14

JAMES WATCHED THE PEOPLE IN the room move around as though they were wind-up toys. Once the police officers had taken Sally's statement and left with a promise to begin the search for Alice, the reality of the situation seemed to sink in with deadly clarity. Sally cried and wrung her hands; Phillip looked near apoplexy.

The officers had been gone but a few moments when there came an insistent banging on the door. Phillip opened it to Helene, who was openly weeping.

"We'll find her," James said to the woman as Phillip drew her gently into the room, wondering how she had heard of the abduction. "They need her alive; they won't hurt her."

Helene looked at him in confusion for a moment. "But she's already dead!"

James felt his heart thump. "What do you mean? How do you know?"

"Because I saw her! I had gone out to get fresh tea at the market, and when I returned the house was ransacked and she was . . . she . . ."

"Alice was at your home this morning?"

"Who?"

"Alice! She's been abducted."

Helene's mouth dropped open. "No, no, I am speaking of my aunt."

James felt his mouth drop open as well. "Elysia is dead?"

Helene nodded miserably and the tears flowed afresh. "I think she must have caught the burglars in the act—they hit her over the head with something and then left. By the time I reached her, she was almost gone. I summoned the doctor, but it was too late."

Sally sat down heavily on the sofa, her gaze stricken. James closed his eyes for a moment. "Come and rest for a bit," Phillip said to Helene and drew her by the arm to the sofa by Sally. "The police have been notified?"

Helene nodded and accepted the handkerchief James handed her from inside his pocket.

"Do you know what the intruders were after?"

Helene shook her head. "I didn't notice that anything was missing."

James blew out a breath and considered their options. Elysia had been murdered and Alice kidnapped. The dilemma before him was how to proceed. They couldn't all go chasing after Kilronomos and Sparks. It would take valuable time, time they didn't have, to mobilize everything. Phillip, however, was beside himself with rage. He had wanted to leave at first light, when they had entered the girls' bedroom at the sound of Sally's moaning.

James's quick trip to the train station afterward had proved fruitful, once enough money had crossed palms. The man on duty had sold tickets to two men—one Greek, one American—and their ill sister, whom the Greek carried in his arms. They had purchased fare to Olympia and left on the morning's first train.

"I am so sorry," Helene said when James filled her in on the details. "This is horrible. Look at what has come from my aunt's obsession with the jewels!"

"But we also brought it with us," James said. "Elysia is not to blame." He was frustrated and more than a little concerned. The group had split, Helene would need support in caring for Elysia's burial details, and Alice was who knew how far away by now.

James glanced at Helene where she sat by Sally, who had taken Helene's hand. He rubbed the back of his head, making his way to the hearth, where Phillip stood with his hands braced on it, white knuckled, looking down at the floor. "This is how we will proceed," James said to his brother. "I will take the next train to Olympia. It departs this afternoon. Helene is going to need help—you remain here with the women, and tell Isabelle and the others what has happened when they return."

Phillip glanced at him askance, clearly disgusted. "You cannot seriously think to leave me behind. I will kill them with my bare hands and save the law the trouble."

"Which is exactly why I'm going alone and you're staying here. We'll not argue about this. I need you here, as does Sally."

Phillip looked over his shoulder at the young woman and straightened with a sigh. He put his hands in his pockets, his jaw working over the words he wanted to say but was restraining. "Very well," he murmured finally. "What do you propose we do when the others return? Wait for you, wonder where you are?"

"I will telegraph you twice daily with updates. This hotel will be the central communication point. You will have to telegraph Isabelle at the location she gave us yesterday when she sent us her update. We can decide our course of action over the next few days." He looked again at Sally, who still appeared a bit worse for the wear after having been drugged with what he assumed was chloroform. "Have we received word from Isabelle yet today?"

Phillip shook his head. "Nothing this morning."

James frowned. Isabelle had said she would telegraph when they were on their way back to Athens. He could only assume that they either hadn't yet found the box or that something had gone awry. "Keep a close eye on them," he told Phillip, motioning to Sally and Helene. "And we'll retain the guards at least until the others return."

Phillip nodded, some of the red receding from his face. He made his way to the couch and stood behind Sally, placing a hand on her shoulders. Sally leaned her cheek against it with a shuddering breath and closed her eyes, large tears dropping from her eyelashes.

"Helene," Phillip said, "there's something we need to show you. Your aunt's obsession with the jewels—it's not merely a legend."

James ran a hand across the back of his neck and turned to his bedroom as Phillip crossed to the safe and opened it. As he readied himself to pack lightly for what he hoped would be a brief trip to Olympia and back, he heard Helene's exclamation of surprise as Phillip showed her the Jewel of Zeus.

***

Isabelle watched from her boarding room window as the ship left the docks and made for open water. She had seen Jean-Louis board, accompanied by a young woman who fit Isabelle's description relatively well and was dressed in one of Isabelle's outfits. She had been headed for Athens anyway, she said, and gladly accepted the payment to stand in Isabelle's place at least until the ship was underway. Jean-Louis would reach Athens in the evening with the box and tell James where she was. James would be angry—that went without saying. Jack would also be angry—assuming she found him alive. He might well be at the bottom of the sea.

Isabelle and Jean-Louis had vacated their small room at the inn and made for the mainland shortly after Isabelle told the Frenchman what had happened to Jack. She hadn't rested easy since; she could only reason that if she had been tailed, they'd have been shot or otherwise by now.

She straightened the blankets on the bed and looked around the small room. All of her belongings were stowed inside her portmanteau. There was a lock on the door, but she was uneasy about leaving anything behind when she went out. She had already placed her money in the small purse she attached to the sash around her waist, and therein lay part of the problem—she needed to blend in. As a tourist, she attracted unwanted attention, although there were admittedly tourists aplenty. Whoever had attacked her and Jack had known enough about them to follow them— the attackers likely had been aboard the steamer to Monemvasia. She had to assume they knew her by sight.

She stashed the portmanteau under the bed, figuring that if someone was going to search her things, she was going to make him work for it. Leaving the room with one last glance over her shoulder, she locked the door behind her and went out into the city streets.

The market hummed with activity: fresh fruits and vegetables, spices, preserved meats and fish, an assortment of cheeses and olives—all displayed in an impressive array. Wandering down the crowded aisles, she turned a few corners and eventually found the object of her quest. Clothing was spread before her in dizzying splendor. Fabrics rich in design and color lay on tabletops and storefront counters. Picking her way through the mass, she eventually pieced together exactly what she'd hoped to find.

Smiling at vendors and gladly handing over her money, she purchased a typical Greek woman's ensemble, complete with large head scarf and comfortable shoes. She made her way back to the boardinghouse, keeping a watchful eye on everything around her.

Back in her room, she made quick work of the new clothing, swiftly buttoning, tying, arranging fabric, and finally donning the head scarf which hid her hair entirely. She retrieved a small sketchbook and a pencil from her portmanteau. Patting the purse at her side that lay mostly hidden by the beautifully embroidered apron she wore over the dress, she gave her room one final glance and left, again locking the door behind her.

Isabelle spent the better part of the day back at Monemvasia, observing people and sipping tea at cafés until she was sick to her stomach. She wandered around the base of the cliffs where Jack might have fallen the night before from the upper level. She made some small, perfunctory sketches of wildflowers in her sketchbook as an excuse should someone wonder why she was loitering about.

Making her way back to the upper level, she traced the path where she'd last seen Jack, looking for something—anything—that might give her a hint as to his circumstances. The ground was punctuated with rocks and pebbles, making the search for telltale footprints laughable.

With a sigh, Isabelle turned and looked out over the brilliantly blue water. She shaded her eyes against the sun and let her gaze wander around the lower level. She drew her brows together as her glance swept over the church they had examined the day before. Who better to ask for help than a priest?

***

James sat on the afternoon train bound for Olympia, thumbing through Ari Kilronomos's diary that Isabelle had left with him. There were notes on contacts the man had had, both in Greece and India. He had also left records of conversations he'd had with clients and observations about people who had snagged his interest, usually for purposes that would suit him.

Toward the back of the book, Ari had jotted a name and an address near Olympia. "There we go," James murmured. If they were lucky, perhaps it would prove to be a relative or friend. It was a place to start at least.

***

Evening was upon Monemvasia, and Isabelle was frustrated. The priest was supposed to have returned from the mainland hours ago. She had sketched so many pictures the little notebook was nearly full, and her stomach had been inundated with more tea than she'd had in a long time.

The lamps were lit, the streets and alleys aglow with a soft yellow light. People wandered—laughing, teasing, eating, and strolling in the moonlight. There were tourists aplenty, but she had yet to spy anyone she felt might have been observing her or dogging her footsteps.

She was considering giving it up for the night and returning to her boardinghouse when she spied a dark shape just outside the double doors to the church. She rose and approached before the man could disappear inside. Jean-Louis had learned the priest spoke passable English, and she was counting on that fact.

"You are the priest, sir?" she said upon reaching the man.

He was tall and thin, with a balding pate and worn features. He looked at her with some surprise. "I am; how may I be of service?"

"I am looking for a friend, a man who was injured last night. I wondered if you might know of anyone who would take in someone wounded?"

The priest looked at her for a long moment. "Come inside," he said and entered the church.

Isabelle followed him and waited as he lit two lamps. "You have a friend, you say?" the priest said.

Isabelle nodded and gave him a brief description of Jack. "I was with him last night and we encountered some thieves. I'm afraid he was shot, and when we ran, I lost him."

The priest was silent. Isabelle had the distinct impression that he was evaluating her character. "I believe you are not telling me everything there is to know about yourself or your adventure last night. My friend at Agia Sophia tells me you are English and traveling with your husband and brother. That others follow your travels. Others we have no wish to see."

She paused for a moment, wondering if she should bother lying. In the end, she settled for omission. "There are things I am unable to tell you, sir, but I am desperate to find my friend. We have others in Athens awaiting our return—I do not wish to go back without knowing whether or not my friend is alive."

"And then you will leave Monemvasia?"

"Yes. As soon as I have my friend with me, whether he be dead or alive."

The older man nodded once. "Come. We have a man in town who is our doctor. I will take you to him."

Isabelle wondered what the doctor would tell her—that he'd found Jack dead? She followed the cryptic priest back outside and around the church, along one street, and then down a narrow alley to a door in a brick building that had clearly seen some years.

The priest rapped quickly on the door, and when it was opened by a man—who was ninety if he was a day—the priest spoke quietly to him in Greek. The wizened old man, stooped, white-haired, and wrinkled, regarded her with sharp eyes through thick spectacles.

He made a motion with his hand and moved back from the doorway, allowing her and the priest entrance. They followed the doctor through a small parlor and into a hallway that displayed three doors. Making his way to the door farthest from them, the doctor again motioned for them to follow.

The light in the room was turned down low, and once Isabelle's eyes adjusted to the muted glow she registered a small bed, a washstand with a basin, and one chair. Jack lay on the bed, his face drawn even in sleep. Isabelle made a quick sweep of the rest of the room, taking in the only ornamentation on any of the four walls—a cross that faced the bed.

"Where did you find him?" she asked the men.

"The doctor has a son who found your friend lying nearly submerged in the water early this morning before dawn. He had been caught up on the rocks at the base of the mountain on the far side. The son brought the man here and then contacted me. We have yet to even know his name. He's not been conscious for well over sixteen hours."

Isabelle approached the bed and squatted down next to Jack's head. She placed her hand upon his brow with a frown. With a shaky sigh, she glanced up at the doctor and priest. "Thank you for keeping him alive."

The doctor spoke in Greek and the priest translated. "He says he removed a bullet from your friend's side. He also noted this man has been shot before, and fairly recently." They both looked at her expectantly.

Isabelle stood and glanced down again at the prostrate form on the bed. "Jack is very valuable to his government. He has faced complications because of it."

"And which government is his?" the priest said. "Is he an American?"

"No." She paused. "He is a Scot. He works for Britain."

The priest nodded. "A man approached me early this morning at the church. He asked about him." He gestured at Jack.

Isabelle's stomach clenched. "Can you describe the man?"

The priest glanced at the doctor before speaking again. "He is one of many who have come to this place— "

The doctor interrupted the priest with a rapid litany of phrases and gestures. While his tone didn't increase in volume, it did in intensity.

The priest pursed his lips and looked carefully at Isabelle. "What do you want here? Why have you come?"

Isabelle considered the men. Any enemies of the King's Men were likely her allies. "I travel with a young woman, a Guardian," she told them quietly.

Even the old doctor seemed to understand her pronouncement. He was the first to recover from her statement and muttered something in Greek to the priest without taking his eyes off Isabelle.

"Guardians are not necessarily unique," the priest translated and nodded as though in agreement.

"This one is," she told them.

The men were quiet for a moment. "The odds are not in your favor, miss," the priest said.

"We have no choice," Isabelle said. "I fear we have stumbled into something that will not leave us in peace until the whole of it is finished." She paused. "It is not about greed for us."

"What of this man?" the priest said and gestured at Jack. "He works for his government."

"At this point he is running for his life. He has no interest in gain— whether for his government or himself." She gauged the men's reactions, wondering if she was going to have to sneak Jack out of the house in the middle of the night after praying for the miracle of Herculean strength. If Jack weren't soon able to move under his own power, she had few options.

Isabelle took a deep breath and fought to keep her voice even. She had rarely won anything by flying into a fit of fury. Tears were often a better alternative, but something about the two men had her believing they could read her every thought. Subterfuge would not only be wasted on them, it would fail. "Do you believe the man who asked after my friend has left town?"

The priest nodded slowly. "He has," he admitted. "I have eyes here that keep me informed. The man is gone. There was another, however, who was found dead this morning at the base of the hill near where your friend was found. The man had been shot three times."

That would explain the exchange of gunfire Isabelle had heard when she'd been hiding in the church. She bit her cheek to keep from smiling. Jack had taken the man down with him. "Do you still have the body?"

The priest blinked at her.

"Where is the dead man?"

"I do not know why you believe you need to see him."

"I need to know whether or not he wears a specific piece of jewelry."

The priest translated to the doctor, who looked steadily at Isabelle before holding a finger in the air and leaving the room. The silence that ensued was awkward. The priest watched Isabelle as though still wondering what to make of her. It was with a sense of relief that Isabelle heard the doctor's shuffling steps return to the room.

The doctor made his way to Isabelle's side and reached for her hand. He turned it palm up, and from a small cloth bag, dropped a gold ring into her hand, one bearing the familiar symbol.

"This was on the dead man," the priest said to her, looking over the doctor's shoulder. When the doctor spoke to her in Greek, the priest translated, "You may as well take it with you. He doesn't want it in his house."

"You don't want it either, then?" Isabelle said to the priest.

He shook his head, his eyes weary. "I'll not have that defiling a holy place. I do not want it anywhere near the church."

Isabelle took a deep breath and slowly released it, her fingers closing around the ring. "How long do you suppose he will be out of commission?" she asked the doctor and gestured to Jack.

After the priest translated, the doctor shrugged and responded. "The bullet passed through his side and his bleeding is controlled," the priest relayed. "He doesn't hear water in your friend's lungs, but until he awakens we won't know how well he might recover."

She nodded, swallowing. How long did she dare wait with him? Was it enough that she knew where he was, that she could leave money for the priest to get him on a boat to Athens when he regained consciousness? Isabelle looked at Jack again and thought of the man who had put the bullet in his side. There were more where that man came from, and if she left now and they returned to finish the job, she would never forgive herself. She closed her eyes briefly and hoped James would understand. She would send a cable in the morning and explain everything.

"Do you have a place to stay?" the priest asked her, his face softening a bit. "The doctor is offering the room across the hallway to you if you need it. Then you will be close to your friend."

"Please extend my thanks," Isabelle said, considering her options. "I would like very much to accept the offer. I need to retrieve my belongings from the mainland. It's just one small bag."

The priest translated and smiled at the doctor's response. "He says that's a good thing because it is a very small room."

***

James entered the room at the inn he'd found in a small town near Olympia. A fruitless afternoon filled with questions about possible Alice sightings had him frustrated and tired. To add insult to injury, the address he'd found in Ari's journal had led him nowhere. A Kilronomos had lived there a few years back, apparently, but the current owner had no idea where he was now. Jack set his bag down on the bed and crossed to the window that overlooked the twinkling lights of the little town.

He was worried.

He hoped he was right, that they wouldn't harm Alice, at least not immediately. But what would happen if she decided not to cooperate? What if she was unable to come up with anything—and surely that was what they wanted from her, her ability to sense the jewels—and they decided she was expendable after all? Truly, what were the odds that they'd return her to Athens? Sparks had shot at Sally in the Egyptian tomb and had been more than ready to kill the lot of them for the jewel. If Alice either proved useless or wore out her welcome, James didn't imagine that her captors would be gentle.

He sighed and readied himself for bed, wondering if he'd be able to quiet his mind enough to actually sleep. Alice was gone, Elysia dead, and they hadn't heard from Isabelle and her consorts for well over twenty-four hours. Of one thing he was certain: Phillip was going to have his hands full when he told the Frenchman that Alice had been abducted.

15

THE DAY WAS LONG PAST by the time Jean-Louis climbed out of the hired hack and pulled his suitcase from the boot. Paying the driver, he turned and made his way into the hotel with equal parts dread and anticipation. He couldn't wait to see Alice but would have given anything to be spared the duty of telling James that he had left Isabelle behind in Monemvasia.

The January air was cool, almost cold. Gas lamps along the street glowed in the darkness, chasing the shadows away as he climbed the steps to the hotel. He glanced in the dining room to see if the others had gathered for dinner. Finding them all absent, he continued to the second floor.

The guards at the door gave him pause; he'd have thought they'd have been retired for the night unless James and Phillip had gone out and left the women behind. Giving them a nod, he turned his key in the lock and entered the common sitting area between the two bedrooms.

Phillip and Sally looked up in surprise as he entered. Jean-Louis noticed several things at once. The room was extremely quiet, which was fairly odd for the group. There were lines around Phillip's mouth that mirrored the tense draw of his brow. Sally's eyes were red rimmed and puffy, as though she'd recently cried.

"What has happened?" he asked, noticing Helene seated near the hearth and looking equally strained.

"Oh, Jean-Louis," Sally said, her face crumbling and tears dropping from her eyes.

Phillip stood and walked toward him, clasping him on the shoulder. Jean-Louis looked at him in consternation. He finally realized who was missing from the room, aside from James.

"Where's Alice?" he asked.

***

Isabelle stood outside the telegraph office, rooted to the spot as she stared at the yellow paper in her hand. She had telegraphed James earlier that morning to apprise him of Jack's status, only to find a message waiting for her.

Feeling slightly weak, she made her way to a nearby bench and sank down onto it, willing the words to change even as she stared at them. ELYSIA MURDERED STOP ALICE ABDUCTED STOP JAMES EN ROUTE TO OLYMPIA STOP PLEASE ADVISE OF YOUR ESTIMATED RETURN STOP.

The abductors could only have been Sparks and Ari, or the Ari look-alike, whoever he was. How on earth had it happened with both Phillip and James present and guards at the door? Had they been out in the city? And what had happened to Elysia?

Isabelle looked up and wondered how the world continually kept in motion when catastrophic things happened. What were the odds that Alice would be rescued unscathed yet a second time? She must be terrified. The first abduction had been of both girls together—she'd at least had Sally to lean on.

Alice had become scrappy, Isabelle had to remind herself. Resourceful. She wasn't the helpless, spoiled young girl they'd first met in India all those months ago. If she could but use her head and her common sense, she might keep herself safe until James could find her.

Isabelle looked down again at the telegram, only to realize she'd clenched it into her fist. With a frown, she absently smoothed the paper against her leg and folded it into fourths, placing it into the small pouch she carried. She tugged a bit at the bow of her head scarf and readjusted it slightly, absently looking for something she could control.

The telegraph operator called out to her, and she returned when he beckoned. He handed her another telegraph and told her in broken English that it had just come across the wires. It was from Phillip, and as she read it, she suffered her second shock of the day. Claire had arrived in Athens, and when Phillip had told her of Isabelle's location, she had hopped on the next available steamer to Monemvasia. She would dock the next afternoon.

Claire. Isabelle had not seen her sister in a very long time. What on earth was Claire doing in Greece? Isabelle looked at the people who milled around, going about their business, and wondered how they kept functioning when her life was in such chaos.

With a deep breath, she stood and resolutely began her trip back to the island and the doctor's house. The sun shone brilliantly, dancing off the blue ocean in glittering winks. It was a struggle to remain focused and vigilant of everything around her when her thoughts turned to worry about Alice, about James should he come across the perpetrators unaware, about Sally's nerves, which surely must be frayed at the turn of events. Not to mention poor Jean-Louis. She closed her eyes momentarily with a wince. He'd been upset enough about leaving Alice behind. Isabelle wondered how he would handle Alice's absence. And Helene must be in a state of devastated shock. Would she help them continue their quest or be disgusted that it may have led to her aunt's death?

And Claire! Isabelle was completely and utterly baffled.

She took a lengthy, circuitous route to the doctor's home in hopes that if someone were still following her, she wouldn't lead him right to Jack. The doctor opened his front door and smiled—as much of a smile as his old face cared to manage anyway—and let her in.

"Thank you," she said to the man in Greek and was rewarded with a slight crinkling at the corners of his eyes. Whether he was appreciative of her attempts to communicate or was amused at her lack of ability, she couldn't be sure. Either way, she was satisfied. Remaining in his good graces was high on her list of priorities.

He gestured toward Jack's room, and he allowed her to walk in front of him. He followed her into the room at the end of the hallway and murmured a word of surprise when they entered. Jack was braced up on one elbow as though trying to get out of the bed. His face was drawn, pinched, and Isabelle heard him groan.

The doctor hastened to gently push Jack's shoulders back onto the pillow, and Jack resisted until Isabelle reached the bed and told him to lie down. He looked around the old man at her face and drew his brows together in confusion. He finally complied, though, and Isabelle nodded.

"We don't want you to rip your stitches," she told him as the doctor moved the blanket away to check Jack's side. When the doctor looked over his shoulder, censuring her for watching the process, she turned her gaze away and looked instead at the lone wooden cross on the wall.

The old man grunted in apparent approval as he examined his handiwork. He spoke a few words that were utterly incomprehensible to Isabelle. When she glanced back, he shook his head and waved his hand in a gesture of dismissal, crossing to the pitcher of water and pouring some into a glass.

"What happened?" Jack asked, clearing his throat after taking a sip of the water.

Isabelle pulled the single chair up beside his bed. "You cheated death yet again," she told him. "It's becoming quite a habit."

Isabelle took the glass of water from his hand, and he leaned back against the pillow. The doctor muttered a few more words at them and left the room. Isabelle wondered if he was going to find the priest to translate.

"How did you end up in the water, do you remember?"

Jack nodded. "I made my way to the far side of the hill. Thankfully, your shot found its mark, and the man chasing me wasn't any faster than I was at that point. He missed another few shots; I turned and unloaded my weapon into him. When I saw the second man exiting the church, I took a running leap, praying to avoid the rocks below. The first man fell a bit closer to the edge, I fear." His easy Scottish brogue was comforting. For the first time in two days, Isabelle began to believe he might live.

Isabelle nodded, her lips twitching into a smile. "You had searched out that spot earlier in the evening. To the far left of the church."

"Yes."

"I had as well. I figured if I had to jump, that would be the best place."

Jack laughed quietly and winced. "I would never be man enough for you, Isabelle Webb. I need a woman who doesn't possess my same skills."

"Silly."

"It is the truth. I believe I would always feel slightly emasculated with you by my side."

Isabelle smiled. "What a horrible thing to say to a woman."

"I salute James completely. He must be very confident in his masculinity. Your intellect, I admire. The fact that you looked for the perfect place to jump from a cliff and into the sea has me feeling slightly queasy."

"If it's any consolation, I was glad I was able to avoid it."

Jack snorted and patted her hand, muttering something unintelligible under his breath. He sobered then and closed his eyes as he shifted slightly in the bed. "Where is the box?"

Isabelle told him all that had happened since they had found it. She wished she could spare him the rest. "There's more," she said and showed him the telegram.

He was silent for a few moments. "So it seems we now face another choice," he finally said. "Shall we return to Athens or go to Olympia?"

"Olympia. And there is one more thing." Isabelle told him about Claire's impending arrival and the fact that they would need to meet her ship at the docks.

Jack opened his mouth slightly and then closed it again. "Will she be amenable to travel and mayhem?"

Isabelle shook her head. "I do not have the slightest clue."

***

Jean-Louis was wearing a path in the carpet, and Phillip watched him with sympathy. His own rage and frustration had kept him awake well into the night, and he was feeling bleary-eyed and edgy. "I cannot just stay here," the Frenchman said to him. "I will go mad."

"I understand," Phillip told him, "but until we hear from James, we need to remain. They may have moved on from Olympia. As ridiculous as it seems, we must wait."

Jean-Louis sank into a chair opposite Phillip and looked over at Sally and Helene, who sat side by side on the couch, examining the box Isabelle and Jack had found. Helene was apparently seeking to distract both of them with details about the box, but Phillip had a hard time making himself care. Thaddeus Sparks had thwarted them yet again, and it grated against him like nothing ever had before. He loathed the man with a passion that would become all consuming if he allowed it. He remembered the threats Sparks used to make against Phillip and James's mother should Phillip try to escape or overpower him. Jack was missing as well, likely dead, and Isabelle had yet to return. She was alone, over a hundred miles away, pursued by the King's Men if the suspicions she had expressed to Jean-Louis were accurate.

Sally—his sweet girl—was emotionally spent, and he wished more than anything he could take the pain from her. In an odd way, it more fully solidified his affections for her. He adored her when she was happy, he was amused at her quirky irritation, and his heart broke when she was sad. He would do anything to help alleviate her pain and realized he never wanted to go a day in his life without her in it.

He knew Deveraux's feelings for Alice were similar, and he could only imagine his level of grief had Sally been the one missing. He tore his gaze from Sally and looked at Jean-Louis. "James will find her," he said. "Or he will summon us soon. One way or another, we'll not have to sit idle much longer."

A knock on the door rendered the room silent, and Phillip rose to answer it. A young hotel bellhop stood in the hallway with a telegram envelope addressed to Jean-Louis. Phillip tipped the boy and closed the door, handing the paper to the Frenchman.

Jean-Louis wasted no time tearing into the message. His face was a mixture of emotions as he looked up. "Isabelle has found Jack, and he is alive. Tomorrow, they leave for Olympia."

***

The Egyptian eyed with distaste the messenger that stood cowering before him. "When did you receive this?"

"An hour ago, sir. I came as quickly as I could."

"Wait here. My man will give you a message to return." The Egyptian turned to his secretary, dictated quick instructions, and then reread the contents of the message he'd received. A box to hold the jewels—and the King's Men wanted it. Very interesting indeed, and very vexing that such a crucial piece of the legend had never made its way to the Egyptian's ears.

"And I want it made clear," he said to his scribe, "that they are not to kill our British agent, Mr. Jack MacInnes, yet. We cannot very well obtain all four items from him if he is dead."

The secretary nodded as he wrote. When he finished the dictation for the telegram, he handed it to the messenger, who bowed and left the room as quickly as his feet could carry him. "Will there be anything else?" the secretary asked of his boss.

"Yes. Our observations of the American women who head the dig near Karnac."

The secretary nodded again. "They still watch the site."

"Very good. I suspect we shall need them for leverage. What of the other young American woman who was supposed to join them?"

"According to the telegram, the old woman redirected her from Egypt to Greece."

"So this younger Miss Webb ought to be arriving there any day now. Make a note that I want her progress tracked as well. She must be a relative of our American spy. Another useful tool, should the need arise."

***

Isabelle walked slowly, bracing her "elderly uncle" as he shuffled along the road near the docks. He used the help of a cane and clearly favored his left side. The loose-fitting Grecian clothing hung comfortably on his frame, his hat nearly obscuring his face. Isabelle scanned the docks for the sister she hadn't seen in years.

A young woman dressed in the latest American fashion made her way up from a ship that bustled with activity as cargo was unloaded and reloaded before leaving again for Athens. Isabelle saw the woman and stopped still, her mouth hanging open in shock.

Jack grunted as he adjusted to the cessation of movement. "What are you doing?" he whispered through clenched teeth.

She swallowed and stared, thinking that surely her eyes deceived her. Claire had grown up. Jack must have noted the direction of her stare, and her suspicions were confirmed by his sharp intake of breath.

"So that would be Claire. You could be standing before a mirror."

16

WHEN ISABELLE'S SISTER FINALLY LOCKED eyes with her, Isabelle was certain it must indeed seem as though they were peering into a looking glass. She imagined that Claire's expression of shock was identical to her own. Claire moved closer to her slowly then finally at a run.

"Belle!" Claire grasped Isabelle's shoulders and then pulled her in quick for a tight hug that took the breath from her lungs and elicited another groan from Jack, this one significantly more pronounced as he was jostled in the exchange.

Claire must have come to her senses and remembered that they had been estranged for over four years because she released Isabelle and stood back awkwardly. "I . . . asked Genevieve about you; she sent for me but had me travel directly here from London."

"Genevieve?" Isabelle's brain felt numb—she could barely string two thoughts together.

Claire nodded with a frown. "I was trying to find you, and she telegrammed me months ago in Chicago—she said you were in grave danger and that she needed me to come right away to Egypt. I'm wondering now if your dire straits were a bit of an exaggeration on her part. You look fine."

"Danger?" Isabelle repeated stupidly.

Jack cleared his throat.

"Ah, and you must be the fiancé Genevieve told me about," Claire said. "A pleasure to meet you, Mr. Ashby, is it?"

"No," Isabelle and Jack said simultaneously.

"No, no," Jack reiterated, extracting his arm from about Isabelle's shoulders, a low grunt escaping as he moved. He introduced himself, offering his hand, which Claire took and shook in a gentleman's grip.

"So if you're not Mr. Ashby, where, pray tell, is he?"

"Olympia," Isabelle said and frowned. Pulling herself together, she reached again for Claire and enfolded her in a stiff embrace. "Well, since you're here to see me," she said as she pulled back and braced an arm under Jack's elbow, "perhaps you might retrieve your luggage and join us for a little train ride. We can catch up along the way." She studied her sister for a moment. "I must admit, Claire, I'm surprised you would come all this way."

Claire narrowed her eyes in an expression that Isabelle remembered altogether too well. "Well, I'm certainly not heartless, Belle. She led me to believe that your life hung in the balance."

"I'm clearly well," Isabelle said. "I'm sorry she implied otherwise."

Claire looked at her quietly for a moment. "I suppose I should return home, then, if you have no need of me," she said.

Silence hung in the air, thick and uncomfortable.

"What nonsense is this?" Jack said, his tone one of forced joviality. "I insist that you join us, Miss Webb. Is your luggage cumbersome? Shall we arrange for help in retrieving it?"

Claire looked at Isabelle for a moment longer before turning her attention to Jack. Isabelle felt churlish and petty.

"I have but one trunk and a portmanteau. I believe I can arrange for them to be delivered to the train station. What time is your train set to depart?"

"Not for two hours yet," Isabelle said. "Perhaps we will wait here while you make arrangements." She glanced at Jack, whose face was pale despite the heat of the day. "My friend would benefit from sitting a spell, I believe."

Claire nodded once. "Yes, by all means. Get him off of his feet. He looks near to swooning. I'll be but a few moments."

Isabelle watched her sister return to the ship, her mind still reeling.

"For the love of heaven, Isabelle, she came thousands of miles to see to your welfare," Jack muttered as they moved to the shade of a nearby shop overhang and sat at a small, round table.

"I know that," Isabelle ground out, caught between irritation at his chastisement and mortification that she had been so readily transparent. "She . . . Claire and I . . . we haven't always seen eye to eye."

"Clearly," Jack said as he slowly shifted in the rock-hard chair. "She is very direct," he noted.

"Yes. That she is."

"Does she leap from cliff tops?"

"Not to my knowledge."

"Excellent."

***

James stood among the ruins of Apollo's temple at Olympia and looked around. He had received information from three different sources that a young woman with black hair and a pale complexion had been seen in the area with two men—one Greek, the other possibly European or American.

The site itself was huge. It had been uncovered by a Frenchman in the late 1800s and was still undergoing excavation. The number of buildings that time had hidden could well be more than most would have imagined. Some of the ruins showed pillars that remained upright, still connected to their ancient floors, and others had toppled and lay across the ground, impressive in girth and design. Grass and wildflowers littered the site liberally, and it was, when not clogged with tourists, peaceful.

James sighed and kept to the shadows, wondering if perhaps Sparks and Kilronomos had spotted him in spite of his caution. Surely they hadn't—if they had, Alice would have seen him too and would have called out. Unless they had threatened her. He was exhausted, hungry, and frustrated. Throwing a prayer heavenward for any little bit of help Providence might be willing to spare, he left the ancient temple and made his way back to his hotel for lunch.

***

Sally traced her finger along the engravings on the ancient box. Phillip had taken to locking it in the safe with the Jewel of Zeus, but every now and again she wanted to look at it. It helped her keep her mind from worrying about Alice. The few moments that she was able to distract herself were a welcome relief. Unfortunately, that feeling was fickle and fleeting. Helene, meanwhile, was making arrangements for Elysia's funeral. It would be a small affair, attended by only family and a few friends. Helene, for her part, seemed relieved to have something to do.

"And what is this here?" Phillip asked Sally as she wiped delicately at her nose, which had become red and most unattractive from too much running and blowing in the last two days.

She appreciated Phillip's attempts to help her. She knew he probably remembered the engraving's meaning from the night before when Helene had explained it to the best of her knowledge. "It is the princess," Sally said. "And these are the three jewels."

She turned the exquisite box and lifted the lid reverently, looking at the three indentations within. "I think we should leave the Jewel of Zeus in here," she said. "We know it will fit."

Phillip raised a brow, clearly skeptical. "I don't know about the wisdom of actually leaving it in there," he said.

"Whyever not?"

"I don't know. That jewel—I hate it. It makes my back hurt all on its own. What will happen if we put it in its magic box and leave it in there?"

Sally smiled. "Magic box," she said and laid her head against his shoulder.

"Yeah, I don't trust it as far as I can throw it," Phillip muttered.

At that, she couldn't help but laugh. "Phillip, I imagine you can throw this box pretty far."

"And I would dearly love to."

Her head still comfortably settled against his shoulder, she slid her arm under his and reached for his hand. He clasped her fingers and softly traced the veins along the back of her hand, placing a gentle kiss atop her head. It was with a sense of blessed relief that she finally felt herself relax enough to approach sleep. It was nearing the noon hour, but she hadn't slept well since Alice had been kidnapped.

She drifted off, only to awake with a start, embarrassed.

"Shhh," Phillip said and placed a hand on the side of her head. "Just rest."

Settling herself more comfortably into the couch pillows, she stretched her legs forward and allowed herself the luxury of sleep.

***

Isabelle secured a sleeping car for herself, Jack, and Claire, whose luggage had been delivered to the train station without incident. Jack was pale, and Isabelle noted a slight wince every now and again that convinced her he needed some rest. He finally gave in when he looked too weary to continue the battle, and Isabelle and Claire went to the dining car for a light lunch.

Isabelle ordered two cups of tea and some pastries from the porter and then took a moment to study her sister. Claire looked well. She had aged some; her face had lost its baby fat and slimmed into graceful, defined lines. The eyes set the two sisters apart: Isabelle's were brown, and

Claire's were an interesting mix of green and blue. Their other features were strikingly similar. Had Claire been as tall as Isabelle's five foot five inches, they could easily have been twins. They had often been mistaken for such, despite the two-inch height difference, and Claire had always complained about the fact that she'd stopped growing when she had.

"How have you been?" Isabelle finally said. Her voice sounded awkward even to her own ears. She had harbored a secret hope for years that she and Claire would someday reconcile. That it might come about as a result of Claire's efforts was a possibility that had never crossed Isabelle's mind.

Claire nodded to the porter when he delivered their tea and food. Settling the napkin on her lap, she stirred her tea, lifting the cup and gently blowing across the top of it. "Fine, thank you," she said and sipped at the beverage with a slight grimace.

Isabelle passed the sugar to Claire, who took it with widened eyes and a grateful nod. "Some things never do change," Isabelle said and accepted the sugar back, adding some to her own tea.

"And how do you spend your time these days? Nursing, isn't it?"

Claire nodded. "I've been working with Elizabeth Blackwell. I have been nursing for five years and will soon attend the medical college adjacent to the New York infirmary. I plan to follow Miss Blackwell fully into the medical field."

Isabelle raised a brow with a quirked smile. "A doctor. Succeeding in a man's profession," she said. "We are two of a kind in that regard."

Claire nodded, her lips curved. "I suspect we've made Genevieve proud."

Isabelle hesitated. "Did Genevieve tell you . . . that is . . . when we were in Egypt, she divulged the nature of our relationship to her—it was certainly news to me."

Claire frowned a bit. "I suppose you're referring to the fact that she is our father's mother."

Isabelle took a bite of her pastry and dabbed at her mouth with the corner of her napkin, using the time to choose her words carefully. "How long have you known?"

"I communicate with her regularly," Claire said. "I suppose it was bound to come out sooner or later. She told me about three years ago."

Isabelle inhaled and exhaled, looking out the window at the passing scenery. "Did you never think to tell me?" she said softly.

"Isabelle," Claire said, drawing her gaze back from the Grecian countryside. "In the first place, you've not spoken to me since the beginning of the war—I never even knew where to find you. And secondly, I didn't think you would be happy to hear it. Neither did Genevieve."

Isabelle winced. That there was some truth to the statement was disappointing. "I spoke with Genevieve at some length in Egypt about it," she admitted. "I was . . . stunned. She was absolutely correct, however, in that I would have been angry. Frustrated. I wanted nothing to do with Papa's family."

"And I wanted everything to do with them," Claire said quietly. She laid her spoon down next to the cup and saucer and placed her hands in her lap. "And if we couldn't have them, I wanted whoever was willing to fill the space. I was angry at you for so very long. I couldn't understand why you wouldn't embrace her fully. It was everything we had needed."

Isabelle let out a soft sigh. "It was easier to be angry. It didn't hurt as much. And I didn't trust her. I couldn't, for the life of me, understand why she had taken us in so completely. Now, of course, it makes perfect sense. I felt . . . responsible for you. I didn't want to rely on others to fill that responsibility. I was frustrated that I couldn't do it by myself." Oddly enough, she had observed the same traits in Sally when she'd first met the defensive young girl. Isabelle had been frustrated with Sally back then, probably unable to admit that she had been much the same way herself.

Claire shook her head. "You were as much of a child as I was."

"That didn't seem to matter. I worried about you constantly. I wanted to buy you things—a home, clothing, good food. Mama and Papa were gone, and I felt I should be able to fill their shoes." Isabelle's voice broke, and the depth of her emotion embarrassed her. She scowled and looked down at her food, grabbing her fork and shoving things around on her plate.

"Oh, Belle. I adored you. You kept me from starving when we lived on the streets. You were everything to me. When Genevieve found us I was relieved that you wouldn't have to shoulder the responsibility all by yourself anymore." Claire paused and Isabelle glanced up to see her shaking her head and sipping at her tea. "And I've missed you. When I couldn't find you at home after the war and Genevieve told me you were here and needed help . . . Well, I suppose she would have said anything to draw me out."

Isabelle smiled. "She definitely would have. But as it stands, I do need help. And I've missed you."

Claire cleared her throat—apparently also in an effort to eliminate the film of moisture that gathered over her pretty eyes. "Enough of this maudlin nonsense," she said. "Tell me what we're doing here."

With a sense of relief at the change of topic to less treacherous ground, Isabelle began the tale, giving Claire the abbreviated version of everything that had happened since the last time they had been together. Throughout the long explanation, Claire interrupted a few times with questions but, for the most part, absorbed the information with an apparent air of equanimity and common sense. It was as though time had erased the bitterness, the hard feelings. Claire no longer appeared as the angrily feisty teenager she had been—there was a maturity about her that was comfortable and had softened the sharp edges. And for her own part, Isabelle hadn't realized how much she'd missed her sister.

"I'm not sure I believe in supernatural silliness," Claire finally said when Isabelle had finished, "but I suppose you're practical enough, and if you believe there is something to it, then perhaps there is."

Isabelle shrugged. "I wouldn't have believed the oddities had I not seen them for myself. There does seem to be a certain amount of the unexplainable associated with the stones," she added in hushed tones. She paused for a moment. "We've encountered danger at every turn, Claire. I don't know that this is the best place for you to be right now; although I certainly appreciate the effort."

Claire stared at her. "The effort? Belle, you're insane if you think for one moment that I'm going to just turn around and go back home now— even though I threatened to earlier. I was relieved you didn't call my bluff." She smiled. "Besides, I can at least be of some service to your wounded friend back there," she said, gesturing with her thumb in the direction of the sleeper car. "Would you like me to take a look at him? I've learned a thing or two since the last time you saw me."

Isabelle nodded and placed her folded napkin next to her plate. "Your expertise would be welcome," she said as she stood. "It's a good thing he was strong before the mayhem began. He's been shot twice in two months."

Claire frowned and fell into step behind Isabelle as they made their way, finding a precarious balance with the sway of the train. "He's a Scot, you say?"

Isabelle nodded over her shoulder.

"Well, he has that in his favor at least. With any luck, he'll be hardy like his forebears."

Isabelle opened the door and stepped onto the platform connecting the dining car to the sleeper car. Wind blew across her hair and whipped her dress to the side. She and Claire crossed into the sleeper, trying to tuck stray hair back into place and shaking skirts back into order.

When they reached the compartment, Isabelle stood to one side and allowed Claire to enter first. Claire approached Jack's side and knelt down near his head. "Mr. MacInnes?" she murmured.

Jack came awake with a start, clutching the wrist she had placed lightly on his shoulder. "Don't fret," she said. "Do you remember me?" She paused for a moment as he continued to stare at her in confusion, and Isabelle saw the moment when the fog cleared his brain and he must have differentiated Claire from her.

"Miss Webb," he said as he relaxed against his pillow and released a shuddering breath. "I might have hurt you."

Claire snorted lightly. "In your condition, Mr. MacInnes, I'm afraid I could best you with one hand tied behind my back."

He smiled and closed his eyes. "Brave words for a little woman." As he shifted on the narrow bed, he winced.

"Are you in much pain?" Claire asked him.

"I've been worse," he said.

"Silly man. Are you in pain or are you not?"

He moved his head on the pillow and opened his eyes, looking at Claire. "Yes. I am in pain."

Claire nodded and turned. "Isabelle, I have a portmanteau with medical supplies. I believe it's stowed next to yours in that compartment behind you. Will you hand it to me please?"

Isabelle retrieved her sister's bag and placed it next to Claire, where she knelt by Jack's side. "I'm going to check the wound, Mr. MacInnes. I also have something I can administer to you for the pain. The only negative with the medicine is that it may make you a bit sleepy. As we have another four hours before we arrive in Olympia, though, perhaps it will be just enough time."

"I'd rather not sleep any longer than necessary," Jack told her. "I need to keep my wits about me."

"As you wish. But perhaps tonight you will consider taking something that will help you get a good night's rest."

Jack nodded. "Perhaps. But the way things have gone on this little journey, I suspect we won't rest long."

17

JAMES KNEW THAT THOSE WHO saw him on the street would think him a man in full command of his faculties. Internally, he was a boiling cauldron of frustration and—if he allowed himself to acknowledge it—fear. He'd had disturbing news about Isabelle via Phillip and Jean-Louis. That the Frenchman had allowed Isabelle to talk him into leaving her made him furious. He had received the telegram the day before, telling him what had happened, and he'd been livid ever since.

He had to admit, however, that Jean-Louis was no match for Isabelle, even on his best day. Between her iron will and scrappy tactics, Deveraux was probably aboard the ship back to Athens before he realized what had happened.

James scowled and entered the telegraph office, making his way to the desk. The little man seated at the telegraph keys gave a start of recognition when he saw James and held his finger up. "Message for you," he said in heavily accented English as he flipped through a stack of papers. He handed one to James with a smile and a nod.

James took the paper and nodded back, making his way to a bench along the wall and sitting before he dared read the message from Phillip. Once he did, he was glad he had sat—the relief left him feeling slightly weak. Isabelle was on her way to Olympia with Jack. Phillip had given her James's location, and she would arrive late afternoon.

He leaned forward and placed his elbows on his knees, reading the telegraph one more time. Shaking his head slightly, he felt a peculiar burning sensation in his eyes and he closed them. The woman was like a cat with nine lives, and she always managed to land on her feet. Nobody had such consistent luck. She also had skill—he'd give her that. But he couldn't wait to get her home. With any luck, she'd choose a less nerve-wracking career. Like fighting fires.

***

"I'm just thinking it may be possible that Sparks is wrong." Phillip sat on the side of his bed and used a shoehorn to shove his foot into his shoe.

"Wrong in going to Olympia?" Jean-Louis asked him as he stood before the looking glass and fixed his tie in preparation for accompanying the women to dinner in the hotel dining room.

"Wrong in going anywhere. I think we're missing something here in Athens."

Jean-Louis frowned. "What could we be missing? We've looked in every museum and antique shop we can find."

Putting on his other shoe, Phillip countered, "But we've been so desperate to search everywhere that we haven't done a very good job of being thorough. Isabelle even mentioned that before you three went south: that perhaps we ought to revisit some of the places we've already been."

"You think the third stone is here in Athens." Jean-Louis turned away from the mirror and regarded Phillip thoughtfully.

"Well, if it isn't, I believe the clues to its whereabouts are here."

"Why?"

Phillip took his turn in front of the mirror and messed with his own tie. "A large portion of Dr. Pearce's papers point to addresses, maps, and anecdotes that originated here in the city. Or fairly close by."

Jean-Louis leaned against the wall and polished his glasses before perching them back on the bridge of his nose. "True, but there are also several pieces of documentation that point to other locations. Monemvasia was very significant."

"Yes, for the box. Not the jewel. If you were going to hide things of value, would you keep them in the same place? The three jewels themselves were scattered to different *countries*. It stands to reason that the third jewel would be nowhere near the box."

Phillip finished with his tie and looked at Jean-Louis—the frown now seemed permanently etched onto the Frenchman's brow, the clenched set of his jaw ever present. "I know you're worried about Alice. I'm worried—I can only imagine how you must be feeling. I think it would help if we keep busy here, try to further this thing along so we can finally be done with it and go home. I believe we should also visit Kilronomos's neighbors. Perhaps they know something that might be useful."

Jean-Louis nodded and looked away, pained. "I am incredibly frustrated waiting here. I want to find her myself."

"James is very competent," Phillip said. "I trust him with my life. He found me amongst all the millions in India. He will find her too. He is much like a dog with a bone when faced with something he wants to accomplish. Not to mention Isabelle. I'd say the two of them together are formidable."

***

Early the next morning, following a simple burial ceremony for Elysia at a nearby cemetery, Sally decided she was of no use to anybody wallowing in the hotel room. When Phillip and Jean-Louis mentioned visiting Demitrios's museum again, Sally had told Helene that they would be joining the men.

There were so many bits and pieces of pottery and statuary in the cluttered room that it all started to blur after a while. Phillip and Jean-Louis spoke to the stout little man about his knowledge of Grecian legends. He knew of the box that held the three jewels—they hoped that perhaps he might know something else that would be of use to them.

Sally wandered down rows of shelves and tables, Helene trailing along behind, seeming equally transfixed—whether by the sheer volume of artifacts or their state of disarray, Sally wasn't sure. Though Helene was still grieving, the fact that she could go out freely without worrying about Elysia's welfare seemed to be a bit of a relief to the woman. She had mentioned as much to Sally on the walk from the hotel. Her life had been occupied caring for her aunt—there had been little time for her own pursuits, and Sally sensed a restlessness in the woman.

Sally absently trailed her finger along a shelf and wrinkled her nose when her finger came back dusty. The old pieces of history deserved better than to suffer an ignominious death among grime and dirt. She stooped to examine a lower shelf that held pieces of carpet, tapestry, and old scraps of fabric. Carefully pulling a few items from the shelf, she rose and placed them on an empty table that stood against a nearby wall.

She ran her fingers over carefully stitched table runners and wall hangings. The colors were muted, and she imagined they must have been vibrant and beautiful in their day. Helene approached her side and looked over her shoulder with a smile. "They're lovely, no?"

Sally nodded, feeling suddenly nostalgic. "My mother taught me to do handiwork," she said, swallowing past the lump in her throat. "Things like these. They're in my trousseau at home. We made them together for me to put in my own home someday. I always thought she would be with me, would help me set up my house, play with my children."

Sally hated the look of sympathy in the older woman's beautiful eyes. Sally had never been good at accepting pity from anyone. "There are many more pieces over here," Sally said, seeking distraction. Making her way back to the shelf, she stooped down, retrieved an armful of items, and returned to the table.

A puff of dust rose into the air when she set the linens down, and Helene laughed, waving at it. "Metaxas needs a maid, yes?" the woman said.

Sally nodded with a smile and dispersed the pieces in front of them. "They really are beautiful," she said wistfully. "I wish I could take them home."

Helene glanced at Metaxas with a quirked brow. "I suspect you would be able to, for the right price. He does sell many of these pieces."

Sally bit her lip. "I wouldn't feel right," she said. "But I would dearly love to. Look! It's blue!" Her heart thumped hard as she spied a piece of faded blue linen in the stack. It had been on her mind to look for the tapestries Elysia had spoken of that fateful night just before they'd gone to the docks.

Helene took one side and helped unfold the fabric. It was roughly two feet wide and one foot tall; wool threads depicted a bridal scene with family and attendants enclosed in an ornate chapel. Curiously, the bride stood alone at the altar a few feet in front of the groom, a white object in her hands.

"Odd," Sally murmured. She softly traced her forefinger along the lone figure of the bride. "Is this a Greek custom? Why is her husband not standing alongside her?"

Helene's brows drew together. She shook her head. "I do not know, but I do believe this is the tapestry that hung in my aunt's house!" She lowered her voice on that last pronouncement, quickly glancing up at Demitrios, who was still engaged in conversation with Jean-Louis.

"You really think so?"

"I was so young, and I couldn't see it clearly because it was much higher on the wall than I was tall. Still . . ." Helene looked at Sally. "I think this is one of the two."

Sally squinted at the fabric, smoothing fraying threads that had begun to pull loose. "It's a shame," she said. "Someone should repair the damage."

Helene nodded. "My mother was once an excellent seamstress. People from all over the region commissioned her to make things for them— beautiful items from decor to wedding attire."

Sally frowned a bit and opened the reticule that hung from her wrist. She pulled out a small magnifying glass and examined the enlarged images as she moved the glass along the stitching.

"What are you looking for?" Helene asked her in a whisper.

"I don't know, exactly, but Elysia said that the instructions for returning the jewels to their home were to be found in the tapestries, yes?"

Helene nodded.

"So I'm looking for . . . anything . . ." Sally passed the glass over the altar, to the ceremony's officiator, and back again to the altar, narrowing her eyes.

"What is that on the altar?" she asked Helene and motioned for the older woman to look through the glass.

"An egg?" Helene said.

She paused, staring at Sally, who returned the expression, equally dumbstruck. "Not an egg," she whispered. "Helene, we have to take this tapestry back to the hotel and study it."

Helene glanced over her shoulder at the men, who were still deep in conversation. She nodded decisively and carefully folded the fabric. Carrying it to Metaxas, she began a rapid-fire discussion in Greek. Sally glanced at Jean-Louis, who followed the exchange with his brows raised. Sally decided she would ask him later about the conversation, but whatever Helene said had Metaxas eventually nodding. Shooting a few parting words at Helene, who looked at him with a complacent smile, he turned to the other two men.

"What is one to do about a woman?" the curator said with a shrug. "Some things are not worth the fight, no?"

Jean-Louis said a few more words to Metaxas and looked with open curiosity at Helene, who had carried the folded tapestry to a table that held the scraps of paper Metaxas used to wrap fragile items. She rolled the fabric in a large piece of paper with deft hands and glanced up at Sally, who moved quickly to her side.

"What did you tell him?" Sally muttered as the men said their good-byes.

"That I am well aware of the fact that he owes the government taxes on a few of the pieces he sold to an acquaintance of mine in England." Helene's smile was smug. "I overheard him boasting about it one day at the market." She shook her head and glanced at him over her shoulder. "Foolish man. He did say others have asked about this piece."

Sally rolled her eyes as she glanced at the man; Phillip and Jean-Louis made their way to the door. "I doubt he even knew where it was," she said. She paused for a moment, thinking, and Helene looked back at her. Slowly, she joined the woman and frowned. "I wonder who else has asked about it." She looked at Helene. "We'd best keep it in the safe with everything else."

***

"Still not here?" James asked the stationmaster. "How far away are they?"

The harried stationmaster processed a ticket for a passenger who was two minutes away from missing his train. "I do not know," he told James. "You wait a moment." He finished helping the next three people in line before finally turning his attention to James.

"The train from Monemvasia," James reminded the man.

"Yes, yes." He looked at a scrap of paper on his cluttered table, running his finger down it. "A message this morning that the train has broken down again and needs further repairs."

"And how far away are they?" James repeated.

"Three hours by train."

James looked into the distance, not really seeing anything. He was uneasy and not sure why. He wanted Isabelle with him again—her group was supposed to have arrived the day before but had been delayed because of trouble with the locomotive. Who knew how long the train would take to repair again? And once that was accomplished, Isabelle and Jack would still be three hours out.

"There are no other trains arriving today that the passengers from Monemvasia might be on?"

The stationmaster shook his head. "Tomorrow, yes. Today, no."

"Thank you for your help," James finally said and made his way down the street in the direction of the hotel. He hadn't walked far when he heard the sound of running footsteps. He turned and paused as a young child ran to his side, breathing heavily.

"Mr. James," the boy said.

"Yes, Abram?"

The ten-year-old boy had made a habit of finding James a few times a day to see if there was anything he could do to earn a coin. James had initially told him of his purpose in Olympia—told him to keep a sharp eye out for Alice—and gave the boy money for doing other small tasks for him, like shining his shoes or buying him a piece of fruit from a vendor.

"I see her! I see your friend!"

"What? Where?"

"Down the last track!" Abram pointed back at the station to a passenger train that had pulled away from the platform.

"Are you sure?" James began running toward the train. Abram ran alongside him, pointing as they gained on the train to the window where the boy said he had seen Alice.

The train was picking up speed, and James was forced to run faster, eventually leaving Abram behind. He was nearly to the window in question when he caught a brief glimpse of black hair on a woman seated next to a man whose arm was against the window. His side ached and his lungs heaved, and he knew he couldn't keep up his pace much longer. Initially he had thought to jump on the train car's rear platform—now he would be happy just to verify the woman's identity.

Please, he thought. *Just let me see her face!*

As luck, or Providence, would have it, the woman turned and glanced behind her—it was enough. He held up a hand to Alice, whose eyes widened before the train sped down the long track and out of sight. Good. She was still alive.

James bent over double and tried to catch his breath. Suddenly, everything was too hot. His suit coat, vest, and white shirt clung to his skin, and his hat was long gone. With his hands braced on his knees, he was still laboring for breath when Abram ran up beside him, carrying James's hat.

"It was her, yes?" the child asked, handing the hat back to James.

James nodded and stood, pulling a handkerchief from his pocket and wiping his forehead with it. "Good work, Abram," he said and handed the boy double the amount he usually paid. "Do you know where this train is going?"

"We ask," Abram said and ran back for the station.

James followed quickly and found himself again standing in line, waiting for the stationmaster. When they finally reached the head of the queue, James had slowed his breathing to its normal rhythm.

"That train," he said to the stationmaster. "The one that just left. Where was it going?"

"Patra," the man said with an irritated gesture at Abram, who was offering to shine his shoes.

James looked at a map hanging on the wall and scrutinized it fruitlessly until the man finally stabbed his finger onto it. "There," he said.

James groaned. It was some distance north, likely two days by train. "And when does the next train to Patra depart?"

The man consulted his train schedule, which was frayed at the corners and yellowed with coffee and tea stains. "Tomorrow morning," he said.

"Time?"

"Five o'clock."

James gave Abram another coin and accepted the boy's chattering company as he walked back to his hotel. There was no doubt he needed to be on the five o'clock train in the morning. The question was whether or not Isabelle and Jack would have arrived by then.

18

HELENE STUDIED THE TAPESTRY ON her lap through spectacles perched on the end of her nose. She ran her forefinger reverently over the neat stitching, the aged fabric. Turning it over, she frowned at the plain linen fabric that lined the back of the piece.

"In a good, quality piece of handiwork, the back should look as neat as the front. We can't see the back with this liner in the way," Helene told Sally as they sat side by side on the sofa in the sitting room.

Sally nodded—she remembered her mother telling her the same thing. Any woman worth her salt would take pride in the product and leave the back of the stitchery neat and tidy, without threads crossing their way over the fabric or dangling in untidy, frayed ends.

"The more I look at this, the more I'm convinced it was Elysia's," Helene said, rubbing the edge of the piece between her fingers. "See here—it has been picked free, but there was a pocket on the top for a dowel."

Helene stood and retrieved her sewing basket, opened the lid, and withdrew a pair of tiny scissors. Sally watched as Helene carefully began picking the stitches that held the tapestry and its back liner together. Before long, she had separated the two enough to fold the lining back and examine the opposite side of the stitchery. Sally smiled. It was immaculate.

Helene ran the edge of the small blade under a few more stitches, revealing more of the tapestry's back image. Sally leaned closer as the bride came into view. Helene paused and stared for a moment at the scene. Lifting it from her lap, she held it higher to catch the afternoon sun that streamed through the window.

Sally gasped as she saw what Helene was looking at. Against the white of the bride's gown, the seamstress had stitched a tiny star onto the lower back of the woman. Helene seemed transfixed—she stared at the small emblem and again laid the fabric on her lap, her finger hovering over it.

"The bride was a Guardian," Helene said and looked at Sally.

Sally leaned forward and studied the star on the bride's back. "How old do you suppose this tapestry is?"

Helene shook her head slightly. "I do not know."

"I wonder if Metaxas would know."

"I would be surprised if he knows where he was born," Helene said. "But it is worth a try. For certain though—we cannot return this to him."

Sally nodded. "We shall lock it in the safe."

***

Isabelle peered out the window as the train came to a halt with a burst of steam and a loud screech. James wasn't in sight, but that didn't mean he hadn't received her message through Phillip that they were on their way. She gathered her bag and Jack's and waited as Claire propped him up and led him into the aisle.

Jack leaned heavily on Claire as they made their way off the train. Truth be told, the train's complications had been fortuitous for Jack—he'd been able to rest fairly comfortably in the inn where the railroad had put them overnight. His coloring was improving, but he was still weak and expressed his disgust about it periodically under his breath in muttered expletives.

Claire was truly the medical professional she was aspiring to be. She was quick and efficient, and Isabelle had given Jack over to her sister's care from the moment they had finished their brief lunch on the train the day before. She sensed Jack's interest in Claire and wondered if anything would come of it. Claire always had been bright in both personality and intellect, with a quick and sometimes wicked tongue. Isabelle was proud of her and comfortable with the inroads they seemed to have made toward a truce that had been long in coming.

Isabelle set the luggage on the platform and turned to take Claire's from her. Jack, using both Claire's support and his cane, navigated the steps and stood on the platform without incident. The only evidence of his pain showed in the small white lines that tightened around his mouth as he moved.

Isabelle squinted into the distance, turning to either side hoping to spy James. A boy stood on the far platform and made his way quickly to Isabelle, holding a sign bearing her name.

"You are Miss Webb?" the boy asked her.

"Yes," she said and took an envelope he offered. The handwriting on it was unmistakably James's. Turning to her reticule that hung from her waist, she fished about for a coin to give the boy.

"No, no," he said. "Mr. James already give me money."

Isabelle smiled. "Well then, I must give you some too. What's your name?"

"Abram, Miss Webb."

"And has Mr. James already left?"

Abram nodded. "He leave this morning. Following the girl, Miss Alice."

Isabelle looked up the street, squinting. "Is there an inn close by, Abram? Perhaps where Mr. James stayed?"

"Yes, Miss Webb. I show you."

Isabelle opened the letter from James and scanned it quickly. "A train for Patra leaves tomorrow at noon," she told her companions. "Looks as though you'll have some more time to rest, Jack."

"I would rather stay on the move," he said, shifting his weight. "We should check to see if there's not another train leaving today?"

"I'm certain James would have thought of it, but I can ask." A quick conversation with an overwhelmed stationmaster confirmed her suspicions. "We go to the inn," she told them when she returned. "And I believe I'll do a little investigating of my own. What would have made them leave suddenly?"

The question nagged her all through the afternoon and into dinner. She had made a cursory examination of the town and resolved to go to the ancient ruins after eating. Abram had told her that James hadn't had any success in finding either Alice or the two men until Abram had spied Alice that morning on the train.

"What were James's tactics, then, do you suppose?" Jack asked as he devoured his dessert and motioned for Isabelle's when she indicated she was done. "Did he ask around town?"

Isabelle nodded. "Clearly he bribed the street children again. Worked well last time."

Claire wiped her mouth with a napkin and sat back in her chair. "I'm not eating my dessert either, Mr. MacInnes. Would you like it?"

He glanced at her askance. "Possibly. My appetite is returning."

"In spades, I should say," Claire observed. "Isabelle, are you still thinking to go out to the ancient ruins tonight?"

Isabelle nodded.

"You have your firearm, I presume?"

"Always."

Jack shook his head between bites of his *loukoumades*. "I don't need a nursemaid," he said to Claire. "You should go with her. Safety in numbers."

Claire looked at Isabelle. "I've never had a man tell me to go out after dark before," she said.

"And likely this is the only one who ever will," Isabelle told her.

Jack huffed in apparent irritation. "You're more than capable of defending yourself, Isabelle, but I should think that if there are two of you, your chances of being accosted are significantly less." He looked at Claire. "I would prefer neither of you go, truth be told, but I know that even at full strength, I'd be unable to keep that one," he motioned at Isabelle with his fork, "from doing whatever she pleases. James is a fool to even waste his breath over it."

"Nonsense," Isabelle said. "I have certainly taken his counsel in the past."

"When?" Jack chewed his dessert and took a swallow of tea.

"Before we met you."

He snorted and looked again at Claire. "As I said. A waste of breath."

"I certainly don't mind coming along," Claire said to Isabelle. "Scrounging around in the dark will be reminiscent of our old days."

Jack raised a brow but refrained from comment.

Isabelle looked out the window at the darkening sky. "I want to see what Sparks saw when he was here. He may have gone out at night or perhaps not. I'd rather not leave stones unturned."

"And this other man with him? You believe you knew him in India?" Claire said.

"Unfortunately. He was responsible for the deaths of Alice's parents there. He partnered with Thaddeus Sparks and abducted Sally and Alice— he was a mercenary in the truest sense of the word. I was certain he had died in India, but unless he has a twin, he seems to be alive and well."

"So you've not met him yet," Claire said to Jack.

He shook his head and looked at her honey pie. She pushed it toward him, a smile quirking the corner of her mouth.

Jack took it from her with a nod. "I haven't met Kilronomos, but I had the misfortune to meet Mr. Sparks in Egypt," he told Claire. "He's the one who laid me up the first time."

"Ah, yes. The first wound from which you've not entirely recovered."

Jack scowled. "I *was* recovering very well, thank you. I barely noticed it at all. And why do you insinuate that the fault lies with me?"

Isabelle laughed out loud until Claire shot her a dark look. Isabelle closed her mouth but failed to stifle the laugh that escaped her nose.

"Of course it's not your fault. I merely view the circumstances from a medical standpoint. Your body needs rest, and as long as you persist in throwing yourself before your enemies, that's not likely to happen." Claire leaned forward, looking at Isabelle intently. "How crucial is this treasure hunt, really? What would be the worst that would happen if you all packed up and went home?"

Jack shook his head, finally done with his round of desserts. "It will never be over if we don't finish it now," he murmured and shifted carefully in his chair. "Alice and Phillip will never be at rest now that the Federation knows they bear the mark. And eventually Sparks and Kilronomos will come to realize we have the first jewel in our possession. All they would have to do is a little investigating at Alice's ancestral estate in England to discover that Lady Banbury shipped the thing to India. When a ransacking of the Bilbeys' personal items in Calcutta proves fruitless, they will know exactly where to turn."

Isabelle nodded. "There are larger issues at play here as well," she told her sister. "There is something odd about the stones themselves. I mentioned it to you yesterday on the train. I fear what would happen should they fall into the wrong hands."

"The ruthless nature of those who search for the jewels keeps me awake at night," Jack added. "It must end here. In Greece."

Once dinner was finished and Jack agreed to rest, albeit bitterly and with a sense of wounded male pride, Isabelle and Claire walked the short distance to the site. Claire muttered that it was probably fortuitous for Jack's sake that he remained behind at the inn—his stomach was bound to rebel from consuming so much rich dessert.

Isabelle looked across the landscape at the pillars supporting nothing but air, the columns that lay on the ground, the large chunks of stone that were once foundations of something massive. Temples built from stone resided in dirt and foliage, awaiting discovery by shovel and trowel after centuries of rest.

The moonlight shone bright upon the ruins, illuminating the landscape in an eerie glow. Crickets provided a steady backdrop of sound, accompanied by occasional scuttling leaves as the breeze wafted across the countryside. The air was cool, and Isabelle drew her shawl close about her shoulders as she walked slowly beside Claire. They entered a structure that boasted several large pillars that were still upright amid several walls and half walls that were in various stages of ruin.

"What exactly happened with Lincoln?" Claire asked quietly as they picked their way across the rubble. "Genevieve told me about your broken leg."

Isabelle shrugged, not really wanting to discuss it. "I had been following Mr. Booth for some time. Had taken a room at Mrs. Surratt's boarding-house. She locked me in my room that night when she realized what I was about. I dropped from my second story window to try and make it to the theater, but . . ." Isabelle frowned.

"Did you lose consciousness?"

Isabelle nodded. "I managed to tell someone who came to my aid, but it was too late." She sighed. "I decided I should probably take a rest from investigative work if I wasn't going to be effective anymore."

Isabelle felt Claire's gaze resting on her. "What is it?" she finally asked.

Claire's expression was soft, gentle. Not at all what Isabelle usually expected from her. "Self-pity does not become you, Belle," Claire said, the bluntness of the words tempered by the countenance that delivered them. "And I should think you ought to have proven to yourself in these recent months that your talents are still intact."

Isabelle nodded. "I do not mean to sound self-pitying. And my mind is healing along with my broken bone. It does still grate at me though. The failure. I doubt that will ever fully leave me at peace."

Claire offered a half smile and looked down as she stepped over a large rock. "Failure was something that never did sit well with you, though, especially with things about which you felt strongly."

Isabelle snorted lightly. "I don't imagine most people are happy with failure."

"Many of us learn to accept it with a certain degree of grace. We learn from it."

Isabelle scowled at her. "I learn from my failures!"

"Certainly you do. After you beat yourself to death with them."

"Claire, I—" Isabelle halted, listening. "Do you hear humming?"

"Humming? I don't—yes." Claire stopped walking. "Yes, I do."

Isabelle narrowed her eyes, turning first to her right, then to her left as she tried to determine the direction of the source. "There," she said as she squinted into a copse of trees.

19

Quietly, Isabelle and Claire made their way to the outer wall of the building, peering around the edge of one of the large columns. The shadow, roughly twenty feet away and clearly illuminated in the moonlight, was small; it jumped atop a large, fallen pillar and walked along it, balancing with apparent ease.

"A child?" Claire whispered.

Isabelle nodded. "I wonder what he is doing alone at this time of night."

"We should ask him."

"And hope he doesn't have older friends lurking in the trees."

Isabelle felt Claire looking at her. "You think he means to spring a trap?"

"Possibly."

"But who would even know we are out here?"

Isabelle frowned. "Someone following us."

"Have you noticed anyone following us?"

"No." Isabelle sighed softly. "That doesn't mean a thing however."

The child soon tired of his skipping game atop the pillar and hopped down, making his way toward them.

"Well," Claire said, "if he means to entrap us, he's taking a forward approach."

Isabelle squinted again into the night. "I think I know who that is," she murmured. As the child grew closer, breaking into a light trot, she nodded. "It's Abram. The boy from the train station."

As Abram approached, Isabelle observed. He was clever—light on his feet and confident in his own skin. The grin that manifested itself as he neared them glowed white against his olive-toned face.

"I know I find you here," he said as he joined the women in the crumbling building. "When people go for a . . . a . . ." He paused, searching for the right word. "A stroll, they come to the temples of the gods."

"And how did you know we were out for a stroll?" Isabelle asked him.

Abram jerked a thumb in the direction of their inn. "Your friend. He tell me."

Claire muttered something under her breath about Jack, and Isabelle ignored her.

"And why were you looking for us?" Isabelle said.

"The old witch in the cottage. She tell my mother about the green eyes."

Isabelle's heart hitched. "The man with the green eyes?"

Abram nodded. "Mr. James say look for the man with green eyes. The old witch talk to him."

"Will you take us to her?" Isabelle asked him.

He nodded. "This way." He turned to leave the ruins.

"Shall we wait for morning? Suppose she is sleeping?" Claire said to the boy.

"She never sleep. Witches no sleep."

Isabelle and Claire walked with Abram as he led them for nearly thirty minutes through trees and bushes, clearings and undergrowth. Isabelle knew they'd never find their way back to the inn without the boy's help, and she hoped he could be trusted. He had led James to Alice's departing train; she supposed that was something.

The cottage they finally approached deep within a thicket was everything Isabelle ever imagined a witch's cottage to be. Like something out of a fairy tale, it blended into its surroundings until they were nearly upon it. A small window showed the interior to be dark.

"You're certain she's awake?" Claire whispered to Abram.

In answer, Abram knocked loudly upon the front door without preamble or delay. When the thin wood panel finally swung open on hinges that creaked, the face answering from within seemed to disprove Abram's theory.

"She's been sleeping," Claire hissed.

A woman who was two hundred years old if she was a day blinked in the light of a candle she held in her hand as she raised it to get a better view of her nocturnal visitors. Her eyes were dark enough to appear black, her hair in wisps under a scarf that matched what appeared to be a long nightdress. A short, croaked question in Greek issued forth from a voice that was rusty from either age, disuse, or sleep. Possibly all three.

Abram answered her quickly and then turned to Isabelle. "I tell her you are sorry for waking her."

Claire gave a disgruntled exclamation, and Isabelle held up her hand to forestall further comment. "Please, Abram," Isabelle said, "will you ask the kind woman what she knows about the man with the green eyes?"

A quick exchange had the old "witch" looking the women up and down before gesturing with a gnarled hand for them to enter.

Claire grasped Abram's upper arm and pushed him inside ahead of them when he moved aside for the sisters to enter first. "I think you should stay with us," Claire told him when he looked up at her with a scowl. "After all, we shall need an escort back to the inn."

Isabelle bit back a smile. For all that James believed Isabelle had a will of iron, he'd never met her sister. Claire would exact her pound of flesh out of Abram one way or another.

They followed the woman into the interior of her home, and she lit lanterns that hung from pegs and were placed on a small, rough-hewn mantel. The lit room showed herbs hanging in bundles from exposed rafters and a long table along one wall that held jars, plants, bowls, and dried flowers. The home smelled earthy and surprisingly pleasant. Soothing.

Claire must have had the same impression, for she examined the surroundings with a quick eye and a slight nod. "Is this woman a healer?" she asked Abram.

He nodded. "She make magic potions."

"For the love of heaven, it's not magic," Claire muttered as she moved to the table and scrutinized a well-used mortar and pestle.

Isabelle drew closer to the woman, who was tossing a small log on a few glowing embers that still shone in the dying fire. "My name is Isabelle," she said as the stooped figure rose to her full height, which came to Isabelle's shoulder.

The woman tapped an arthritic hand to her chest. "Desma."

Abram spoke to Desma, who nodded and spoke to Isabelle. Abram translated for her. "She meet the green-eyes man at the ruins. He travel with a . . ." Abram frowned and scrunched his face. "Guard."

Isabelle raised her brow. "A Guardian? Did the man tell Desma that his companion was a Guardian?"

Desma nodded her head when Abram asked her. He then told Isabelle, "She know Guardians."

Isabelle looked at Desma, whose clear, dark gaze met hers without blinking. "What did she tell the green-eyed man?"

Abram listened as Desma spoke, then he turned to Isabelle. "She tell him go to Delphi. The oracle know everything."

"The Oracle at Delphi?" Claire said. "That is ancient history. There isn't an oracle at Delphi anymore, and when there was—well, she was a charlatan."

Isabelle felt herself tense as she thought of Alice being dragged about Greece by two men who cared for her well-being only because of what they wanted her to find. "Did the Guardian look well?" she asked Desma directly.

Through translation from the young boy, who yawned and was finally showing signs of fatigue, she answered. "She seem brave," Abram said. "The witch say the Guardian is brave."

Claire frowned at the boy. "Does this woman know you call her a witch?"

On impulse, Isabelle reached into her reticule and pulled out a bundle of cloth. She opened it to reveal the ring she'd received from the doctor in Monemvasia. Closely watching Desma's face, Isabelle held it out for her to see.

Desma looked down at it and swiftly up again at Isabelle. Her uttered response was harsh and urgent, and Isabelle had no trouble understanding the woman's meaning.

"She say that bring danger," Abram said, looking at the ring but taking a small step back. "It is enemy to the Guardian."

Isabelle nodded. It made sense—the King's Men were enemies of the Guardians. They wanted the jewels for their own use, and a Guardian's purpose was to keep them from unworthy hands. The ring itself brought trepidation to those who knew the history behind the legend.

"Does she know where the stone is?"

Abram spoke to the woman as he smothered another yawn, and Desma looked at Isabelle with her dark eyes. "She not know," Abram told Isabelle.

"Why did she help the man with the green eyes? He is not a nice man."

Desma regarded her with a raised brow as she answered, and Abram said, "Who say she help?"

Claire moved forward then into Isabelle's line of sight. "She sent them on a wild goose chase?"

"So it would appear," Isabelle said, relieved on one hand but anxious on the other.

"Thank you for your time, Desma," Isabelle said, and she took the woman's gnarled hand.

A long Greek phrase in response had Isabelle looking at Abram for translation one last time. "She say people meet at Delphi. The enemy go soon to Delphi."

Isabelle felt her blood run cold. "She sent a Guardian to the enemy? Why?"

Abram answered when the woman responded, lightly tapping her chest. "Because the oracle know everything."

***

The train left the station promptly at noon the following day, and Abram waved at them with a grin on his face, still moving his arm as the train turned the corner and Isabelle could no longer see him. Settling back into her seat, Isabelle regarded the couple seated across from her. Claire sat facing forward because she was prone to motion sickness, and Jack looked a little worse for the wear, pain making him pale again. He had refused Claire's offer of laudanum, though, determined to keep his wits about him.

Isabelle pulled her diary out of her bag and flipped back over the scores of pages that contained her reflections, notes on odd happenings, and observations of the players in the game that had begun on a steamer bound for Bombay. She wondered how the group in Athens was faring. Fairly certain Jean-Louis wouldn't go off half-cocked, she was more worried about Phillip's temper. Knowing that Sparks had bested them yet again wouldn't be something that would sit well with the young man. She wondered how James had convinced his brother to remain behind when he had chased after Alice and her abductors.

Isabelle puzzled over the mystery of the King's Men and their role in the legend as opposed to the Federation. How many entities were actively searching for the jewels? And how on earth had the Egyptian Federation head muscled his way to the fore of something that had likely begun and would end in the region of Greece? And what of Elysia? She felt a pang of sadness at the old woman's fate.

"Jack," she said softly, tapping her pen on her lip, "were there any Greeks involved in the Federation? You mentioned the Egyptian meeting with powerful men from other counties."

Jack shook his head and winced as the train swerved over a piece of uneven track. "There were representatives from the Far East and Turkey.

Also several from both northern and southern Europe, although they all rarely met at once. None from Greece."

"Do you remember him ever speaking specifically of Greece?"

"Not particularly, other than the fact that it was common knowledge that one of the stones was likely hidden here."

"And he never mentioned the box?"

"Never. I doubt he knows it exists."

Isabelle pursed her lips in thought. "But the King's Men know about it," she murmured.

Jack drew his brows together and he shifted in his seat. "What are you thinking?"

"I'm wondering which group poses the bigger threat. The King's Men seem a step ahead of the others."

"Does it matter really?" Claire said. "It doesn't sound as though either group is too friendly. He's been shot by both."

Jack dipped his head in acknowledgement. "I doubt many can boast of such a privilege."

Claire looked at him for a moment before turning her attention back to Isabelle, who saw Jack fight a grin.

"It doesn't seem to matter which is the bigger threat—they're both deadly," Claire said to Isabelle.

"They are," Isabelle admitted, "but one knows more than the other. I wish we had someone planted on the inside of the King's Men."

"Let's assume that the only information they had beyond the Federation's is the existence of the box," Jack said in an undertone as he leaned forward slightly. "As it was, they didn't know where it was located."

"They knew it was at Monemvasia," Isabelle said.

"But hadn't found it. It makes me wonder how useful their resources really are. You and I found it in one night."

"That may be, but they didn't have the map; we knew specifically to look for a building in the shape of that mausoleum. And at any rate, they seem to have intimidation fully on their side. The priest and doctor on the island were truly spooked by the ring."

"*Someone* saw the map. Your stateroom had been broken into."

"Again, I feel compelled to mention that they shoot people," Claire said, pointing at Jack. "Seems to me our choices are simple. We must find that last stone before the other zealots lay hands on it. And then we run your Sparks fellow to the ground to retrieve the jewel he stole from you in Egypt."

"What a novel idea that is," Isabelle said, casting her sister a look. "I wonder that I didn't think of it myself."

"Wait," Jack said and sat up a bit. "Run Sparks to the ground . . . We can likely assume they left the Egyptian jewel behind in Athens, I should think. Why would they carry it with them? Kilronomos has a home there that they will certainly return to."

Isabelle nodded and then briefly closed her eyes. "And who do we have in Athens that will sneak into the home to search for it?"

"Deveraux and Phillip." Jack's shoulders drooped slightly.

"Phillip would do it," Isabelle said, "but I worry about his lack of penchant for stealth. He and his brother are rather . . . not stealthy."

Claire's eyes widened slightly, and she cast a quick look over her shoulder. "Not to mention the fact that if he should be arrested, you'd be facing a sticky mess! I suppose you have a plan to move him swiftly through the Greek judicial process?"

"I have government contacts," Jack said with a lift of his shoulder.

"You're a Brit!"

Jack scowled at Claire. "I am a Scot, madam."

Claire breathed loudly out through her nose, her lips tight. "My point is you had better hope your friend suddenly becomes exceptionally good at thievery and subterfuge because the legal ramifications could be enormous. He might never make it out of some fetid Greek jail."

"Why must it be 'fetid'?" Jack asked Claire, who glared at him.

Isabelle watched the exchange with a fair sense of amusement. She'd never seen Jack at his flirtatious best, and she had to assume, for all of Claire's bluster, that her sister wouldn't last for long against it.

Claire sat back in her chair and shook her head. "You do not take my point?"

Jack sobered. "I do take your point. And I agree—any illegal stealth needs to be done either by me or your sister," he said with a motion of his head toward Isabelle.

Claire looked at him for a moment before responding. "You truly believe what you're saying."

Jack glanced at Isabelle, who watched the exchange with a slight smile. "You've never told her exactly what your profession involved?"

"Not in so many words."

Jack turned back to Claire. "There are times, dear lady, when the end justifies the means. This is most assuredly one of those." He leaned his head back and closed his eyes, shifting a bit in an apparent attempt to get comfortable.

Claire looked at Isabelle, who shrugged. "What kind of trouble did you find yourself in?" Claire asked her.

Isabelle also leaned back and attempted to find comfort as the train continued its way closer to James, and hopefully, Alice. "All kinds," she answered. "But not always life threatening."

Claire snorted lightly. "Well that's something, I suppose." She nudged Jack lightly on the arm. "And when this is over, what will you do? Go back undercover and continue risking life and limb?"

Jack opened one eye and looked at her. "I'm considering my options," he said, "and hoping I'm still alive when this is over. Perhaps I ought to hide out in the States for a while. I've blackened the eye of a man who thrives on power. He's not likely to forget it."

Claire examined him for a moment, chewing on her lip. "Then you must endeavor to keep yourself safe. Or hope your wounds are not such that I can't treat them."

"I have a hard time imagining anything you can't treat, Miss Webb," Jack told Claire and again settled back with his eyes closed.

Claire flushed and refrained from further comment.

Isabelle smiled.

20

SALLY OPENED THE DOOR TO the hotel sitting room with a frown. The person on the other side had been banging on it for all he was worth. "Mr. Metaxas?"

The antique shop owner stood in the hallway, his posture rigid, his face a flushed red. "The tapestry," he said without preamble. "I must have it."

"Come in, come in," she said and stood to one side, her mind spinning. There was no possible way she would surrender the tapestry to the man—the fact that it bore a depiction of a Guardian made it important to their cause even if they weren't certain exactly why. She would have to placate the man until Helene was ready for the day. The older woman was still in the bedroom, dressing for breakfast.

"Sit down, please," she said in her most gracious Southern hostess manner, gesturing to the sofa and chairs. "Would you care for some tea?"

"No, no tea," he said and walked toward the sofa, turning again to Sally. "The tapestry. I must take it back to the museum."

She placed a hand on his arm, gently propelled him forward to the sofa, and took the chair adjacent to it. Indicating again for him to be seated, she waited with a patient smile until he finally huffed and sat down.

"Now then," she said. "What can I help you with?"

He stared at her for a moment, mouth slack. "The tapestry," he finally said, enunciating each word carefully. "I must take it back to my shop."

"I'm afraid we don't have it, but you're welcome to join us for breakfast. We'll be going downstairs soon—the dining room is just lovely here. And I've found the food to be exceptional. Have you dined here? I'm sure you'll agree with me that the menu is a delight. We've yet to find its superior in any other establishment in Athens. The chef must be ever so accomplished. Small wonder, really, that so many Europeans frequent this place year after year."

Demitrios Metaxas stared at her, his mouth hanging with significantly more slack than before. He looked to one side, his brow furrowing, and shook his head slightly before returning to the topic at hand.

"You do not have the tapestry?"

Sally heard the bedroom door open. "Oh, good! It's Helene. We can now go to breakfast."

Helene's eyebrows rose when she saw Demitrios, who rose as she entered. "Mr. Metaxas," she said to him in English, "what a pleasant surprise."

His complexion darkened and he gestured at Sally. "I need the tapestry. She tell me you no longer have it."

Helene nodded without missing a beat. "That is correct."

Sally rather hoped the woman would continue with an explanation of where they had supposedly taken the tapestry because she herself had yet to fabricate anything plausible.

Demitrios waited a heartbeat before asking, "And where *is* it?"

"We loaned it to a man from the new archaeological museum near Syntagma Square. He claims to have superior cleaning methods."

Metaxas's face turned purple, and he exploded into a diatribe of Greek, likely none of which was complimentary. The veins in the man's neck stood out, and Sally examined them, transfixed, wondering if one would rupture right before her eyes.

Sally turned when she felt a hand on her elbow. Phillip stood at her side, with Jean-Louis directly behind him, straightening his cuffs. She looked at the men, trying for a sense of bright innocence she hoped Metaxas would believe if he happened to look her way.

Phillip wrinkled his brow at her in question, and she shook her head ever so slightly.

By this time, Helene was answering the man in Greek, and Jean-Louis closely watched the exchange. That was a good thing because she could hardly wait for a translation of the whole loud mess.

"Mr. Metaxas," Sally finally said when there was a break in the heated verbal foray, "why, exactly, do you need the tapestry? It's beautiful, yes, but there are many others in your museum that are much more striking. The one we borrowed from you is rather bland."

Metaxas looked at her, his nostrils flaring—likely with the attempt to draw in enough air to keep from swooning. The thought of the stocky man swooning very nearly made her laugh.

"Miss," he said through teeth that snapped back together as he appeared to search for the right combination of words, "the tapestry, it is very . . . old."

"Well, certainly," Sally said as she took her gloves from her reticule and pulled them onto her hands, "but everything in that museum of yours is old. Surely that's why you call it a museum." She waved one freshly gloved hand at him and added, "And what is another old, musty tapestry, more or less?"

He glared at her as she smiled brightly and made her way to the door. "Perhaps a nice spot of tea will be just the thing to freshen your perspective on the matter," she said. "Do say you will join us!"

Rather than respond, he cast a hot look at the lot of them, spending an extra few blistering moments on Helene before storming from the room in a huff. The sound of his angry footsteps on the marble stairs echoed for a bit before dying out.

Sally drew in a deep breath and released it with a shuddering sigh. "What will we do when he realizes that nobody at the museum near Syntagma Square has it?"

Helene managed a smile. "I suppose we have time to think of something credible," she said. "But you, Miss Rhodes, were brilliant."

Sally raised a brow. "I'm not so certain of that. I managed to make him very angry."

Phillip's mouth quirked into a smile. He drew her gloved hand to his lips and placed a kiss on her knuckles. "You kept him from knowing we still have the tapestry. And in so doing, bought us some time. We may need to shift our plans. Find a different hiding place for the items in the safe."

Phillip was impressed with her, and Sally felt an inner glow that spread warmly throughout her body. It took away some of the sting from constant worry about Alice's welfare. Sally had experienced very little over the past few days that had made her smile.

Jean-Louis pulled a key from his pocket and followed the others into the hallway, locking the door behind them. Sally turned back to wait for him as Helene started down the stairs, laughing as Phillip stumbled and then caught his balance, making a lighthearted remark about being an oaf among swans.

"What did Metaxas say?" Sally asked the Frenchman.

"That somebody wants the tapestry—it's one of two, which we knew, and a person in a position of some apparent prominence is after him to locate them."

"He certainly was angry about it," Sally said, running her hand along the polished brass handrail that lined the wall going down the stairs.

"I believe it was more than anger." Jean-Louis paused. "I think he is afraid."

That gave Sally pause. "Afraid of whoever wants the tapestry?"

Jean-Louis shrugged as they turned a corner at a landing and continued to the main floor. When they reached the others, Sally saw Leila approach Phillip with an envelope. Sally's heart skipped a beat as she joined him quickly, looking over his arm as he tore into it. Jean-Louis and Helene circled around him as well, and Sally wondered if they all held a collective breath.

"It's from Isabelle," Phillip said and quickly scanned the contents of the telegram. "They are on their way to Delphi, following James, who is following Alice, Sparks, and Kilronomos." He shook his head slightly, a muscle working in his jaw. Sally knew what it cost him to remain behind when what he dearly wanted most to do was tear after Sparks.

***

The frightening man again cornered Leila when she was alone, dumping trash in the large container behind the hotel. "I am doing everything you ask," she said, backing up with her palms out. If only her father were still alive! He would best the brute with a cloth covering his eyes. She tried to hold that image in her mind, remembering when her father had been vibrant and strong, and willing herself to be as tenacious as he had been.

"Have you found the information I need?" he asked, still stalking toward her.

Leila stopped shuffling backward and stood her ground. "Yes, I saw the telegram myself. They are traveling to Delphi."

"When are they to arrive?" Leila knew she would hear that low, gravelly, accented voice in her sleep for the rest of her life. He was Egyptian—she was certain of it.

"Likely tomorrow."

The man studied her face for a moment, his eyes narrowing. She fought to keep her chin up and her back straight. He eventually reached into his coat pocket and withdrew a small object, holding it out to her. She reached her hand forward, and he dropped the thing into her palm. Her nostrils flared slightly in anger and dismay as she looked at Theo's favorite spinning top. He kept it in a box near his bed and spun it most evenings on the rough-hewn dining room table as the two children talked over the day with their mother, who worked tirelessly into the night dyeing her beautiful fabrics. Theo liked to see how long he could keep the toy spinning before it tilted into the cracks and ridges on the table.

"See that you remain available—they will eventually be forced to return," the man told her and finally turned his back, leaving the alley and disappearing around the corner, hidden from her view.

***

James stood at the base of a hill at the ancient city of Delphi. The serpentine path stretched before him and wound its way up to the Temple of Apollo. He hadn't seen a sign of Alice or her abductors since crossing the Gulf of Corinth earlier that morning. He knew they were a day ahead of him and would likely be staying at an inn or boardinghouse close by, but knowing where they were ultimately headed gave him a place to start.

He wandered the path, turning to look down at the large amphitheater where countless plays and orations had occurred through the centuries. He knew that the actual ground upon which he stood was no older than the dirt and rocks at home, but the fact that ancient inhabitants had left such an impressive and indelible mark behind left him in awe in spite of himself.

Ruins dotted the hillside and valley; buildings of varying shapes and sizes provided numerous tourists plenty of fodder for discussion. Some walked with natives of nearby towns who led tour groups for a small fee—James had been approached by a few earlier—and he couldn't decide if he was grateful for the large number of people in the area. On the one hand, he would be able to hide in the crowds. On the other, so could Sparks and Kilronomos.

James continued his walk up the side of the hill. What could possibly be their motivation for traveling to the ancient ruins? Were they hoping to find an oracle still in position over the crack of steam in the opening of the temple floor? And if they did think they would find someone who would tell them whatever they needed to know, why did they need Alice?

The thought stopped him cold in his tracks, and he looked up toward the Temple of Apollo. Hopefully, they'd just abandon her if they didn't need her anymore. Or perhaps they still had a role for her to play. Either way, he felt a sense of urgency: time was running out, and she had to be found.

He continued his climb, making his way to the building so many had sought throughout the centuries. He would spend a considerable amount of time in the shadows until they showed themselves. Surely they wouldn't waste time getting there—if nothing else they had proved to be rash and quick to act. James cast another glance around the hillside and assessed his surroundings, hoping to turn that to his advantage.

***

"He has a basement in that shop of his, you know," Helene said to Sally, Phillip, and Jean-Louis as they strolled the market streets in an attempt to keep from going insane pacing the hotel room. Sally decided it was working. Barely.

"Who does?" Jean-Louis asked her.

"Demitrios."

"How do you know this?" Sally said, turning her attention toward the woman and away from a collection of scarves at one of the market stalls.

"I was a child when Metaxas's father owned the museum before he died and left it to Demitrios. The father acquired the building soon after he finished school, opened the shop—which he liked to call a museum, as does his son, but we all know Demitrios will sell anything for the right price—and set to work collecting antiques. He purchased several large pieces from my parents' belongings after they died, telling me that he would store them in the basement until he made a place for them in the main room upstairs. He has yet to bring them up, and I find myself wondering what else he might have hidden down there."

"Do you suppose he knows?" Sally said, wrinkling her nose. "He wasn't aware of that tapestry until we showed it to him. If his storage room in the basement is as cluttered as his display areas, he likely hasn't a clue." And if the basement were as dusty and musty as she imagined it to be, she was certain she never wanted to set foot in it.

"I wonder if he does indeed have the other tapestry," Jean-Louis said quietly as he gently urged the group forward and away from the possibility of curious ears. "We know there are two and that the one we took was one of them. Suppose he has the other and doesn't realize it?"

"And what does the other one depict?" Phillip asked, guiding Sally around a group of people who were haggling over the price of a piece of jewelry. "Who needs it and why?"

Sally's brow wrinkled. "It is supposed to tell the Guardian how to return the jewels to their home. But all we see in the tapestry is what looks to be a bridal procession. Is she supposed to place the jewels on some sort of altar?"

"I think I would like to look at the tapestry again," Jean-Louis said. "Perhaps it will tell us nothing without its companion piece, but I believe it deserves a second look."

The walk back to the hotel was quick and fairly quiet, and it was a subdued group that climbed the stairs to the second floor. Sally led the group and was first to see that their door was wide open and the hotel concierge was inside, gesturing madly and speaking rapidly to one of the hotel staff.

They must have heard Sally's squeak of surprise, for they turned toward her with halted speech and frozen expressions. What stunned her the most, however, was the destroyed painting that hung crookedly on the wall over the safe.

21

Isabelle and Claire stood at the railing of the steamship that carried them across the Gulf of Corinth. Claire had bullied Jack into taking a brief nap for the duration of the trip—Isabelle figured he finally acquiesced just to shut Claire up.

"What do you remember learning about the Oracle at Delphi?" Isabelle asked her sister as the wind picked up and whipped across the deck. The waves below the ship were white capped and active, and Isabelle wondered how Alice had fared when she had crossed the gulf with her abductors.

"I actually studied Greek mythology in school. If I remember correctly, Zeus was looking for the center of the universe. He released two birds, and they met at Delphi. There's a crack in the earth there, where vapors rise and where oracles through the years sat on tripod stools and told the future. Priests would then interpret it, which is laughable because I'm sure they interpreted it however they pleased."

Isabelle nodded. "What are the vapors, exactly?"

"Most people speculate now that they're noxious and the silly oracles were out of their minds when they babbled." Claire rolled her eyes. "I would babble too if I were breathing in poison gas."

Isabelle pursed her lips, thinking. "If I were Sparks and I believed in the supernatural, where is the one place at Delphi where Alice would be useful to me?"

Claire turned her gaze from the open water and studied Isabelle. "Surely they wouldn't put her over that steam pit."

"I think that's exactly what they'll do."

Claire squinted a bit. "But I thought Alice was already useful to them because of the star on her back. Leads her to the jewels or some such?"

"I may be wrong," Isabelle said. "But truly, think of it. This is a man driven by signs and magical jewels and people who bear the mark. Does it not stand to reason that he would believe her capable of acting as an oracle?"

"None of this stands to reason," Claire said, looking out over the water again. "I cannot believe I've finally arrived on the other side of the world and have yet to do any real sightseeing."

Isabelle smiled and glanced around the deck, her old habits resurfacing. People had strolled and wandered, coming to the railing and again retreating in the time that Isabelle and Claire stood there. One man, however, remained. He moved a bit but rarely more than five feet to one side and then back again. When Isabelle had routinely scanned the deck, he had seemed to be at ease, looking over the water on the other side of the ship.

He looked familiar, and that was the problem. She knew she'd never formally met the man, but his face was one she knew she'd seen over the course of a few days. He was handsome, midforties, she assumed, with a head of thick, black hair that was shot through with only just an occasional strand of gray. She remembered him because his handsome face and confident swagger were unmistakable.

Turning her attention back to the water, she gave a mental head shake. Their enemies should have known better than to send a man who didn't blend into the background to shadow them. She would scoff at his ineptitude were it not for the fact that what the man lacked in skill, he probably made up for in deadly intentions.

And she knew that because a glint of sunlight flashed on a ring he wore—a ring like the one Isabelle had in her stateroom. Furthermore, if she had to guess, she would wager that he wanted the box she had sent back to Athens with Jean-Louis.

***

Phillip brushed past the others and into the room, his heart pounding at the sight of the painting that swayed crookedly over the safe. The hotel manager stood openmouthed after a hastily silenced conversation with his assistant. A third hotel employee stood at the window, looking down into the street.

"What has happened?" Phillip asked the manager.

In the confused jumble of explanation that followed, what surfaced gave validity to the fears they'd had all along regarding Dr. Pearce's papers. Two people had broken into their room and had used a duplicate key from the front desk to open the safe. The concierge had stepped away from the desk for a moment and when he returned had become suspicious when he noticed one of the men coming out from behind the front counter and climbing the stairs.

The concierge alerted the manager, and with another employee they had surprised the burglars mere moments after they had entered the room, at which point one of the men had hastily placed the painting back over the safe and the two had made for the window and jumped to the lawn below. One of the men, according to the hotel employee who had rushed to the window, had hurt his leg in the fall and could barely run away.

Jean-Louis made his way to the window and looked out, only to have the employee shrug and tell them that the men were long gone. Phillip, meanwhile, hurried to the safe and removed the painting. "Why bother to hang this back up?" he muttered.

"We surprised the men very much," the manager said in his broken English. "They look very afraid; they put the picture back on the wall and jump out the window."

Phillip examined the safe, which was closed and locked. "Do they still have the key?" He turned and looked at the manager, whose pale expression belied his anxiety.

"I am afraid yes."

Phillip looked at Jean-Louis, his jaw tightening. "That was an unforgivably close call. We should have moved the things days ago when we first considered it." Turning to the hotel employees, who had gathered miserably by the door, he thanked them for their help and told them he would like to make a formal police report.

Nodding, the men left the room and closed the door quietly behind them. The silence that followed was prolonged and painful. Phillip pulled a key from his vest pocket and inserted it into the safe. For one horrified moment he envisioned the safe empty, but with a fair amount of relief, he noted that the documents, black journal, alabaster box, and stone were still in place.

"We can't leave the things in there," Sally said, removing her gloves with a frown and making her way to the safe. Peering inside, she studied the contents for a moment before turning to Helene. "What would you suggest?"

Helene frowned. "Elysia used to say that valuables were better hidden under rocks than locked in someone's safe. Are these things going to be protected anywhere?"

"I myself, would suggest the bank." Jean-Louis caught Phillip's eye. "We clearly can't leave them here in the hotel. I do not believe they would be protected even in the main lockbox inside the offices downstairs."

Phillip rubbed the back of his neck, closing and locking the safe, all the while wondering why he even bothered. The thought that they should have moved to a different hotel altogether had plagued him since Alice's abduction; their enemies had found them at their current location though. What were the odds that they could move about the city undetected?

Helene sank down onto the sofa, rubbing her forehead with a weary sigh. "Elysia would say it is the King's Men at work."

"What do you believe?" Sally asked.

Helene dropped her hand and looked at each of them. "At this point, I'm afraid she would have been correct. I cannot imagine who would stand to gain from robbing the safe other than those who search for the jewels. The King's Men have many eyes, and I am not necessarily surprised that they have been following your activities."

"But what do they *want* with the jewels?" Sally said over her shoulder as she hung up her bonnet and returned to sit next to the other woman. Phillip stood to her side and placed a hand on her shoulder, his thoughts churning with worry over the items in the safe and concern that he wouldn't be able to keep Sally from harm. She placed a hand on top of his and patted it as though in reassurance.

Jean-Louis looked thoughtful, pensive. "They want the jewels to open the treasure trove," he said. "Do you remember what Elysia said? The stones lead to the treasure's location."

Phillip gaped at him. "The jewels will provide access to the princess's hidden fortune? I don't think I caught that part. No wonder people are willing to kill for them. All this time I thought they wanted the jewels for the value inherent in them alone."

Helene frowned a bit. "I do remember Elysia saying that." She looked back at Phillip and Jean-Louis. "There are moments when she was much more lucid than others."

"And how would you have defined that moment?" Jean-Louis asked.

"Lucid. Amazingly enough, I believe she may have been correct."

***

Isabelle paid the innkeeper, a proprietress of a tiny lodging place at Delphi, and thanked her for securing them a room despite the sudden influx of travelers to the city. The inn was simple and rustic but clean. The farmer who had given them a ride from the dock in his donkey cart told them it was where all the Europeans stayed. They pieced this much together with their Greek-to-English phrase book. They just smiled and nodded when they didn't understand him.

The main floor consisted of a small reception area with doorways that branched off into a dining room and kitchen. There was one bedroom at the inn, apparently, that wasn't spoken for, and it was on the second floor. It was unfortunate that Isabelle would have to share a room with her sister and "brother-in-law," but what else was to be done? Isabelle agreed with the woman and thanked her again.

"Congratulations, you two are now a married couple," she murmured to Jack and Claire as she joined them near the stairs. "And I am intruding on your marital bliss. We all must share a room."

Claire gaped at her while Jack seemed to accept the news with an equanimity that spoke of a man who had certainly been in worse scrapes. He grinned at Claire and offered her his elbow. "My lady," he said.

Claire stared at his arm for a moment before narrowing her eyes. "It is I who should offer you an arm. I doubt you'll be able to climb these stairs."

"Nonsense. I am healing at an amazingly rapid rate."

"You are not. It was all we could do to help you down the gang-plank."

Isabelle picked up her bag with one hand and hefted Jack's in the other. "Up," she ordered the arguing couple. "We have plans to make."

Claire picked up her own bag and took Jack's arm, only to support his weight as they climbed the stairs. Isabelle couldn't discern the exact nature of Claire's muttered comments as they made their way to the second floor, but she was fairly certain she heard the phrase "taking advantage of your situation." Jack's answering response was tinged with humor he didn't even bother to hide. Were it not for his pale complexion and an occasional wince of pain, Isabelle might have thought he was putting on an act.

They made their way to the room, which was far enough down the hallway to avoid the hustle of the lobby and busybodies who might wonder why the husband and wife acted so strangely around each other.

Who knew, though? Perhaps they wouldn't raise suspicion at all. Isabelle smiled as she looked over the room and spied a sofa that would serve Jack well enough.

"What are our plans, then?" Claire said as she placed her bag on the bed.

Isabelle set down Jack's and her luggage and stretched. "I'd like to go out and get the lay of the land. Look around, familiarize myself with the town, and perhaps ask a few discreet questions. Maybe someone has seen a crazy, green-eyed man and a native Greek dragging around a terrified British girl."

"More likely an angry British girl," Jack said and sank down onto the sofa with a mild grunt. "I don't imagine Alice remaining terrified for long."

Claire frowned. "Do you suppose they would really parade her around during daylight? I should think she might scream or raise a ruckus."

Isabelle shook her head and made her way to the window, scanning the ground below and weighing the possibility of jumping without breaking another leg. "They are clever—at least Sparks is. He knew just how to threaten Phillip, who is easily twice his size, to not only keep him from alerting anyone, but to keep him from even thinking of running away."

"What on earth did he say?"

"Threatened Phillip's mother with all kinds of horrible things. Promised that if Phillip didn't do exactly as he said, he would go back to Utah and do his worst."

Claire made a noise of disgust and opened her bag. After dipping a clean handkerchief in medicinal alcohol and rubbing her hands with it, she withdrew a small container that Isabelle had come to recognize as a salve Claire routinely put on Jack's wound. Jack must have noticed her intent, because he groaned and squirmed to rise from the sofa as Claire approached with an assortment of supplies.

"Sit," she ordered and began to remove Jack's suit coat.

"Honestly, woman, that stuff smells foul."

"It does not. It smells medicinal."

"Yes. Foul."

Claire gave him a flat look and pulled his shirt from his trouser waistband. He slapped her hands with a scowl and pulled the fabric free himself.

"It's preventing infection," Claire told him as she examined his side once he'd lifted his shirt.

"And it stings."

Isabelle smiled and moved to Claire's side so as to get a better view of the wound as Claire unwrapped the dressing. "It is a sad day indeed to see a man brought so low. I don't believe I heard you complain this much after being shot. Either time." Isabelle looked closely as Claire gently probed the edges of the wound with her fingertip.

"That speaks volumes, does it not?" Jack clenched his teeth together as Claire gently cleaned the area with another cloth dipped in alcohol.

"It does look better, Claire," Isabelle said, impressed. "Where did you find that salve?"

"It's better if he doesn't know."

"What do you mean by that?" Jack twisted to look at Claire's face.

"Sit up straight; you're compressing things."

Jack looked up at Isabelle, his eyes wide.

Isabelle shrugged. "I'm sure it's fine, Jack. If anything, I believe you're healing more quickly than last time. I'm going to go walk around a bit outside while you finish."

Claire nodded. "Come back when you're done, and we can make plans for dinner."

"You do realize I have the full backing of my government," Isabelle heard Jack tell Claire as she turned to leave the room. "If I come to harm at your hands, it's likely to cause an international incident."

Claire's answering snippet had Isabelle laughing to herself. "We've dealt with you before. Perhaps you've not noticed that in my country we do not salute the Union Jack."

22

SALLY LOOKED AT PHILLIP AND Jean-Louis as she and Helene ate dinner with the men in the hotel restaurant. She decided there was no time like the present to plead her case. "Helene and I need to get into Demitrios's basement."

As she had anticipated, both men paused in their eating, forks poised midair. "Why?" Phillip finally said before placing his food carefully in his mouth.

"We know what to look for," Helene answered for Sally.

"We also know what the tapestry looks like," Jean-Louis said. "I do not favor the idea of the two of you wandering around in the museum alone."

Sally lifted a shoulder. "If we're alone, there really is no risk at all, and if you and Phillip keep watch outside or upstairs, we shall be fine."

"Sally," Phillip said, "I cannot in good conscience condone something that might bring you harm. There's no need for you or Helene to place yourselves in such a position when Jean-Louis and I are better equipped to handle the unexpected."

Sally felt her veneer begin to crack. "Phillip," she said, leaning in close, "I will not sit in the hotel room with a guard at the door when I should be out doing something productive. I know exactly what that tapestry looks like—I think about it all the time. I dream about it. I could describe it in minute detail to you right now. If the companion tapestry is in the museum, Helene and I will find it." She sat back in her chair, relaxing the death grip she held on her fork. "Besides, my gun will stop an assailant just as easily as will yours."

"The hope is that we can avoid shooting anyone at all," Phillip said.

"Alice is gone," Sally hissed, feeling her nostrils flare and her face heat. "I may never see her again. I will not sit under lock and key any longer." She glanced at Jean-Louis and felt a pang of regret at her choice of words when she saw the muscle work in his jaw before he finally took a drink, followed by a deep breath.

"Sally, that is precisely the reason you need to remain under protection," Jean-Louis said quietly. "One of you missing is enough."

"Jean-Louis, you are not hearing what I am saying—" Sally began.

Phillip held up his hand and seemed, for a moment, very much like his older brother—and not just in appearance. "I understand," he said. He looked at her with his blue eyes, and her heart tripped in her chest. "I understand, but I don't like it."

He wiped his mouth with his napkin and sat back in the chair, nodding once. "The four of us will go to the museum, Jean-Louis and I will keep Demitrios distracted, and the two of you . . . " He took a deep breath and shook his head once. "The two of you will go down into the basement."

***

Isabelle, Jack, and Claire returned to their room after dinner in the inn's dining room. Isabelle checked the purse that attached to the waistband of her skirt to see that her small pistol was still in place. She hadn't bothered with her Greek clothing—the small town was so overrun with tourists that she decided she might stand out more trying to look like a native.

"I do not relish the idea of staying behind while you two go out," Claire told Jack and Isabelle. "Do you really need someone to remain here at the room, or are you merely trying to keep me from harm? Or from interfering?"

Isabelle exchanged a glance with Jack and wondered at the wisdom of trying to fool her perceptive sister. "Truthfully, my first thought was to keep you safe. If you remain here, I will worry less. These men we are chasing—they are not pleasant. They are rash and ignorant but regrettably clever."

"I do appreciate that," Claire said, remarkably unruffled. "I must ask though—do you intend to separate?"

Isabelle looked at Jack, who answered, "The two of us?"

Claire nodded.

"Most likely," Isabelle said.

"Then might I suggest that you will need help," Claire said to Jack. "I hate to offend your masculine sensibilities, but you are not maneuvering well on your own."

"I do not think you hate to offend my masculine sensibilities at all."

Isabelle pursed her lips. "She may have a point, Jack. I don't know though, Claire. I would never forgive myself if you were hurt."

"We went to the ruins at Olympia at night," Claire pointed out.

"But I knew Sparks had already left the area."

"You're forgetting I wandered the same streets you did all those years ago."

Isabelle chewed on her lip for a moment, and when Jack opened his mouth to say something, she said, "Very well. You may accompany Jack."

"Isabelle!"

"Jack, it makes sense."

A muscle worked in the handsome Scot's jaw. "I am not at my best—if I can't take care of myself, I certainly cannot keep someone else safe. We may as well remain here."

"I would come along to aid you, Jack, not the reverse," Claire said to him as he wandered to the window with the help of his cane and looked out over the darkening countryside. "It seems to me that when dealing with men who aren't averse to shooting people, you are living on borrowed time. You need to find this girl, and I am not seeking to tag along merely to have an adventure. I would just as easily stay here in front of the fire and read a novel. You need help."

Jack winced at her mention of Alice, and Isabelle tightened as well. Her sister was right; they didn't have much time left.

Jack nodded. "So be it."

Isabelle gave him a quick look to be sure she still detected the ridge of his weapon holster under his jacket. "We need to remember that James is here as well," she said, shrugging into a light cloak and grateful that winters in Greece were mild in comparison to the northern United States. "I telegrammed Phillip when we arrived, apprising him of our location. I'm hoping to hear back from him soon and that he has James's address."

Jack nodded and absently checked his weapon before making his way to his bag and retrieving a small box of extra bullets, which he placed in his suit coat pocket. Rotating his head, he said, "I have a sudden urge to find a priest."

"Nonsense," Claire said, pulling on her shawl and fitting her gloves into place. "There will be time enough for confessing when you're an old man."

Jack shook his head. "I'm beginning to believe the grim reaper is camped out on my doorstep."

"Well then, he can wait a bit longer. There are plenty of others he can visit, I'm sure." Claire turned to Isabelle. "What are you thinking we should do first?"

"You could ask me that, you know," Jack said.

Claire turned her attention back to him. "Very well. What are *you* thinking we should do first?"

"I thought I would follow Isabelle's lead."

Isabelle laughed. "Now that's a first. When have you not had an opinion on our tactics?"

Jack grinned. "I know I'm safe in suggesting it because I'm fairly certain we are of one mind."

"Go to the ruins."

He nodded. "Indeed. I suspect at some point we will find those idiots trying to hold her over the steam crack in the temple. Stands to reason they would do it after dark."

***

Sally watched to be sure Phillip and Jean-Louis had fully engaged Demitrios in conversation before she and Helene escaped out of the main room's back exit and onto a landing that pointed to staircases leading both up and down.

"Does he live upstairs?" Sally whispered to Helene as they approached the wooden railing that bore chipped paint and years of wear.

"No, he lives around the corner," Helene answered as she glanced up the stairs before moving to descend those leading to the basement. "I'm not certain what he keeps up there. Might be his offices, I suppose."

"If that's the case, I would assume he's already checked up there for the tapestry," Sally whispered as they slowly crept down to the basement, which lay entirely in darkness.

"He's convinced it's not here," Helene answered softly, running a hand along the wall as she led the way into the blackened void at the end of the last stair. "We may be on a fool's errand."

"It must be here," Sally said. "What are the odds the one tapestry would be by itself?" Sally had searched the shelf in the main room where she had found the first tapestry but to no avail.

"I don't know," Helene murmured, inching her way down a hallway. "The stones are not together though."

"Hmm. There is that," Sally said, feeling slightly deflated. She had been so certain they would find the tapestry.

"But we'll not know until we look," Helene said, her voice lifting in what Sally was sure was a sense of forced optimism for her sake. "Do you have your candle?"

"I do. Is it safe to light it now, do you suppose?"

"I believe so. I cannot even see my hand before my face."

Sally withdrew a small candle from her purse and struck a lucifer match to light it. The resulting glow was a comfort but also disconcerting because the light it provided around them only made the blackness beyond seem more pronounced.

"Here is a door." Helene ran her fingers down the dark wood until she found the doorknob and glanced back at Sally. "Shall we hold our breath?"

Sally was holding her breath already, and she nodded in response. "I can pick the lock if we need to, but it's been a while," she whispered. Isabelle had taught her the skill as a way to pass the time when Sally had been recovering from a nasty illness in Virginia.

Sally closed her eyes as Helene turned the doorknob. The opening door sounded loud in the silence, and Helene paused and held it open only a scant inch before slowly easing it forward. Sally winced as the hinges creaked, sure Demitrios would come storming down the stairs.

The space between the door and the frame was finally wide enough to allow them entrance, and Sally stepped in first, holding the candle high. When Helen followed her inside, Sally chewed on her lip for a moment while she debated whether or not to close the creaky door. If they left it open and someone came downstairs, they would see the flickering light of the candle within the darkness as surely as if the women announced their presence and invited the world to enter.

"If we hear someone on the stairs," she finally whispered to Helene, "I will extinguish the flame."

Helene nodded her approval and took a look around the room. From what Sally could see, it was densely packed with pieces of furniture, both large and small, stacked to the ceiling; shelves upon shelves of tapestries; papers; and shadows that looked like an odd assortment of statuary and pottery.

Sally took a deep breath and looked at Helene, who was examining the room with a furrowed brow. "Where should we start?" she asked the older woman.

Helene absently placed a hand on her hip and with the other tapped a fingertip against her lip. "We should begin with the shelves on the far wall to the right and do our best to quickly go through the room. Clearly he has not had a woman anywhere near this building in quite some time," she said with a shake of her head.

"Has he never married?" Sally asked as she led the way to the wall Helene had indicated.

"No. He was promised to a young woman when he was younger, but she left the country with her parents and never returned."

Sally sniffed the air. "Do you smell something?"

"What does it smell like?"

"An extinguished flame."

"Perhaps from when you blew out the match."

Sally nodded and squinted in the dim light as they approached a series of shelves that were stacked from floor to ceiling with fabrics of all shapes and sizes. Helene exhaled a quick breath and began at the bottom shelf, flipping through ends of tapestries, draperies, half-finished samplers, and woven fabrics.

They systematically made their way from floor to ceiling, right to left, trying to be as thorough yet quick as possible. A couple of well-placed boxes served as footstools for those things that lay high and out of reach. Sally was relieved as she monitored the candle closely that there would be plenty of wick to spare yet silently cursed each time she tipped it slightly and dripped hot wax onto her hand. One good thing was that the bulk of the tapestries and fabric were varying shades of brown. If they looked carefully enough, the blue just might stand out.

Five minutes turned into ten and then twenty. They had worked into a good rhythm when Sally heard a noise—barely a whisper of sound— from the far side of the room. She touched Helene's shoulder, not sure if she wanted the noise to be a human or a creepy-crawly animal. Her heart pounding in her throat, she bent close to the woman's ear and whispered, "I don't think we're alone."

23

HELENE GRASPED SALLY'S ARM FROM her crouched position at a lower shelf and stared at her, her eyes wide. "Are you sure?" she mouthed the words.

Sally nodded and motioned over her shoulder before quickly extinguishing the candle, plunging the room into complete blackness. Again placing her lips next to Helene's ear, she whispered, "I heard a noise in the corner."

Helene stood and drew Sally's arm through hers, pulling her close. The older woman began moving toward the back of the room, and Sally felt a moment of panic as instinct screamed at her to make her way for the door, which she knew was still open a crack. She pulled against Helene, her breathing accelerating until the woman again drew her in close and placed a hand across her mouth. "Listen," Helene whispered almost soundlessly against Sally's ear, and Sally made an effort to calm herself, nodding.

The silence was so pronounced it roared, and Sally felt her nerves stretch taut to the breaking point. Perhaps she had imagined the noise? How silly if there was nothing in the room but maybe a mouse. One minute turned into two and then became three. Sally resigned herself to the fact that she had likely been imagining things when something brushed against an item on the shelf near the front of the room. Whatever it was crashed to the floor, and the sound was followed by a muffled exclamation of frustration.

Helene slowly began to work her way along the back wall, pulling Sally with her an inch at a time. The darkness was suffocating—Sally breathed slowly in through her nose and out through her mouth and tried to keep from shrieking in terror and running like a madwoman for the door. She tried to imagine what Isabelle would do, and she figured that Isabelle would think carefully before doing anything rash.

Very well. She could think carefully. She began to see the reason in Helene's retreat to the back of the room as she heard another whisper of sound approaching the front corner of the room where they'd been working. Whoever was in the basement with them must have figured they would run for the door

Helene continued moving, inching her way with a firm grip on Sally's arm. The darkness felt thick against her skin. She imagined someone coming upon her from behind, and she breathed in through her nose, feeling the terror bubble up inside her throat as she bit back a scream.

They had walked through the abyss for what seemed an eternity before Sally heard a light thump as Helene stopped abruptly. She heard Helene exhale as the older woman turned them ninety degrees and up along the far wall of the room. A shuffling sound along the back wall had her heart tripping over itself, beating ever faster as she felt the other person in the room following their progress.

Helene increased her speed, and Sally lifted her skirt to avoid tripping over it, hoping that if Helene was holding her other arm out to avoid hitting anything that she wouldn't fall on her face. It wasn't long before Helene stopped again; this time her hand connected with something on one of the rickety shelves, and it fell to the ground with a crash. A small cry escaped Sally's lips as Helene tripped over the object that had fallen, taking Sally down with her in the process.

Sally opened her mouth to scream when she heard the other person moving up the middle of the room, another low, muffled curse as he apparently connected with something solid and then opened the door. From the faint light beyond, she caught sight of the large shape of a man just before he exited the room and closed the door behind him. The sound of a key in the lock had her gasping as she scrambled to her feet and fought her way through the debris on the floor to where she'd seen the door. Smacking her palms flat against it, she groped for the doorknob and turned it, rattling it as though her efforts would somehow force the lock open.

She heard a scrape to her right and looked at Helene as a match flared to light, eventually coming to rest on the wick of the candle she held in her hand. Helene stood and walked gingerly over what Sally could only assume was broken pottery, handing Sally the purse she'd dropped when she ran for the door.

"At least we still have light," Helene said and brushed dust and dirt from the bodice of her dress.

"What are we going to do?" Sally whispered. She'd been locked inside an ancient Egyptian tomb, but that hadn't been as horrifying as this was because she'd been unconscious for some of it, and besides, Isabelle had been with her. Sally doubted Helene could pick a lock.

Sally stared at the other woman. "*I* can pick a lock," she said, feeling some of her courage return.

Helene regarded her for a moment, and Sally sensed the tapping of her foot. "I think that while we're in here, we ought to take advantage of it."

"No! Whoever was in here will come back!"

"I don't think so. Not right away at least." Helene again took hold of Sally's arm and quickly moved back to the wall where they'd been. She held the candle aloft as she began quickly scanning the tapestries and fabrics stacked on the shelves. "Whoever was in here wasn't supposed to be, any more than we are. I think he locked the door to keep us from following and discovering who he was."

"But suppose he tells Demetrios we are down here?"

"Then he will be forced to admit that he was too. Someone with Demitrios's permission to be in this room wouldn't be scouring about in the dark with a tiny candle. As we are. That was probably why you smelled the extinguished flame when we neared the back of the room. He must have blown out his own candle when we opened the door."

Sally nodded reluctantly as she joined in Helene's rapid search, despite her misgivings. "We should have brought a lantern. I don't know, Helene. We can hardly see anything. This may be a lost cause."

"We must try," Helene said, holding the candle closer to the shelves to better see the fabric. "We may not find another opportunity." Working in tandem, they finished the first wall, pulling out pieces of tapestry that appeared to be the least little bit blue or gray.

The shelves along the back wall contained statuary, pottery, and various shards in differing shapes and sizes. Helene moved to the other side wall where they'd so recently run and said over her shoulder, "The only other fabric in this room is along these shelves. See?" She held the candle out as she walked, shielding the flame with her hand and showing Sally that the interior shelves and tables filling the center of the room contained objects of wood, plaster, and glass.

Sally followed the flickering light as it moved down the room, fearing the dark enough to scurry quickly after Helene to avoid being left alone. Another ten minutes of quiet, rapid searching finally led to a small scrap of pale blue, just protruding from a pile of cloth on a low shelf.

Helene lifted the stacks above it and pulled it out, sucking in her breath as she held it closer to the flickering light. It was a stitched depiction of a volcano erupting in fury, black smoke rising in the air and lava cascading down into the deep blue threads of the sea.

"It's similar in style," Helene breathed as she moved the tapestry through her fingers to examine the picture. "And size as well."

Sally squinted as she took one end of the fabric and held it taut so they could examine it, carefully maneuvering the candle closer, when she noticed a white-threaded square outline just below the surface of the water against the side of the volcano that stretched down to the ocean floor. In the square were three ovals—one purple, one orange, and one blue.

Helene noticed it too and stared at Sally, her mouth open. After the space of a few heartbeats, she blinked and closed her mouth. "We cannot let this out of our sight." She folded it carefully and motioned for Sally's purse, which Sally opened with one hand, fumbling awkwardly until Helene helped her. Placing the fabric gently inside the purse, she closed the snap and handed it back to Sally.

Sally opened the purse, fishing around for the small box Isabelle had given her. "I need my tools."

"Tools?"

"Yes. To pick the lock."

Carefully tiptoeing around broken glass and pottery on the way to the door, Sally bent to the lock and began working at it. A few moments later, she heard a satisfying click. With a grim smile, she straightened and looked at Helene then closed her eyes and carefully turned the knob.

***

As Isabelle, Jack, and Claire left the inn, Isabelle pulled her cloak collar tight about her neck against the cold. She had felt chilly and tired all evening, and being outside in the temperamental weather only seemed to exacerbate her discomfort. With a frown, she gathered her thoughts together.

From the innkeeper, she had learned that the ruins of Delphi were located exactly under their feet. Archaeologists were excavating to prove what local lore had insisted all along—that the town itself was built atop an ancient one that had contained beautiful temples and structures to commune with the gods.

"Supposedly," she said as she looked down over the town from their vantage point midway up the hillside, "archaeologists are petitioning the government to move this entire town so excavations can begin in earnest."

"I wonder how the residents feel about it," Claire said as she buttoned her coat up to her neck.

"According to our innkeeper, some are in the process of selling their property, but others refuse to move."

"Did she say where the oracle performed her magic?" Jack asked.

"Up." Isabelle pointed at the pathway that led upward, noting that the moonlight illuminated a few of the ruins that had already been unearthed—the tops, anyway. Much of the buildings' structures were still under the ground. "But she's not entirely sure. It's what the locals believe though, and there are pillars up there that some people insist belong to the Temple of Apollo."

"Does the steam still come up from the ground?" Claire asked as they began their walk up the path that twisted serpentine across the hillside.

Isabelle shook her head. "No, and some suggest that there never was any credibility to the steam theory."

Jack frowned. "Credible or not, legend holds that it came from the Temple of Apollo, so I would assume that will be where we find the crazy men and Alice."

Claire looked up the path as they continued climbing. "And do we have a plan should we happen upon them?"

Isabelle also cast her gaze upward, wondering who, if anyone, they would find behind the homes and small establishments that dotted the hillside. The buildings were clustered together in some places and standing sentinel beside recently excavated relics in others. When they reached the position on the path where the temple's pillars protruded from the ground, she felt a stab of disappointment that there was nobody else around.

The temple foundation was in the shape of a large rectangle, boasting pillars in two of the four corners. Between the tall pillars, along what must have surely been the outer walls, were other pillars, whose tops had been broken, standing at varying heights above the dirt that entombed them. One corner of the structure was roped with thin twine and staked into the ground in a manner that was reminiscent of archaeological plots she'd seen in Egypt. Someone was definitely trying to unearth the ancient temple, and she wondered how long it would be before the government supported the decision to move the town. As she looked over the hillside,

Isabelle noted several buildings in various states of recovery, their pillars a dim white in the darkening light of the sky. When it was excavated in its entirety, Delphi would be a sight to behold.

Claire's line of thought must have mirrored her own; Claire drew in a breath as she too cast her eye over the town and down the hillside. "I do believe that might be an amphitheater," she breathed, pointing to a bowl-shaped area down below the streets of the small town. "This is incredible."

Lights flickered inside the town's buildings as the darkness continued to fall. The countryside was awash in a sense of cozy ambience, yet the brush of cold wind against her face had Isabelle shuddering. Clouds were gathering, and she watched with a sense of foreboding as the dark wisps moved over the face of the moon. The world was hushed, and in the space of a few heartbeats, the coziness was replaced with a chill that had nothing to do with the weather.

At the base of the hill was a small street lined with homes that remained dark, as though the occupants were either out or already bedded down for the night. A series of shadows entered the home second from the end—Isabelle counted what she believed to be at least four people approaching from the side, but she was high up on the hill and the light from the moon was growing increasingly dim by the moment. She blinked, wondering if she'd seen anyone at all, and when the house remained dark, she frowned and pursed her lips in thought.

"Did you see that?" Jack murmured beside her, and Isabelle glanced at him, following his gaze to the house in question.

"Thought I was imagining it," she admitted. "How many did you count?"

"I can't be certain. Five?"

"Where?" Claire whispered, straining her eyes against the dark.

"There," Isabelle said and pointed, and even as she did so, another two shadows crossed from the other side of the dusty street and approached the front of the house, from which point Isabelle lost the visual. When she didn't see the shadows continue down the street, she was left to assume they'd also entered the building.

"They could just be locals," Claire said, hushed.

"They could. But it seems rather odd that they would approach in groups, silently and under the cover of darkness. And light no candle inside."

"There," Jack said as the tiniest sliver of light shone from one of the rear windows facing them. "The curtains must be drawn." As though someone inside had heard his comment, the sliver vanished almost as quickly as it had appeared. The light had either been extinguished or the curtains pressed more closely to the window frame.

Isabelle slowly began descending the path, her eyes focused on the house, now almost entirely invisible as the moonlight was completely obliterated and the first fat drops of rain began to fall. Jack and Claire fell into step behind her, and Isabelle turned to Jack as they continued down the mountainside.

"I will approach the house and listen at the window," she told him. "You and Claire stay back in the trees and watch."

Jack made a sound as though he might argue but seemed to change his mind and instead said, "Very well. And if you're discovered—do you intend to enter the house, or would you rather we stop it before it progresses that far?"

"I'll go in," she said, flipping her cloak hood up and over her head, feeling the weariness hit again and wishing she could just return to the inn and crawl into bed.

"I don't suppose you'll let me devise a different plan for you," Claire muttered as she too covered her hair and pulled her scarf closer about her chin.

"I will take care," Isabelle said. "And if they threaten to kill me, I'll tell them I have information about the oracle."

By the time the trio reached the bottom of the hill and approached the street, the rain was falling steadily, gusting with cold blasts that had Isabelle clenching her teeth. Jack cursed under his breath as his cane slipped in a puddle of mud and Claire pulled him to her side, wincing when he groaned in pain. Isabelle considered telling her sister to bodily force the man back to their inn, but she knew he would never go.

Waiting until they were secreted in a copse of trees at the rear of the house, she finally approached it from the side, quickly making her way through the rain. The noise of raindrops hitting the roof of the house, the trees, and the packed dirt around the base of the house made it impossible for Isabelle to hear anything that might have been said inside as she leaned next to the window where they'd seen the brief glimpse of light. She gritted her teeth in frustration and crept around the side and out of Claire and Jack's line of sight.

Stopping at the windows by the front, darting past the door, and creeping to the corner of the house, she was very nearly around to the other side when an arm circled her waist from behind and a hand clamped down over her mouth.

24

SALLY AND HELENE REACHED THE main floor of Metaxas's museum without incident and heard Jean-Louis and Phillip conversing rather loudly with Demitrios. As Sally peered around the corner, she caught Phillip's eye. With a quick motion of his head, he indicated the front door, and Sally and Helene slipped behind Metaxas, who was gesturing wildly and speaking to Jean-Louis in rapid-fire Greek.

Night had fallen and was thick upon the city. Sally pushed the museum door open and stepped out into the fresh air, breathing deeply for the first time in over an hour. Her relief was short-lived; a man stepped from the shadows, and she saw the glint of a knife blade just before he pressed it to her side and pulled her with him away from the building.

"Your purse," the man said in heavily accented English.

"No, I—" Sally gasped as the knife point pierced her skin through her dress and the layers of underclothing beneath it.

Helene followed them as the man dragged Sally to the side of the building, which was hidden from the street with trees and brush. Helene called out loudly and rushed to Sally's side, pulling her away from the man.

Sally cried out as she felt the knife slip deeper into the flesh between her ribs.

The man barked something at Helene in Greek, and Helene stopped for a moment, torn. He repeated his phrase, and Helene, her face a mixture of anger and horror, dropped Sally's arm. Helene snarled something at Sally's assailant, and he laughed shortly then issued another sharp command.

"Give him the purse," Helene told Sally.

Sally stared dumbly at the woman, her mind a myriad of tumbling thoughts. She finally focused on the one giving her the most grief. "Tell him to remove the knife from my side and I will give him the purse."

The man issued what must have been a threat, for Helene blanched, her pallor clear in the light that filtered through the trees from a full moon. "Now, Sally, or he will push the knife in completely."

Sally handed the man her purse, making eye contact with him briefly before he snatched the bag from her hand and sharply withdrew the knife. She gasped and put her hand to her side, sick at the warmth she felt spreading over the fabric of her dress. The assailant turned and ran through the trees to the back of the museum.

Helene caught Sally as she began a slow descent to the ground, shock wreaking havoc on any logical thought. "I'm bleeding," she murmured as Helene hauled her up against her side and, drawing Sally's arm about her neck, bodily dragged her back around to the front of the museum, where she promptly began screaming for Phillip and Jean-Louis.

***

Isabelle was satisfied to hear a muffled grunt from the man who had grabbed her from behind as she jammed an elbow back into his midsection. His grip loosened enough that she turned and tried to catch herself midstomp when she realized who the man was.

"James!" She couldn't help her hiss of surprise, and her aborted attack on his instep was only partially effective—she still slammed into the side of his foot with her heel. "Are you insane?" she whispered furiously in his ear as he bent over double.

Grabbing his arm, she began running for the trees at the back of the property where Jack and Claire were hidden. He followed quickly, to his credit, and once they were safely out of sight, she risked a look back at the house. To her immense relief, it was quiet; if anyone inside had heard them, they hadn't come outside to investigate.

The trees offered some protection from the cold wind and rain but not much. Isabelle gripped James's upper arms and stared at him in shock. He returned her gaze, breathing heavily and rubbing his midsection.

"You fool!" she whispered. "I was preparing to shove your nose into your brain!" She threw her arms around his neck in a rush, and he gathered her close, lifting her into the air.

"I'm glad you didn't," he said in her ear as he set her back on the ground.

"Why didn't you just show yourself?" Isabelle's hood had fallen back, leaving her face exposed to the weather. She blinked raindrops out of her eyes and examined him, drinking in the sight and realizing how much she'd missed him.

"I was hoping to whisper quickly enough in your ear that it was just me," he said, running a hand through his sodden hair and shaking the rain off his hand. "You move too fast."

Jack lightly cleared his throat. "Claire," he murmured, "this is Isabelle's fiancé, James Ashby."

James turned to Jack and Claire, who he seemed to be noticing for the first time, and stared at Claire with his mouth open. Looking at Isabelle and back again at Claire, he shook his head slightly.

"There are two of you?" he said to Isabelle.

"You've heard me speak of my sister. She came all this way to see me."

James drew his brows in confusion as he extended a hand first to Claire and then to Jack. "Good to see you're well," he told the other man.

Jack nodded his head and then gestured toward the house. "We will explain everything later. Who's in there?"

James turned back and looked at the house as though remembering his purpose for being out in the rain, and the three gathered close to him to hear over the storm that was building in intensity with every passing moment.

"I was hoping Alice would be in there," James said, "but I don't think she is. I've been looking for them, but I don't know where they're keeping her. I happened to see Kilronomos leaving a tavern up the hill and followed him here. People have been arriving for the last twenty minutes."

"Roughly how many?" Isabelle asked.

"I'm not certain, but I counted seven after Kilronomos arrived."

Isabelle chewed on her lip for a moment and looked at the house, still quiet and dark. "We wait until he leaves and then follow him," she finally said. "Presumably he'll lead us to wherever they're keeping her."

"Unless we see a repeat of our adventures in India," James muttered.

"What happened in India?" Claire asked.

Isabelle nodded slowly. "That's right. I'd forgotten—Kilronomos went to Delhi while his accomplice took Alice and Sally to Calcutta."

Claire stared at Isabelle, an incredulous frown marring her brow. "This has happened before?"

Isabelle blew out a breath and reluctantly nodded. "Unfortunately."

"And the girl is how old?"

"Seventeen." Isabelle scowled at her sister. "It's not as though we solicit this—trouble has dogged our heels since we left England for Bombay."

Jack shifted his weight and leaned heavily on his cane with a slow exhalation that he appeared to try to mask. Her mind made up, Isabelle turned to Claire. "You take Jack back to the hotel," she said. "James and I will finish here."

Jack glared at her. "Nobody is taking Jack anywhere, Isabelle; you are not my mother."

"The four of us can't follow anyone without being seen, and you need to get off of your feet. You'll be of no use to anyone if you don't heal. Besides, James and I can cover ground much more quickly by ourselves. An added benefit—we keep Claire out of harm's path."

Claire scoffed at that and turned to Jack, taking his arm and securing her hood against a fierce gust of wind. "Do you see how she does it? In one fell swoop, we are to suppose we're doing each other a favor. Manipulative. I had forgotten that about her."

Isabelle bit the insides of her cheeks as Claire turned Jack toward the path that led to the inn. James seemed to follow her line of thought when he murmured, "That's rather the pot calling the kettle black."

Isabelle looked up at him, so relieved to be with him again that it nearly dispelled the anxiety she felt over whether or not Kilronomos would lead them to Alice. James returned her perusal and put a hand behind her neck, pulling her close for a kiss that warmed her to her toes. She was about to tell James that he shouldn't be kissing her as she felt a cold coming on, but she heard a sound coming from the house. Voices? An argument?

With a finger to her lips, she crept out of the safety of the trees and ran back toward the house with James on her heels. She leaned her ear near the window, making certain to remain out of sight should someone move the curtain. There were several voices—she could hear differing tones—but was frustrated that the entire conversation was in Greek. What had she expected? For a moment, she regretted sending Jean-Louis back to Athens, although the image of him standing in the rain and eavesdropping on a conversation conducted by less than reputable men was not one she could fully form in her mind.

James had flattened himself against the wall beside her and shrugged when she glanced at him. The conversation inside flew so rapidly that she wasn't sure even Jean-Louis would have been able to follow it.

They were fine at the back of the house as long as none of the men crossed their path upon leaving. Motioning to the house next door, Isabelle nudged James, and they broke into a run through muddy puddles and rain-slicked vegetation. Once on the far side of the house next door, Isabelle collected her thoughts and hoped that the residents—if there were any—slept soundly.

"Very well," she said quietly and clasped her hands together in an attempt to warm them through her wet gloves. "The house has just the one door at the front. We'll stay here and peer around the corner. When Kilronomos leaves, we follow at a safe distance. The trick will be to follow him without the others taking notice. On any other night, we could simply be a couple out for a moonlit stroll."

James nodded in agreement, and the two crept to the front of the neighboring house, peering around the corner and settling in to wait.

"Do you remember Ari mentioning a brother?" James said in her ear as he squinted in the rain.

Isabelle shook her head. "Why? Was there something in his journal?"

"He mentions the name Adelphos in a couple of places, and when I was following him here, he seemed different than I remember."

"Different how?"

James shrugged. "Thinner."

"He may have lost weight. Being attacked by a jungle snake might have a way of doing that."

"Shorter."

Isabelle opened her mouth and then closed it again. "Hmm," she finally said.

"I don't know that I can pinpoint it exactly. But definitely different. I don't think this man is Ari."

***

Sally's side was on fire, and she gasped as the midwife placed an iodine-soaked rag against her skin. She was lying on the sofa in their hotel sitting room. When they left the museum, Helene had sent word to a midwife friend that she was desperately needed. When the woman had pronounced the girl would live, that the knife had penetrated merely an inch into her ribs and just required some stitching, Sally wasn't certain she believed it.

The police had just left, taking Helene's and her account of the incident and promising to examine the grounds outside the museum for clues to the assailant's identity. Sally also gave them a good description, through Helene, of her purse. Aside from the loss of the needlepoint, she was despondent at the thought that her lock-picking kit was gone. It had been a gift from Isabelle.

Sally noted Phillip hovering behind the woman, looking alarmingly pale. He paced a small area of the room until Helene finally told him to sit down before he fainted. "There's just so much blood," he mumbled and finally sat, leaning forward and placing his head in his hands.

"I'm fine, Phillip," Sally said, swallowing. "It hardly hurts at all."

Phillip groaned quietly but otherwise remained silent.

Jean-Louis stood slightly apart from the group, his hands in his pockets and the look on his face something Sally couldn't define. *Anger* was the closest she could come.

The midwife said something in Greek to the men, and Jean-Louis nodded. "Phillip, we need to leave so that she can attend to Sally."

Phillip raised his head, and Sally met his gaze. "I shall be fine, honestly, Phillip. Go out and get some fresh air."

Phillip nodded and rose with a sigh. Looking slightly unsteady on his feet, he made his way to the door with Jean-Louis, and Sally caught a glimpse of the police guard just before the door closed and she heard the key turn in the lock.

The midwife said something to Helene, and the two of them helped Sally to sit up enough that they were able to remove her clothing down to the light cotton chemise she wore against her skin. The fabric on her side was drenched in red, and Sally felt light-headed looking at it.

The midwife must have noticed Sally's dismay; she shushed the young woman gently and eased her back down onto the sofa, using a pair of scissors to cut the fabric away from her wound. Sally tried to imagine pleasant things, tried to picture herself somewhere beautiful and warm, but all she could conjure was the face of the man who had stolen her purse. She had seen him before, but the memory hovered on the edges and wouldn't crystallize.

Helene sat down on the floor near Sally's head and held her hand. She explained that the midwife was deadening the wound with a mixture of herbs so that Sally wouldn't feel the pain of the stitching. Suddenly, thinking of the man who had abducted her was a welcomed diversion.

"I think I know the man," she said to Helene.

"The man who did this?"

Sally nodded. "I don't remember where I've seen him. He didn't look familiar to you?"

Helene shook her head. "He was in the shadows—I couldn't see his face."

"What are we going to do? We need that tapestry." Sally felt the deadening poultice being applied to her side, and within moments the pain subsided and a blessed numbness settled in.

Helene snapped her fingers and released Sally's hand, crossing the room to her bag and returning with a notebook and pen. "We need to try and remember everything that we saw in the needlepoint."

"Oh dear. It was so dark and we didn't see much."

Helene opened the book to a blank page and began drawing a rough version of the image that had been so deftly sewed onto the fabric. She lifted her book so Sally could see it, sketching as she talked. "The volcano rose like this, and the lava spilled down the side and into the ocean." With a quick glance at the midwife, Helene continued, "And then there was this under the water about so far." She drew a rectangle with three ovals inside it.

Sally considered the drawing for a moment, wondering what kind of details they hadn't managed to see in the dark of the museum basement. She wished for a moment that they still had instant access to the other needlepoint. They had placed it and the other items from the safe in a secure lockbox at the bank down the street where they had conducted the business of currency exchange upon arriving from Egypt.

She closed her eyes, visualizing the original tapestry she had spent so much time studying. She remembered it showed the bride approaching the altar, and the right edge of the scene displayed a sandy color that ran off the edge of the fabric. Now that she had seen the other half of the entire scene, it made sense. The sand on the first image was a beach.

But why would the bride have been carrying the box in the first depiction, and then the box was under the ocean in the next? She mentioned it to Helene, who paused in her sketching and pursed her lips. She tapped the pen against the side of the book, clearly thinking.

"What was the bride wearing?" Helene asked Sally in a low tone, and Sally wondered if she was uncomfortable talking about the subject in front of the midwife even though the woman apparently couldn't understand English.

Sally frowned, trying to think in spite of the fact that, although she was numb, she still felt the pull of needle and thread through her flesh.

She suddenly felt slightly woozy. "The bride was wearing . . . was wearing a white gown and veil."

"A veil or a crown?"

"A ve—" Sally paused. "A crown?"

"We might have imagined her as a bride because she had the head-piece on, but suppose it's not a bridal headpiece?"

Sally tilted her head against the couch cushion to look at Helene. "What are you saying?"

"Suppose she's not a bride at all but a princess. We did find it odd that not only was the groom not at the altar, but he trailed behind her."

"So he wasn't a groom. Who was he, then?"

"Perhaps he wasn't friendly. We need to look at it again."

"What are you thinking?"

Helene glanced at the midwife again and then murmured, "We need to look again at the first tapestry."

25

By the time the men vacated the house next door, the storm had increased in its intensity to include flashes of lightning and ear-splitting thunder. Isabelle seriously doubted she'd ever again be warm. The dark shadows crept quietly into the night, a few of them casting furtive glances over their shoulders in a manner that Isabelle would have found comical had she not been convinced they were up to absolutely no good.

There were nine men total who left the small house and dispersed into the dark. She was certain that one of them was the same man who had followed them across the Gulf of Corinth, and she wouldn't have been surprised to see the man who had been aboard the steamer and given them his cryptic prediction about the volcano. The storm was an advantage if for no other reason than that the men turned up their collars and pulled down their hats, not noticing Isabelle and James, as they pushed against the wind to return to their homes.

James touched Isabelle's arm and pointed at a trio of men, the last to leave the meeting, who walked past the couple's position against the wall of the neighboring house. Isabelle squinted into the pounding storm, only just managing to catch the profile of the middle man when lightning flashed and temporarily lit the night. With a brief nod to James, she acknowledged seeing Kilronomos and waited until the men had reached the end of the street before darting after them, James close on her heels.

The men crossed several streets and began making their way to the very edge of the town, where a few taverns and a smattering of lodging houses sat together against the base of the hill. Isabelle knew a quick moment of terror when a bolt of lightning split the sky so near she could have sworn she heard a sizzle. It must have frightened Kilronomos and the other men as well; they quickened their pace after looking upward when the thunder crashed mere seconds after the lightning hit.

Isabelle and James took refuge behind an abandoned building as the men slowed their flight. They finally reached a nondescript house on the deserted street, and one of the men fumbled with a key in the lock, eventually shoving the door open and allowing the other man and Kilronomos to enter before him. With one last look over his shoulder, the man went into the house and closed the door firmly behind him.

Isabelle studied the home, taking in the exterior structure, the dim light shining from a window on the second floor, the lanterns that were lit on the main level a few moments after the men entered. Everything else ceased to exist as she tried to determine the best way into the house. There were no clear footholds at the front or sides of the house—no trees tall enough to see into the windows on the second floor. She might find something useful in the backyard, but with the rain still falling in buckets, anything she climbed or stood on might be too slick to hold her.

"Why don't you go back to your inn and change into something dry. I'll wait here and watch the house," James said, turning her to face him. He tugged her cloak together at the front in spite of the fact that it did absolutely no good. With a shrug, he traced her cheek with his finger and leaned down to place a quick kiss on her lips.

Isabelle shook her head. "I wouldn't be able to sit still," she told him. "Knowing that you were out here in the rain and Alice might be in that house." She chewed on her lip for a moment as she studied the house again. "I need to get inside."

James groaned and pulled her back to a small, closed shop that boasted a little front porch. Taking refuge under it, Isabelle drew a deep breath that came out in a cold shudder. They would be sick by morning if they waited outside all night in the elements. She was forced to acknowledge that she had been well on her way to illness before even leaving the inn.

"Isabelle, you are not going inside that house." James brushed ineffectually at the rain on the front of his coat, which was soaked through and smelled of wet wool.

"I need to see if Alice is in there before they offer her up as some sort of sacrificial gift to the gods. The windows on the main level have curtains covering them, and accessing the second floor is out of the question in this weather." Isabelle fought to keep her teeth from chattering, knowing full well that if James knew the extent of the chill she felt, he'd haul her up over his shoulder and forcibly take her back to the inn.

"At least let me go in to look for her, then," James said.

Isabelle looked at him with eyelids at half-mast. "James, you're as stealthy as an elephant."

He had the gall to look affronted.

"It's going to have to be me," she said. "Jack is in no condition to do any reconnaissance—or rescue, if it comes to that."

James's eyes narrowed. "I suppose Jack is stealthy."

"Well, not now. Usually, yes," she said, distracted, looking out again at the house and into the rain. Turning her attention back to James, she noted his expression and paused. "I do need your help though, James."

"Oh, do you now," he said, his tone dry as he leaned a shoulder against one of the porch's posts. "Tell me, dear, what it is that you're going to have the useless fiancé do."

A corner of her mouth quirked into a smile she fought to tamp down. "You're not useless. You're large and strong. And if Alice is in there and we awaken the men while trying to escape, I'll need you to come in, guns blazing."

"Guns blazing."

"Or fists flying."

"Why do I get the impression that you're trying to fabricate a task for me? And one that doesn't require much skill or finesse, at that?"

Isabelle smiled. "Now you're just being silly."

"No, I'm not. You think I'm a big, witless monkey."

She laughed. "If I thought for one moment you really believed that, I'd feel sorry. You know I think you're wonderful." Isabelle sobered as she looked at the face that had become so beloved to her. "I've missed you." She silently cursed as she felt her eyes sting. She never had been one for excessive emotion, and that she was as vulnerable to it as any other woman was irritating.

He reached for her and pulled her in close, and she willingly pressed her face against his soggy, scratchy overcoat. "Don't ever leave me again," he said, and she felt the words reverberate in his chest. "I cannot tell you how hard it was to leave Olympia, knowing you were only a few hours away."

She closed her eyes and tried not to tremble from the cold. For one brief moment, she wished they were far away, lounging somewhere warm and already married so she could crawl into bed beside him and consider never leaving that spot. Would it be so much to ask? With a deep sigh, she pulled away and instantly missed the contact.

Isabelle sat down on the edge of the porch, which offered paltry shelter from the storm but allowed her to dig in for the long haul as she watched the house, whose windows still glowed with lantern light. She felt James's gaze on her for a few moments before he too sat down on the wooden planks. Taking her hand in his, he stripped the wet glove from her fingers, removed his glove, and entwined his fingers with hers. He lifted their hands and kissed the back of hers, his eyes closed and soft lips lingering there for much longer than any chaperone would have deemed appropriate.

With a sigh, he tucked their hands inside his coat against his heart and, with Isabelle, watched the house.

***

Jean-Louis observed as Phillip stood for the third time and wandered around the hotel parlor, which was just off of the main lobby. Not that he blamed the man; circumstances were spiraling out of control, and they weren't any closer to locating either jewel. Alice was enduring who only knew what. He was finding himself angry and frustrated, two emotions that had been largely foreign to him until he embarked on a crazy journey with kind people—who had befriended him and drawn him into their quest—and met a young woman who had stolen his heart with her zest for life and willingness to learn everything she could.

The night clerk at the front desk entered the parlor and handed Phillip a telegram. "This came earlier today for you, but you were out."

Phillip nodded his thanks and tore into the envelope, and Jean-Louis moved to his side to read over his shoulder. With a stab of disappointment, he read that James had made it to Delphi but hadn't yet seen any signs of Alice. His throat felt uncomfortably tight, and he wandered slowly over to the hearth, looking down into the flames.

Jean-Louis heard Phillip greet someone and turned back to see the midwife, satchel in hand. She nodded to them both and told Jean-Louis that Sally was sleeping and that she would be fine. For at least a week she was to rest, not exert herself, and limit her diet to broth and tea, with perhaps a crust of bread or biscuit.

Jean-Louis translated for Phillip, who held his hand out to the woman and grasped hers in thanks. Jean-Louis also extended his hand to her and thanked her profusely, nodding when she told him to send a messenger for her if Sally worsened. He watched the old woman leave the room, relieved for Sally's sake but still heavy hearted.

He glanced at Phillip, who was wiping his forehead with a hand-kerchief. "If they've not found Alice by tomorrow night, I'm going to Delphi," Jean-Louis told his friend. "I cannot wait here any longer."

Phillip looked at him for a few moments before finally nodding. "I understand. I wonder if you would help me do something tonight though."

"Anything. What is it?"

"First, we need to tell the guards to remain at the door upstairs for at least another hour. Then, I need *you* to stand guard outside Kilronomos's house for me."

"While you do what, exactly?"

"See if the Egyptian jewel is inside."

***

Isabelle closed her eyes briefly, unable to control the shivering that wracked her frame.

"Enough, Isabelle," James told her and began to stand, tugging on her hand. "I'm taking you back to the inn."

"No, James, wait." She pulled him back down and nodded toward the house they'd been watching for nearly ninety minutes. All the lights had been extinguished for the last half hour. "Just a few more minutes, and then I'll quickly get in and see if she's there."

"Belle, at this point you're no stealthier than I am. Look at you." He placed an arm around her shoulders and briskly rubbed her arm, gently pulling her head against his chest with his other hand. She winced as he pulled back in shock.

"You are on fire," he stated flatly. "We're leaving."

"We may not get another chance," she hissed at him, frustrated that he'd discovered she was running a temperature. Her body ached from head to toe. "James, we must do this now. I've certainly been worse off than this. I once did surveillance near a Southern spy's home for two days in a mosquito-infested swamp. The malaria I dealt with afterward wasn't particularly pleasant. "

James closed his eyes and quickly shook his head as though to dispel the image. "I thought the bulk of your work took place in ballrooms and parlors."

She hesitated. "Mostly."

He held up a hand. "I don't need to know anymore." Looking down the street at the still-dark house, he drew his brows in thought. "What are the odds they are asleep?"

She expelled a breath and rubbed her forehead, feeling light-headed. "Probably not very good—something big is happening, and I doubt they're going to rest easy."

James looked at her. "And you want me to let you go into their house."

She gave him what she hoped was a bright smile. Unfortunately, it felt sickly. "Trust me." Isabelle stood and stepped off of the porch and into the rain, which still fell steadily, hoping he didn't notice her slight wobble to the right.

Some of the clouds had shifted slightly to allow streaks of moonlight to pierce the black. The street was blessedly deserted; she wondered how many of the homes had already been vacated to accommodate the excavation of ancient Delphi. James caught up with her in two easy strides and took her hand firmly in his. Poor man—he probably still hadn't decided whether or not to bar the door when she approached it.

The house loomed ahead of her at the end of the street, her vision narrowing and expanding in a strange display of distorted reality. She blinked and focused on the building, wishing it would hold still for at least a few minutes.

They reached the home next to the one in question and stood behind the shelter of a tree that only just reached James's head. If it were light out, the sight would be laughable, and Isabelle absently wondered if people would believe she'd been a professional spy.

She reached inside her cloak and pulled out the purse attached to her waist. With fingers numb from cold, she opened it and withdrew the small lock-picking kit. James put his hands on her shoulders, and she looked up, blinking at the rain as her sodden hood dripped water onto her face.

He kissed her once, hard, and reached into his inner pocket for his gun. Pulling the hammer back, he grimly asked her, "Do you have your gun?"

She nodded and removed her outer cloak to reduce her bulk; she then unbuttoned her skirt and stepped out of it and the fluffiest of her petticoats, leaving one thin slip over her drawers. Pulling her gun from the coat pocket, she handed all of her clothing to James, who looked at her slack-jawed before closing his mouth and taking the pile of fabric.

She tied her purse at her waist again, and crossing the distance from the tree to the house, she glanced quickly up at the windows on the second floor and then down at those on the main level. Everything remained dark and still. She was torn between gratitude for the moonlight, which would help her see things better in the house, and frustration that she now glowed like a ghost in her white underclothing. With a sense of urgency, she knelt at the lock and got to work.

Blessedly, instinct ruled her hands and stilled her nerves as she began working on the lock. Rain quickly soaked through her shirt and slip; the fabric clung uncomfortably to her fevered skin. Her fingers fumbled slightly with the cold, and she was forced to repeatedly wipe water from her eyes, but she eventually heard the light click that signaled success. She opened the door by degrees, slipping inside when it was only just wide enough for her to fit.

She stood inside the house and waited for her eyes to adjust to the dark, which wasn't much worse than it had been outside. Water dripped steadily from her, and she knew she'd leave a trail through the house, but short of borrowing a towel and clothing from Kilronomos, she had no other options.

The front windows were unadorned; moonlight filtered through the sheer curtains and illuminated the interior. Immediately before her a staircase rose up against the right wall to the second floor, and to her left was a parlor. Inching her way slowly across the tiny foyer, she made her way into the parlor and crept across the room, keeping her back to the wall.

There were dying embers in the fireplace, and the room was sparsely furnished with one small settee and a chair. She continued along her quiet path, her arm bent at the elbow, the gun in her hand resting up at her shoulder. Rounding a corner, she peered into a small kitchen that was also, thankfully, empty of people. She returned through the parlor and stood for a moment at the bottom of the stairs, listening for noise on the second floor.

Ever so slowly, she placed one foot on the first stair and, keeping her back to the wall, began a methodical climb up the staircase. Taking extreme care to ease onto each wooden step, she kept a light touch as she ascended and avoided excessive noise on creaky spots.

Once at the top of the stairs, she paused and examined the landing. There were two doors, both closed, and she hesitated, wiping her brow with her wet sleeve as she continued to shiver. The gun in her hand felt slick, and she switched hands, rubbing her palm on the fabric of her slip, which was also wet. Choosing the door closest to the stairs, she placed a hand on the door handle and applied pressure by slight degrees until she felt the mechanism slide back into the door.

She leaned her forehead against the doorframe and quietly inhaled and exhaled before inching the door open enough to peer inside. The room was small and contained two beds. A quick glance at the rest of the space showed nothing else on the floor except a dresser with a lamp. Both beds held sleeping men, and she stared for a moment, trying to identify whether or not either was Kilronomos. One man shifted slightly in his sleep and snored a bit. When he moved, a shaft of light glinted off a mostly bald head, and the other man was clearly blonde. Kilronomos was a handsome Greek with a head full of dark hair. She slowly pulled the door closed and released the handle a fraction of an inch at a time.

Finally stepping back, Isabelle turned toward the other door and performed the same slow procedure again, wishing she felt normal. She wondered how she would get Alice out of the house if the girl were drugged or otherwise incapacitated. She could barely function herself.

The second room held two beds, both occupied, and a lantern on a table in between that must have been the earlier source of light. The person on the left she identified as Kilronomos; James was correct though—there was something different about him. Perhaps it was just the low light or maybe the fact that she was afraid she was hallucinating as her fever escalated, but he didn't look the same.

She turned her attention to the person in the bed on the right—the lump under the covers indicated that someone was definitely there and probably had been when the other three had been at their clandestine meeting across town. Would they have left Alice alone for any length of time? And where was Sparks?

Instinct screamed at her to leave—it was inconceivable to think that not only had the men left Alice alone in the house, but that she now calmly slept in the same room as one of her abductors. Isabelle never left stones unturned, however, and the thought of exiting without being certain that the other person wasn't Alice grated on her.

She crept quietly into the room and slowly skirted the bed, nearing a wardrobe that was situated in the corner. As she inched her way closer to the bed, her foot pressed on a floorboard that squeaked, and she froze, horrified, as the person in the bed stirred and turned upon the pillow so that she saw his face.

It was Sparks, and Isabelle held her breath and waited for him to open his eyes. He mumbled something unintelligible and tossed for another moment, causing Kilronomos to stir. With a swift drop to the floor, Isabelle hid behind Sparks's footboard and prayed both men would remain asleep.

"What is the problem?" Kilronomos muttered to Sparks, who murmured and then coughed in his sleep.

Isabelle made herself as small as possible, angled as far away as she could be from the Greek's line of sight and still remain hidden from Sparks. She didn't dare shift or try to make herself more comfortable, and soon her feet began to tingle from squatting in an awkward position.

She closed her eyes and leaned on her hand, still carefully holding the gun and grateful that she at least possessed enough wherewithal to keep from shooting herself. Her head was beginning to pound and throb behind her eyes, and she very nearly gave in to the temptation to cry.

"What is the time?" Kilronomos said, still sounding groggy but more awake.

"I do not know," Sparks mumbled.

Isabelle heard Kilronomos shuffling around in his bed and listened as something scraped across the nightstand. "It is one o'clock," he said, and she heard the audible snap of a pocket watch. "You were supposed to stand watch! Why are you in bed asleep?"

Sparks stirred in the bed, and Isabelle shrank farther into a ball, slowly inching her way across the floor as the man moved, using his noise as cover for her own.

"I only wanted to sleep for a moment," Sparks said, his voice gravelly. "I was forced to stand watch over her last night too if you'll remember."

"Shh, you'll awaken the others," Kilronomos hissed.

Isabelle slid on her behind around the corner of the bed, and as Kilronomos stood and Sparks sat up, she quickly slid underneath the bed, flattening herself as much as possible. She had an inch of room between herself and the boards beneath the mattress, and she held her breath as Sparks stood. She looked at his bare feet and wondered what he would think if he rounded the corner of his bed and realized there was a puddle of water where she'd sat dripping.

"It doesn't matter," Kilronomos said. "Just go down and be certain she's still there."

"Where is she going to go?" Sparks's tone was harsh, and he walked to the foot of the bed, grabbing a pair of pants from the bedpost and thrusting his feet into them. A rustle of fabric must have involved the removal of a night shirt and donning of his daytime attire as he stood, blessedly, away from the puddle of water at the foot of the bed.

"Do not wake the others," Kilronomos growled at Sparks, who had sat back down on the bed and shoved his feet into his shoes. "They will not be happy to realize you've left your post."

"I do not care one fig for your King's Men," Sparks whispered furiously. "This was never to have involved anyone but you and me. I've a mind to just take the girl and leave without the lot of you."

"That would not be wise, my friend. This is much bigger than you are. Make certain she is ready—we leave in one hour for the temple."

Isabelle closed her eyes briefly and offered a quick prayer of gratitude as Sparks left the room without noticing anything was amiss. She'd left the door open—she was lucky he hadn't realized that he had been the last one in the room for the night and had closed it behind him.

Kilronomos whispered what sounded like a muffled curse and walked to the door. He paused for a moment at the threshold before lifting one foot and rubbing the bottom of it on his leg. He tested the floor again, tapping his foot against it, and slowly turned, following Isabelle's path until he reached the far side of the bed where she'd scooted underneath. She turned her head awkwardly, bumping her nose on the floor, and looked out at the man's feet. What were the odds he'd just assume Sparks had gone outside and tracked the water in before going to bed? Probably not very good, and Isabelle felt a sheen of perspiration on her forehead that she wiped awkwardly with her sleeve.

The Greek walked back around to the table between the beds, and she turned her head again to follow his movement. She heard a match strike, and the clink of glass against metal signaled the lighting of the kerosene lamp. The floor soon glowed; Isabelle's eyes hurt from the sudden light, and she felt a stabbing pain in her forehead protesting the invasion. Kilronomos's feet stayed by the side of the bed for an eternity, and with agonizing slowness, he lowered himself to the floor and looked beneath the bed, setting the lamp on the floorboards.

Isabelle held her gun steady when she met his gaze. "If you don't move too quickly," she told him, "I won't shoot you."

26

JAMES STOOD OUTSIDE THE HOUSE for so long in the cold, feeling like a fool, that by the time he saw light flickering in the upstairs window, he was strung tighter than a bow. If she had found Alice or was safely hidden, he didn't want to rush into the house and ruin her efforts. He should have insisted that she give him a time limit.

A pebble bounced close to his foot, and he glanced down at it with a frown. Another followed, this one hitting him in the back of the leg, and he turned around. He saw shadows behind the house he stood next to, and when he narrowed his eyes he recognized Jack and Isabelle. No, not Isabelle. This woman had her clothes on.

Jack motioned to him, and James cast a quick glance at the upper window of the house. He then made his way quickly through mud and puddles of water to the couple hiding.

"He wouldn't stay at the inn," Claire Webb whispered with a quick gesture at Jack. "I tried."

"How did you find us?" James asked the pair and looked again back at the house.

"Us? Where is Isabelle?" Jack said, taking his hat from his head and shaking the water from it.

"She's in there," James told him, gesturing with his head as his arms were still full of Isabelle's coat and skirts.

"Naked?" Claire's brow shot high.

"More or less," James muttered. "She's been in there for over twenty minutes."

"We've been wandering all over town for the last hour," Claire murmured. "We would have walked right by you had that house not drawn our attention with the lighted window. She is inside looking for the young lady?"

James nodded. He hesitated to admit the next. "Isabelle is ill. She is running a temperature, and I'm concerned she may have bitten off more than she can chew this time." He glanced at Jack. "She doesn't listen to me."

Jack cast him a glance that looked suspiciously sympathetic. "Isabelle listens to Isabelle." He paused. "But to her credit, her instincts are expert. I've never seen the like, male or female."

James felt the hot stirrings of jealousy climb up his spine, and he tamped them back down. Gritting his teeth, he took a deep breath and glanced at Claire, who looked so much like Isabelle it gave him pause.

She smiled at him, if somewhat grimly. "She is incredibly intelligent. And far too brave for her own good," she said quietly. "Always was."

James nodded at her. "I know. And this time I am extremely concerned. I've never seen her so—" He shifted the clothing, and when Claire extended her arms, he gratefully deposited the pile of fabric into them. "I am afraid she's very sick. She won't be performing at her best. I don't know how long to wait before going in."

Jack glanced at Claire. "You see? I'm glad we came back."

James looked at the Scotsman with a flat expression and tried to maintain his calm. "I would have managed on my own."

"Of course."

"Very well then. What do you suggest?"

Jack studied the house for a moment and then opened his mouth to speak, only to interrupt himself by motioning toward the front door, where people were emerging. Three men stood at the doorway, conversing in harried tones. After much angry gesticulating, two of the men left and walked down the road, and the third went back into the house, slamming the door.

"That cannot bode well," James muttered, feeling the discomfort rise—equal parts of frustration and fear.

"It's probably time I go in," Jack said and withdrew a pistol from the holster he wore over his shoulders underneath his great coat.

"I'll go in," James said to him, already moving from the shadows and toward the house.

"Someone needs to follow those two," Jack told him as he caught his arm and pointed at the men moving quickly down the street. They were very nearly out of sight.

"You follow them," James told him. "I'm going to get Isabelle."

Claire cleared her throat. "And where would you like me to go?"

James threw a head nod toward Jack. "You'd better go with him. He can hardly walk."

Jack cursed under his breath and gestured at Claire. "Hurry then. They're almost to the corner."

James strode to the front door of the house where Isabelle was, without looking back once at Jack and Claire. They could walk to the moon, for all he cared. His focus had narrowed considerably, and he had only one aim.

***

Phillip looked at the Kilronomos home with some trepidation. The house stood vacant in the dark of the night—no lights—and as far as he and James had been able to ascertain earlier from studying the house, the Ari look-alike lived alone. There was no aged mother or grandmother, no wife or children. He licked his lips and wondered how Isabelle had ever grown accustomed to exploring people's homes without their permission.

"Very well then," he told Jean-Louis. "I will go inside, and you stay out here to make certain nobody enters the house. If someone does, send me a signal."

Jean-Louis frowned and whispered, "What sort of signal?"

Phillip ran a hand across the back of his neck. "I don't know—a bird call. Can you do a bird call?"

"What sort of bird?"

"Any bird!"

"An owl, then."

Phillip nodded. "Good. An owl." With one final look up and down the deserted Athens street, he crossed to the side of the house that he and Jean-Louis had just examined. There was a window open just an inch. Glancing across the street at Jean-Louis, who gave him a firm nod, Phillip placed his hands inside the frame and began pulling upward on the window. It moved just enough to give him hope, and he continued lifting, wincing when it creaked.

Nobody came running to sound an alarm, and he continued until the window was raised enough to allow him to slither inside. He walked his hands along the floor until the rest of his body followed and his feet touched the ground. Jumping up and dusting himself off, he looked at his surroundings and tried to make sense of the room.

Withdrawing a tin of matches and a small candle, he gave himself enough light to look around and claim his bearings. He was inside a small parlor that housed a seating arrangement around a tiny fireplace hearth. Closer inspection showed furniture that had once been expensive but was now worn and faded.

"Where would I hide a jewel?" he murmured quietly as he began walking the perimeter of the room, his hand cupped around the small flame and hoping that passersby wouldn't know Mr. Kilronomos was out of town and his home should have been empty. Phillip began checking boxes that sat displaying cigars or cuff links. Looking carefully at the hearth, he leaned down to test the ridges of bricks with his fingertips, hoping one would give way and reveal a hidden compartment. He lifted furniture cushions and throw pillows, held what few paintings there were on the walls to one side to check for an elusive safe.

Finding nothing, he continued his search through a small kitchen and two bedrooms, which were sparsely furnished, with only one bed and chest of drawers in each. Feeling a bit of daring at the fact that he'd yet to hear an owl hooting outside, he used his candle to light a lamp in one of the bedrooms.

He lifted the mattress on the bed, careful to tuck the blankets back into place, and turned to the drawers. Each held nothing more exciting than a few pair of socks, handkerchiefs, and a total of two shirt fronts. Exiting the room with a real sense of frustration, he extinguished the light and performed the same routine in the second bedroom.

The results were the same until he came to the bottom dresser drawer. Inside it were neatly stacked papers, and he withdrew them, sitting on the floor. They were letters, mostly, but written in Greek. With a sigh of frustration, he realized he would need Jean-Louis to translate, and he wasn't sure he wanted to steal the letters outright.

With a mild curse, he stood and strode from the bedroom to the front door, which he unlocked and opened, then beckoned to Jean-Louis, who still stood sentinel across the street. When the Frenchman reached the front door and hurried inside, his eyes were narrowed, and he threw up his hands as Phillip closed the door.

"What could you be thinking?" Jean-Louis whispered at him in a clear fury.

Phillip motioned for him to follow and returned to the bedroom, which was still lit by the lamp. "Read these," he said, and Jean-Louis snatched them from his hands with a glare.

Jean-Louis carried the papers closer to the light and began reading, his finger trailing over the lines of script. "I do not know every word," he said with a creased brow, "but it is a letter to one Adelphos from Ari, addressing him as his brother." Jean-Louis looked up at Phillip. "This means we are not dealing with the same man you knew in India."

"So it would seem that Ari did die that day in the jungle with Isabelle." Phillip rubbed his jaw. "What does the letter say?"

"Just that Ari believes he is on to something that would make them wealthy, that he had a client in possession of something valuable she was going to sell to a business associate in India."

"Sparks." Phillip's nostrils flared of their own volition. "Ari met him after killing Lady Banbury en route from England to Bombay, and then he insinuated himself with James and Isabelle, befriending Alice and her father. He later shot Lord Banbury and chased Isabelle into the jungle where she saw him bash his head on a rock."

"I do not understand why Lady Banbury was a client in the first place. Alice and I haven't discussed much about her parents' deaths." Jean-Louis frowned and pushed his spectacles up slightly up on the bridge of his nose, a gesture Phillip was coming to recognize as the Frenchman's contemplative tell.

"She hired Ari through people she knew in London to provide proof that her husband was being 'indiscreet,' shall we say. Ari provided the proof but killed the other woman and her child in the process. He then went after Lady Banbury in London to exact her promised payment, which she thought to gain through the sale of the Jewel of Zeus to Sparks. As we know, that never happened because her trunk was shipped to Calcutta by mistake, even as she was returning to her husband and Alice in Bombay."

Jean-Louis nodded. "And James and Isabelle found the jewel in the trunk after Lord Banbury was killed and Alice and Sally had been put aboard the ship to Egypt."

"Yes, which is where we met up with you. And you know the rest."

"But Sparks believes the Jewel of Zeus to be in India still, isn't that correct?"

Phillip nodded. "Thank the high heavens he doesn't know we have it. You were there when he took the one we found in Egypt."

Jean-Louis frowned and shuffled the papers he still held, scanning a few more. "More of the same, really. He tells Adelphos that their fortunes are about to be turned, that they would soon restore the family's wealth.

No mention of parents—we might assume they've already passed. Oh, and in this letter he tells Adelphos about the legend and the jewels in some detail."

Jean-Louis paused, his frown deepening before his eyes opened wide. "What is it?"

"Look at this—it is addressed to Adelphos, from someone other than Ari, and gives him instructions on where to begin attending meetings and . . . ceremonies . . . I believe. But look at the signature at the bottom."

Phillip moved to look at the bottom of the page over Deveraux's shoulder. The name he didn't recognize, but the symbol that accompanied it in a dripping of red wax he certainly did. "That may have been made with a ring," he said, "or a similar stamp." Running a hand through his hair, he stepped a few feet away and exhaled on a whistle.

"This means," Jean-Louis said, his voice strained, "that Adelphos Kilronomos is one of the King's Men. And he has Alice."

27

ISABELLE KEPT THE GUN TRAINED on Kilronomos as she backed out from under the bed on the opposite side and quickly raised her arm as she stood, prompting him to lift his hands into the air.

"Where is Alice?" she asked, her throat scratchy and beginning to ache. Her gun arm was steady, but she wasn't certain she could keep it so for long. The gun suddenly seemed to weigh a hundred pounds, and she tightened the hand holding it.

"We can discuss this civilly," the Greek said, "for I certainly will not tell you anything if you keep pointing your weapon at me."

"You're not Ari."

"What do you know of Ari?" The man's face flushed crimson in the lantern light, and the veins in his neck stood out.

"I know he's dead." She pulled the hammer back on the gun as he moved closer to the bed. "Where is Alice? You're keeping her in the basement? Is that what I heard you say?" Her arm dipped, and she placed her other hand under the weapon to steady it.

"Dead? How do you know he is dead?" He advanced closer, and she lifted the gun from his chest to his head.

"Walk out of the door ahead of me, and take me to Alice," she said.

He moved so quickly in his rage that she didn't see it coming until it was too late. He slapped hard at her hands, forcing her arms up as her finger pulled the trigger, sending the ball into the plaster behind his head. Diving over the bed, his shoulder to her midsection, he drove her into the floor and brought his fist down repeatedly on her wrist, effectively wrestling the gun from her hand.

Isabelle saw a blanket of stars in the ceiling and fought to stay conscious. He had knocked the air from her lungs and pinned her so completely that she couldn't draw a breath. The back of her head felt as though she'd been hit with a hammer, and she realized he'd probably broken at least one of the bones in her wrist.

She heard thundering footsteps on the stairs and realized with a sick flash of humor that she had been correct in her assessment: there was nothing stealthy about her fiancé.

✦✦✦

The sight that greeted James from the open door of the upstairs bedroom nearly drove him to his knees. Isabelle lay sprawled on the floor, Kilronomos rising off of her with her gun in his hand. The man turned, and James ducked out of the doorframe as Kilronomos swung the gun wide and fired a shot. He screamed for James to drop his weapon onto the floor and slide it to him.

James held the gun carefully between two fingers to show he wasn't touching the trigger and slowly made himself visible again through the open door. Isabelle struggled to push herself onto her elbow, and in dismay James realized she was hurt or she would have taken the Greek to the ground by now as diverted as his attention was on James.

"Put the gun on the floor and slide it to me, or I will shoot her in the head," Kilronomos told James, his breath heaving.

"Here," James said and slowly bent to the ground. "I am giving you the gun. You leave, and I will take her out of here."

"Leave?" Kilronomos barked a laugh. "No, no." He rubbed his brow with one hand and reached down to grasp the gun that James slid to him, even while keeping the other trained on Isabelle. "Do not move!" he yelled at Isabelle as she sat up. She raised her palms and scooted back until she leaned against the wall.

James's blood roared in his ears as he looked at her and cursed himself a thousand times a fool for ever letting her enter the house. Kilronomos motioned to him with the gun and directed him to the far bed, where the Greek had James sit.

"You have somewhere to be, do you not?" Isabelle asked him, her eyes closed and her left hand cradling her right arm. "You're going to let that fool Sparks take care of the matter?"

"What do you know of it?" he snarled at her through gritted teeth.

"I know you are to have Alice up at the temple in less than an hour. And I would presume you have several men here in town with you that will be displeased if you fail to appear with her."

Kilronomos wiped at his brow with the back of his hand. "How do you know my brother is dead?" he barked at Isabelle.

"We don't know he's dead," James said, drawing the man's attention away from her. "We last saw him in India, and he may well be alive. He met with an accident, but his body was never recovered." James didn't believe for a moment that Ari was alive. That Isabelle had clearly provoked him so readily spoke to her state of mind.

Kilronomos breathed heavily through his nose as he looked at James. He remained silent, and James pressed his advantage.

"All we want is the girl. We will go our way and you can go yours."

The Greek's eyes narrowed in response. "The girl is the key to the treasure," he said. "We have traveled a long way for this moment."

"Adelphos!" A voice from the stairs called out, but the Greek maintained his focus on James and Isabelle.

"Take her up," he answered. "I will be along shortly."

"What is happening up there?" James recognized the voice as Sparks's and he tensed.

"Nothing you need concern yourself with."

Isabelle laughed, but it was weak. "You really are insane to leave matters to him," she said. "And if you kill us, our country will hunt far and wide until you are shot before a firing squad. I am an agent for the United States government."

James maintained a neutral expression. To his knowledge, she was no longer officially a spy. She certainly seemed convincing in her tone.

Adelphos looked at her with a derisive scowl. "Am I to believe that the United States uses women for its spies?"

"It doesn't much matter what you believe," she said and winced as she shifted her position. "But if you kill us, it will not go well for you."

A feminine scream pierced the night just outside the house, and James moved to stand, only to have the Greek roar at him to be still. Adelphos pulled the hammer back on the gun and pointed it at James's head.

"He'll never make it all the way up the hill with her by himself," Isabelle said, her voice calm, nonthreatening. "What if she continues to scream? The whole town will come out to see who is being molested."

"Stop talking!" Kilronomos rubbed at his eyes with the heel of his hand, and James watched him carefully.

"In fact, I wonder that someone hasn't come already to investigate the gunshots fired in here. Probably won't be much longer until the constable comes around. I met him tonight. Nice fellow. Seems concerned that his town maintain its integrity despite the pending relocation."

James glanced at her and then turned his attention back to the agitated man who, by now, was pulling at the collar of his nightshirt. He was volatile, and Isabelle was walking a very fine line with her tactics.

"I suppose the most surprising thing of all is that there were only two bullets in my gun. I realized it after I'd already entered the house."

Kilronomos glanced at the gun in his right hand, and James sprang at him, using the full force of his weight and strength to plow the man back into the wall behind him while shoving the gun arm up. The weapon fired again, and James was beginning to lose hope that there really was a constable who would come around to investigate. How many shots had to be fired before the law intervened?

He slammed the Greek's hand repeatedly into the wall until the gun clattered to the floor, and James pummeled at his midsection until he heard a crack. Pulling his arm back, he landed his fist on Kilronomos's face, heedless of the give of the nose and the resulting blood that spurted far and wide.

His fury was blind and brutal. It wasn't until he heard a soft voice in the corner that his tunnel vision widened again to take in the room around him.

"James, enough."

He allowed the unconscious man to slump down the wall into a heap on the floor and turned to Isabelle, breathing heavily and finally beginning to tremble.

"I do not want to visit you in prison here." She swallowed with a wince, and her voice sounded scratchy. "And we do not have much time. We must be on our way after Alice and Sparks."

He stumbled forward and fell on his knees beside her, gently gathering her into his arms and shaking so much it frightened him. He placed a hand softly at the back of her head and felt a knot that had risen to an alarming size. His movement nudged the arm that she still held cradled, and she moaned.

Pulling back, he framed her face with his hands and tried to steel himself against the sight of the tears that pooled in her eyes and fell down her cheeks.

"You must go and find Alice," she whispered. "I will follow along, but you must hurry. I don't know what they'll do with her when she can't predict the future. Or tell them where the stones are."

"Do you really know the constable?" James asked her as he slowly released her and stood, crossing to the wardrobe and searching inside.

"Yes, actually. That much was true."

James noted a belt and a pair of suspenders, which he quickly pulled from the compartment. Turning to Kilronomos, he clenched his jaw at the mess he'd made but knew he'd do the same thing over again, given the chance. His hand ached, but he nudged the man onto his stomach and, ignoring the stabbing pain through the back of his hand, tied the man's hands together then his feet.

By the time James was finished, Isabelle had risen to her feet and was moving toward him slowly. He retrieved both guns and pocketed them then reached toward her and circled her shoulders with his arm while fishing in the wardrobe for something to cover the ill and injured woman. He finally laid hold of a thin jacket, which he retrieved, draped across her shoulders, and gently maneuvered so she could thread her arms through.

"James, please go ahead of me," she said, her voice giving out as she jostled the wrist she'd been cradling.

He'd never heard her plead so desperately and it tore at his heart. "Jack and Claire are out there. They followed the other two men who left the house, and my guess is that they're already up at the temple."

Her tears fell steadily as they made their way down the stairs and out of the house. "This will all be for naught if she is harmed. I wish I had started in the basement."

"Did you know there was a basement?"

"No."

"Well then."

As they stepped back out into the night and the rain, which was thankfully falling in mere sheets instead of buckets, James looked toward the house where he'd parted from Jack and Claire. "I wonder if she left your clothes," he thought aloud and began guiding Isabelle as quickly as he thought she could move to the neighboring home.

"James, just go!" The bite was back in her voice, and he had to admit relief. "I will never forgive you if she is harmed and you could have stopped it!"

He looked down at her face, which was raised in abject fury.

"I don't need my clothes! See, they aren't even here. If you won't go, I will." She pulled away from him and began to walk down the street, hurrying more than he knew was comfortable for her. With a curse, he caught up with her as she swung her arm down only to gasp and pull it back up against her chest. She broke into a slow trot and gained her bearings by looking toward the east and up the hill where the Temple of Apollo stood.

James knew she couldn't maintain her pace for long, and as she began to slow, she breathed hard. Frustrated beyond words, James looked around for someone—anyone—who could help. He thought of waking a local and asking for the use of a mule and cart, but the time involved would likely be at Alice's expense. The streets were completely deserted, and as they hurried along, he despaired of finding any other options. And he knew Isabelle would literally collapse before abandoning Alice.

He tried a new tactic. "Are we near your inn?"

She coughed, the sound coming from deep within her lungs. She nodded after looking at the streets crisscrossing the hillside. "There," she pointed.

"You go to your room, and I will continue to Alice. I can move faster without you."

She hesitated but only for a moment before nodding. He wondered that he hadn't thought of that bit of manipulation earlier. If she thought she was slowing the rescue effort, she would swallow her pride and step aside.

They rushed to the building she identified as her inn, and he bustled her inside, grateful to see lamps still burning and the figure of a woman in the reception area. The woman gasped and rushed to Isabelle's side, which was all he needed. Leaving her in the proprietress's capable hands, he turned and went back out into the storm.

***

Alice was angry. She hadn't had a decent bath in three days, hadn't been afforded the use of a mirror to fix her hair, and the trail Sparks urged her up was muddy. Her feet were soaked—the shoes and clothing her stupid captors had provided for her after they'd abducted her in Athens—in her nightgown, no less—were ridiculous. The dress was two inches too short, and the shoes were old and made of soft material that did nothing to protect her from the ground.

They had dragged her across Greece, forcing her to traipse through more ancient spots than Zeus himself had seen, and plagued her with questions about whether or not she "felt anything." They cajoled, bribed, and threatened, and in the end, promised to return her to her friends in

Athens if she would help them locate the Jewel of Hades. The fact that her reputation was now completely ruined was a reality that hovered in the back of her mind, but she held it there, unable to contemplate the thought of Jean-Louis's reaction should she ever really return. He would be disgusted, and she was tempted to flee Athens—once the Idiots took her back—and to book passage to England with the promise that the captain would be compensated upon their arrival in London. She could return to her family's estate and live the rest of her life in furious misery with a guardian uncle and brothers she didn't know. Of course, her family would probably learn of her soiled reputation as well, and she would be forced to become a nun and live a sequestered life in the hills somewhere.

With these thoughts swirling around in her head as the rain fell against her cloak—the one item of quality the Idiots had managed to secure for her—her eyes burned and she clamped her jaw down hard, determined to never let them see her cry. Adelphos—clearly Ari's brother—had been secretive in Olympia before they left, sending telegrams to Athens and informing his highly valued acquaintances about an emergency meeting in Delphi. He'd gotten a strange gleam in his eye after speaking to the witch in Olympia. He never did tell her or Sparks what the woman had said, but whatever it was had lit a fire under him, to be sure. And now there was a whole host of Idiots descending on the town of Delphi—she had heard them coming and going from her cold, damp room in the basement.

They climbed higher on the hill, Sparks's fingers digging into her arm as though she'd try to run away. She supposed he had some cause— she'd attempted it more than once since they'd taken her from the hotel in Athens, but Adelphos had finally guaranteed she'd never do it again when he hit her, hard, and threatened worse. He had then promised that if she helped them, they would return her to Isabelle. And Jean-Louis.

Whom she could never have now.

She stifled a frustrated scream as the thoughts continued to batter her nerves and tears still threatened. In an act of defiance that served to soothe her wounded pride, if nothing else, she ripped her arm from Sparks's grasp and hissed at him that she could climb the hill by herself without any help.

The odious man looked a bit taken aback, but he didn't argue with her. She glared in disgust at his emerald-green eyes, the color discernible even in the dark, and wondered how she'd ever thought him charming in the least. He'd been aboard the steamer that transported Alice and Sally to Egypt, but he'd called himself by a false name. Now that she knew his true colors firsthand, she was repulsed. He was nothing more than a treasure-hunting, money-grubbing, pathetic little man.

She slipped twice and fell to her knees, snarling at Sparks when he'd attempted to haul her to her feet, before finally reaching an area on the mountain behind several homes and ruins. The four pillars of the structure rose into the sky, with several shorter ones lining the sides. Her heart stuttered when she glimpsed shadows—men in dark clothes and black hoods—standing on the ancient floor of the place. She quickly counted seven and shivered as the rain finally penetrated the thick layer of her cloak.

One of the men struck a match, the man next to him sheltering it with an umbrella while they applied the flame to the wick of a small lamp. Alice wiped at the droplets of rain that dripped from the edge of her hood and caught her breath as the light glinted off of a ring on the hand of the man who held the umbrella. She suddenly realized who Adelphos's important acquaintances were.

Think, think. Alice believed she had a basic understanding of what Sparks and Adelphos wanted her to do at this strange place. They had spoken of the oracle in hushed tones ever since leaving Olympia, and she remembered enough of the legend from her mother—who had liked strange legends—that she began formulating a plan.

28

JAMES HUNG BACK FOR A moment, taking in the scene at the Temple of Apollo and the surrounding hillside. There were homes and shacks nearby—plenty of places to hide—but he needed to hear what was being said and actually see Alice. Quietly skirting the edge of the ruins, using an older building as cover, he inched closer to the tableau that was barely visible in the darkness.

One of the hooded men standing in the group inside the temple pillars lit a small lamp, and it cast enough light that James saw Alice's face clearly illuminated. He closed his eyes briefly in quick gratitude that he at least knew where she was. He continued walking the perimeter, giving the temple a wide berth as he kept an eye out for Jack and Claire while wondering if the two men they had followed had actually come up to the temple.

His questions were answered soon enough as he rounded the corner of an abandoned shack and saw Jack and Claire quietly watching the proceedings as Jack checked his pistol. Tossing a pebble at their feet in the same manner they'd used earlier on him, he put a finger to his lips when they looked his way.

James approached them and nodded toward Alice. Jack answered him with a grim nod of his own and moved his gun under his coat to keep it out of the rain. Jack motioned James closer and put his lips next to James's ear.

"We must get her to the hotel, where we can hide her until morning. I don't know where we'll find a conveyance to take us to the train station or the harbor at this hour," Jack whispered.

Claire touched James's sleeve, and he looked at her. "Isabelle?" she mouthed.

James placed his hand over hers and nodded. It seemed enough for the moment—she didn't ask for an explanation. Claire too seemed wretchedly cold and miserable, and he wondered if she'd have made the trip to find her sister had she known what would be involved. He had to give her his respect, however; she could easily have stayed behind at the inn.

Jack caught his attention again and whispered to him, "We watch for the right moment."

James nodded his agreement and inched his way closer until reaching the front corner of the shack, knowing that the world beyond the lamp likely appeared black to those standing near it. The man holding the umbrella was speaking to Sparks, his accent heavy and his tone sharp, made all the more eerie by the fact that his face was hidden. The hoods had slits for the eyes to see through, but nothing else.

"Where is Kilronomos?"

"He is taking care of some business," Sparks told the man. "Where is Metaxas?"

The man with the umbrella paused. "Also taking care of business. He sends us with instructions to relay the prophecy back to him when the telegraph office opens. You should hope your oracle is worth the trouble. The King's Men rarely meet outside the Parthenon."

Metaxas? James grimly wondered which brother was the associate who was apparently the head of the group. Baltasar or Demitrios?

Sparks stiffened at the man's words, and James had to give him credit for having bravado if not common sense. "And you should be grateful I am allowing you to take part!"

The man with the umbrella faced Sparks for a moment before laughing softly. The men around him closed in subtly, and James felt Jack and Claire approaching Sparks from behind. James was beginning to wonder how they were ever going to extricate Alice when the young woman herself raised a hand.

"The oracle receives her revelations alone," she announced. "You will not listen or watch as I seek the gods."

Sparks, standing just to her left, moved to take her arm, and she slapped it away forcefully. James's brows shot up—clearly she had an ace up her sleeve.

"You will not touch me," Alice shouted at Sparks. "Any of you! If you want your prophecy, you will comply with my conditions!"

The umbrella man paused, the silence broken only by the falling rain. He finally spoke in Greek to the others and they slowly began to back away. When they stopped at the edges of the wall of pillars, she made a shooing motion with her hands.

"All the way," she stated. "Into the dark. And extinguish the lamp. I must have complete darkness and solitude." When they hesitated, she barked a command at them in Greek, and James's brows rose sky-high. Jean-Louis would be proud. The girl did indeed seem to have an ear for languages.

Alice followed her one-word command with a full phrase of words in Greek, her tone sharp. Whatever it was she said had the desired effect—the men melted into the shadows to the side of the temple, Sparks reluctantly on their heels when she angrily told him to make himself scarce.

James glanced at Jack, whose gaze followed Sparks and the King's Men as they retreated, and whose mouth moved as he quickly counted them before they disappeared fully into the dark. When Jack returned his attention to Alice, there was a quirk of a smile tugging at his lips.

Alice began murmuring nonsensical phrases, and James thought he saw her lifting her arms to the sky. Her voice rose and fell, and from sound alone he realized she was circling the perimeter of the ancient temple floor. She continued the pattern for several minutes, occasionally shouting a word or two, and James wasn't certain, but he thought he heard some French thrown into the mix.

Her intent slowly dawned on him, and he grabbed Jack and pulled Claire in close. "She's going to jump down the far side onto the path below," he whispered. He turned and tore back around the side of the shack and raced for the path, for the first time that night truly grateful for the darkness which hid his descent.

Alice's voice continued to rise and fall, but she grew increasingly more hushed in her tirade. James felt himself smiling as he tore down the path and was very nearly at the exact spot below the front of the temple when Alice leaped unhesitatingly down roughly fifteen feet and landed with a *woosh* of breath in front of him.

"Alice! It's James," he whispered to her as he helped her rise from the mud where she'd slid on her side a good two feet.

"James!" Alice squeaked and threw her arms around his neck.

Squeezing her tightly, he turned and continued down the path, half dragging her along with him until she caught her footing and began running with a limp she probably hadn't even noticed in the rush of adrenaline that propelled her forward. He clasped her hand and caught sight of Jack and Claire, who raced onto the path behind them.

Any sense of relief he felt was short-lived; an angry shout from above told him the King's Men realized she'd escaped.

***

Sally flipped through Jack's grandfather's journal by the light of a small lantern on her nightstand, trying to focus on something other than the pain in her side that was keeping her awake. She lay in her bed, and Helene occupied Alice's. Not wanting to awaken Helene, she blew out the lantern, taking the journal with her into the sitting room where two lamps still burned low. Phillip and Jean-Louis had yet to return from whatever escapade they had dreamed up together, and she was caught in an odd maelstrom of worry, pain, and a laudanum-induced fog.

Sitting on the sofa, half reclined, she read over the anecdotes and notes Dr. Pearce had made, hoping something might jump out and catch her attention. He had utilized every last inch of space in the black book, writing notes in margins and scribbling names, addresses, and bits of information inside the front and back covers. She tipped the book to one side then the other and then flipped to the back inside cover and did the same.

There was a seam along the inside of the back cover that aligned with the crease. As she opened the book more fully, the seam gaped and she thought the end paper had come loose from the hard cover. It proved to be a pocket, and she ran her finger along the edge, slipping it inside. Encountering a piece of folded paper, she pulled it out of the pocket and looked at it in happy surprise.

"Something new," she murmured and unfolded it. She chewed on her lip as she examined the writing—clearly Dr. Pearce's—and was frustrated that the meaning wasn't immediately apparent. It seemed to be an address in Piraeus, followed by one word in Greek. She frowned at the paper, wondering why the doctor had written the address in English but not the word beneath it.

Sally tapped the edge of her finger against the paper and wondered if she dared wake Helene. She really did not want to wait until morning to ask her about it.

"You should be asleep, young lady," Helene told her as she opened the bedroom door and joined Sally on the sofa.

"I couldn't sleep, but I did find this." Sally showed Helene the paper. "This was here in this folder." She indicated the envelope in the journal as Helene took the paper from her hand. "What is that word on the bottom?"

Helene scanned the paper and wrinkled her brow in thought. "It means 'under sea.' Literally 'sub marina.'"

"And this is an address in Piraeus?"

Helene nodded. "It seems to be."

Both women glanced up at the sound of voices at the door, followed by a key scraping in the lock. Jean-Louis dismissed the guards for the evening as Phillip pulled the key out of the door and pocketed it.

They seemed surprised to see the women awake—Phillip locked eyes with Sally and moved to her side, taking her hand and kneeling next to her.

"How are you feeling?" he asked.

"I am much better," she said. "I just cannot sleep. And I found something else in Dr. Pearce's journal."

Jean-Louis closed the door and locked it from the inside then joined the group. "What did you find?"

Helene handed him the paper, and he studied it for a moment, brows drawn. "Under sea?"

When Helene nodded, he said, "We should visit this address in the morning." Jean-Louis removed his spectacles and rubbed his eyes.

"Where have you been?" Sally asked Phillip.

His response had her dropping her mouth open. "You entered Ari's house?" She paused. "A pity I couldn't loan you my lock-picking kit."

"He isn't Ari," Jean-Louis said, sounding bone weary. "He is Adelphos, Ari's brother. And he's one of the King's Men."

Sally digested the information slowly, wishing her brain didn't feel so fuzzy. "And he has Alice, a Guardian."

Phillip nodded, his lips pressed into a tight, thin line.

"Have we heard any more from James?" Sally asked.

"Just that he is at Delphi but hasn't yet found her."

"And we don't know if Isabelle is there yet?"

"No. The last we heard from her was when she left Olympia with Jack and her sister."

A sick feeling in the pit of her stomach hit Sally, and she struggled not to cry. She knew men hated it when women cried, and everyone had enough worry without trying to soothe her fears. She couldn't suppress the images, though, of Alice in the hands of one of the King's Men, who were after the jewels and reputedly not at all that nice to Guardians, and of Isabelle, who might very well be lost at the bottom of the Gulf of Corinth. Why hadn't Belle telegrammed upon arrival at Delphi? Perhaps the reason was because they had never arrived.

"We cannot just wait here indefinitely," Sally said, worried, and glanced up at Jean-Louis's set features.

"No," he agreed, "we absolutely cannot. In fact, if we do not hear from them by morning, I am taking the next train to Delphi."

***

James and Alice hid in a narrow alley near Isabelle's inn as several of the King's Men ran past. James waited a few moments and then glanced out from behind a building to be certain the path was clear. Jack and Claire had peeled off as soon as the foursome left the uppermost trail, and James assumed they were well enough hidden, as he hadn't heard any ruckus to indicate otherwise.

Still grasping Alice's ice-cold fingers, he tugged her back out onto the main street, ran with her to the front door of the inn—which he opened quietly—and led her in before closing the door behind them.

The main room was lit with two lanterns that cast a welcoming glow, along with a fire in the hearth that spread much-needed warmth. Isabelle was seated next to the fire, dressed in fresh clothing, and the inn's proprietress paused in the act of drying Isabelle's hair with a towel. She took in Alice's bedraggled appearance with a cry of dismay and a rapid litany of Greek as she approached them.

Alice, meanwhile, ran toward her friend, who slowly stood and nearly fell over backward when Alice threw herself into Isabelle's arms. Alice began crying then and was blubbering something when she paused and placed her hands on Isabelle's cheeks. "You are absolutely on fire!"

Isabelle rolled her eyes and pulled Alice's hands away. "Just from sitting near the hearth."

James should have realized the woman wouldn't be tucked into bed. He opened his mouth to say something, but she spoke first.

"Where are Jack and Claire? I've secured transportation to the railway station, but we must leave before morning. The others will surely leave then, and I would prefer we already be well out of town."

The innkeeper fussed over Alice, pulling the sodden cloak from the girl's shoulders. Isabelle told the woman she had clothing Alice could put on, and the woman seemed to understand as she nodded and started toward the stairs with Alice. Isabelle followed but turned back to James and placed a hand on his arm.

"Well done," she said with a smile. Her eyes were fever bright, and she looked flushed although she still shivered involuntarily.

"Go back to the fire for a moment," James said to her and tried to nudge her toward the hearth. She resisted and instead turned to follow Alice and the innkeeper up the stairs.

"I need to get some clothes for her," she said and moved away before he could protest. "We must be on the road within the hour."

29

The telegram was brief but welcome. RETURNING STOP ATHENS BY TOMORROW MORNING STOP HAVE ALICE STOP.

Phillip showed the paper to Jean-Louis, who closed his eyes briefly with a sigh. He then relayed the message to Helene as the threesome stepped out into the bright Athens morning sunlight.

"This way," Helene said and pointed to the left. The hotel carriage waited by the curb to take them to Piraeus. They had left Sally behind under police guard as a precaution. She had been unhappy with the decision, as Phillip had expected she would be, but her wound was still raw, the stitches too fresh. He didn't want to risk hurting her further.

"Helene, I have wondered something," Jean-Louis said to the older woman once they had settled in and the carriage pulled forward. "What is it, do you suppose, that the intruders were hoping to find that morning in your aunt's home?"

Helene winced slightly but remained composed. "I have wondered this myself." Shaking her head, she stared into the distance for a moment before continuing. "The tapestries perhaps? I remember them hanging on her wall, after all, and we know that they are an important piece of the puzzle."

"But we hadn't even seen the first one at that point. In fact, nobody seemed interested in the tapestries until after you and Sally found the one at the museum." Phillip frowned and lifted a shoulder. "Might there have been something else of interest in Elysia's home?"

Helene nodded with a shrug. "I suppose so—clearly they were searching for something."

"Isabelle mentioned that there was a man Elysia once ejected from her home because he wore a King's Men ring."

She nodded again. "She may well have made enemies of them ages ago. And there was something I didn't mention to Isabelle at the time—I believe that man was the senior Metaxas."

Phillip raised a brow. "As in the father of Demitrios and Baltasar?"

"Yes. Now that I think further on it, there always seemed to be a kind of animosity there between their family and my aunt. Having been gone all those years, though, I don't know the extent of it."

"And what were the King's Men looking for?" Phillip said, thinking aloud.

Jean-Louis looked at him with a slight nod. "The jewels."

Helene's mouth fell open, and she looked at the men for the space of a few moments before closing it and shaking her head. "Surely I would have known."

"Would you?" Phillip asked. "You said she was often less than lucid. Perhaps she did have one and had forgotten."

Helene rubbed a hand across her forehead, her brow creased. "She would have told me about the jewels if she'd had any of them," she murmured.

"Perhaps she did," Jean-Louis said, "and you weren't aware."

"What do you mean?"

"She babbled much, yes? And talked of the legend intermittently. She may have had the stone, even told you where she'd placed it, and you might not have been aware."

Helene pursed her lips. "I will ponder that for a while."

They rode in silence until they reached the docks.

***

Jack stood near his seat on the train as it waited at the platform, the final call going out to passengers scurrying along the side. He kept a close watch on those in the group; Claire sat in the window seat next to his; Isabelle and Alice sat just in front of them, with Isabelle closest to the window; and James was directly across the aisle. They were all exhausted, and Isabelle's face was still flushed with fever. Once they had arrived at the train station an hour's donkey-cart ride away, Isabelle had let him and James assume the details of the rest of the excursion to Athens.

It was nearly lunchtime—he was gratified to feel a rumble in his stomach. Since receiving the gunshot wound in Monemvasia, his appetite had waxed and waned, and he needed his strength. Running about Delphi in the rain the night before had nearly done him in. He glanced down the train aisle, wondering how long after departure the food cart would make its way to them.

Jack turned his attention to the platform outside, his eye skimming over people who waved at others that were boarding the train. His gaze stopped on the profile of a man he'd not seen since Egypt. Backing out of the seat and into the aisle, he moved slightly to the right, still keeping the man in sight. The man ranked high in the Federation; that the Egyptian had sent him meant they were earnest in their pursuit of Jack.

He felt a chill as he realized that the man must have followed him from Delphi, which meant he had trailed him in the ancient city and Jack hadn't even been aware. The blast of the train whistle and then the subtle movement of the train provided a small measure of relief as he realized the man wasn't boarding the train.

They had, as a group, been careful—they had separated upon arrival for the subsequent thirty-minute wait for the train that would take them to Athens and kept a vigilant eye out for Sparks or for any who seemed to fit the limited visual recollections they had of the King's Men. The three women all wore clothing purchased at a hefty price from the innkeeper as to better blend in with the locals.

The Federation's man looked behind him in frustration, and Jack was grateful for the crowd on the platform. With any luck, he wouldn't be aware that Jack had boarded the train until it was well on its way. The Federation did not look kindly on spies or turncoats. He wondered if he'd actually be able to return to England—he'd joked about that somewhat with Claire but was now seriously contemplating the fact that it might be wise to formulate a plan for when they finished their quest.

Once Jack and Claire had arrived back at the inn the night before, Alice had filled them in on her happenings since being taken from the hotel in Athens. She confirmed that Sparks and Adelphos wanted to use her to ferret out the third jewel and that they assumed it would likely be hidden in a place of historic significance—like Olympia or Delphi. She had also learned that Sparks had taken the second jewel—the one from Egypt—and put it in a deposit box at the bank in Athens.

Jack figured he could telegram his superiors in London in order to have the stone released into his care, but that would work only if the Greek authorities were in agreement. The only way they *would* agree was if they had no idea what was in the box. And explaining to *his* government why the stone disappeared after he took it from the box was going to be interesting. He couldn't very well tell them they were going to destroy it to protect the world from foes who wanted it for evil purposes.

With a sigh, he resumed his seat as the train gathered speed and the man on the platform disappeared. Claire looked at him with a raised brow and he smiled.

"What is the matter?" she said.

"I saw an old friend."

When she would have pressed further for details, he shook his head and nodded forward to Isabelle. "I don't want her worrying right now about anything else," he whispered.

Claire looked at her sister with a frown and a nod.

"Do you know what ails her?"

Claire pursed her lips. "I believe so—she is coughing now, and I believe the fever is a symptom of a lung illness. She was always extremely hardy—I hope that once we get her back to her hotel she can rest a spell so it will pass." Claire checked her pocket watch. "She needs more tea—I wonder when they will bring the cart."

Jack looked down the aisle again. "It's on its way." He glanced at Claire, who continued to eye Isabelle with apparent concern. He hadn't known Claire long, but he knew her to be pragmatic and practical. He didn't figure she would waste energy worrying unless she needed to, and the fact that she was now was unsettling.

30

HELENE CONSULTED THE PAPER AGAIN and looked up at the row of small buildings along the dockside. "It's this one," she said, pointing, and Phillip looked at the shack in question. It was old, to be sure, but tidy. It did seem to lean slightly to one side—by fractions of a degree, really—and he felt his expression turn dubious as he examined the structural integrity of the thing.

He glanced at Jean-Louis, who was eyeing the building similarly.

"Well then," Helene said, squaring her shoulders. "We do not have all day now, do we?"

"I suppose not," Phillip said. "Perhaps a few more minutes wouldn't hurt though."

Helene made a *psh* sound and with a wave of her hand dismissed the concerns. She marched along the wooden planks that led to the shack's front door, and Phillip and Jean-Louis were left with nothing but to follow her or look pathetically afraid.

The door opened to show a short man, whom Phillip judged to be in his seventies, with white hair and a wide smile. "Yes?"

The man spoke English? Phillip stepped forward and offered his hand. He apologized for interrupting his morning and then paused as he wondered how to broach the subject.

"Sir, a friend of ours has some documents from his grandfather, and your address was listed among them. Might you know of a Dr. Pearce, by chance?"

"I was beginning to worry," the man said. "I thought I might have to track Jack down myself before he ever found that piece of paper."

Phillip wrinkled his brow. "Sir?"

The man chuckled. "I am Dr. Pearce, dear boy."

The stunned silence that greeted the old man's pronouncement hung thick in the air for long moments before Dr. Pearce motioned impatiently for them to follow him into the shack. Phillip glanced at Helene and Jean-Louis, who looked as flabbergasted as he felt.

Dr. Pearce motioned to a small table and chairs, and the men waited for Helene to sit before taking a chair.

Phillip didn't feel comfortable censuring an elder, but he did feel compelled to point out to the older man that Jack had grieved for his grandfather—had there been no other way to meet up with him in Greece? And how had he known that Jack would be there?

Dr. Pearce sighed, his expression momentarily downturned. "I do regret the deception," he said, "but it was necessary. Too many people were discovering my activities in building the submersible—people who were more than merely curious—and once I realized I was being hunted for my knowledge and files, I decided I would need to fabricate my own demise. Shortly afterward, I heard from Jack, or rather Andrews heard from him, just before I was set to leave England and bring the submersible here to finish her. When Jack requested that my papers be sent here, I thought it the perfect solution. And timely as well."

Jean-Louis nodded. "Mr. Andrews sent a letter explaining what had happened. And when the papers arrived here, they were in a state of disarray. It has taken us some time to decipher everything."

Dr. Pearce winced. "And now Andrews is gone. I regret that perhaps most of all. He was a good man. The legend has taken her share over the years."

"But why are you here now?" Phillip asked. "You certainly didn't know Jack had met us and that we were searching for the jewels."

The old man sighed. "I have been a student of the legend of the jewels for many, many years. And from more than one source I have seen predictions about the jewels coming together at the eruption of a volcano. In November of last year, I read in a scientific journal that Santorini is showing signs of doing that very thing, and suddenly the pieces seemed to fit together. The next thing I knew, Jack was cabling Andrews that he was on to something and needed my papers. I had already begun work on the submarine and decided that the time was likely at hand."

"Jack will be so happy," Helene said then.

Phillip was skeptical. "It was a big gamble."

The doctor nodded. "It was. But do you smell the sulfur in the air? It has been building for two days now. And according to the local authorities, Santorini has begun spewing ash and rock."

"We don't have all of the jewels. We have only one," Phillip told the man, hating to burst his bubble.

"I have hope," Dr. Pearce said. "And now you're here; you found me. I pray my efforts have not been in vain."

Phillip looked at Helene and then Jean-Louis. "No," he finally said. "Your efforts have not been in vain. I'm returning to the hotel, but you should accompany Jean-Louis and Helene to her home. Jack is taking care of some business, but he and James will be there in one hour."

***

Isabelle couldn't blame James for telegraphing ahead from their final train transfer for Phillip to have medical help available for her when they arrived at the hotel in Athens. Ordinarily it would have peeved her in the extreme, but she was just ill enough to figure that summoning the energy wouldn't be worth it. Claire, for her part, was irritated that James had assumed they would need more expertise than she could provide, but she did grudgingly admit that the old midwife who had also helped Sally had done no more or less than she would have.

Claire sat next to Isabelle's bed now, and Isabelle murmured a contented sigh when her sister placed a cold, fresh cloth on her forehead.

"I suggest you do not even think of getting out of this bed until tomorrow morning."

"I could never sleep for twenty-four hours, Claire."

"You can, and you will. I will be your eyes and ears and apprise you of everything that happens."

Isabelle felt her eyelids droop. They were so heavy. Every limb felt heavy. The last conscious thoughts she had were to wonder what had happened with Adelphos and whether or not Sparks would immediately return to Athens.

***

James told the Athens police exactly what had happened to Alice, and they planned to contact the constable in Delphi to check on Kilronomos. Sparks, however, was another matter. It was a shame they had been unable to apprehend him, but it was good to know that the Jewel of Poseidon was locked up at the bank. Jack was speaking with the British embassy in an attempt to have it turned over to his care.

Jack met James outside the police office and shook his head. "The locals won't authorize it."

James took off his hat and ran a hand through his hair, releasing a frustrated breath. He massaged the back of his neck, where he felt a dull ache settling in. "There is no possible way we will be able to get it out of a bank," he muttered. "I have no idea where to go from here."

"Well," Jack said as he motioned with his head and started walking, "we may have to follow Sparks when he returns. Provided he doesn't wait around for Kilronomos to be released from the Delphi constabulary."

The men walked in comfortable silence through streets that were becoming familiar. The temperature was pleasant, the sun bright overhead, the sky azure. James took little notice, however; Isabelle was in bed, sick, and he knew it must be severe to keep her down. Helene had mentioned that she wanted to look for something at Elysia's house, and there was no way Isabelle would miss it unless she was really not doing well.

It didn't take long to cover the two-mile distance to Elysia's house, and Jack knocked on the front door when they arrived. Helene answered, and with a long look at Jack, she let them in the house.

Helene had two guests: Jean-Louis and an older gentleman. When Jack noticed the man standing near a chair where he'd likely been sitting, Jack whispered, "Papa?"

Jack rushed to the old man and embraced him, mumbling almost incoherently that he was supposed to have been dead. When the initial shock had finally worn off, the group sat, and the doctor told them his story.

"I've done some of my own spying around Athens," Dr. Pearce said when he finished his narrative. "I don't know what you've been up to, but I at least knew you were here. I was going to give you one more day to find the address at the docks before knocking on your hotel room door. It would have been risky though. The people who wanted my files are the same who have been tailing you. I've seen them."

Helene was fidgeting in her chair, and she rose, walked to the back of the house while Jack peppered his grandfather with more questions, and then returned. She cast an eye about the parlor where they currently sat, frowning.

"What is it?" James asked her, and the others fell silent.

"I think somebody has been through the house again since I cleaned it last week. Things have been moved, rearranged," she said, her face creased in concern.

"Do you know if anything is missing?" James asked her.

"No, I don't think so. And that's not why I wanted to come by with you today. Jean-Louis suggested that my aunt may have told me about the legend without my realizing it, and I started thinking about all of the times she talked of her beautiful jewelry." Helene turned and with a crook of her finger led all of them into her aunt's bedroom. "I found her jewelry box—the one she used to let me look at as a child—in her hiding place under the bed." She lifted a small wooden box for the men's perusal, and James looked inside.

There were just a few pieces that, to James's untrained eye, didn't seem priceless. There was a tangle of silver necklaces, a pearl, a gold brooch, and a gold band. There were also three other rings. He supposed they were probably sentimental in nature and the old woman must have had her reasons for keeping them.

Helene plucked the three rings from the box and held them open in her palm. He didn't notice anything unusual about them until she set the box down and placed the rings, side by side, on her fingers.

They were oval in shape and were three distinct colors: an iridescent purple, a brilliant orange, and a deep blue.

James looked at Helene's expectant expression. "Are these meant to represent the jewels?"

She nodded. "I believe they are. She only ever wore the blue one, but I don't know why."

"Do you remember your aunt saying anything specific to you on the occasions she let you look at this box?" Jack asked her as he studied the rings.

"She told me they were special, that some of her jewelry had been in the family for years. She said they were as precious to her as her rock garden."

James wrinkled his brow. "Her rock garden?"

Helene nodded. "She maintained a beautiful garden in the back, and woven through her plants and herbs is a path that consists of rocks she picked up when she was out and about. Sometimes the sizes appealed to her, other times the colors or unusual designs."

"Helene, was Elysia a Guardian?" Jack asked her.

Helene stared at him. "I don't think she was—surely I would have known!"

"Would you? Why did she have such a complete knowledge of the legend? She was almost reverent in her approach to it."

James watched Helene's expression change from disbelief to incredulity to shock.

"Could she have been?" Helene whispered. "She was the firstborn daughter, just older than my mother. Of course I never had occasion to see if she bore the mark . . ."

"Will you show us the rock garden?" James asked.

Helene raised a brow and nodded. She replaced the rings in the jewelry box and led the way through the small house and out a back door onto a patio area whose plants showed the evidence of their mistress's obvious care. They were planted in an L-shape around the back and side of the patio, and running through the beds was a rocky path that wove and twisted as a river might.

James moved closer to the path, inspecting the rocks and realizing that, although they varied in size and color, they were all oval or egg shaped.

"I always thought she loved her rock garden because it reminded her of places she had been." Helene bent down and touched a stone, pink in hue, with her forefinger.

Jack and Dr. Pearce walked down the other leg of the rock garden, carefully looking at the collection of stones. "That may be," Jack said over his shoulder, "or perhaps she had other reasons."

"I hardly know what to look for," she said and scanned the small, carefully created pathway.

"A pattern perhaps," James said as he stooped closer to look, "or a break in a pattern possibly."

"Or a single blue stone," Jack said quietly, and James straightened. He and Helene moved to Jack's side and looked over his shoulder to see a small stone, similar in shape to the others in the path, but it was the only deep blue rock in the entire collection. It was smaller than the Jewel of Zeus or Poseidon, not at all iridescent, and lacked the mystical qualities the other two seemed to possess, but the fact that it was the lone blue stone in a sea of other colors seemed significant.

Holding steadily to his walking cane, Jack bent down and carefully moved the rock. A few stones that had lain next to the blue one slid and moved into its place. Jack scooped them out of the way and smoothed the dark earth beneath. He looked up at Helene and asked, "Do you, by chance, have a small shovel?"

***

Sally and Phillip had gone down to the hotel dining room for a late breakfast, and Alice sat with Jean-Louis in the sitting room of the hotel suite. She stared into the fireplace and refused to look at him. She knew if she did, she would burst into a million tears. When he finally sat next to her on the settee and took her hand, she felt her eyes begin to burn anyway.

"Why will you not speak to me, Alice?"

The pain in his voice broke her heart. "It is better if we just remain the most casual of friends, Jean-Louis," she said and cleared her throat in an effort to sound calm and unaffected.

"I will certainly respect your wishes if you are not interested in being courted. I asked Isabelle if I might."

Alice smiled, still looking forward. "I suppose she would be the one to ask."

"Alice." His fingers tightened on her hand, and he tugged at it. "Please, will you look at me?"

She finally turned to look at him, his handsome face nearly her undoing.

"Have I mistaken your interest in me?" he asked.

She opened her mouth to say yes, to try to push him away for his own sake, but couldn't force the word past her lips. Closing her eyes briefly, she shook her head.

"Then why are you sad?"

"I . . ." The words clogged in her throat and a tear slipped out of her eye. "Jean-Louis, you deserve to court a woman who does not have a ruined reputation."

Bless the man; he looked genuinely baffled. "Ruined reputation?" He blinked at her behind his endearing spectacles.

"Yes," she said, finally feeling some fire beneath her sense of utter humiliation and turning her face again toward the hearth. "I have been in the company of two men for several days and nights, completely unchaperoned! You would do well to keep better company."

He was silent for so long that she glanced at his face, which stared back at her in apparent shock. His jaw grew taut then, and his grip tightened. "Did they hurt you, Alice? Did they . . . dishonor you?"

"No," she said, feeling her face burn but grateful for the truthfulness of her statement. "They did not. I think the fact that I am a Guardian had them slightly awed."

He released his breath and brought her hand to his lips. Closing his eyes, he kissed her knuckles and said, "That is good. I should hate to have to kill a man."

She smiled at him sadly. "I would certainly never expect you to. And truly, Jean-Louis, your mother will want you to court a woman of good standing."

He shook his head. "Actually, my mother was a woman of the evening. She died when I was an infant, and I was raised by the vicar and his wife."

She blinked at him, searching for an appropriate response.

"Perhaps now it is you who should search for a more appropriate suitor," he said.

"No, no," she said. "I am surprised, that's all."

"I am legitimately adopted into the family. I have no scandal attached to my name," he said, placing one palm on his chest. Pausing, he continued, "Alice, I have been in a state of agony and worry for your safety. I have been angry and frustrated . . . and very, very afraid."

Alice felt the tears gather again, and he placed his thumb on her cheek and wiped away the moisture as it escaped. Leaning forward, he kissed her softly, gently, and she melted.

Pulling back, he caught her gaze with his own, which she could have only described as fiercely determined. "I cannot endure it again."

She nodded and placed her palm alongside his cheek. "I shall endeavor to never again be abducted."

"Will you walk with me down the street a bit? There's someone I would very much like you to meet."

***

Jack used the small spade Helene had found on Elysia's potting bench to gently chip into the earth, which was hard packed and in need of watering. After watching him for a moment, Helene disappeared and then returned with a watering can, which she tipped a bit and allowed a rainbow of water to spill down onto the ground.

The moistened earth gave way a bit more easily, and he kept working at it, wondering if his supposition was nothing but foolishness. He was very near admitting defeat when the spade struck something solid with an odd thud. Using his fingers and digging through the soil, he fought with the dirt until he had a good enough purchase on the object that he was able to pry it loose.

It proved to be something solid, wrapped in burlap. Glancing up at James and Helene and his grandfather, who looked at him with wide eyes, Jack slowly unwrapped what he immediately recognized as the

Jewel of Hades. The stone was brilliantly blue, fit snugly in the palm of his hand, and was perfectly oval in shape.

He looked up to see James staring down at the thing, his mouth slightly ajar. "All this time, and it's been buried here in your aunt's backyard?" James looked at Helene, dumbstruck.

"I believe I should sit for a spell," Helene said and sank to her knees. James hastily caught her arm and supported her as she folded her legs under her and placed a hand to her forehead. "I simply do not know what to say or think."

"May . . . may I?" Dr. Pearce stared at the stone in Jack's hand.

Jack nodded and handed it to him and then looked over his shoulder, quickly scanning the yard and the open door leading back into the house. They were very exposed, vulnerable. The last time they had found a jewel, Sparks had shown up and taken it.

"If someone has been in the house recently, he may return or be watching it as we speak," Jack told the others. "We should go." Handing the jewel to James, Jack turned back to the spade and quickly refilled the hole. As best as he could, he rearranged the earth and the rocks covering it so that it looked undisturbed. The plain blue rock that had led them to the jewel, he handed to Helene, after which he tipped some more of the water from the watering can onto his hands to clean them off.

James helped Helene to her feet, and Jack retrieved his cane, his senses on alert. The stakes had just been considerably raised.

***

Isabelle had slept for a time but was congested from her head down into her chest. She felt as though someone had filled her completely with cotton, and she heard the illness in her own voice when she spoke. Her throat and voice were raw, and she sounded as though she had a clothespin on her nose.

She leaned up on one elbow as the midwife tipped some broth on a spoon into her mouth.

"I have already given her some, and she can drink it rather than sip from a spoon," Claire said to the woman, standing with hands on hips. "She needs to sleep. The fever is finally breaking."

Isabelle raised a hand to her sister. "I'm doing much better," she said, wishing she sounded convincing. She needed to get out of the bed. "What I would really like is some fresh air."

"The weather change," the midwife said, her voice low, and Isabelle turned her attention fully on the woman.

"I'm sorry?"

The woman gestured to the sky and said something in Greek.

Claire made an exasperated sound though, to her credit, she seemed to be trying to stifle it. Isabelle waved her hand at Claire and sat up more fully in the bed.

"The weather change," Isabelle repeated to the woman and watched her closely.

The midwife spoke again in Greek and, apparently frustrated, set down the bowl of broth and gestured with her hands, moving them from her lap, upward and out.

"Claire, will you please see if Jean-Louis will come in here?"

Claire nodded and went to the door. She returned in a few moments, perplexed. "He's not here."

"Did Alice say where he went?"

"Alice isn't here either."

Isabelle's heart thudded in alarm. "What do you mean?"

"I mean, she is not here."

"Will you check downstairs in the dining room? Perhaps they went to see Phil and Sally." Isabelle swung her legs around and put her feet on the ground, a wave of dizziness sweeping through her head.

"Isabelle, you stay in that bed!"

"I can't, Claire. And when you're downstairs, will you please send Sally up? I need to see that tapestry again, and I don't know where she put it."

31

JAMES, JACK, HELENE, AND AN older gentleman Isabelle had never met returned to the hotel before Phillip and Sally returned from the dining room. Isabelle was dressed, combed, and in the sitting room when they arrived, and she hoped she didn't look pale.

They entered looking wild-eyed and hunted; Jack looked out into the hallway twice before closing the door and locking it.

"What is it?" Isabelle asked without preamble.

James put his hand into his inner coat pocket and withdrew something. He approached her quietly, and she tried to read his expression. She took the object from him when he offered it and looked down to see the Jewel of Hades resting quietly in her hand on a piece of old burlap.

Isabelle couldn't catch her breath, for reasons having nothing to do with her ailment. "Wha—where—"

Helene sat down next to her. "Buried at my aunt's house."

Isabelle remembered the midwife in the bedroom who was gathering her supplies and packing up her bag of medicines. Isabelle hurriedly folded the burlap back around the stone and handed it to James just as the old woman entered the room. He slid it back into his inner coat pocket without comment.

Helene, looking harried, stood and greeted the woman, walking with her to the door. As the midwife began talking, Helene looked back at Isabelle.

"She was trying to tell you something about the weather?" Helene said.

Isabelle nodded. "I mentioned the need for fresh air, and she said something I couldn't quite make out."

The midwife tugged on Helene's arm and continued speaking, again gesturing with one hand as she had to Isabelle.

Helene turned again to Isabelle, her brow creased. "A volcano?"

Isabelle's heart beat faster. "I thought that was what she was trying to tell me." She looked at James. "Just like the man on the steamer from Egypt. He said something about Santorini erupting."

"Ah, yes." James glanced at the midwife, and Helene escorted her to the door, unlocking it and speaking to her gently while patting her arm. The old woman left just as Sally and Phillip returned to the sitting room, with Claire on their heels, sounding a bit winded.

It was with a fair amount of understandable shock that Isabelle greeted Dr. Pearce when Jack introduced him to her. Her mind swirled with the oddity of her current reality—and as much as she wanted to hear the full story, of both Dr. Pearce and the discovery of the third jewel, her anxiety over Alice's whereabouts had climbed steadily. When Claire confirmed that she had looked in all of the common rooms of the hotel to no avail, Isabelle closed her eyes in frustration.

"We just brought her back! What could they have been thinking to go out alone?" Isabelle was caught between anger and fear; neither emotion was one she particularly enjoyed.

As though her comment had caused them to materialize out of thin air, a key sounded in the lock and Jean-Louis and Alice entered the hotel room, hand in hand, with Alice looking becomingly flushed.

"Where have you been?" Isabelle said as she stood.

Alice looked up at Jean-Louis, beaming, and then turned her attention back to the room. "We are married!"

A stunned silence fell thick in the room, and Isabelle's head began to throb. "Everyone sit," she said, and to her surprise everyone did.

Sally recovered her voice first and jumped up from her seat with a squeal. She rushed to Alice, groaning and grabbing her side, and threw her free arm around Alice's neck.

Isabelle supposed she shouldn't be surprised. She had seen the union coming—she had only assumed they would court for a year or so. Or five. Jean-Louis had a look about him, though, that spoke of grim determination. She had known that his return from Monemvasia to Athens only to find Alice gone would not sit well with him. A reluctant smile twitched at the corner of Isabelle's lips, and when the Frenchman met her eyes, searching her face for approval, she saw him relax.

"Congratulations," Isabelle said over Alice and Sally's chatter. "We can discuss the particulars later. For now, we have much to talk about."

Alice paused and frowned, placing a hand at the small of her back. If there had been any doubt about the authenticity of the jewel, it could now safely be put to rest.

"Are you not wearing your necklace?" Isabelle asked her.

"The clasp is broken—I left it here."

"We are going to need to fix it," Isabelle said.

They had the Jewel of Zeus and the Jewel of Hades. Now all they needed was the Jewel of Poseidon.

***

Jack and Phillip waited in the shadows of the train station and watched each passenger disembarking, gathering luggage, embracing loved ones, and moving on down the platform to waiting family carriages or hired cabs. The duo had been watching the station since midafternoon, when the group had decided they needed to find Sparks, who could lead them to the jewel. Jack only hoped the man would withdraw it from the bank upon his return. Surely he must be nervous by now—the constable in Delphi had confirmed that he was holding Adelphos in the local jail until further word from the Athenian authorities. That meant Sparks was on his own.

"I don't know how you can stand this," Phillip muttered. "Surveillance is for the birds."

Jack spotted a familiar figure exiting the train—one of the last to do so. The man carried a solitary satchel and looked harried. "And sometimes it pays big dividends, my friend," Jack told Phillip with a clap on the back. "There's our man."

Phillip emitted a low growl, and Jack wondered if he was going to have to restrain the man. "Not yet," Jack murmured. "You'll have your chance to exact your pound of flesh but not until we have the jewel."

"I wonder if he will go straight to the bank." Phillip watched the man with narrowed eyes.

Jack stood and began following Sparks, Phillip close on his heels. They weren't far from the center of the city and Syntagma Square, close to the bank and police station, both. Jack weighed their options as Sparks turned in the direction of the bank rather than Adelphos's house. If they took the time to alert the police, they risked losing Sparks—there was no guarantee he would return to the house. Jack wasn't certain he trusted Phillip to follow the man alone while he found an officer, and he knew that if he tailed Sparks while Phillip went to the authorities, he might not be able to keep up if a chase should ensue. He was feeling stronger but still required the use of his cane.

Sparks was proving to be nothing if not predictable. He went straight to the bank, which was five minutes from closing time; withdrew something from his deposit box; placed it in his coat pocket; and left, looking furtively around himself as he walked. The darkness had now fully fallen, and Jack and Phillip were able to follow the man in relative stealth, hiding in the shadows and staying far enough behind that when Sparks looked over his shoulder, their identities were unclear.

Sparks stopped at a sidewalk café, purchased a pastry and a cup of coffee, then continued on his way to Adelphos Kilronomos's house. Jack knew that Phillip and Jean-Louis had been inside the place, and he had to admit a grudging respect—he wouldn't have thought either of them capable of pulling it off. The benefit of it now, of course, was that Phillip had a knowledge of the layout of the home. Their best chance for obtaining the jewel would be while Sparks slept.

"What will his next move be, do you suppose?" Jack asked Phillip.

Phillip shrugged a shoulder. "He has the one jewel—the intelligent thing would be to cut his losses and run. He's greedy though, and now that he knows there are three, he may just be stupid enough to stay here and try to find the one from Elysia's garden. He believes the Jewel of Zeus to still be in India."

Jack took a deep breath. "Our best plan, at this point, is to get inside the house again. Do you believe you can do it?"

"Of course."

"I should rephrase that. Can you do it without killing the man in his sleep?"

"Now that I can definitely do. I want him looking me in the eye when I plant my fist in his face."

"Wonderful," Jack muttered.

"I won't do it tonight," Phillip said, his tone implying more than a little regret. He glanced up at the sky and sniffed the air. "Do you smell something odd?"

Jack wrinkled his brow as he also inhaled through his nose. There was something . . . something . . .

"Sulfur. Just as your grandfather said."

Jack looked ahead at the man they trailed, who was turning onto the streets of Adelphos's neighborhood. Something was definitely wrong. If not wrong, he supposed, then it just wasn't quite *right*. He attuned himself to the surroundings and realized he wasn't hearing the usual night sounds—no animals or insects, nothing that provided the familiar backdrop of the city at the end of the day

They fell back farther as Sparks neared the house; then they hid in the shadows as the man withdrew a key and unlocked the front door. With a final look over his shoulder, he entered and closed the door behind him.

Phillip looked at Jack, who nodded once. "And now, we wait again," Jack told him. "There is a yard just there across the street with a fair amount of coverage. I suggest we make ourselves comfortable."

The time passed slowly—the minutes seemed to last twice as long as usual, and Jack felt a sense of restlessness and urgency that grew increasingly uncomfortable. Finally, after the light in the house had been extinguished for nearly forty minutes, Jack nodded at Phillip, who stood and stretched stiff muscles.

Jack rose a little more slowly and put his hand on Phillip's shoulder. "Now," he said and paused. "You must be quiet. Please, for the love of heaven, be quiet."

Phillip huffed and looked a bit offended. "I've done this once before, you forget."

"There was nobody in the house at the time."

Phillip, to his credit, tipped his head to the side in acknowledgment. "I will be as quiet as a mouse," he said. "Not to fret."

"Right. Well then, off you go."

***

The hotel sitting room was again a hub of activity as the group waited for Jack and Phillip to return. Dr. Pearce filled in all of the missing holes and gaps that the mystery of his documents had produced.

They were killing time, really, and Isabelle still felt as though her head was nothing but soupy fog. Her chest burned when she coughed, and she cursed the timing. More than once since returning from Delphi, she had reviewed the events that transpired in the small house when Adelphos discovered her, and she cursed her clumsiness at the whole mess. Had she been feeling well, she would never have made so many mistakes. If James hadn't been there . . . She gritted her teeth at the thought. She didn't like having to be rescued.

Seeking to distract herself from the unpleasant thoughts, she turned her attention to the young women seated adjacent to her on a small sofa.

Isabelle watched Alice's face as she explained the reason for her hasty elopement.

"He said he wanted to be by my side day and night, and I realized I wanted nothing more. When he told me he'd already made arrangements with the license—he procured it the day after I was abducted!—and asked if I would be willing to buck convention, I told him yes, absolutely I would!"

Sally clasped her friend's hand. "That is so very romantic," Sally said. "I think you made the right decision. And I heard he booked the room next door for the two of you." They leaned their heads together and giggled, Alice's face turning beet red.

Isabelle had her own opinion on the matter—she wasn't sure she was comfortable with Alice being in the next room and not in one that adjoined the suite. She was forced to admit that Alice had been abducted from the suite, however, and was probably safer sleeping in the same bed as her husband than in a twin bed next to Sally's.

Isabelle rose and slowly paced the room, looking over Jean-Louis's shoulder as she passed his chair. They had gone to the bank to retrieve the items from the safe deposit box earlier in the day, and Jean-Louis now studied the tapestry that depicted the Guardian offering the stones to the volcano. It was the only explanation they could come up with, and as Isabelle pieced the bits of the legend together, she finally understood Dr. Pearce's need for the submersible. He confirmed her theory when she asked and made mention of a sketch he had seen years earlier of the tapestries themselves. The wording on the sketch had said, "Returning home," and while cryptic, it had made perfect sense to him.

If the tapestry was to be believed, they needed to jettison the jewels under the water at the volcano roughly fifteen feet below the surface, according to Dr. Pearce's best guess. The legend stated that the ancient city had been buried under water—if the jewels were to be returned to that spot, they would need the use of the odd ship. They couldn't very well go to Santorini and stand on the shore if the volcano was erupting, and in a conventional ship, there was no guarantee the jewels would reach the right spot.

Where the right spot was, exactly, was up to Alice to determine. On impulse, Isabelle turned to Dr. Pearce, who was in quiet conversation with James at a small seating area in the corner of the room. They looked up as she approached, beginning to rise from their seats, and the doctor smiled at her.

"You have a question for me, I can tell."

She returned his smile and motioned for them to sit. "Please, I need to stand and stretch my muscles. And I do have a question for you. How did you determine the proper way to dispose of the jewels from a sketch?"

He sighed a bit and his gaze turned contemplative. "I visited Athens many years ago as a student, and I saw the sketch in an old bookshop. The sketch was part of a diary that was full of symbols and pictures someone had written on paper that was so aged it was thin and in danger of ripping apart. But the picture itself was very clear—more so than the tapestry, even," he said, motioning to Jean-Louis.

Isabelle felt her eyes widen. "Do you have it?"

His face fell. "To my everlasting regret, I put it down and then was distracted by a fellow student who wanted me to come and see a parade that was moving down the street. When I returned to the store some time later, I couldn't find the book, and the shop owner had no idea what I was talking about. When I later learned of the legend, I realized what the book had been and thus began my obsession. I never forgot that image—of a Guardian returning the jewels to the ocean—and knew when I heard of effective submersible designs that it would be the only way to properly do the job." He smiled. "I've had the shack at Piraeus rented for twenty years while I perfected the craft."

"A pity you never did find that book," James said.

Dr. Pearce nodded. "Aside from the jewels themselves, it was the one thing I really did want to see again."

Isabelle smiled at the gentleman, so glad for Jack's sake that his grandfather was still alive. And the doctor's reaction to the two jewels that rested in James's pocket had been priceless. He had been in absolute awe, his eyes filming over with tears when he held one in each hand. He had questioned Alice about the mark, marveling at her as though she were the goddess Diana. And Alice, for her part, had charmed him and conversed with him until all of his questions were answered.

Alice had come so far from the young woman she had been when Isabelle had first met her. Had it been eight whole months ago? The time had flown, and yet Isabelle felt as if she'd known each of the players in their little entourage for an eternity. She worried about the outcome of the whole endeavor and realized that, even had she not been so sick, she'd still not likely have had much of an appetite.

"What is it?" James asked her softly.

She turned to him and realized he'd been quietly studying her. "So many things can go wrong," she murmured.

"Yes, and yet so many things can go right," Dr. Pearce said to her with a gentle smile. "All we need is the third jewel. As soon as we have it, we will head for the docks and leave on the steamer ferry carrying my sweet *Betty*."

Isabelle's lips twitched. "*Betty*?"

"Yes. Named for my first love. I was seven years of age, and she was a grand fifteen. I was heartbroken when she eventually married the baron's son."

"She wouldn't wait for you, hmm?"

"No. Alas, she was ignorant of my very existence."

James cleared his throat a bit. "Your *Betty*, then. She is seaworthy? You are certain?"

Isabelle understood his concern. Alice had said that she wanted Isabelle to accompany her and the doctor when the time came to return the jewels to their former home. Jean-Louis had understood, thankfully. He seemed to realize that Isabelle had become the mother Alice had always needed. The young woman had been a bundle of nerves when the doctor had explained what he believed the process should entail, and when Isabelle had agreed without reservation to be with her, Alice had visibly relaxed.

"My *Betty* is tight as a drum and very fast," the doctor assured them. "With the help of some hired hands, I secured *Betty* in the ship this afternoon, and I calculate that we will be at sea for five hours before we reach Santorini, at which point we will launch *Betty* into the water and be on our way."

"She's been tested, then?" James pressed.

"Indeed. Admittedly not under an exploding volcano, but still—in normal conditions she's done very well."

James's face took on a slightly green hue and Isabelle laughed, which then precipitated a coughing spasm that had her turning away from the men as she tried to control it. James handed her his handkerchief from behind, and she took it, dabbing at her mouth and nose. To her great chagrin, the room was silent and all eyes were on her.

"For heaven's sake, I'm fine," she croaked out.

Nobody seemed to believe her, but they had the grace to remain silent. That she felt her fever rising again was a fact she decided to keep to herself. "Sally, why don't you ring for some tea and biscuits. Phillip and Jack should be back soon, and we can all have refreshments before we embark on our journey.

32

PHILLIP STOOD IN SPARKS'S BEDROOM, frozen in one spot because he'd stepped on a floorboard that creaked. The jewel was in the room; there was no doubt about it. The star-shaped birthmark on his back itched, and there was a slight burn that was just enough to cause discomfort.

Sparks turned in his sleep, mumbling something unintelligible, and Phillip rolled his eyes. His hatred of the man nearly choked him when he remembered the things Sparks had said to him to coerce him into continuing their farce of a quest all those months ago in India.

When all was quiet again, Phillip eased his way over to the coat stand where Sparks had hung his overcoat. A quick search of the bureau drawers had yielded nothing, and Phillip wondered where he might put the jewel himself if he were trying to hide it. The coat pockets were empty, and Phillip ran a hand through his hair in frustration. It was when he turned his head back toward the sleeping man that Phillip realized where he would place the jewel if it were up to him.

Creeping ever so slowly toward the bed, Phillip moved with agonizing care until he was at Sparks's side. He looked down at him for a moment, his nostrils flared in distaste and anger. With as much stealth as he could muster, he slowly reached his hand down and placed it at the edge of Sparks's pillow. Sliding his fingers forward a fraction at a time, he was about to admit he'd been wrong when his fingertip touched something solid. He continued inching his hand forward until he was able to just grasp the stone with his fingertips.

Holding his breath, Phillip pulled the stone out from under the pillow and had it fully in his hand when Thaddeus Sparks opened his eerie green eyes and stared at Phillip, who was less than a foot from his face.

Phillip jumped back in horror and ran to the door as Sparks gathered his wits about him and shouted, scrambling to disentangle himself from the bed sheets. Phillip slammed the bedroom door closed as he heard Sparks crashing to the floor; he ran down the hallway and out the front door.

He heard Sparks screaming behind him, and he made his way nearly across the street when he saw Jack and changed his mind. He tossed the stone to Jack and hissed, "Go!" before turning back toward the house and then running down the street in full sight of Sparks, who wasted no time in tearing after him.

He ran through the streets, recognizing the maze of alleys and walkways as he grew closer to the Acropolis. Racing up the path to the ancient ruins, he hoped he'd drawn Sparks far enough away from the house to give Jack a clear shot at returning to the hotel.

***

Jack was so surprised when Phillip tossed him the jewel that he nearly dropped it. Fumbling for a moment, he finally grasped it and withdrew farther into the shadows as Sparks raced out of the front door and down the steps, stuffing his foot into a shoe as he ran. Jack waited until both men were out of sight, and then he turned and ran in the other direction for the hotel. The first few spats of rain hit his face as he ran, and he wondered if they would see a repeat of the bad weather that had plagued them in Delphi.

It was slow going—his side hurt and he was fatigued by the time he arrived, but he made good time considering his limitations. Climbing the stairs quickly, he entered the sitting room, where eight pairs of eyes turned and looked at him.

"I have the jewel, and Sparks is chasing Phillip." Jack tried to catch his breath.

Sally and James both rose from their chairs at his pronouncement, and he winced, thinking after the fact that he probably could have been a bit more gentle with his delivery. They didn't have the luxury of time, however.

"We need to alert the police," Isabelle said.

"I'm going to find him," James added, making long strides toward the coatrack by the door.

"James, no," Isabelle said. "You don't know where he is."

"Neither do the police." James withdrew his weapon from his coat pocket, checked it, and then shrugged into his overcoat.

"She's right," Jack said to James as he moved to leave the room. "Phillip will return here before you could ever find him."

"Which direction were they headed when you saw them last?"

Jack looked at the man, whose determination was clearly written on his face. "East. My best guess is that he'll head for the Acropolis."

James was off without a backward glance, and Jack closed the door behind him, wondering at the best course of action. Before he could formulate a thought, however, there was a knock on the door.

"What on earth?" Isabelle said and moved to his side.

As his hand was still on the doorknob, Jack turned it to see one of the hotel errand boys. "Down in the lobby," the boy said breathlessly. "You must come!"

"Who?" Isabelle asked.

"Miss Petrojanis."

Jack looked over his shoulder at Helene, who approached the door and spoke to the young boy in Greek. The boy answered back in a flurry of expression and animated gestures.

Helene looked at Jack, her expression grim. "It is Demetrios Metaxas. He is here and has been injured."

Jack turned to Jean-Louis and his grandfather, whose presence he had just registered. "You remain here with the young women." The Frenchman nodded his agreement, and Jack followed Helene and Isabelle down the stairs after the errand boy.

The noise in the lobby increased as they descended, and they heard the museum owner before they reached the main level. When they finally did, Jack had to stop short to keep from running into Isabelle, who had bumped Helene. The older woman stood with her mouth agape at the sight of a bleeding, bruised Demitrios.

When the man saw her, he turned his attention from the hotel manager, who was trying to usher him outside. Demitrios rushed to her side and spoke to the three of them, looking at Jack and Isabelle with equal measures of urgency as he talked.

Helene put a hand on his arm and apparently told him to slow down and repeat himself because he swallowed and rubbed a bloody handkerchief on his swollen lip then spoke more deliberately.

Helene's face drained of all color, and she looked at Jack and Isabelle. "His brother is the leader of the King's Men. Demitrios stumbled upon them making plans to sabotage the submersible."

***

Phillip reached the top of the Acropolis before slowing his pace and deliberately allowing Sparks to catch up to him. He planted his feet, but Sparks still took him to the ground with his momentum. The rain splashed down in earnest now, and the smell of sulfur hung heavy in the air.

Sparks got a few good shots to Phillip's midsection before Phillip could muscle the fight into his favor and roll Sparks onto his back. He vaguely registered pain in his hand as he hit the man's face but ignored it as he exacted several months' worth of vengeance.

Phillip finally stood and looked down at Sparks, who was breathing heavily and rolling onto his side. He would have to drag the man to the police station, but he was more than willing to. He only regretted having left his weapon back at the hotel, a move which had been unforgivably stupid.

Apparently, Sparks hadn't had the same oversight. What Phillip had assumed was loss of consciousness had been Sparks's efforts to roll on his side so Phillip wouldn't see the gun he pulled from his pocket. Phillip registered the weapon seconds before Sparks aimed it at him and fired. He jumped out of the way and rolled behind a pillar edging the Parthenon as Sparks rose to his feet.

"Where are you, Ashby?" Sparks said, winded. "Come out now and I won't return to Utah and visit your mother."

Phillip closed his eyes and gritted his teeth. His mistake had been easing up. He should have pummeled the man to death.

"I want the jewel back. It belongs to me!"

Phillip listened through the rain as the voice moved closer to him. He slipped behind the next pillar and waited. Peering carefully around the side, he looked into the darkness, waiting for Sparks to get close enough. A flash of lightning illuminated the ruins just enough for Phillip to see Sparks moving toward him. He inched his way out from behind the pillar and jumped at Sparks, shoving the man's gun arm up.

Spinning him around, Phillip smashed Sparks's back up against a pillar and smacked his hand against it to force him to release the gun. When it clattered to the ground, the fight began again in earnest.

Sparks hit Phillip hard enough to knock his breath out and shoved him back while Sparks dove to the ground and felt around for the gun. Phillip charged at him, and when Sparks stood, Phillip shoved him out of the interior of the Parthenon and near the edge of the plateau.

"Give me back the jewel, Ashby! You had no right to take it from me!"

"You took it from us!"

Rain fell steadily, and wind whipped into Phillip's eyes, distracting him enough that he didn't see Sparks's fist coming at his face. The blow that landed on his jaw had him seeing stars, and he stumbled backward. He was dangerously close to the edge, behind which was a rocky drop of two hundred feet. Stumbling and slipping on loose rock and dirt, he caught his balance and moved away from the edge.

Sparks caught him again on the side of his head, and Phillip fell to his knees. When the man moved closer and grabbed at Phillip's coat, attempting to search the pockets, he had enough presence of mind to elbow Sparks in the stomach. Phillip stood groggily and tried to focus in on the man's face, which had doubled in his vision.

Sparks grabbed Phillip by the lapels and twisted Phillip's necktie so that he was choking. "Where—is—the—jewel?"

With his last ounce of strength, Phillip head butted his captor on the bridge of the nose and felt immediate relief as Sparks's hold on his clothing released. Sparks fell backward, losing his footing and slipping over the edge of the precipice and onto the rocks below with a scream.

Bloody and bruised, Phillip breathed heavily as he carefully made his way to the side of the Acropolis, where another flash of lightning illuminated Sparks's broken body on the rocks below. The startlingly green eyes were open and lifeless.

Phillip turned at the sound of footsteps and a shout. James ran toward him and pulled him away from the edge, looking down into the abyss. "Is he down there?" he shouted at Phillip over the storm.

Phillip nodded.

"Is he dead?"

"Yes." Shock replaced his numb rage, and he soon found himself trembling with relief. "He's dead."

***

Isabelle considered the group of people in the room, knowing that the decisions they made in the next few minutes would be crucial. Demitrios was sitting in a chair at the hearth, a bandage wrapped around the worst of the cuts on his head; the bruising would take several days to fade, and she wondered at the little man's tenacity—he'd taken a beating and still managed to warn them of his brother's plans. It crossed her mind briefly to wonder if it was all a ploy—that perhaps Demitrios was part of a conspiracy intent on leading them into a trap—but she dismissed it with no other reason than that it didn't feel right, and she trusted her instincts.

She was worried about James and Phillip—there was nothing to be done for it though, and it couldn't be helped. They would have to manage without the brothers and hope James would find Phillip before Sparks killed him. Her stomach clenched in knots, and she forced her mind away from a haunting image of Phillip lying dead on the streets of Athens.

A knock on the door interrupted her thoughts, and she moved to answer it, admitting Leila, who carried up a tea tray, along with another young girl who stood behind her holding a second tray with small sandwiches and a few pastries.

Alice and Sally rose to set up the trays, probably grateful to have something to do. Leila, true to form, took the teapot and poured an amount into a cup for Jack. He took the cup and saucer from her absently, and Isabelle wondered if the girl would ever be at ease around him. For all that she seemed to adore him, her skittishness never seemed to abate.

"Phillip!" Sally's declaration turned Isabelle's attention toward the door, where James and Phillip entered, wet from the rain and the younger brother looking a little worse for the wear. Sally set down the teapot she had taken from Leila, and Alice was obliged to steady the tray as Sally launched herself at Phillip. He closed his arms around her and buried his face in her hair, his eyes closed.

Isabelle looked to James and he gave her a nod. "The police are retrieving the body," he told her as he approached, running a hand through his wet hair and shrugging out of his sodden overcoat. She looked again at Phillip, who showed evidence of cuts and bruises. There would be time for details later.

Taking a deep breath, she took stock of their circumstances, shivering a bit with the fever she felt returning. She quickly told James and Phillip what had transpired with Demitrios. "He just told us that the King's Men have been following us and they know about Dr. Pearce. Baltasar's right-hand man at the gun shop was the one who accosted Sally and stole the second tapestry. Once they had it, they pieced together the significance of the submarine and are planning to somehow sabotage it around midnight."

James pulled his pocket watch from his vest and checked the time. "That's in an hour. And there's something else—the air outside smells heavily of sulfuric acid."

Isabelle's brows drew together as she looked at him in question.

"I believe our volcano is active," Jean-Louis said.

Jack set his saucer and cup untouched back on the tea tray with a frown. "We need to leave now. We have the jewels, we have the box—we must get Alice to Santorini."

Alice turned to Isabelle with wide eyes. "You will go with me, yes?"

Isabelle nodded. "Of course."

Claire had moved her way across the room from where she'd been sitting with Helene, and she subtly took one of Isabelle's hands and felt the palm with her fingertips. When Isabelle looked at her in surprise, Claire whispered, "You're warm again, Isabelle. You don't look well."

"I don't have time for that," Isabelle whispered back. "I'll lie down and take whatever medication you think I need when we return."

"Do you want me to accompany you in the submersible? Is there enough room?"

Isabelle shook her head, half listening in on the other conversations in the room. "There's room for just the three of us. I'll be fine."

She turned to join the others when Claire grabbed her arm. "Belle," she said, swallowing.

Isabelle gave her sister her full attention, a bit irritated until she saw the look of distress on Claire's face.

"Belle, I just found you again, and—"

Isabelle hugged Claire impulsively and whispered to her sister, "I will be fine, and when the night is over, we will be back in this hotel room again together."

Claire pulled back and brusquely made a show of shaking some nonexistent dust from her skirt while surreptitiously wiping a finger at the corner of her eye. "Very well then," she said and straightened her shoulders, looking at Isabelle with watery eyes. "I suppose I shall have to take care of that one." She nodded a head toward Jack, who was leaning heavily on his cane as he talked to his grandfather and James.

Isabelle smiled, though it felt somewhat grim as she and Claire joined the men. "He's tired. We're all tired."

"Very well then," James said as he turned to Isabelle. "We will all go to the docks with the jewels. We keep them separate as agreed. You have the first one?"

Isabelle nodded.

"Alice, you have the one we just found at Elysia's?"

Alice nodded as well and patted her pocket.

"Jack, you have the one from Sparks?"

"Yes. Who has the box?"

Jean-Louis lifted the cloth bag that held the box Jack and Isabelle had found in Monemvasia. "Remember," he said, looking at his new young bride and handing it to her, "do not place the stones into the box until it is time to jettison them from the submarine."

Alice swallowed visibly and nodded her head.

James turned again to Isabelle. "You, Dr. Pearce, Alice, and Jack will leave in the ferry carrying the submersible. We will see you off and then come back here to the hotel until you return."

Isabelle nodded and took stock of the others in the room. By this time, the young women and Helene had gathered around to listen to the plans. Helene looked back over her shoulder at Demitrios, who still sat staring into the fire.

"Did he know about his brother before this?" Isabelle asked her.

Helene shook her head. "I don't think so. He knew his brother was a follower of the legend, but I do not believe he knew Baltasar was the head of the King's Men. Demitrios seems to be rather in a state of shock." Looking at Isabelle and then the others, her lips pursed; she looked back at Isabelle. "I will stay here with him. If his brother comes looking, he will need help."

Isabelle quirked a brow. "You will hold them off by yourself?"

Helene smiled. "I too have a pistol." She patted her dress. "I've carried it with me since Sally was attacked."

Isabelle nodded at her, and Helene joined Demitrios by the hearth.

"If you're hungry, eat now before we leave," Sally said as she went back to the tea tray and took a healthy bite out of a pastry.

"I couldn't eat a bite to save my life," Alice muttered, and Isabelle couldn't agree more. Whether from nerves or her illness, she wondered if she'd ever again have an appetite.

Isabelle was fetching her cloak when she noticed Leila still hovering in the room. While the girl certainly danced attendance on Jack, she didn't usually linger so long after delivering tea. Isabelle's eyes narrowed as she moved to approach Leila; something wasn't right.

Leila stood near the door, the other serving girl having long since left the room. Isabelle cursed the oversight—she ought to have noticed. She was nearly upon the young woman when Leila's face took on an expression of sheer horror as she stared at someone in the room. Scrambling, she turned around and opened the door, dashing into the hallway.

Isabelle glanced at the group as she bolted for the door to give chase. There didn't seem to be anything unusual that would have warranted her reaction. James and Jean-Louis were finishing the last of their cups of tea; Phillip had a pastry in each hand as he returned from his bedroom in a dry overcoat, a fresh coat for James slung over one arm; and Alice straightened the collar of her coat and helped Sally into hers. Helene and Demitrios stood now, making their way to the door to accompany the group as far as the lobby, and Helene wrung her hands, although her face held its practical expression well enough.

Dashing out onto the landing, Isabelle spied Leila, who was running down the stairs and was out of the hotel's front door by the time Isabelle reached the lobby. She was winded and light-headed. Bracing a hand on the wall, she stared for a moment at the closing door and realized she'd never catch the girl in her current condition.

With a silent curse, she made her way back up the stairs and stood at the doorway. Movement seemed to slow as she studied the tableau before her. James and Jean-Louis—placing cups and saucers back on the tea tray. Phillip wiping confectionary sugar from the side of his mouth. Sally and Claire, who must have seen her mad dash out the door, looking at her in question and walking toward her.

Time stilled as she looked over at Jack, who was helping his grandfather shrug into his coat. The entire room seemed to slow its movement until the figures in it were virtually frozen as Isabelle watched.

James placing his cup and saucer on the tea tray.

James placing *Jack's* cup and saucer on the tea tray.

Jack's tea, which Leila poured specifically for him, that he didn't so much as sip. He had placed it on the tea tray, and James had picked it up.

Time returned to normal with a sickening rush, and Isabelle put a hand on the doorframe. "James," she whispered as her fiancé accepted the dry overcoat Phillip handed him and shrugged his wide shoulders into it with easy, masculine grace.

"James!"

The others stopped in their tracks and stared at Isabelle, whose breath now came in short gasps. "Did you drink that whole cup?"

James looked at her, his brow creased in a frown. "Yes. Why?" He reached her side and grasped her arm. "What is it?"

Had she imagined the whole thing? He was fine. Isabelle shook her head slightly and stared at the tea tray. James was watching her closely, as was Jack by this time.

"What is it, Isabelle?" Jack asked her.

"I don't know . . . nothing."

"What is it?" he repeated.

"Leila always pours your tea, yes?"

Jack shrugged a shoulder. "Yes, I suppose."

"She's fawned over him since our arrival," Sally said. "I've felt rather sorry for her to be so obvious."

"You've not been ill?" Isabelle asked, wondering if she were losing her mind.

"Not at all. What are you suggesting? That she's been slowly poisoning me?" As he said the words, the color drained from his face.

Claire shook her head. "You would have felt the effects by now," she said. "We would think you were coming down with an illness. The only problems you've suffered have been as a result of the gunshot wound. Is that correct?"

Jack nodded and looked at Claire. "I haven't felt the least bit ill."

They all looked back at Isabelle, who stared into James's face. Feeling her eyes begin to burn, she shoved her way through the crowd of people at the door and picked up the cup she'd seen James holding. Running a finger along the bottom of the cup, she came away with fine particles of something that might have been from the herbs used to make the drink.

Claire came to her side and looked at the cup and Isabelle's finger. Claire had already donned her gloves, so she pulled one from her hand and drew her finger through the cup as Isabelle had. Touching the tip of her tongue to her finger, her eyebrows knit together as she then rubbed the particles between her thumb and forefinger. With a slight shrug, she said, "I don't taste anything unusual, but that may not mean anything."

"It doesn't taste like the tea herbs either though," Isabelle said, lightly placing her finger on her own tongue.

Dr. Pearce cleared his throat. "Ladies, I fear we are running short on time."

Isabelle placed the cup back on the saucer and shook her head. Claire frowned and looked at the cup for a few protracted moments before making her way to the door. "No odor, no discernible taste . . ." Isabelle heard Claire murmur.

Isabelle withdrew her gloves from a pocket in her cloak and pulled them onto her hands, which shook. James took her elbow as she reached the door, and she looked up again into his face. "You are well?" she whispered to him as they descended the stairs, feeling her eyes welling up again. She blinked back the unshed tears and wished her inner voice would stop screaming that something was wrong.

James nodded and glanced at Isabelle, his face creased in concern before checking his watch again as the group reached the lobby. "We do not have much time at all," he said grimly. In a quick rush, Jean-Louis asked the concierge about securing two cabs despite the late hour. With the promise of additional coin, the man agreed to roust the hotel's drivers.

Isabelle was chilled despite the layers of clothing, and when they stepped outside, she shivered in the gusts of wind that swept the rain into visible waves. The group waited under the hotel awning, and Isabelle felt Claire was watching her closely. She wanted to be able to convince her sister that she was fine.

After several long minutes, the first of two cabs drew up, and the driver climbed down and opened the door, handing in Alice and then Sally. He was holding out a hand for Isabelle when she heard James cough behind her. The cough turned into a choking sound, and she whirled around.

There was white foam at the corner of his mouth, and as Isabelle flew to him and grasped his arms, his knees buckled and he began to fall, still choking and gasping for air.

"No! No!" she screamed, staggering under his weight. "Do something!" She looked at Claire, whose eyes were round with shock.

Claire rushed to Isabelle and grabbed James as the chaos erupted. Phillip braced his brother from the side and began to lower him to the ground.

Someone was pulling on Isabelle's shoulders as she clutched at James's jacket. "Leave me be! Stop!" Her voice was raw from the illness, and the horribly raspy, screeching sounds she made only added to the unreality of the moment.

Jack placed an arm about Isabelle's waist from behind and yanked her away from James with a force that left her gasping for air. He righted her and spun her to face him, grabbing her face roughly in his hands. "We must go," he said, punctuating each word. "Get Alice to the submarine, and rid the world of those infernal jewels."

Her tears fell in a torrent, and she felt her knees begin to give way. Jack grabbed her shoulders and shook her as she sobbed. When she tried to move toward James, Jack hauled her roughly up and against the side of the carriage where Alice and Sally sat, numb with shock. Sally, her eyes huge in her determined face, rushed down from the seat in the carriage to the group gathered around James, listening as Claire gave out orders in rapid, succinct direction. Isabelle heard the words "my medical bag upstairs" but couldn't wrap her brain around the moment. Pausing, Claire raised her head and shouted, "Isabelle, go!"

Phillip had tugged James's tie loose, talking to his brother in low, rushed tones, and Helene ran out from the hotel, where she'd apparently gone to fetch two large glasses of water. Jack shoved his shoulder into Isabelle's abdomen, lifted her off her feet, and heaved her into the carriage next to Alice. Dr. Pearce climbed in and then Jack, who followed Claire's command to leave with them.

The carriage pulled away with a lurch, and Isabelle looked out of the small window, her hands splayed on either side. With a shuddering sob and tears that blurred her vision, she watched the crowd gathered around her fiancé in the pounding rain until the carriage turned a corner and the scene was gone.

33

"CLAIRE IS VERY GOOD, VERY efficient," Jack told Isabelle as the carriage rattled through the night and toward the docks at Piraeus. "She will induce vomiting; he will be fine."

Isabelle looked up at Jack and wondered if he was trying to convince himself or her. He looked pale and shaken in the dim light of the carriage lantern. Holding her breath for a moment and biting down hard on her lower lip to keep the wracking sobs from coming, she took the handkerchief Dr. Pearce offered her. She wiped at her eyes, hiding for a moment behind the snowy white fabric that was monogrammed with the doctor's initials.

Arms crept around her from the side, and Alice pulled gently on Isabelle's head until it rested on the young woman's shoulder. Isabelle allowed herself a few more moments of terror and grief before sitting straight and wiping her nose. Taking a few deep, shuddering breaths and quietly blowing them out, she threw a prayer heavenward and willed her heart to slow. That it refused didn't come as a surprise.

She glanced at Alice, who touched a hand to Isabelle's cheek with a sad smile. "Your fever has returned, Belle. When we finish this horrid task, we will put you to bed and take care of you."

Isabelle returned a tentative smile when she noticed a slight, nearly imperceptible wince cross Alice's features. Still wiping at her running nose and trying to clear her throat enough to speak, Isabelle finally said, "Alice, your back."

Alice nodded with a shrug. "It isn't so abominably bad."

"And we forgot to take the time to fix the clasp on your talisman." It was with a sense of relief that Isabelle realized all three jewels had made it into the carriage, and Alice still held the sack with the ornate box. Claire, bless her, must have remembered Jack held the Egyptian jewel in his pocket, and thus her insistence he get in the carriage with them.

"All three stones together," Isabelle said, clearing her throat as tears still burned in her eyes. "It must feel awful."

"Well, in truth I cannot say it feels fine, but I can bear it for the time necessary."

Jack checked his pockets and withdrew his weapon and a stash of ammunition. "How long did you say it will take from the docks to Santorini?" he asked his grandfather.

Dr. Pearce's face was a study in worry. That he had been affected by the scene outside the hotel was evident. He cleared his throat. "Five hours. The ferry is quick. She travels at thirty knots."

Jack nodded and pocketed his gun and bullets, leaning his head back against the seat as the carriage made its way to the water. Dr. Pearce patted Jack's leg in reassurance a few times before turning and looking out the window on his side of the carriage.

It was on the tip of Isabelle's tongue to ask him how on earth he had a steamship that could travel at thirty knots when most of the ships of the day were considered fast at eighteen. Realizing that the man also had a completely seaworthy submersible that was powered with clockwork gears and cans of compressed air somehow made the question irrelevant.

The minutes ticked by in silence, punctuated occasionally with Isabelle's shaky, involuntary indrawn breaths that were a residual of her violent sobbing. She couldn't remember a time when the tears and grief had come that hard. Even losing Lincoln, horrifying though it had been, paled in comparison to the fear that gripped her heart and again flooded her eyes with hot tears as they neared the docks.

She blinked them back and drew on reserves of emotional numbness that had served her well during the war. Her sister was smart, and Isabelle could only hope that Claire would be able to preserve James's life.

As they disembarked from the carriage and gave the driver permission to return to the hotel without them, Jack, Dr. Pearce, Alice, and Isabelle made their way toward a dock near the doctor's boathouse. Isabelle had yet to see the submarine, and even now it seemed she would have to wait. It was situated in the bay of Dr. Pearce's speedy ferryboat, which they wasted no time in boarding.

Isabelle scanned the surroundings for signs of life other than seagulls and the occasional splashing fish. It appeared they had managed to beat the King's Men to the docks, and with any luck, they would be able to outdistance their pursuers should they give chase.

Isabelle glanced around when they entered the darkened wheelhouse. "Who is going to captain the ship?" she asked the doctor.

"I am," the little man answered her, and he set about the business of readying the craft for departure. "And Jack also knows how."

She glanced at Jack, a brow raised.

He nodded with a slight shrug. "It has been some time," he said, "but I believe I remember well enough." He made his way outside and removed the ropes that kept the boat moored to the pier. At Jack's signal, Dr. Pearce lifted anchor as the ship shuddered to life.

"So we should definitely be able to outrun any other ship that might follow us, then, yes?" Alice asked the older man.

"In theory."

"I'm sorry?"

Dr. Pearce looked at Alice. "We are carrying extra weight with the *Betty* on board. She does, unfortunately, slow us a bit."

Isabelle closed her eyes briefly. As Jack came up the steps to the wheelhouse, she turned to him and asked, "Did you see anyone out there?"

He shook his head. "Not on the docks, but I believe I saw lanterns on an approaching carriage."

"I wonder if Metaxas has access to a ship of his own," Isabelle murmured as she moved to look out of one of the wheelhouse windows. The ship pulled away from the pier and began, sluggishly, to fend her way out to open sea.

"Now then," Dr. Pearce said to Alice, "I know the way to Santorini. I have my charts and instruments. But once there and loaded into *Betty*, you will be the one to lead us."

Alice looked at him for a moment before finally nodding but quickly frowned as the boat continued on her path. "We are going the wrong way," she said.

Dr. Pearce smiled. "Not for long. Just until we get to the open water." The little man beamed at the girl. "You do know the way."

Jack approached Isabelle, his demeanor weary. "Isabelle, I owe you an apology for my rough treatment back at the hotel. I—"

She placed a hand on his arm and gave it a gentle squeeze. "It needed to be done, Jack. I harbor no grudge. I was nearly out of my head."

"Nearly."

The corner of her mouth quirked into a smile in spite of herself. "Very well. Completely."

"But understandably so."

The smile fell and she nodded.

"You must trust your sister. You left him in good hands."

"Yes. I did." She frowned as she considered something that hadn't fully struck her in the moments after she realized James had been poisoned. "Leila has been working for the Federation."

"Yes. That seems quite clear now, doesn't it? And here I thought the poor girl was just besotted the whole time. It seems I have an exaggerated sense of my own worth."

"Her nerves were real enough. She was never at peace around you—I wonder if she had been coerced, blackmailed perhaps. Threatened in some way," Isabelle mused.

"We must find her when we return," Alice said with a scowl. "I cannot imagine what could have been horrible enough for her to be convinced to kill someone."

"I don't know that we *should* find her for any reason other than one," Isabelle said. She pursed her lips for a moment. "We need to convince the Federation that she's done her job."

"If they had someone watching the hotel and saw James react to the poison and not me though, they will know," Jack said.

"Then perhaps we should make sure you do not return from this venture," Isabelle said.

He nodded slowly.

"We smuggled Lincoln into Washington, after all," she said. "We can find a way to keep you hidden. Get you out of the country."

"But then you likely cannot return home," Dr. Pearce said from his position at the wheel as he set their heading for Santorini.

Jack sighed. "There is that." He made his way to a bench that lined the wall and sat down. "Ladies, I beg your forgiveness for seating myself while you both still stand."

"Psh," Alice said and waved a hand at him.

"There are staterooms below us," Dr. Pearce told the women. "Just a couple, and they are plain but serviceable. Perhaps you both might get some rest?"

Isabelle looked at Alice, who seemed anything but tired. Determined perhaps, and a bit terrified, but not the least bit sleepy. "Come and keep me company," Isabelle said to her. "It will keep me from thinking too much."

Alice took Isabelle's arm in her own, and together they walked down the stairs and into the hallway below the wheelhouse. There were four doors, and opening the first they saw a small cabin with two beds.

"Perfect," Alice said and entered first, using the light in the hallway to find the lantern hanging by the door. She lit it with a box of lucifers hanging in a carved wooden match holder next to the lamp, and a warm glow soon spread far enough across the room that it felt a bit less dreary. "Would you rather I extinguish the light when you're settled?" Alice asked and removed her traveling cloak.

"No," Isabelle said. "I would prefer the light tonight."

Isabelle must have finally fallen asleep—in spite of her own misgivings about her ability to—because when Alice gently shook her shoulder, she had to force her eyes open. They were puffy from crying and felt gritty and sore. There was something wrong—she knew it in the back of her mind—but couldn't place it. With a sudden rush, she remembered James lying on the street, and her heart sped up uncomfortably.

With a light groan, she forced herself into a sitting position and took a deep breath before looking at Alice, who watched her with gentleness. "I should be caring for you right now, Alice," Isabelle murmured.

"You've always cared for me from the moment we met. Allow me to take a turn." Alice smiled at her, suddenly looking more mature, more like a woman and less a girl. She was married—mercy, had it only been a day?

"You've yet to even have a proper wedding night," Isabelle told her.

Alice blushed and rolled her eyes. "Time enough for that later," she said.

"Do you have any questions?"

Alice's jaw dropped open. "About my *wedding night?*"

Isabelle nodded with a shrug.

"Belle, we are about to embark on a perilous—what do you know of it anyway?"

"Enough."

Alice quirked a brow.

Isabelle smiled. "I have friends who talk."

Alice shook her head with a laugh. Grasping Isabelle's arm, she gently pulled. "Come. We need to go to the wheelhouse. Dr. Pearce says we're nearly there."

Isabelle squinted as they left the stateroom. "What is that noise? Thunder?"

"Mmm, no. That would be our volcano."

34

"I AM AFRAID WE HAVE encountered a bit of a complication," Dr. Pearce said as Alice and Isabelle climbed the stairs into the wheelhouse.

Isabelle looked at him and drew a deep breath. "You don't say."

"We have ourselves some company here on the high seas."

"What? How can you tell?" Isabelle asked him.

He pointed behind them out the rear wheelhouse window. "Do you see the lights?"

Isabelle and Alice both looked through the glass and noted lights on the horizon. Isabelle turned back to the doctor. "How much longer until we are close enough to launch *Betty*?"

"Ten minutes, fifteen perhaps. The problem lies in that we must drop anchor and remain stationary until we launch. That leaves Jack as a sitting duck in the water until we are clear and he can move out." The old man's hair was slightly ruffled, and his tie had been pulled loose. He checked his instruments for the third time in twenty seconds and looked out ahead of the ship at the expanse of black water.

Isabelle followed his gaze and tilted her head up as she caught sight of a red glow, coming ever closer, accompanied by the noise and the smell of sulfur heavy in the air. Lava spewed into the sky and rolled down the surface of the mountain, which itself was invisible in the dark.

Jack climbed the stairs to the wheelhouse and joined them as they looked at the eruption in awe. "The machine is set to go," he told his grandfather. Placing a hand on the older man's shoulder, he added, "You're certain about this? We can't just get close enough and toss the jewels overboard?"

Dr. Pearce shook his head. "We do not want to take unnecessary risks—suppose they do not get to the right place and some fortunate diver comes upon them at a later date. No, we have one chance, and we must do it right the first time."

"Are you certain that the lights from the boat behind us belong to our enemies?" Alice asked.

"Given the state of our luck, I would assume so," Jack answered for his grandfather. "We noticed them shortly after leaving Piraeus, roughly thirty minutes out. The only reason they haven't caught us is that, even loaded down with *Betty*, we still travel with slightly more speed."

"Surely many ships leave from Athens on a regular basis," Alice said. "Perhaps the authorities are sending resources to evacuate the people."

The doctor shrugged. "One can hope; however, the volcano has been spewing rock, ash, and lava for a while. According to the dockmaster, most of the locals have been evacuated already."

"When we reach our heading," Jack said, "we must not waste any time. How quickly can we put *Betty* into the water?"

"It is simple, just as I showed you." Dr. Pearce glanced at Jack, worry stamped on his features.

"I can care for myself. I'm beginning to think I'm indestructible."

"That might just be true," Isabelle told the older man, who still watched his grandson in concern. "He's been shot twice."

"Papa, it's what I do." Jack gave the man a sympathetic glance, and Isabelle understood. It was difficult to assuage the worry of loved ones when the profession involved such an element of danger.

"Perhaps we need to find you a different line of work." Dr. Pearce smiled a bit and took a deep breath. "Well then, I believe we are close."

Isabelle looked out of the window again, amazed to see indeed how close they were to the exploding mountain. The rumble was constant, and Isabelle noticed large areas of the sea's surface splashing, huge boulders displacing water as they were flung from the volcano's core and out into the night.

"Whatever you do," Isabelle told Jack, "do not get too close to the island. We'll resurface to find you sunk."

Jack nodded. "One of the scientific ships sent from Athens to study the volcano was hit by a large rock just two days ago. They haven't even managed to find any wreckage."

Isabelle frowned, worried, as she looked again at the melee outside.

"Here we are, then," Dr. Pearce said. "I believe this is a good spot."

Jack reached into his pocket and handed his grandfather the stone he still carried. "You care for this one, then, Papa," he said and clapped the man on the shoulder.

Isabelle watched from inside the submarine as Jack, standing on the lower deck of the ferry, worked the automated lever that lowered the submarine into the water. Dr. Pearce and Alice sat in the front two seats, and Isabelle sat between them and slightly behind. As they entered the water and moved away from the ferry, Dr. Pearce illuminated one forward light, which cast the world in an odd glow. As the submarine began to descend and water slowly crept up and over the craft's single window, Isabelle saw Jack watching them from the ferry until the ocean closed over them and they continued to drop down into the dark, roiling abyss.

With a loud whir and a flip of several switches, *Betty* accelerated and began propelling herself through the water. It was with a fair amount of alarm a scant few minutes later that Isabelle heard the whistle of artillery—a sound she hadn't heard for well over a year—muffled and distorted by the water. A projectile crossed just in front of the submarine, and Isabelle thought she heard the older man swear under his breath. Maneuvering quickly, Dr. Pearce forced the craft to accelerate, shoving them momentarily back into their seats.

Alice took a shaky breath and opened the cloth bag that held the beautifully translucent white box. Isabelle had collected the three stones just before climbing aboard *Betty*, and she now withdrew from separate cloth bags the Jewel of Zeus, the purple one from India; the Jewel of Poseidon, the orange stone from Egypt; and the Jewel of Hades, the blue rock from Greece. Spilling them carefully into her lap, she traced a finger over the three smooth ovals before scooping them up and handing them, one at a time, to Alice, who placed them into the box.

The jewels fit into the indentations inside the box as though the container was made for them, which, of course, it had been. The box itself seemed to glow—although Isabelle convinced herself that the fever was playing tricks on her mind. It was a study in beautiful color—the white of the box, the brilliance and translucence of the stones themselves. The hum that had always been lightly present with each jewel when in proximity of either Alice or Phillip now intensified. A buzz rang in Isabelle's ears, and she knew from a quick glance at Alice and Dr. Pearce that they also experienced the strange sensation.

A second, muffled explosion sounded from behind *Betty*. Isabelle wanted to ask Dr. Pearce what sort of defensive maneuvers the submarine was capable of performing but figured she would know soon enough if they were forced to evade.

"That way, to the right," Alice said, and the doctor obeyed her without hesitation. Isabelle bit her tongue, thinking the girl must know what she was talking about despite the fact that they now were skirting around the red slashes of lava she saw falling down below the surface of the water, slowing as they cooled.

Isabelle thought she heard a loud boom from above and behind them, and she closed her eyes, hoping Jack hadn't just been blown out of the water. She was beginning to think that if they all made it out alive it would be the most amazing of miracles. Dr. Pearce must have heard the noise as well because he winced but remained steadfast in following Alice's directions as she continued to have him skirt the island, farther and farther to the eastern side.

"Closer," Alice said, and Isabelle glanced at her. Her gaze was focused; her hands, which clutched the box, were white-knuckled.

The submarine angled to the left, and Alice frowned. "Farther forward, now to the left again."

There was a red glow ahead, showing in the dark beyond the reach of the submarine's light. Alice leaned forward in her seat, a sense of urgency clear in her movement. "As close as you can," she murmured to the doctor.

"I must swing about this way," he told her, "so that we face the island. Then we can jettison the stones straight ahead." As he was shifting the craft, cutting back on the propulsion and maneuvering so that the back end began to swing out and to the right, a large object crashed into the water close enough to the submarine that it was moved backward on a huge wave, spinning and turning it so that the beam of light swung wide, illuminating the black expanse of water and rendering their one point of visual, stable contact invisible.

"Where is the island?" Alice said, craning her neck around to the back, clearly having forgotten that there wasn't a window behind them.

The doctor grunted in frustration as he tried to stabilize the ship.

"What was that?" Isabelle murmured.

"A rock," he replied, his tone terse.

Alice's face turned a shade of green, visible even in the dim light that reflected back into the submarine.

"Oh dear," Isabelle said and placed a hand on Alice's arm. She glanced to her right and left, wondering if there wasn't something aboard the craft that was cold and portable for her to place on the back of Alice's neck to abate the seasickness that she should have guessed would return.

"I'm fine," Alice said, staring out the window and breathing shallowly in and out.

Dr. Pearce stole a glance at her as he fumbled with the controls. Another loud boom from above elicited a muttered curse, and Isabelle closed her eyes, hating the feeling of helplessness that crept up her spine and settled into her brain. James had been poisoned, Jack likely blown up, and they were going to die in a small, metal coffin beneath the waves of the Mediterranean.

"Belle," Alice said with a tremor, and Isabelle reached forward and grasped her hand.

"We will be fine," she told the young woman. "This will be finished soon, and you'll be with your husband again before you know it."

Alice managed a small smile. "My husband," she whispered. She took another bracing breath and visibly tried to steady her nerves.

Isabelle felt a sense of disorientation herself as the doctor fought the current and attempted to muscle the submersible back into position. Between the rocking of the ship and the buzzing from the jewels, she wondered how Alice hadn't already lost her dinner all over her lap.

"There," Dr. Pearce breathed as the island again came into view. "Are we in the right place, dear?"

Alice nodded and looked down at the box and opened the lid. "They are beautiful," she murmured. "I hate the necessity of this."

"Indeed they are beautiful," Isabelle said. "Now close the lid and hand them to the doctor."

He shook his head. "She must be the one to place them into the tube." He looked with an expression of what seemed to be longing on his face. "I have spent the better part of my life in the study of these jewels," he said. "I regret the necessity as well."

Alice nodded and snapped the box shut. There was a latch, and she fastened it securely. Eyes closed, she placed a kiss on the ancient box and looked to Dr. Pearce, who spun a metal wheel that swung open and revealed a hatch at the front, just below the instrument panel.

Alice placed the box inside the opening and closed the hatch, turning the wheel until it was shut tight. Dr. Pearce pointed to a large metal button next to the wheel and nodded at her.

With a final glance at the doctor and then Isabelle, Alice closed her eyes again and pushed the button. The box was propelled through the tube leading to the outside of the craft and was visible as it shot forward into the beam of light that illuminated the water to the black surface of the island, down which red lava continued to flow.

Isabelle watched, spellbound, as the projectile neared the mountain, which, in the submarine's light, showed a large fissure in the side. Alice reached back and clutched Isabelle's forearm, her nails digging into the skin. They visually tracked the jewels' progress as they entered the fissure with deadly accuracy.

Alice turned to look at *Betty*'s other two occupants. "That's it?"

Before either could answer her, an explosion ripped through the side of the mountain that threw the submersible back, tumbling it end over end and around, tossing the three from their seats and violently into the top and sides of the ship.

When the machine finally righted itself, Isabelle lay stunned for a moment before she finally had the wherewithal to push herself up from where she had sprawled onto the floor. Her head ached abominably, and she felt a warm trickle down the side of her face.

"Belle?" Alice's voice was tentative, but Isabelle was glad to hear it.

"I'm alive," she answered and shoved herself up into her seat, wiping at the blood that now poured in a steady stream. "Dr. Pearce?"

When the doctor didn't respond, Isabelle reached over to where his form had landed back in his seat. He leaned against the side of the craft, silent. Perhaps more alarming, however, was the fact that Isabelle felt water against her foot.

"Dr. Pearce?" Alice's voice took on a near screech.

Isabelle winced and placed a hand on Alice's arm. "Be still for a moment," she said and tried to restrain from screaming. She leaned forward and placed two fingers on the doctor's neck. The pulse was thready but still evident. Breathing a sigh of relief, she considered their options.

"How closely were you watching him drive this thing?" Isabelle asked Alice.

"What? *What?*"

Isabelle debated the wisdom of telling Alice she suspected there was also a crack in the fuselage. "Well," she finally said, "help me get him out of that seat and into mine."

Alice looked at her with huge eyes. Mutely, she nodded and leaned over with Isabelle, helping her drag the dead weight of the little man out of the captain's seat. Isabelle's wrist throbbed from where Adelphos had smashed it. She gritted her teeth to keep from groaning and was gratified instead to hear a groan coming from the doctor.

"Oh, good," Isabelle said, "you're still with us, Dr. Pearce."

He opened his eyes and squinted at Isabelle. She continued to gently move him into place and he cried out. She immediately stopped and spread her hands wide. "Where?"

"My arm," he said. "I fear it may be broken."

Isabelle's fear rose a notch as she felt warm water continuing to rise in the bottom of the submarine—slowly but clearly steadily as it now touched her ankle. The doctor must have also realized it because his eyes opened wide and he lifted his foot.

Isabelle moved forward and climbed into the captain's seat. "You're going to have to instruct me, and I don't know that we have much time."

"Water. There's water in here," Alice stammered and looked down at her feet.

"We will be fine," the old man murmured and leaned forward. "We must surface. Then we will see Jack." With his good arm, he pointed toward the controls and began instructing Isabelle, who followed explicitly.

She was relieved to feel the ship begin to rise, and it wasn't long before they broke the surface of the water, the world above coming visible by degrees as the ocean receded away from the front window. The explosion within the volcano had thrown them much farther than she had realized, and she squinted for any sign of the steamer.

"We traveled a fair distance around the island," the doctor said. "Take the controls and point us in that direction. Here—push this and this."

Isabelle did as he said, and *Betty*, bless her, began to move forward, crack in the hull notwithstanding. She was sluggish, however, and water continued to seep in by degrees.

"It's hot," Alice said. "The water."

"Yes, it would be," Dr. Pearce said. "There are points around the base of the volcano and in the caldera where the water is said to be boiling."

Lovely, Isabelle thought. Drowned *and* boiled to death. Steadily, they made their way across the waves, occasionally moved and bumped by rocks that continued to spew forth from the erupting mass beside them. Not wanting to alarm Alice further, Isabelle refrained from asking Dr. Pearce if he was a praying man. The odds of a large boulder hitting the submarine were huge as close as they were to the land.

Rounding the corner of the island, Isabelle strained to see if Jack was still where they had left him. It was with a fair measure of panic that she spied a boat in flames, and she knew from the indrawn breaths beside her that her companions had seen it as well.

Isabelle's heart sank. Not only did she feel a stabbing sense of grief for Jack, she realized that as clever as she was, and for all of the harrowing experiences she'd had in her life, their options may well be spent. To try and swim ashore, should the submarine sink, meant almost certain death from exposure to the boiling, toxically mineral-laden water. If Jack and the ship were gone, their only hope, and it was slight, was to try and reach the nearest island before *Betty* was completely incapacitated.

"My boy," Dr. Pearce murmured as they drew slowly closer to the steamer that burned like a beacon on the water. "Oh, Jack."

Isabelle's eyes burned as the grief swamped her in waves. James. Jack. Their own lives in peril. Had it all truly come to this? She had landed on her feet more times than she could count, and Isabelle wondered if her luck had finally run out. The one consolation was the destruction of the jewels. At least their efforts would not have been in vain.

"Circle around more to the right," Dr. Pearce told Isabelle, his voice heavy. "The nearest island will be on that side."

Isabelle nodded and attempted to maneuver the wounded craft, which protested but finally submitted, hobbling around the burning ship. Looking closely at the water at the base of the steamer, she watched for signs of life. Her heart sank as she glanced up to see the prostrate form of a man, hanging limply over the railing.

Her breath caught in her throat. She didn't want to point the man out to the other two. As they moved a bit closer, however, she noted the clothing on the dead man. His white pants were clearly visible through the railing, and unless Jack had changed his trousers, it must have been someone else.

"That is not my steamer," Dr. Pearce suddenly said. "The hull is different."

Isabelle slowly nodded as she followed around the side, the sickening sound of the clockwork gears faltering as the submarine struggled to keep moving. The steamer was indeed different, and she also noted the presence of another man farther along on the deck and then the gruesome sight of a charred body floating in the water.

"Where is Jack?" Alice wondered aloud.

"There!" Dr. Pearce pointed to the right, and as *Betty* drew her final, gasping breath, the water climbing steadily higher inside, their steamer came into view, with a familiar figure at the bow, waving his cane.

35

THE TRIP BACK TO ATHENS was excruciating. Isabelle had staunched the flow of blood from the gash on her head, but her headache increased—it hadn't entirely abated from the night before when Adelphos had tried to shove her through the floor—adding to her sense of misery from the fever and "lung condition," as Claire had called it. She was congested, her nose continually running, and when she tried to blow it as delicately as possible, she felt as though a bomb were exploding in her skull.

Worse than her physical discomfort, however, was the numbing fear that had wrapped its cold fingers around her heart and was squeezing until she thought she would die. It was the longest five hours of her life— unable to sleep or even rest, she stayed in the wheelhouse with the others, alternately standing next to Jack at the wheel and sitting on the hard bench that offered little comfort.

The other steamer, Jack had told them, had been captained by Baltasar Metaxas. He had been equipped with a full battery of weapons that he used without hesitation to fire on both Jack's steamer and the submersible, just after it had dipped below the surface. Jack had maneuvered the ship away as soon as the submersible left and, thanks to its advanced speed, had been able to put some distance between himself and the King's Men but not before a few shots of ammunition had ripped through the lower deck.

Withdrawing the captain's spyglass, Jack had taken a good look at the men aboard the ship with Baltasar and saw drama among the crew. The Federation's man—the Egyptian's right-hand, whom Jack had seen on the train station platform during their return from Delphi—was brandishing a weapon at Baltasar, clearly seeking for the upper hand in their one last desperate attempt to get their hands on the jewels.

One of Baltasar's men fired a bullet into the back of the Federation's man, and he dropped to the deck, not moving again. The most amazing part, Jack had said, was when the volcano seemed to explode from deep inside, spewing out streams of lava and enormous rocks that crashed against the base of the island and into the water. A huge, black boulder had landed on Metaxas's ship, and the bulk of his ammunition promptly ignited, sending a fireball shooting into the sky. Jack had returned to the site, but there were no signs of life—and he confessed he wasn't certain he would have taken any survivors aboard at any rate.

Dr. Pearce was in pain but seemed at peace, as did Alice, who sat near the older man for the majority of the trip. He told her of his research, of the part the jewels had played in his life.

Late morning was upon them and in full swing when they finally reached the familiar dock at Piraeus, and Jack positioned the boat close to the pier, where Isabelle jumped and helped a dockworker to secure the boat. The hired conveyances were already operating for the day, transporting people back and forth to the city, and once the ship was in place, her engines quiet, the four piled into a carriage.

Isabelle leaned back against the cushion, her head rocking with the movement of the carriage, her fist unconsciously clenched tightly in her lap until Alice took it in her own hand and laced their fingers together. Alice didn't say anything but allowed Isabelle to squeeze her hand for the thirty-minute ride into the heart of Athens.

As they pulled up alongside the front of the familiar hotel, Isabelle looked at the spot on the ground where James had lain the night before. She sat for a moment, and the others waited. The carriage driver jumped from his seat and opened the door, flipping the stairs down into place.

"I don't want to go in," Isabelle finally admitted with a murmur.

Jack moved then and stepped down first. Reaching a hand up to her, he made a beckoning motion with his fingers when she made no attempt to join him. "Let's go inside," he finally said in his lilting brogue. "I want to have a good, long look at your sister."

Laughing a bit in spite of herself, she took his hand and climbed down the few steps to the street. Alice followed, and with great care Jack helped his grandfather alight. They were a sorry looking sight as they entered the hotel lobby, and the concierge, in some alarm, asked if they needed medical assistance.

Dr. Pearce's Greek was passable enough that he was able to explain the injury to his arm, and he then translated the message that the hotel would arrange transportation to the hospital. Dr. Pearce wanted to see the others, though, and his true thoughts weren't difficult to discern; he wanted to know whether or not James had survived.

As they climbed the stairs to the second floor, Isabelle realized they could have just asked the concierge about James, but if he was gone, she didn't want to hear the news from a stranger. Jack had his copy of the hotel room key, and he inserted it in the lock, glancing at Isabelle, his expression inscrutable, and opened the door.

Sally reached Isabelle first and clasped her in an embrace so tight that Isabelle couldn't breathe. She looked over the girl's shoulder to see Phillip, his eyes red rimmed but relief showing in his face.

"You made it," he said and enfolded Isabelle in a hug when Sally released her and moved on to Alice, who finally, after everything was said and done, broke down and cried. Jean-Louis entered the sitting room from the men's bedroom and reached Alice, lifting her from her feet and holding her close.

"James?" Isabelle whispered to Phillip.

"In here," he said and led her by the hand into the men's bedroom.

James lay upon his bed, his face pale. But his chest rose and fell in a rhythmic pattern that had Isabelle collapsing in relief. Phillip caught her as her knees bent, and he led her to the chair that sat near the head of James's bed.

"We've all been keeping watch on him," Phillip told her. "He made it through the night, which was what had concerned Claire."

"Strong as an ox, that one. Treated him with water, ipecac, and charcoal. The rest he's done on his own."

Isabelle turned at the sound of a voice in the doorway. Claire entered, wiping her hands on a clean white cloth, and she reached down to place her palm on James's forehead. She also peered into his eyes by lifting his eyelids, nodded once, apparently satisfied, and turned to Isabelle. She smiled then and reached down to wrap her arms around Isabelle's shoulders and plant a kiss on her cheek.

"Oh!" Claire said as she pulled back. "And you, my friend, are finally going to submit to my ministrations."

"Give me just a few minutes, please? I need to be with him. Besides, Jack wants to see you."

"Did he tear his stitches?" Claire asked, frowning.

"No. He literally wants to look at you."

Claire raised a brow, and Isabelle was gratified to see a light blush stain her cheeks. "Well, I suppose I should see if he needs anything."

Isabelle smiled at her. "I believe he's going to accompany his grandfather to the hospital, so go now." She gave Philip and Claire the abbreviated version of events that led to Dr. Pearce's broken arm.

Claire turned immediately for the other room, and Phillip squatted down next to Isabelle's chair. "I am so very, very glad that you are safe," he told her. "I was the reason for this whole, huge mess, and had something happened to you—"

Isabelle placed her palm on Phillip's cheek. "I wouldn't change a thing even if I could. I would never have met your brother otherwise, so thank you."

Phillip leaned forward and kissed her forehead. "Do you want me to get anything for you? Are you going to go to your room now?"

"No. I'm staying here. You may leave and close the door."

His brows lifted significantly, but he refrained from comment. The corner of his mouth quirked into a smile. He made his way to the door, glanced back at her, and whistling a tune, left, closing the door behind him.

Isabelle looked at James, who had yet to awaken. Finally removing her cloak, gloves, and shoes, she climbed onto the bed next to him and laid her head on his pillow. Placing her hand on his chest, where she felt the steady beat of his heart, she closed her eyes and slept.

36

THE DAYS THAT FOLLOWED THE return of the jewels to their home were consumed in the healing of the sick and wounded, sending telegrams, and talking with local authorities and British and American embassies. Jack spent considerable time with each entity, describing the attacks on the steamer by those known as the King's Men and his witness of their subsequent deaths. Scientists on a steamer from Athens arrived the following morning at Santorini and confirmed not only the accident but the cause as well.

Isabelle finally consented to retreat to her own bed, where she slept for twelve hours without waking once. Afterward she still coughed and sniffled, but the fever abated and she felt marginally refreshed. Claire insisted on splinting Isabelle's right wrist, which was painfully sore and nearly black from bruising but wasn't broken.

James regained his strength quickly enough, especially given that he had been poisoned with arsenic, and Jack's gunshot wound from Monemvasia was still healing nicely, much to Claire's satisfaction.

Dr. Pearce's broken arm was set, and a particularly large lump on his head from the somersaulting submarine was attended to. He was relieved to have his files again in his possession, although he contemplated destroying the lot of them to discourage future treasure seekers who might take it upon themselves to resurrect the legend. As it stood, any who were knowledgeable about it would have to continue to wonder where the jewels were hidden and if they'd ever be found—there was no way to tell the world they had taken it upon themselves to send the jewels to a watery grave at the base of a volcano. Jean-Louis had visibly blanched at the thought of the files being destroyed, and he offered to take them to France and secure them away if the doctor decided he had best be rid of them. The stones themselves were gone—there was nothing Jean-Louis could do about that, he told Dr. Pearce—but the thought of destroying so many years of meticulous work was the straw that broke the camel's back and was more than he could stomach. The doctor turned the files over to the Frenchman, who secured them reverently in a locked portmanteau.

Alice and Jean-Louis, for all that they were newlyweds, still managed to carve out a considerable amount of time for their friends; the couple had plans to return to Jean-Louis's home in France. Alice was at peace, clearly happy with her new husband, who looked at her with adoring eyes. Isabelle would have found it supremely irritating had she not felt a sense of relief that Alice would be loved and cared for very well.

Phillip was bruised but otherwise no worse for the wear after his altercation with Sparks, who had been taken by the police to the city morgue, where officials began the process to coordinate with the American embassy and locate Sparks's next of kin. Adelphos Kilronomos was still rusticating in the Delphi jailhouse, awaiting the pleasure of the judicial system in Athens, where Alice had given testimony regarding her abduction.

Phillip asked Sally to marry him, and she cried and said, "Yes!" sounding very much the Southern belle. He had secured a simple gold band as a symbol of the engagement at the same jewelry shop Jean-Louis had found Alice's band. Both girls were giddy and obnoxious in their joy, and Isabelle was happy with it.

Jack, James, Phillip, and Jean-Louis had found Leila and told her that they would not press charges for attempted murder if she agreed to inform any who might follow in the Federation informant's footsteps that Jackson Pearce was dead. She readily agreed and also understood the stipulation that should she default on her end of the agreement, the Athens authorities would be notified of her activities. Leila, for her part, was relieved that her family was no longer in danger. Jack telegraphed the head of the Federation in Egypt, using the name of the man who had been sent to kill him, and reported that the attempt on his life had been successful.

In a bizarre twist, Jack later received a telegram from the British embassy in Cairo. Jack's identity had been tortured out of the only employee who knew Jack's true identity as an agent of the Crown. The employee had died of his injuries, and as an act of revenge, the man's son had slipped into the Egyptian Federation head's compound and killed him in his sleep. Jack could only hope that with the head of the snake cut off, the rest of the body would eventually stop twitching and be still.

Jack, for his part, had smiled at Claire's suggestion that New York was a very nice town and had taken her up on her offer to show him around before she settled in as a medical student with Elizabeth Blackwell. He mused aloud that he might try his hand at detective work in America, given that he wasn't entirely sure he would be safe back at home. Isabelle, on the second night after returning from Santorini, had left from the dining room for their suite to retrieve a clean handkerchief and spied Jack and Claire locked in a passionate embrace in a dark corner of the hotel hallway. She had immediately turned around, hoping they hadn't heard her approach. Isabelle didn't let on that she'd seen them, but she was glad that, if things progressed, her sister would spend her life with a very good man.

Isabelle now stood at the top of the Acropolis and looked out over the ancient city of Athens. She wore a beautiful new Greek dress—white with blue accents, starched to perfection, with flowing skirts and embroidered hems. The beautiful gossamer veil that Elysia had worn on her wedding day adorned Isabelle's head and hung beautifully down her back in waves. She held wildflowers, tied together with a soft ribbon, in her hands, the right one still in a splint. James stood next to her and looked as handsome as ever in a black suit specially tailored for the occasion. The priest that Alice and Jean-Louis had visited stood with them and spoke the words of the wedding ceremony in heavily accented English.

As they exchanged vows, Isabelle felt tears burning in her eyes, yet again, in gratitude that she and James were both alive, whole, and finally getting married. When he had awoken and taken his turn sitting by her bed while she slept, he had decided there was no chance in Hades he would be willing to spend another two months in travel and not be legally and morally allowed to hold Isabelle in his arms all night. When she had asked whether his mother would be hurt that they didn't wait until reaching Utah to be married, he declared that she would be thrilled to have two daughters as well as her sons returned to her unscathed.

Claire, throughout the ceremony, was very teary but denied it after the fact. She told Isabelle she would take the time later in the evening to write their grandmother, Genevieve, a long letter explaining the adventures that had erupted around them, literally, since leaving Egypt and promising that they would visit her in Boston when Genevieve returned home.

The celebration that followed the ceremony was lavish and wonderful, put together by an elated Helene, who was thrilled to have been witness to it. They held the festivities at Elysia and Helene's home, which had been scrubbed and shined to perfection. Demitrios Metaxas hung close by the woman's side all evening—Helene had told Isabelle earlier that Demitrios "needed the influence of a woman in his life," not to mention someone to organize and clean the frightful mess of his museum.

Helene told Isabelle that, after some coercion, Demitrios had admitted to her that he'd been aware his father had been one of the King's Men and he knew that Baltasar had shared that obsession with the jewels and hidden treasure. But Baltasar had hidden the fact that he had become the head of the King's Men in the last year. Demitrios, by helping Isabelle and the rest find the answers they sought, had unwittingly brought his brother into the fray and placed them all in danger. It was finished, though, and Isabelle could only be grateful to the museum owner for his help and loyalty to them at the end, when his brother had wreaked havoc. She expressed her thoughts to Demitrios, and his swollen mouth stretched into a wide smile.

When Isabelle was so tired she could no longer dance and so full of delectable food she was sure she'd never manage another bite, James informed the crowd of friends and local neighbors that he was taking his bride back to the hotel. They were showered with rice and white flower petals as they ran to the carriage that whisked them quickly to their temporary home.

Isabelle was content as James pulled her onto his lap in the carriage and then, upon reaching their new, private room in the hotel, lifted her and carried her over the threshold. He kissed her soundly before setting her on her feet and rolled his eyes at her when she suggested he might catch her illness—although it seemed to be in its final stages.

"I love you, Isabelle Webb Ashby," he said to her as he removed her shawl and headpiece and laid them carefully on the bed. He drew her to the French doors that led out onto a small balcony and opened them wide. Gathering her close in his arms, he said, "The universe goes on into eternity. That is how much I love you. I have adored you from that first moment I rescued you on the docks in London, and I will adore you forever and ever."

Would she never stop crying? She'd shed more tears in the last few weeks than she'd squeezed out during the course of her entire life to that point. "You didn't rescue me," she said, her lips quirking into a smile, and she tipped her head back to look at him. "I had the situation well under control."

He thumbed one of the tears that escaped her eye and shook his head with a grin. "You drive me to insanity."

"Forever?"

"Forever."

"I do have one concern."

He frowned. "What is it?"

"I am your only wife, yes?"

He closed his eyes and laughed. "Yes."

"Forever?"

"Yes. Forever. My one and only."

Author Notes

I DON'T LIKE TO TAKE liberties with my historical fiction as it concerns real places and times. However, it becomes necessary to do so, at times, to help the plot move forward. In this book, I tweaked a few things for my benefit.

First of all, extensive excavation at Delphi began formally in 1892. My supposition, from what I've been able to find, is that in 1866 very little of the ancient ruins was visible above ground. I did try to stay true to this but had to push the excavation forward a bit so that my characters would have places to run and hide.

The railway system in Greece was not nearly as extensive in the interior of the country as I imply. But to put my characters on horses and stretch their journeys into months instead of days just didn't work. So I fudged. And on top of that, there are places where I have them crossing by train as the crow flies, where I'm not sure there are railways even now.

I like to tell myself it's fiction and therefore okay. I hope you don't mind too much.

Author Bio

Nancy Campbell Allen (N. C. Allen) has a degree in elementary education and has been writing for fun since the third grade. Her first book was published in 1999, and she now has eleven books to her credit—four contemporary romance and seven historicals, including the award-winning Civil War series Faith of Our Fathers—and plans to write until the day she dies. She loves to read, travel, and spend time with family and friends. She has completed two half marathons and is trying to talk herself into doing another one. Nancy lives in Ogden, Utah, with her husband and three children, although one recently married, moved out, and brought a son-in-law to the mix. She still maintains that this does not make her old.